That Last Summer

Sara LaFontain

26 TREES PRESS, TUCSON, ARIZONA

26 Trees Press
3661 N. Campbell Ave #379
Tucson, AZ 85719

Publisher's Note: This is a work of fiction. Names, characters, places, and incidents are a product of the author's imagination. Locales and public names are sometimes used for atmospheric purposes. Any resemblance to actual people, living or dead, or to businesses, companies, events, institutions, or locales is completely coincidental.

Book Layout © 2017 BookDesignTemplates.com
Cover Design: Leigh McDonald
Editors: Karen Dale Harris, Amanda Slaybaugh

That Last Summer/Sara LaFontain. -- 1st ed.
ISBN 978-1-7326857-1-0

To Ryan Williams,
With all my love.

Chapter One

Present Day: Whispering Pines, May 2013

Cara could still feel the phantom indentation of a ring on her finger, even now, six months after she'd removed it. Sometimes she found herself smoothing the empty space with her thumb, trying to rub down the absence, erase its lingering presence.

She'd tried to give the diamond ring to Phil's mother after the funeral. Elaine insisted she keep it, not understanding that it was a noose, a shackle, an unwelcome tie to an engagement she'd never wanted. When she slipped it off her finger for the final time, there had been nothing but relief.

It doesn't matter, you'll always be mine, his voice intruded in her thoughts, yet again. Half a year had passed, but she still let Phil take up too much real estate in her mind. She gritted her teeth and reminded herself to focus on the present.

His ghost was wrong anyway. She could move on, she was strong enough. That's what she was doing right now, with her current vigil watching out over the chill waters of Lake Superior for the arrival of the ferry from the mainland.

"It's just a coincidence that I'm here," she planned to tell Sam when he arrived. "I happened to be in the area, and noticed you on the ferry." That was her cover. She didn't want to admit she'd made the half-mile walk from the Inn at Whispering Pines just to see him. She didn't want to admit that she'd braided her hair in a way she knew he liked, freshened her makeup, and waited with butterflies in her stomach.

What would it be like to see Sam again? Would he be different? Would he be glad to see her? Everything had changed since the end of last summer's tourist season, when he'd boarded the ferry and left the island without saying goodbye. Her last memory of him was his back as he stood rigid, clutching the rails, refusing to turn around.

They hadn't spoken in months, even when she needed him, even when she'd emailed him, promising to break up with Phil, offering to give him what they both wanted. He'd never responded. He was the only one who hadn't sent condolences either, not one single word. There had been nothing but radio silence.

Cara had spent weeks planning what to say to break that silence, to find a way to reconnect. She wanted to clear the air before they both returned for the summer tourist season on Whispering Pines, but then a phone call from her uncle shattered her heart.

"Sam's taken a job in Denver this summer, so I've written an ad to find a replacement," Paddy said, oblivious to the effect his words had on her. "I'll email it to you before I post it."

Seeking chef for exciting culinary opportunity, seasonal position with possibility of extension. Must be single, attractive, heterosexual male, late twenties to mid-thirties.

She laughed at that, and of course changed the ad before it ran. They might have needed a chef to replace Sam in their kitchen, but she didn't need her uncle to act as matchmaker. She wasn't really ready to date again, and sometimes she wasn't sure if she ever would be.

Even without Paddy's additional conditions, the chefs who applied were uninspiring. It was tough to find someone available to take a limited five-month position, and the applicants, almost entirely freshly graduated from culinary school, lacked the experience necessary to run a fine-dining establishment. She suggested to her uncle that they change the restaurant concept, despite the universally positive reviews, into something more casual, something any diner cook could handle. The idea seemed to make Paddy ill—the restaurant was his late partner's baby, his legacy, and Paddy didn't want to let that die too.

After all the phone calls and emails, they finally found a potential new hire, and Paddy began making arrangements for a tasting interview. And then it all changed again. Cara was vacationing with her cousin in Thailand when she received the news.

Hey, Cara-

Might not need to interview that chef. I got a message from Sam saying he's changed his mind and wants to come back. Are you OK with that? I don't know what happened, but I noticed some animosity between the two of you last year. If you don't want him here, just say the word, and he's gone. Let me know ASAP. Also, tell Amy I said hello, and you girls need to get off the beaches and explore more of the country. Bring me back something interesting! Love you!

Paddy

She sent her response before she could consider it. Of course she wanted Sam back, she assured her uncle. That was the best solution for everybody. It would be better than training someone new, and Sam, despite his other faults, really was a superior chef. She would be able to handle his presence.

That's what she was doing now, right? Handling his presence? The ferry was coming, and as it got closer she scanned the passengers on its decks. There weren't many. Tourist season didn't officially begin until next week, so the ferry-goers were either islanders returning home from mainland jobs, or perhaps a few summer employees coming back for the start of the season. Sam should be easy to spot, taller than most of the crowd, with his broad shoulders and mop of dark curls. She couldn't find him though.

After the ferry docked, she waited, watching the passengers disembark just in case. Maybe she'd missed him, maybe he'd been sitting somewhere out of sight, and she'd see his familiar grin and startlingly pale blue eyes. But no. He wasn't there.

"Hey, Cara," called Vivian, the ferry master. "This was only a passenger run. Were you waiting for cargo? I'll have some boxes for you in the morning."

"Actually, I was hoping you brought me a chef."

"Sam? Sorry, he's not here. Was he supposed to arrive today?"

"I thought so, but maybe I got the dates mixed up," Cara said. Was it possible he changed his mind again? She knew their friendship had been destroyed, but what about professionalism? What about loyalty to this island and the people on it? What about the contract he signed promising to return?

"You never mix anything up." Vivian tipped her head to the side and studied her carefully. "Cara, I hate to say it, but you're not looking well. I know you've had a rough few months. If you ever need to talk, I'm here for you. Anytime, I promise."

Cara smiled at the offer. She had known Vivian for two decades. She was a mother figure to all the islanders, and a force to be reckoned with to all others.

"Thanks, but I'm fine." That was a lie, of course. But she would be fine, someday. Someday when she eradicated the ghost of Phil from her mind, and the memories of his hands from her throat.

Angel, I'll never let you go, his voice whispered.

Chapter Two

Ferry's Landing, May 2013

A kick woke Sam out of a disjointed dream. A kick, and the sounds of someone yelling at him for trespassing. He sat up groggily and rolled the brim of his knit cap up off his eyes.

"Oh. Sammy, it's you!" Vivian was the source of his rude awakening, which was reasonable since he was occupying the bench outside of her office. "What the hell are you doing?"

"I missed the last ferry, so I slept here. Sorry," he told her. He had sprinted from the bus depot to the ferry docks only to see it disappearing over the lake. After cursing for a few minutes, he'd wandered the streets of Ferry's Landing, and eventually came to the conclusion that sleeping on a bench was preferable to paying for a hotel.

"You know about the hidden office key, right? I've got a couch for islanders who miss the boat," she reminded him. He did know about that, but since he wasn't sure of his reception, he hadn't wanted to risk it. He almost said as much, but she beat him to it.

"Look, you may not be one of my sons, but you are one of my boys. You're always welcome here. Now give me a hug, and then you can earn free passage if you help Duncan and Everett load some cargo. Most of the boxes are for your inn anyway." Her weathered face broke into a grin. "But in the future, if you want a ride, you bring me some food. I've missed your cooking."

Sam laughed and accepted her offered hug, relieved by her welcome. He hadn't known what it would be like returning this year. Whispering Pines islanders loved their gossip, and he wasn't sure what consensus they'd come to about him.

When the ferry finally pushed out from the mainland dock, Sam let out a breath he didn't know he was holding. From the minute his plane landed in Duluth, he couldn't wait to make it back to the island, back to the crisp pine-scented air and the laid-back vibe that permeated everyone who resided there.

He tried to tell himself that it was some intangible essence of Whispering Pines that drew him back every summer, even though the pay wasn't as high, even though he'd received other offers—real career offers, as his ex-girlfriend reminded him— even though the five-month position meant he had to cobble together other temporary work the rest of the year. He found a sense of relaxation there, a sense of peace.

But truthfully, he came back because of shining brown eyes with golden flecks that took his breath away.

No, he couldn't let himself think about that, about those eyes, and the way they looked into his soul; and the way they'd found him lacking.

The ride took twenty minutes, and at the halfway point the island finally appeared. He told himself the wind caused the tears in his eyes, and he tried to wipe them away surreptitiously. He always loved the approach, seeing the land as it seemed to curve around the horizon, the bold white tower of the lighthouse discernible first, followed by the village slowly coming into view, turning from a dark smudge into individual buildings. He inhaled the scent of the pines brought in on the cold breeze.

He stepped back from the rails, feeling almost overcome with the bittersweet emotion of returning to the place he thought of as home, but a home where his welcome wasn't guaranteed. In stepping back, he almost tripped over his bag, and one of Vivian's boys saw him.

"Hey, Sammy, might want to watch your footing. It's a rough crossing." Everett laughed good-naturedly, and Sam casually flipped him off. An easy camaraderie existed between the locals and the summer employees. They were all in it together, dealing with the massive influx of tourists that descended in hordes on the small island.

Sam lifted his duffel and placed it on a seat where he couldn't trip over it when anyone important could see.

Funny how the duffel contained almost the sum total of his possessions. *You're thirty-two years old and everything you own fits in one bag*, his ex-girlfriend's voice complained in his head. Last year, she gifted him an enormous rolling suitcase that turned out to be quite expensive, rather unwieldy, and far too large to shove into his half of the closet. He preferred the beat-up old duffel that he could cram under his bed in the small staff house room he shared with his friend, Sato. Lizbet had been wrong anyway. Everything he owned didn't fit in one bag. He also had a nice set of skis and cold weather gear stored in his brother's Las Vegas garage. *Two bags, then*, he could almost hear her say contemptuously. *That's all you've got to show for yourself?*

Was it as bad as Lizbet always expressed, him owning so few things? He wasn't sentimental. All that truly mattered to him were his knives and his recipe binder. Everything else was replaceable. He didn't care about his clothing; he didn't own a car, or furniture, or anything of value. Most other chefs had collections of pots and pans and other kitchen accoutrements, but he wasn't picky; he could cook with anything. He always believed it was better not to have too many material possessions: it made it easier to walk away.

But walking away when things got rough was a habit he was trying to break. That's why he came back here, wasn't it? Last September when tourist season ended and he boarded on the ferry to leave, he never planned to return. Why would he, when she made it so clear he wasn't wanted? And last year, instead of watching the island fade into the distance, he'd turned resolutely toward the mainland, refusing to look back. He'd told himself he didn't want to see if she watched him go, and worse, he didn't want to see if she didn't.

Individual boats were discernible now, not many of them docked this early in the season, although he thought he recognized Matteo's speedboat already in the water. And now the buildings were coming into focus, though, of course, the inn wasn't visible from this side. There, on the road above the docks, he spotted what he had been looking for—a flash of bright blue. One of the inn's electric carts? Maybe. Yes. *It's probably Paddy*, he thought, the owner driving down to pick up the supplies. Not her. He couldn't let himself get his hopes up.

The ferry came ever closer and now, yes, yes, there it was. The blue cart stopped and two women got out, causing Sam's heart to beat faster. Not Paddy, it must be the O'Connell cousins. He suppressed a grin—she came after all. At this distance, he still couldn't tell them apart, but he could make out their long brown hair and matching dark blue Inn at Whispering Pines jackets. Closer, closer. One of the women started jumping and waving excitedly. That energy level could only belong to Amy. So that meant Cara was the one with her arms crossed, leaning against the cart. Did she see him? Was she even looking?

As a test, he raised a hand in greeting, and so did she. A flush of adrenaline surged through him. Cara was there, and she was watching him. He immediately regretted not renting a room last night. He should have showered, shaved, cleaned up a little. What had he been thinking?

Amy ran to greet him and jumped into his arms almost as soon as he stepped off the boat. "Sammy! You came back! We missed you! But I wish you opted for a later trip. Getting up this early can't be healthy for anyone."

He smiled and hugged her back. Amy's exuberance was both welcome and unexpected. His last contact with her had been a scathing email she inexplicably sent last November, and he had heard nothing since.

"Get off me, woman. You're crazy." He put her down and turned to her cousin. "Cara, it's good to see you."

They stared at each other for what felt like an eon, but it probably lasted no more than a few seconds. She smiled suddenly, stepping forward, and he was finally able to hug her too.

"I missed you, Sam." Her voice sounded muffled against his coat.

He took a deep breath, inhaling the clean strawberry scent of her shampoo. Sometimes things didn't change. God, but he still wanted her. He held her tightly, probably an instant too long as he felt her pull back. Cara. She was here, and she was speaking to him. This might be a good summer. Maybe coming back was the right choice after all.

"You really missed me?" He looked at her with what he hoped was an intent and meaningful expression. He tried to keep from smiling, tried to maintain the seriousness of the moment. There were so many things he wanted to say, so much he wanted to convey to her ... if only they weren't standing out in the open at the docks, if only her cousin wasn't watching, if only things hadn't ended so badly last summer.

"You have no idea how much," she said, with her sweet smile he knew so well. "Amy's been doing all the cooking and she's experimenting with what she's calling Indian-Italian fusion, and it's pretty awful. We need you back in the kitchen."

Chapter Three

Two months earlier: Aspen, early March 2013

The end of ski season is approaching, and Sam's future is unfolding before him. There are two contracts sitting in his email inbox. One is for summer employment as the executive chef at the Inn at Whispering Pines, in case he decides to come back. This is where he's spent the last three summers in the best kitchen he's ever worked in. He's not taking it, though. He can't. It would hurt too much.

The other is from a highly-rated fine dining restaurant in Denver, where he could take a full-time, year-round job as sous chef. A permanent position with a salary and benefits. A career.

He starts to look at apartments in Denver. He has been living in Aspen while cooking at a ski resort, which is crazy expensive, so he and seven other seasonal workers are crammed into a one-bedroom apartment. The whole place smells like sweat and grease and dirty feet, and Sam is one of the unfortunates who sleeps on an air mattress in the living room. The apartment is always full of alcohol, skis, and snowboards, and there isn't enough room for everybody to be home at once. He is not there right now. He's at his girlfriend Lizbet's.

Somehow, she can afford her own two-bedroom condo, despite working only part-time as a ski instructor and spending the rest of the time racing Sam down black diamonds. He suspects a trust fund is involved, but he's never cared enough to ask. He just likes to occasionally spend the night with her, enjoy the smell of freshly laundered sheets, and have room to actually cook breakfast in the morning. He is using her computer now, for his apartment search.

Lizbet comes out of the bedroom, tossing her long blond hair. "Samuel, aren't you coming to bed?" she asks. Her voice sounds like whining, but he knows it's the tone she uses when she's trying to sound sexy.

"Later, Lizzy" he tells her, and she wrinkles her nose in distaste at the nickname.

"Studio apartments?" She sits down on his lap, facing him. "You should be looking for a bigger place. I'm thinking about joining you."

He is dumbfounded. Yes, she's technically his girlfriend. Yes, they are sleeping together (and have been on and off for the past two years). But neither of them has ever discussed a serious future, and he never thought that she'd go with him. It never occurred to him at all. In fact, he was kind of looking forward to a fresh start.

"You want to move to Denver with me?" he asks, and perhaps deliberately, she misinterprets the tone of his question.

"Oh, Samuel, I'd love to! I thought you'd never ask." She starts to kiss his neck. "I can't believe we're finally moving in together! Come to bed, let's celebrate." Her hand traces a line down his chest, and he stops her before she can get any lower.

"Later," he tells her again, slightly annoyed this time but feeling guilty for sounding so rude. "Later, I promise."

He kisses her cheek, and she sticks out her lip and pouts. The expression is not as cute as she thinks it is. She flounces off to bed, warning him she won't wait up much longer.

Sam continues searching Denver apartments, still looking at small studios. He could live there, right? Denver is a nice city. He could live there and work and move on and forget about other things ... things like the golden glints in Cara's eyes, and the sweet scent of Cara's hair, and how it felt to caress her face, and how big and shiny and terrible her stupid engagement ring looked on her finger. That day in the rain, had he imagined everything? Had he imagined their connection? How could she not see how wrong she was, how right he was? How they belonged together? He knew how he felt, how strongly he had felt for years. He was sure he saw those feelings reflected back at him, but she had chosen to run away.

She was married by now. His sister-in-law had called in December, telling him that a wedding invitation with a Whispering Pines postmark had arrived for him. "Shall I open it and read it to you," she had asked, sounding excited, "or wait and send it with the rest of your mail?"

"No," he had told her. "Don't open the envelope. Just throw it away." He should have told her to burn it.

Weeks later, an email came from Sato, his island roommate: *Hey, haven't heard, you coming to the wedding?*

Can't make it, he had replied. *Sorry.* Though he wasn't sorry. Travel halfway across the country to see the woman he loved marry someone else, someone who, in addition to being not-Sam, was also horribly wrong for her? No. He couldn't do that.

Too bad, was hoping to see you. I'll send pics! Sato had responded, and that email had recently appeared in his inbox as well, WEDDING PICS!!!!!, the subject line read, and Sam couldn't bring himself to open it, couldn't stand to look at pictures of his friends having fun, dancing, eating cake, Cara in a wedding dress vowing to love, honor, and cherish someone else. No, he would never torture himself by opening the message.

Now he sits at Lizbet's computer, thinking. He needs to move on. He needs to move to Denver, alone. He needs to stop tormenting himself by dreaming about the woman he lost.

In a reckless, masochistic moment, he checks to make sure Lizbet isn't coming out and opens an incognito window, types in the address to Amy's blog, *Always Amy O.* He doesn't want to see anything about Cara, but he can't help himself. It might be painful, but a part of him is craving it, if only to look at her face again. He used to read the blog all the time, not just because Amy was Cara's cousin, but because she was his friend and she lived an unusual and interesting life. He stopped last fall, refused to check in on his old friends at all. He couldn't because what if Amy posted about the wedding? Surely she helped plan everything. Surely she was the maid of honor, threw Cara a shower and a bachelorette party, and took her dress shopping. And Amy always wrote about everything. She bragged that her life was lived completely openly, so she would have shared every excruciating detail. He didn't want to know any of it, as if by avoiding the knowledge he could go on pretending he might one day have a chance.

I'm only looking, he tells himself. *Just a peek.* The most recent post on Amy's blog, written only a few hours ago, jumps out at him.

Alright y'all, I'm going to need some help. I don't usually do polls here, but everyone should have a voice, right? Democracy and all that. My contract at the resort here in Thailand is up, so I'm rather impatiently waiting for my awesome cousin Cara to arrive. (If you're new to this blog, and want to know who Cara is, check out THAT EASTER WE ALMOST DIED and HOW TO DRIVE A SOCCER TEAM WILD.) Cara is on a flight to Bangkok at this very moment, and we're going to spend the next six weeks backpacking around (and spending all the money we earned over the winter), and she needs to have some fun. She's single and ready to mingle (and oh, does she ever hate when I use that expression!!). She's been in a bit of a rut, and I need to snap her out of it, get her back on the old cowboy. (Yes, I know. Cara told me the expression is 'back in the saddle,' but how does that make sense? We're from Texas; we know that real ladies ride cowboys.)

So here's the issue: a group of absolutely gorgeous Italian men is staying at the hotel up the road, and there is also a trio of hot Australian surfers a block away near the beach. For Cara's first night in town, who do we cowboy-up with? Italians or Aussies? Vote below! Poll closes when Cara arrives (and don't tell her I did this!!!!).

Sam leans back from the computer. He can't breathe. His chest is tight as though he's having a heart attack. Is he hallucinating? What does *single and ready to mingle* mean, exactly? Is she actually single, as in unmarried, or just traveling without her husband? Is she still engaged? Is Amy exaggerating for effect? He rubs his eyes, looks again. The words are the same. *Single and ready to mingle.* It doesn't make any sense.

He goes back to his email, clicks on WEDDING PICS!!!!! In the first one, smiling and wearing a black tuxedo, is Sato. And in the next, in a long white dress, is Margaux from the bakery. It hits him like a sucker punch. Sato and Margaux were dating last summer, and Sato started spending most nights away from the staff house and waxing rhapsodic about the future, but this . . . this is not what he expected. He scrolls through the images. Sato and Margaux dancing, Sato and Margaux cutting the cake. It's Sato's wedding. He can feel blood rushing through his entire body as he continues to click through the pictures. There, finally, there's one—Cara, with her arms around her Uncle Paddy, smiling for the camera, no fiancé in sight and no ring on her finger. Sam's head is spinning.

Back to Amy's blog. The first comment on the post, appropriately enough, from IslandSato: *Gonna need more info here, Ames. Cara likes tall, dark, and handsome. Maybe add some pics of the choices?* More comments, many from people with Italian names writing disparaging things about Australian surfers. Cara is actually single? Sam can't catch a breath. Cara is single. This changes everything.

Back to his email. And before he can think about what he's doing, he types a response:

> *My situation has changed. If your offer still stands, I'd like to come back this summer. I'll get the contract printed, signed, and mailed tomorrow. I've got some new recipes I want to try. Can we schedule a call to talk wine pairings? Also, please keep me informed on any staffing issues. Are you still considering hiring a pastry chef?—Thanks, Sam V.*

Chapter Four

Two months earlier: Kata Beach, Thailand, March 2013
Blog post from Always Amy O:

Ok, poll results came in, in favor of the Italians. Fabio might think I didn't notice that the majority of them came from the same ISP address, but believe me, I did. (Very sweet, btw.) Anyway, Cara showed up, looking way too pale after spending an entire winter sitting in the Canadian dark, and immediately informed me that: 1) she was a bit jet-lagged and 2) she's not going to obey the whims of a bunch of internet strangers and 3) she wanted to hear some Australian accents.

So Cara and I went out with the Aussie trio. Dinner, drinks, dancing, extremely loud club music, more drinks. You know, the usual. I don't want to gossip too much (also, I don't know details, damn my close-mouthed cousin), but last I saw her (DAD! STOP READING THIS RIGHT NOW!), we were both drunk and skinny-dipping with some lovely well-built surfers. Don't worry, she was safely back at the hotel this morning. Hungover, but hey, that was the plan anyway.

Now we're here, lounging on the beach while a charming Italian man brings us drinks and provides foot massages. (Fabio just read that bit over my shoulder and laughed at me. But then he went and got me a drink, so score!)
It's fabulous having my cousin with me again. She's my very best friend and the platonic love of my life, which is good because for five months a year we are roommates in a tiny house on a remote island with not enough interesting people to en-

tertain us. (I'm directing that at you if you're reading this, IslandSato. And I'm kidding.)

True story though, one problem I always have when spending time with my cousin is that people seem to think that we are twins and like to make lewd suggestions as to what they'd like to do with us. Even this morning, despite us looking quite hungover and miserable, we had a creepy older man walk past us on the beach, stop, do a double take, and then suggest a threesome because he's always wanted a three-way with twins. This is how you know Cara is awesome: she smiled at the guy, told him that would be wonderful, and grabbed Fabio's hand and said, "Me and my twin brother are definitely in! What's your room number?" I was briefly afraid that Fabio was going to get punched in the face, but instead, the rather embarrassed-looking would-be lothario cussed at us and walked away while we all laughed.

It's a bit ridiculous, but this is not the first time we've received such invitations. However—and this should be obvious to anyone with half a brain—my cousin Cara and I are not twins. Our fathers are identical twins, so I guess we're genetically closer than regular cousins, but we were born to different mothers. My younger brothers are identical twins, as are my younger sisters; however, I was born alone. (Cara just muttered, "And you'll die alone too" because she is old and bitter.) As a secondary thing, neither of us are into incest either.

I don't think we look that alike anyway. We both have long brown hair, but hers has reddish highlights, mine doesn't. Her eyes have gold flecks, mine don't. (I'm plainer than her, I guess.) Also, I assume you can tell by just by looking at our faces that I'm much more fun than her. She would agree with this statement. Hell, I'm more fun right now since I'm drinking a super boozy cocktail (thanks again, Fabio!) and writing this on a stolen laptop, and all she's doing is lying on the beach drinking water (seriously, water!?!?) and reading a book about 'eco-friendly hotel development planning,' of all things. (Fabio would like me to correct this because he says I'm merely borrowing his laptop, so I was compelled to point out that it is extremely rude to read over someone's shoulder, even if you are, as he claimed, safeguarding your property from an [amazing, smart, sexy, beautiful] American thief.)

But enough complaining. We are here, on a gorgeous beach, with a gorgeous man (still need one for Cara though—only non-sleazy applicants please), and we have six weeks to relax, get tan, get drunk, and get Cara's groove back before we are off to the cold Midwest to once again open the beloved Inn at Whispering Pines. Good times.

Chapter Five

Whispering Pines, May 2013

Cara listened to Sam unpacking in his room on the other side of the staff house common area. He was always a bit of a neat freak, she remembered, and as soon as he arrived he always wanted to put everything away exactly in its place. Last year she'd sat on his bed and chatted with him, watching as he carefully and precisely folded every article of clothing. This year, she didn't feel welcome. He'd been standoffish when she'd picked him up at the ferry, and she'd noticed a minute hesitation before he hugged her.

That was fine with her though—she had the same hesitation. Nerves had set in last night, when she got back from the docks and checked the voicemail. *Hey, it's me, Sam, um, Sam Vervaine. I just missed the last ferry, so I'll be arriving tomorrow morning on the first one. You don't need to pick me up or anything. I can walk. I just wanted to let you know. Okay, um, bye.*

She'd played the message over and over listening for nuance and trying to analyze the feelings it brought up in her, until Amy came looking for her and she had to pretend she was hearing it for the first time. Now he called, she thought almost bitterly. She'd hoped to hear from him months ago, and there was nothing. She thought she could steel herself, face him without ... without what, exactly? She wasn't sure what she felt anymore. There was a sense of betrayal, a sense of sadness, but at the same time there was hope.

This morning when the ferry arrived, Amy acted like her usual overly excited self and started jumping and waving like a lunatic when Sam came into sight. Cara hugged herself tightly and shrank back. She wanted to be stoic, and strong, and proud, and pretend that he hadn't hurt her. But the second he lifted his hand and waved to Amy, she felt something melt. Damn it, she had missed him.

Amy was the one who held up the conversation the entire way back to the inn, including when they stopped at Margaux's coffee shop for a quick breakfast. Cara and Sam sat back and let Amy chatter on while they both seemed to search for the right words to say. Sam's eyes kept traveling to the empty space on Cara's left hand. He looked like he wanted to ask something, but the next voice Cara heard wasn't his; it was the other one, the voice that she had been trying to avoid. *I think you're lying when you say there's no one else,* Phil said. *We could have been so happy together, Cara. You ruined everything.* She hid her hand under the table out of Sam's line of vision, but even without his eyes on it the guilt came flooding back.

It didn't matter though, none of it did. She lay back on her bed and through the open door she listened almost wistfully to the sounds of Sam as he moved about his room, unpacking and occasionally tripping over things. She reminded herself of her therapist's words: *You can't change other people, Cara. You can only change how you react to them.* It was good advice. She needed to stop reacting to Phil's voice in her head. She had to stop letting it bother her, stop letting him ruin her.

Fortunately, her cousin was there to distract her from thinking too much about the past, and Sam, and what the future might or might not hold for them.

🌲 🌲 🌲 🌲 🌲

"Well, I feel much better," Amy announced, stepping out of their shared bathroom wrapped in a robe.

Cara couldn't help but laugh at her. "I'm glad you feel better, but I'm still going to make fun of you."

"You said you'd turned on the pool heaters," Amy respond-ed and shivered theatrically, though her skin had regained its color and her lips were no longer tinged with blue.

"Most people would dip a toe in first," Cara reminded her, "rather than shouting cannonball and jumping in. Also, most people would know that it takes a while to heat an entire swimming pool. I told you I turned the heaters on, I didn't say the water was warm yet."

"Whatever. It didn't kill me. It was kinda fun. Like one of those polar-bear swims people do. Most people would miss out on an awesome experience." Amy began combing out her long hair. "Hey, can you believe that guy?"

"What guy? I only saw one idiot in the pool."

"Very funny. You know I meant Sam, that guy. I'm still mad at him," Amy dropped the comb and started making faces at herself in the mirror.

"You sure didn't act mad when we picked him up."

"You know I hug everybody. Besides, we're friends. I can be excited to see him while still being mad and thinking he's a colossal jerk."

"I'm sure he had a good reason not to call." Cara didn't want to keep poking at that wound. She had never told Amy exactly why Sam had cut himself out of her life, so she hadn't been able to explain his lack of contact.

She thought back again to that day in the rain when it all went wrong. She still remembered his hands on her face, the way he brought his forehead down to hers, how he looked in her eyes with a terrifyingly intimate intensity. His hands, so warm. His breath. The way he told her he loved her and whis-pered her name. And she clutched handfuls of his jacket, supporting herself against him because she was afraid her legs wouldn't be able to hold her up. And the way she pushed him away as soon as he tipped his lips down to hers, how she shoved at him and stumbled backwards. The wounded look he gave her. "I'm engaged," she had cried out, as if he hadn't known and he looked at her with an expression so full of pain.

"You're with the wrong man," he said, and she turned away, even though she didn't want to, even though he was right, even though she wanted nothing more than to fling herself into his arms. But instead she abandoned him and ran off into the rain, feeling empty and conflicted and so very lost. He avoided her for the next week, the final week of tourist season. And that was the end, it was all over. His contract was up, and she drove him down to the ferry. He wouldn't look at her. She was actually surprised when he sat in the front seat, surprised he didn't ride in the back as though he was just another guest she had to chauffeur down to the dock. As he took his over-sized suitcase out of the cart, he finally did look directly at her.

"You getting married?" he asked, and she nodded.

He stared at her for a moment and then shook his head and walked away. He boarded the ferry and strode straight to the far end, looking out towards the mainland. She watched the whole time while the workers loaded the cargo, while the last passengers scrambled aboard, and while the ferry pushed off and took him from her life. He stood perfectly upright, rigid, and never once turned around. Maybe if he had, she would have broken. Maybe she would have yelled for him to come back. And maybe he would have; maybe he would have made the return trip right away (or, in her fantasy, he would have dived into the water and swam back in a daring romantic gesture straight out of the movies). But he didn't, and she didn't, and months later she'd heard from others that he'd taken a job in Denver and she would never see him again.

"Everybody else called or emailed or sent flowers, and he didn't." Amy twisted her hair into different styles while continuing her complaint. "He's a selfish jackass. All he had to do was pick up the phone and say, 'I'm sorry for your loss.' Five words, that's all. It's not difficult to be supportive. He does look kinda hot though, with that new haircut. I mean, I'm disappointed he did that, but those curls were a bit too much. He looks better without them. If I were single, I'd at least give him a try, make this the Summer of Sam."

Cara hoped she was joking. "I liked the curls. And *Summer of Sam* is a movie about a serial killer; I'd rather you not get killed. We're not going to be able to hire someone to replace you this close to the start of the season."

"Yeah, that's the only reason you want to keep me alive. The hiring process is awful. Hey, speaking of hooking up, have you given any thought to your own love life this summer, now that you're single? Oh, maybe this will be the year you finally get with Matteo?"

Cara laughed so hard she snorted. "I believe Matteo is damaged goods, Miss Drunken Fling 2009. Not interested. Plus, when we were eleven, he wiped a booger on me. That sealed his fate for all eternity. I will never be attracted to him."

Matteo was the only other kid in her grade at the school she attended during the two years she and her mother lived on the island. They were best friends back then, and remained quite close throughout the years. But she always considered him to be more like an annoying brother, which made him off-limits and irrevocably unattractive, even if he hadn't carried on a two-week love affair with her cousin.

"Ok, fine, not Booger Boy. Still, it would be nice to find you a fun fling, since that didn't actually happen on our trip. I don't expect you to just get over Phillip, but, come on, I know you. You need someone to kick start your love life, get some of your needs met, if you know what I mean. Have a fling, or find a rebound guy you can date all summer and then dump in September. Maybe there's some potential at the Village Hotel? I think Bernie is bringing in a couple of new staffers. Or the ferry brothers are both single, if a little young. You could be a cougar. Or what's the name of that steelworker over on Gallery Row that always flirts with you?"

"Or how about none of them? I'm not ready to move on. You know that." She would have been, maybe, if the man she was interested in reciprocated that interest. But he hadn't called.

I'm the only one who will ever love you. Phil's voice jumped unbidden into her head again, and she closed her eyes and shook her head, determined to ignore him.

Chapter Six

Three years earlier: Sevilla, Spain, November 2010

It is another post-tourist season trip. This year both Cara and Amy have temp jobs starting in January. Flush with cash from a summer saving on Whispering Pines, plus some good contract work through Amy's marketing business, they have decided to spend their break in Europe. It is not their first time, so they have lots of friends to visit and things to do. Right now, they are in Sevilla, where Kelsey, one of Amy's old roommates, lives.

They take turns choosing what to do when they travel. The morning is up to Cara, and she chooses to spend it in the Parque de María Luisa, her with her sketchbook, Amy with sunglasses to hide the fact that she is napping.

Cara has always liked to draw, though she's not talented enough to make a career out of it. She had a show once in the community center on Whispering Pines, which was thrilling but not at all lucrative. It doesn't matter. She does it because she enjoys it; it's a relaxing hobby, and a fun way of documenting her life. Her current passion is drawing the foreign landscapes where she and Amy are traveling, but changing the people in them to her loved ones. The older couple by the fountain become her parents, smiling and holding hands. The homeless woman yelling at a flock of doves transforms into her stepmother—petty, but satisfying. A man walks by with a dog, and she quickly sketches him as Matteo and adds several additional dogs to round out Matty's pack. The tourist snapping photographs of the Mudejar Pavilion is her Uncle Paddy, and the man sitting alone reading a book becomes that executive chef they've just promoted, the one with unsettling blue eyes and a strangely disarming smile. And, of course, draped on a bench sleeping with an arm flung dramatically out is her beloved Amy.

Amy's nap gives Cara time to finish a rather nice preliminary sketch—she'll fill in more details later. Eventually, though, Cara gets hungry enough that she nudges her cousin awake so they can go eat lunch.

Amy always prefers activity to observation, so that afternoon Cara sets aside her pencils and they wander around getting lost in the winding medieval roads of the Barrio Santa Cruz. Now it is nearly evening, and time to meet Kelsey for drinks followed by a late dinner. They leave the Barrio and are arguing about the fastest way to get to their meeting spot when, from the corner of her eye, Cara sees a man stepping off the curb into the path of a bus. The bus is not stopping. She is close, no more than an arm's length away, and she is fast enough to knock the man over onto the sidewalk and keep him out of the road.

Ten cuidado, amigo, be careful friend, she tells him in Spanish, and he stares at her, holding his head. She suspects he hit it on the ground. She looks for assistance, and a police officer who saw what happened comes running over. She speaks to him rapidly in Spanish, makes sure the man is getting help, and jumps into a taxi that Amy somehow managed to hail. They make it to their destination, and the incident is largely forgotten.

The next day, Cara and Amy are supposed to join Kelsey again, this time at a bar popular with foreigners. Kelsey wants to introduce them to some American tourists, friends of her cousin or some distant relation who happen to be in the area. The O'Connells are running late, which is not unusual for them. Amy met a man at a club the night before, and they are having a little trouble ditching him. That sometimes happens with Amy; she is too friendly for her own good.

When they arrive, they can't find Kelsey. Presumably, she remembers they are always late and planned accordingly, so the cousins order drinks and go sit at a table to wait. There are a lot of American accents in the bar, and they shamelessly eavesdrop on other conversations. One is particularly interesting: at a table near them, a man is telling the story of a beautiful Spanish woman who saved his life and then disappeared. "She may have been an angel," the man says, seemingly seriously, and his friends laugh.

"She can't be an actual angel. I got her picture. See," says one of the other men, the loudest of the group. He is holding an extremely large and expensive digital camera, one that Cara suspects will be stolen before the end of his trip. "I was taking shots of the crowd. This is her, right, getting into this taxi?"

Another American voice. "No, *that's* her."

"That's what I said, that's her, look at the picture."

"No, I mean that's her. Hey Phil, your Spanish girl is at that table right over there."

Cara suddenly realizes the men are talking about her. She and Amy exchange a look, she raises an eyebrow, Amy subtly nods, and they wordlessly agree, yes, they are Spanish.

The man named Phil comes over to their table, staring at her almost reverently. No one has ever looked at Cara like this before. He is handsome, she notices, and his eyes are kind.

"You saved my life," he tells her.

Cara smiles pleasantly, tipping her head to the side and giving him a quizzical look. Amy just looks perplexed. They don't speak a word of English.

Phil blushes. "I'm sorry, no Spanish. Ummm ... *habla inglés*? Ummm ..." He glances helplessly at his friends. None of them speak the language either, and so one of them resorts to the American trick of increasing his volume to make his English more understandable.

Amy shakes her head, shrugs, and casually gestures to the now-empty wineglasses on their table. This, the Americans understand, and one of them immediately heads to the bar, coming back with more drinks. "I didn't know white or red, so I got two of each." He holds up four glasses shouting loudly, "WHITE AND RED!"

Cara takes both reds, "*Vino tinto,*" she corrects gently. "*Gracias.*"

Amy takes the whites, pours them together into one very full glass and begins to drink. "*Cierra la puerta, por que yo no tengo naranjas,*" she tells them in a friendly tone. She speaks French and some Mandarin, but not Spanish, that's Cara's language. But it doesn't matter. The men don't understand that she told them to shut the door because she doesn't have oranges. The cousins could say whatever they want; these men would never notice.

Phil is still trying to speak to them. He runs a hand through his hair, and Cara represses the sudden urge to reach out and smooth it back down. "Ummm . . . my friend um, my *amiga* is coming, and she'll translate. I just want to thank you for saving me. THANK YOU!"

"*De nada,*" Cara replies, saluting him with one of her wine glasses. She doesn't know how much longer she can do this. Amy's face is turning red, and she looks like she's about to choke.

Kelsey arrives and starts making her way over to them. "Oh, you've already found each other," she says in surprise.

"Yes, we found her. This is the Spanish woman who saved me yesterday," Phil tells her excitedly. "You have to translate for me. Tell her she's beautiful and amazing, and I owe her my life."

Kelsey looks at the cousins and back at Phil. "The Spanish woman . . ." she repeats doubtfully, looking at Cara.

Amy finally cracks and starts laughing hysterically.

Cara gives up the charade and offers Kelsey the second glass of red wine. "Here, you may as well take this," she says, and it takes the men a moment to notice that she is speaking English. "Wait, Kels, are these the Americans you wanted us to meet?"

Chapter Seven

Whispering Pines, May 2013

On Sam's third night back, Paddy invited his five full-time staffers to a night out before the season started. It would likely be the only time all of them would be able to hang out away from the inn together. They went to The Digs, the island's only real bar. It was still uncrowded this time of year, but Sam knew that in a couple of weeks it would be near impossible to snag a table there.

Sam was happy for the opportunity to go out. He hadn't had any time with Cara, had hardly seen her really, since she spent her days in the inn's office doing paperwork while he was busy preparing the restaurant kitchen. He thought maybe a night of drinking would loosen things up, and maybe give him the courage to say what he wanted to say. He managed to maneuver his way into sitting next to her at the table, and he shamelessly kept 'accidentally' bumping his leg into hers.

"So is this everybody?" Tyrell asked, looking around the table.

Sam had been surprised to meet him when he arrived. Nobody told him they were getting a new employee. Apparently, Hannah, who had worked with them for the past two summers, accepted a permanent position elsewhere, and Tyrell had been hired to replace her.

"We're the important ones," Amy told him. "Sammy has a kitchen staff and some waitresses, but they're all part-time. And we have housekeeping, of course, and a couple of on-call people who fill in, but again, part-time. We're the ones who put in a million hours a week and do all the real work."

"Amy is bad at math," Paddy reassured Tyrell. "I don't work you that hard. Slightly less than a million hours a week. But your schedule will be packed and irregular. That's why I give you room and board on top of salary. It's to make up for all the uncompensated overtime. Trust me, you'll all earn your end-of-season bonuses."

Sato returned from the bar balancing a pitcher of beer and a stack of glasses. He looked softer than Sam remembered. He'd gained a little weight and had an overall countenance of contentment. "I don't get room and board. You should give me a raise," he said, joining the conversation.

"Nice try. You can move back into the staff house whenever you want. And don't think I don't know how much you eat." Paddy began pouring the drinks.

"Not happening. Sato snores. Tyrell doesn't." Sam crossed his arms and leaned back, bumping into Cara's arm. "I'm perfectly happy with the arrangements this year."

They discussed business for a while, planning out the upcoming season. There were several weddings scheduled, and the entire property was almost fully booked from mid-June to mid-August. Finally, Paddy finished all the logistics he wanted to go over, and announced he was heading home, to his little cottage behind the inn.

"Drink all night, do whatever you want," he told them, "But I already told Timmy not to put it on my tab."

"Not even my drinks? But we're family!" Cara exclaimed in mock horror.

Paddy pulled a twenty-dollar bill out of his wallet and threw it at her. "That should get you drunk, my dear. Goodnight, everyone be safe."

"He seems like a good boss," Tyrell commented as they watched him depart.

"He is, and we need to listen to him," Amy announced. "Paddy said he wants us to drink all night, so let's get started. Cara, you buying the next round? I know you can afford it."

"Actually, she's not." Sato told them all. "And I'm not paying for any drinks either. Anyone who didn't bother to come to my wedding is buying for everybody tonight. You owe me. Even you Ty, and I don't care that you didn't know me then."

"Hey, I was working in Thailand," Amy protested. "I couldn't get time off, but I sent a gift. That should count for something."

"It's fine. I'll buy the next round." Sam stood, but before he walked to the bar, he leaned over as close to Cara as he dared to get and whispered loudly. "Lend me twenty bucks?"

She turned to look at him and for the first time he was able to see that under her tan she appeared tired and her eyes lacked their usual sparkle. Her smile was still sweet though.

"Oh, Sam, if you don't have the money, tell Tim to send the bill to the inn. I'll be happy to deduct it from your first paycheck."

When Sam came back with drinks, he saw that he had been replaced. There was a blond man in his seat, leaning back with an arm draped all too familiarly across the back of Cara's chair. *Damn it, Matteo*, he thought in irritation.

"Hey, Sammy, welcome back," Matteo greeted him. "I'm taking Cara and Ty out kayaking tomorrow. Want to come? We could use a fourth." Matteo owned Cap'n Rentals, offering bikes and kayaks for rent as well as guided tours. He was a true local, born and raised on the island. Sam always liked hanging out with him, but he couldn't help but be annoyed that Matteo had usurped his proximity to Cara.

Although the outing sounded fun, Sam couldn't join them. He had too much work. He and Paddy had been going over menus, and he had some experimenting and perfecting that he wanted to do. There was a lot of prep that went into reopening a seasonal restaurant.

"I'll go," Sato volunteered. "I just need to check with my wife first."

"Check with your wife? Oh, Sato, you've changed," Amy teased.

"You wish you had someone to check with," Sato retorted with a grin. He really did appear happier than ever before.

Married life suited him, Sam thought, with a brief pang of envy.

"How the mighty have fallen," Matteo said sorrowfully. "You should have seen this guy. All winter, I couldn't drag him out to do anything. Marriage is a killer." He jerked suddenly, like he had been kicked under the table, and his faux-sorrow transformed into a guilty expression. "Sorry Cara, I didn't mean that."

Her smile appeared strained. "Don't worry about it." She turned to Ty. "So, Ty, you've been here four days. What do you think of our little island so far?"

"It's not that little," Ty replied. "I know I need to do everything possible to learn this place before the guests arrive, but I'm worn out. Paddy sent me out on the hiking trails all day, and now my leg hurts. It'll be nice to sit down and paddle tomorrow instead."

"The real one or the robot one?" Amy asked innocently.

Tyrell demonstrated his ability to deliver a spectacular eye-roll. "For the millionth time, it's not a robot leg. Those don't exist. It's just a prosthetic. It doesn't do anything."

"That's what he thinks." Amy shook her head and looked at the others. "One day, when the robot wars start, he's going to be surprised as to what side he's on and how little control he has over it."

"Oh, Amy, quit teasing the new guy," Cara chastised, but before Ty could thank her she added, "You'll want to be on his good side when the robots make us their pets."

"I'll make you my pet," Matteo leered, and everybody but Sam laughed. "No, I'm kidding. I don't even want to joke about it. When you broke off our engagement, you broke my heart, Cara."

"Shut up Matteo!" Amy snapped immediately.

"You two were engaged? I thought ..." Tyrell started to ask, but that was the point when Cara punched Matteo in the arm and called him a liar.

"What? It's true," Matteo insisted. "Don't pretend you don't remember."

"I remember," Amy said. "I remember how much trouble you got in for giving your mom's engagement ring away."

"I don't think I'm familiar with this story," Sam looked from Matteo to Cara. He'd never heard anything about them being involved. He knew Matteo hooked up with Amy once— he bragged about that encounter every year—but Cara, too? How many broken engagements did she have?

Cara rolled her eyes and focused on Ty. "I lived here for a couple of years as a kid, and when I was eleven and my mom and I were moving back to Midland, Matteo took his mother's engagement ring from her jewelry box, gave it to me, and said that if I came back to the island, he was going to marry me. Believe me, I did not say yes." Matteo started to protest, but she cut him off. "And then once we were there, I took the ring to school to show Amy. She said it wasn't a real diamond, and we needed to test it by cutting glass."

Amy shrugged. "It seemed like a good idea at the time."

"Yeah, until you said we had to pry the stone out and use the bottom of it—"

"That was the sharpest part!"

"Maybe, but how would we know since you dropped the damn thing on the gravel playground?"

"Wait," Sam interrupted. "You lost the stone for Matteo's mom's ring?"

"Oh, it gets better," Cara continued. "When I got home from school that day, my mom asked for the ring because Mrs. Capen called and said I stole it."

"I eventually told the truth," Matteo interjected.

"Yeah, but first I got in trouble. And my mom was furious when I gave her the ring without the stone."

"Well, I was grounded for a month, and my parents made me sell my bike and my brand-new kayak to pay for a new stone, so it was worse for me," Matteo countered.

"But, wait, the story gets better," Amy continued. "Four years later, my little sister Mandi came home from school all excited because she found a crystal on the playground, and it was that goddamn diamond. But since Matteo already had bought a replacement, we kept it. I think it's still in my jewelry box back home."

"Seriously?" Tyrell looked skeptically from Amy to Matteo. "I was believing you up until your sister found the stone."

"Oh, every word is true," Cara promised. "Especially the part where I rejected Matteo."

"Yeah, you brag about that too much. Breaks my heart." Matteo shook his head morosely. Then he cheered up surprisingly quickly for a man who had just been reminded of perpetual rejection. "Doesn't matter. There are hundreds of women out there looking for some island loving. Ty, are you single? Sammy and I have had a lot of success here. The tourists love us, right buddy?"

He tried to high-five Sam, but Sam shook his head and left him hanging. He felt the need to defend himself. "Hey, I've had no success lately. At least, not at getting what I really want." He carefully looked at Cara when he said it, but she had turned to say something to Amy and didn't seem to notice.

Later, when Matteo went home to walk his dogs, Sam, Sato, and Tyrell moved to stools at the bar and leaned against it to watch as Amy and Cara started doing shots.

"Those girls can drink," Tyrell commented.

"I'll let you in on a secret," Tim the bartender told them conspiratorially. "Every time Amy comes up to buy a round, she gets vodka for Cara and tap water for herself. She doesn't want to get too drunk, but she wants Cara to enjoy herself. Meanwhile, Cara thinks she's going to have to take care of drunk Amy later, so she's doing the exact same thing. Neither of them knows it."

"You going to tell them?" Sam asked, raising an eyebrow.

Tim shrugged. "They tip well, so I'll probably keep my mouth shut on this one."

Tyrell observed them with amusement. "Are they always like this? I need to know what I'm getting into, working here this summer. I've never lived with women before. I don't know what to expect."

"Nah, they're just blowing off some steam," Sam said. "Once tourist season starts they work pretty hard and don't have time for stuff like this. None of us do."

"Yeah," Tim chimed in. "He's right. Summers are busy. My bar gets packed, especially during the Fourth of July weekend, and around PrideFest."

"Oh, that's right, I just read an article about that," Tyrell nodded. "So it's a good one?"

"PrideFest?" Tim put his elbows on the bar and leaned closer. "Yeah, it's fantastic. Lots of fun people, and it's family friendly. That's what brought me here. Came for the festival, fell in love with the island, and bought the bar. I've been here ever since."

"Oh yeah?" Tyrell turned around on his stool to face the bartender. "Were you staying because of the island or because you met someone special?"

At that point, Sam tuned them out. As much as he enjoyed attending the annual celebrations, spending hours at a grill for a barbeque did not appeal to him nearly as much as creating refined dishes in his well-appointed kitchen. He thought of grilling as a craft, and he preferred cooking as an art.

He watched Amy come back for another round, and wondered when he would finally be able to talk to Cara. Would it be tonight? Or should he wait until she was sober?

Sato clinked his beer against Sam's, interrupting his train of thought. "Cheers, man. I didn't get the chance to say welcome back. Glad you came."

"Me, too," Sam smiled. "I think it's going to be a good summer. Hey, listen, I should apologize for missing your wedding."

"No worries, I know it's tough to travel mid-season." Sato waved a hand dismissively. "I understand. You were busy at the resort. Wedding was beautiful though. I'm not usually into that kind of thing, but Paddy set everything up, and at a discount, too. I think he was using it as a test run."

"A test run for what? We have weddings here all the time. Didn't he say there are ten this summer?"

"You didn't hear?" Sato gave him a quizzical look. "Paddy's thinking about staying open year-round. Only on weekends, I think."

Sam was surprised. Throughout the inn's ninety-year history it had always only been open from May to September. After that, the tourist trade dried up and most of the businesses on the island shut down. The summer residents and workers left, and only the hardiest locals stayed to endure the long, cold winter. It never seemed feasible to Sam that they would decide to stay open longer.

"That would be ... interesting." Sam wondered about the restaurant, and what that would mean for his own job security. If they were open all year, they wouldn't need a seasonal chef, would they?

"It'll be great for me." Sato grinned. "You know how work dries up around here in the winter, and I need to earn some more money. I'm going to have a family to support soon. It's not just the inn, either. The Village Council has been meeting to discuss details a lot lately. Matteo, you won't be surprised to hear, is strongly in favor of winter tourism. I think he gets lonely. But yeah, the hotel, the bed and breakfasts, everywhere but the campgrounds are excited about the idea. Paddy's thinking winter weddings, company retreats, and they've all been talking about a holiday festival. I think Amy's going to help set that up. You know her. She's already halfway through designing some sort of marketing campaign."

Sam continued watching Cara and Amy. They were playing darts and laughing with some people Sam recognized as summer employees from the Village Hotel. He idly wondered if those employees were considering sticking around for the winter. This might change everything. This really could be his last summer on the island. He needed to make it count.

Chapter Eight

"Whiskey?" Even though it was barely mid-morning, Paddy didn't wait for an answer. He poured a glass and slid it across the desktop to Sam.

They were in his office behind the lobby reception desk where he conducted all his business. Most of his business seemed to be delegating things to Cara and drinking whiskey. Sam liked meeting with him there to discuss menus, food orders, and, of course, Paddy's favorite subject, island gossip.

"I'm glad you changed your mind and came back," Paddy said. "I need you in the kitchen. Plus, Cara doesn't sit in my office and drink whiskey with me. Doesn't like it. I even got rum for her once, and she was all, 'Uncle Paddy, I'm not going to sit here drinking straight rum with you when we need to go over these accounts.'" He delivered the last bit in a prim falsetto that sounded nothing like Cara.

Sam laughed. "You need to work on your impressions. You didn't sound nearly Texan enough."

"I save my best Southern accent for when I'm quoting Amy. It annoys them both more that way." Paddy took another sip of whiskey. "Listen, before we start going over menu plans, we're going to have a little talk about Cara. I want to make sure that whatever sourness was happening between you last year is over. I can't have my general manager and executive chef not speaking to each other."

"Everything is fine," Sam promised. "Seriously." Privately, he thought he wasn't the one with a problem last summer. Sure, he'd stopped speaking to Cara, but she was avoiding him anyway, so it didn't matter. It hardly counted as not speaking to someone if they weren't around to notice.

"Do you want to tell me what happened between the two of you?" Paddy folded his arms across his chest and looked at Sam appraisingly.

Sam almost felt like he was back in high school, sitting in the principal's office, waiting to find out his punishment. He looked down at his hands and didn't respond, unsure of what he should say.

After a long moment, Paddy slapped his hand down on the desktop, making his framed pictures jump. "Damn it, she wouldn't tell me either. You know I like gossip."

Sam sighed. He did not want to have this conversation with his boss. "Look, Paddy, it wasn't a big deal. I just told Cara that I thought marrying Phil would be a mistake, and she disagreed with me. We argued over it. That was all." Obviously, that wasn't all, but it was all he was willing to say.

"Oh, well in that case ..." Paddy topped off Sam's glass. "You said what we were all thinking. I knew she wasn't actually going to marry that guy. So did Amy. We had a bet going as to whether Cara would ever start planning the wedding. I lost, by the way. I tried really hard to get her to ask me to host it here, but she never took the bait, and now I owe Amy a case of wine. Under the circumstances though, she's not tried to collect. Did you have a chance to meet Phil when he visited here last summer?"

"Oh, I met him." Sam almost laughed at the memory. Phil was pretentious and possessive, and Sam rather enjoyed needling him. "He didn't seem like Cara's type."

"No, no he didn't." Paddy shook his head. "It's a shame what happened to him though." Sam was about to ask for details about the breakup, but thought the better of it. He decided he'd rather give Cara the opportunity to talk about it herself.

Paddy changed the subject. "Hey, did you have fun at the bar last night? What do you think of your new roommate?"

"Tyrell?" asked Sam. "What's not to like? He's easygoing and he makes his bed every morning. And he doesn't put up with any of Amy's nonsense, so I think he'll be a good fit here."

Paddy leaned forward. "Don't tell anyone I asked this, but does he take off his leg when he goes to bed? That's not the kind of thing I can ask directly, right? I was just wondering about that."

"He takes it off. But I don't think he'd mind you asking." Tyrell had been surprisingly open about the mechanics of his prosthetic limb, though he was rather reticent about the accident that caused him to need it. Despite Amy's multiple attempts, all he would reveal was that he deployed with two good legs and came back with one.

"You know who I got him for, right? Did you figure it out?" Paddy asked, pouring himself yet another whiskey. "Hey, next time you come in for a meeting, bring a bucket of ice so we can drink this properly."

"Got him for? What?" Sam had no idea what Paddy was talking about.

"I'm a matchmaker, Sam. I've owned this inn for almost thirty years and I've fixed up dozens of my staffers. I always know. It's like Sato and Margaux. I hired him for her, and look what happened. That's why I always made him do the bakery runs instead of you."

"Sato has worked for you for ten years. And wasn't Margaux married to someone else for part of that?"

Paddy winked. "I play the long game, Sam. Love doesn't always take a direct path."

"Alright, I give up. Who'd you get Tyrell for?" *Please don't say Cara, please don't say Cara.*

"If you can't figure it out, I'm not going to tell you. I knew the minute I interviewed him. You'll see though. End of the summer, I bet Tyrell sticks around. Just wait. He's going to become a permanent resident."

Damn it, he must be talking about Cara, if what Sato had said about the winter season was true. Tyrell didn't just come to replace Hannah as a Guest Services Specialist, he came to replace Phil as a lover. Sam took a deep breath. He was up for the competition.

Then another thought crossed his mind. "If you're such a matchmaker, who'd you hire me for?" If not Cara, then who? It certainly couldn't have been Amy, could it? He watched Paddy's face.

Paddy leaned back, and his eyes narrowed before he let out a laugh. "You? Sam, I hired you for Geoffrey. He wanted to retire, and he needed someone he could train as a replacement. Why? Who'd you think?"

🌲 🌲 🌲 🌲 🌲

After the meeting with Paddy, and drinking some water to combat the whiskey, Sam got back to work. Most of his supplies weren't in yet—Paddy didn't want to spend money on fresh ingredients until they were ready to be used—so Sam set himself the task of arranging the restaurant seating. During the winter, patio furniture was stored in there, and all of the dining furniture was stacked against the walls covered in sheets. Fortunately, someone already had pulled out the patio furniture, so he started on the tables and chairs. It surprised him when Sato wandered in to help out.

"I thought you'd decided to go kayaking with everybody else. What are you doing here? Margaux wouldn't let you go?" Sam teased.

"Nah, I let Timmy go in my place. I thought he'd have more fun than I would. Besides, who would help you if I went? Not Amy, that's for sure. She's not gonna dirty her hands with manual labor." Sato yanked sheets off and threw them in a pile. Sam had been neatly folding and stacking them because, until he saw Sato's nonchalant attitude, he had forgotten that they were going to be sent to the laundry rather than stored away for the summer.

While they worked they chatted a bit, and finally Sam got up the nerve to ask something he was curious about. "Hey Sato," Sam said, trying to sound casual. "What do you think about me and Cara?"

"Nope, I'm not playing this game." Sato tossed another sheet on the pile.

"What game?"

"Look man, I'm friends with both of you, plus she's my boss. Don't ask me to take sides in whatever you're fighting about."

"I . . . we're not fighting."

"Yes, you are. You guys went from being best friends and hanging out all the time to you completely cutting off contact with her last summer. And don't deny it, everybody knows. Hell, we were all surprised you came back."

"Seriously, we're not fighting," Sam assured him, though he honestly wasn't sure if that was true. He hadn't really had time to talk to Cara yet and to work things out between them. He planned to though. He was going to take her out to a nice dinner and tell her he meant what he said last summer when he told he loved her, and she'd . . . well, he didn't know what she'd say, but he had his hopes. "To be honest with you Sato, she's the reason I came back this year. You know, now that she's single . . ."

Sato stopped working and stared at him. "You're kidding, right?" That was not the response Sam expected.

"Come on, Cara and I are great together, you even said it. Best friends, right? You've seen us. So yeah, she's single and I'm single, so I think it's time we give it a shot."

"Man, that's a terrible idea. What happened to that Colorado girlfriend you always string along?"

"Who, Lizbet? We were never serious, and anyway, we broke up." Sam had ended things with Lizbet in mid-April, or rather, she dumped him when she found out he turned down the Denver job.

Apparently, without his knowledge, she had already signed a lease on a two-bedroom apartment and started making arrangements to move them both there. She had been furious with him, and after a plate-throwing screaming tirade, she kicked him out of her condo. He was actually relieved when she initiated the abrupt ending. He had been planning to do it anyway, but he was terrible at that kind of conversation. He hated to hurt people's feelings. Technically, he had never broken up with anyone. He just sort of disappeared on them. Eventually, they realized the relationship was over without him having to go through any difficult conversations and drama.

"I mean it, Sato. I'm serious about this." Sam didn't like the way Sato was looking at him, his face a mixture of skepticism and concern. "I really am. I'm planning on taking Cara somewhere romantic, maybe somewhere on the mainland if Paddy lets me borrow the inn's van. There are some restaurants I wanted to try anyway."

Sato just shook his head. "My advice, speaking as Cara's friend, is to back off. Wait until the summer season starts and find someone else. You of all people know there are always plenty of available ladies."

"I'm not interested in anyone else. I'm only interested in Cara."

"That's a bad idea. And if you decide to ignore me and ask her out anyway, I think you should wait, man."

"Why? Do you know how long I've waited for her to be single? And I'm sure I had something to do with it. There's always been something between us. I know she feels it, too. She has to."

"Sammy, I strongly doubt you had anything to do with the engagement ending, unless you're the one who killed her fiancé."

"He was murdered?" Sam was both horrified and incredulous. He'd just assumed Cara was the one who'd called the whole thing off—hopefully because of what he had told her, hopefully because she knew she was with the wrong guy, and because she couldn't marry someone else when she had such a deep connection with Sam. It never occurred to him that her single status could have been created by anything other than her choice.

"No. Well, I don't think so. I was kind of joking. I don't know the exact circumstances of his death. Cara wouldn't say, and nobody at the funeral would talk about it either."

"You went to his funeral?" Sam had a hard time processing this. Why hadn't he heard about this? Why didn't anybody tell him? He could have sent flowers or at least a card, or something. Cara must think he was the biggest oaf. No wonder she hadn't sought him out at all since he'd been back.

"Of course I went. He lived in Chicago, remember? It was like a nine-hour drive, but we took the inn van. Paddy had to go, to support his niece, and a bunch of us islanders went too, for the same reason. Hell, Matteo even went, in spite of the panic attacks he gets every time he sets foot on the mainland. There were a lot of people, hundreds maybe. And I remember

Phil's parents asked Cara to eulogize him. She was crying too hard, so Amy said a few words instead, something about the cycle of life. And Cara was still wearing her engagement ring, but she doesn't wear it now. So give her time. Give her a chance to heal and to mourn. I don't think that's the kind of thing someone gets over quickly, and it's only been six months."

They worked in silence for a time, setting the chairs and tables back in their usual locations and making sure they were all still in working order. Sam was thinking hard about Cara, and her fiancé's death, and how all he wanted to do was find her and hug her and tell her how sorry he was, and how he'd be there for her.

Finally, Sato spoke again. "Just in case you're still considering asking her out, you know the island hierarchy, right? Year-round locals run everything, and they protect their own. And Paddy's one of their own. And so is Cara. You don't want to mess around with her."

"Cara doesn't live here year-round."

"No, but she did for a couple of years as a child. And her grandparents once owned the inn, and everybody remembers her mom. She's a Whispering Pines daughter. Summer employees rank higher than tourists, and people always like you—possibly because of the barbeque sauce you make on the Fourth. But we all know you, Sam. And, no offense, you're kind of a dog."

"What? No, I'm not!" Sam was astonished. That was not how he thought of himself, not at all. At least, not anymore.

"You are. Remember the first summer you were here? Weren't you living in the hostel in town but never actually sleeping there? And everybody knows the story of you and the night clerk at the hotel. Oh, and what about those two waitresses who actually got in a fight over you? I'm sure there were some others, too. You made a reputation for yourself on a small island full of people who love gossip and don't have anything else to talk about the rest of the year."

"That is all exaggerated, and that was only one summer," Sam protested. "I'm different now. You know that. You and I shared a room for two summers, and not once did I bring anyone home. Hell, last summer I didn't even think about hooking up with anyone."

That last bit was a tiny lie. He had spent far too many nights thinking about who he wanted to hook up with, if she wasn't wearing that damn engagement ring on her finger. Maybe he had made an unfortunate first impression when he arrived on the island, but he'd worked hard to change his image, and he had thought he succeeded. Apparently, the island's collective memory for gossip was longer than he had imagined.

"We're not allowed to bring people back to the staff house," Sato corrected, "so that's not really evidence of anything but your ability to follow rules. And don't lie to me about last summer—everyone saw you and Amy making out at the bar."

"No, we didn't. I kissed her on the cheek, one time, and only because a guy was harassing her. I was just pretending to be her boyfriend to make him go away. That's all. I can't help it if the local gossips blew everything out of proportion." Amy had shown up at The Digs to pick up a cart load of aggressive drunken guests who seemed to think that she came to party with them. Sam didn't regret stepping in, even if apparently all of the witnesses misunderstood the situation.

"Still, everybody thinks of you as that guy. And don't say it's the same with Matteo. His track record with tourists is more forgivable because he's a local. Plus, everyone knows he makes half of it up. So in him it's just, you know, how he is, whereas in you it's a moral failing. But the point is, if you were actually interested in Cara, you would need to do a lot of proving yourself to everybody else."

"That's ridiculous," Sam argued, frustrated by the utter unfairness of everything Sato said. "Cara can make her own decisions. When she's ready to date again, I'm just going to ask her out and not worry what people in the village have to say about it."

"Except then you are the dog they all think you are, taking advantage of a vulnerable local girl whose fiancé just died. Then you're a predator. Do you want everyone in town warning her off you and banding together to destroy your relationship?"

"What is this, a cheesy eighties movie? You don't seem to believe me, but I really do like her. I *like* like her. I'd even go so far as to say I'm in love with her. I meant what I said—I came back this summer for her. I've known for a long time that she and I belong together. In fact, that's the real reason I didn't make it to your wedding." He was getting frustrated. He had never told anyone—other than Cara herself—how he felt about her, and that had gone just as badly.

"My wedding took place a couple of months after Phil's death, and Cara was there. If you liked her as much as you claim, you could've made a move then." Sato held up one hand. "Not that I would have advised it then either. I'm just pointing out some flaws in your logic."

"I'm a little embarrassed to admit this, but I never read your invitation." Sam explained how he'd thought it was for Cara's wedding. "That's why I sent your wedding gift so late ... because I didn't know it came from you. Hell, if I hadn't seen a blog post from Amy about Cara being single, I would be in Denver right now."

Sato shook his head, unconvinced. "I guess that's why you didn't send her any condolences when Phil died? Did you somehow miss all those emails? And Amy said she contacted you directly, and you didn't call her back. We all thought you were being kind of a cheap jerk when you didn't contribute to the flowers we sent."

"I didn't know about any of that," Sam insisted. "If I knew, I would have done something. But I never got any emails . . . oh wait. Crap." He knew what happened.

Last fall, on a night when he felt particularly sorry for himself, he set up an email filter redirecting any message containing *Phil* or *Phillip* and *Cara* straight to the trash. Drunk and maudlin, he wanted to avoid hearing about the wedding . . . and when he sobered up he hadn't bothered to change the settings. In fact, he hadn't thought much about it until Renee Phillips at work complained that he missed her Valentine's Day party and he discovered the rerouted invite in the trash. By then it would have been too late.

"You're right, Sato. I am a jerk."

Chapter Nine

Two years earlier: Whispering Pines, July 2011

Sam has never been in love before. He's dated, of course, and he's had more than his fair share of hook-ups, but he's never actually loved anyone. He's not sure it's in his nature. Sure, he'll commit to a woman as long as the sex is frequent and she doesn't ask too much from him emotionally, but the only times he's said 'I love you' were heat-of-the-moment responses to similar declarations, and were instantly regretted. That's why he can't quite classify the feeling he has sometimes around Cara.

She's his boss and his housemate and she has a boyfriend, three characteristics which mean he should feel nothing for her whatsoever.

But he is about six weeks in to his second summer on Whispering Pines Island, and it seems like there is something shifting inside of him. He doesn't ever think about his life outside the island. It's like all of his past has disappeared and he is nothing more than the person he is here, the man who looks into gold-flecked eyes every morning and feels content.

Today something is off, though. Something has cracked his perfect peace: Cara is missing. Five days a week, he is in charge of breakfast for the inn's guests, and those same five days Cara opens the reception desk. And on each of those days, they follow the same routine: Sam wakes, takes a fast shower, and makes coffee. Some of this effort is for his roommate, Sato, who on three of these days is up early and grabs his coffee as he heads down to the village bakery to pick up fresh bread and pastries for the guests. The rest of the pot is for Cara. Sometimes he also cooks her pancakes or scrambled eggs, or if he is in a particularly fancy mood, a frittata. No matter what it is, she says thank you and blinks her beautiful sleepy eyes at him while they eat together.

This morning everything is all wrong. Cara's coffee is on the table, but it is her cousin Amy who comes stumbling bleary-eyed out from the door to the women's bedroom.

"Well, you're the wrong person," Sam says in surprise.

"Aren't you a charmer in the morning?" Amy collapses into a chair. "How do y'all get up so early? Hey, whose coffee is this?"

"That's Cara's," he tells her, looking back at the now-closed bedroom door. Where is she? Already his mood begins to sour.

"Oh, good, then I'll drink it." She picks up the mug and also picks up on the expression on his face. "What? Cara has a terrible cold. She's not leaving our room today. Paddy said I have to take the morning shift because he doesn't get out of bed before nine." She takes a sip and makes a face. "Yuck! Sammy, that is not coffee! That's just sweet milk that was walked past a coffeepot. Gross. Is there any real coffee?"

"That's how Cara likes it," he informs her a bit defensively. He wouldn't drink that crap either, but Cara always smiles and tells him it's perfect.

"I know, she has no taste. But you're a professional, you should know better. How do you take your coffee?" Amy is looking around as if for another cup, perhaps hoping she can cajole him into giving her his. Then she has the nerve to get up and try to start another pot without even asking.

He doesn't like to be too possessive, but this is kind of his kitchen. She should let him do it. "Coffee destroys taste buds and stains teeth," he says. "It's destructive. But I'll make you some and I'll even make you eggs, if you sit down and stop touching stuff in my kitchen."

"I don't think you know much about taste buds," she says, but she does retreat back to the table. "They regenerate, you dummy."

"I think you don't understand the importance of a chef maintaining a clean palate," he mutters under his breath.

Why is he in such a bad mood? Usually, this is the best time of the day. Usually, he sits and relaxes and doesn't feel this tightness in his mind, this tenseness in his muscles. The whole interaction with Amy has put him off-balance, and he can't figure out why. They're friends; they hang out often enough. But this is a bad morning. Something is wrong, and he just can't get his head on straight.

After the breakfast service, and still feeling off-balance, he heads into the restaurant kitchen and starts preparing soup. Cara has a cold, so he starts with chicken noodle. Then he remembers that Cara is from the Southwest and likes spicy foods, so he makes a tortilla soup with green chilies as well. Then he thinks that maybe her throat hurts, so he also makes a corn chowder. It's sweeter and might be more soothing than the others.

Hannah wanders into the kitchen in search of food while he is finishing up. "What's with all the soup? You catering something?" she asks as she helps herself to leftover breakfast pastries.

"It's for Cara. She has a cold," he explains.

Hannah starts to laugh. "Dude, you made her four pots of soup? You do know she has a boyfriend, right?"

"Three. The flavor on the tomato soup isn't quite right. And it's not too much. I didn't know what kind she wanted, and the leftovers will keep. Soup freezes. And yes, I know she has a boyfriend." His response is a bit defensive. It's not like he's doing it because he wants to sleep with her. He's just being nice. That's what he does here—he takes care of people's culinary needs.

That's not to say he hasn't thought about what it might be like to sleep with Cara. He's thought that about all the women he works with; it's his nature, he can't help it.

Hannah would be loud, he's sure of that. And Amy, he knows she's bouncy. She'd probably always want to be on top. And Cara ... well, he has had many ideas about her. She always seems so calm and professional, but there's a wickedness in her; he's seen it in her eyes. Oh, and she likes to be in charge. He's watched the way she handles temp staff during inn events. That must carry over into the bedroom, and he likes that. He likes a woman who takes control, who can tell him exactly what she wants him to do. *Tell me what you want,* he would whisper, and she would. She'd give specific instructions.

And he's good at following instructions. He'd try whatever she asks, and when they were done, she would lie against him, and he would breathe in the smells of sweat and sex and strawberry shampoo, and maybe she would kiss the bite marks on his shoulder (he thought maybe—hopefully—she'd be a biter), and then they would doze off. Later, he'd make her breakfast, or lunch, or dinner, and she'd sit across from him, and maybe she'd have put on nothing but one of his T-shirts, and he would reach across the table to feed her bites of food and ...

He realizes he is fantasizing and Hannah is staring at him, amused.

He puts the three best soups into thermoses and takes a tray up to the staff house. It's his first time actually entering the women's bedroom, and he carefully backs through the door because of all he's carrying. It takes a moment for his eyes to adjust to the dim light, but then he finally sees Cara, lying on a bed looking miserable. "I hope you've come to kill me," she croaks in a hoarse voice, and he laughs.

"I've come to make you better," he replies, and she smiles, and immediately the bad mood of the morning dissipates and all is right in the world again. He describes her options and is not surprised when she chooses the tortilla soup first.

"You didn't have to do this," she tells him as she struggles to a sitting position. She looks wretched. Her nose is red and she sounds like she can't breathe very well. There is a wastebasket full of used tissues next to the bed. Poor Cara.

"I wanted to do it," he assures her as he sets up the bowl of soup on the lap tray. "You need to get your strength up." He looks for a place to set the extra thermoses and notices an enormous bouquet of flowers on a dresser.

"From Phil," she says, but he would have guessed that.

"That's a lot of pollen. Soup is better than flowers when you're sick." Sam then realizes what he's doing. He's trying to show that he's better than her boyfriend. What he really wants to do is climb into the bed next to her and gently sponge off her face, stroke her hair, feed her soup, and let her drift off to sleep in his arms . . . oh. That's it.

It turns out, he does know what it's like to be in love.

Worse, he knows what it's like to be in love with someone he can't have.

Chapter Ten

Whispering Pines, May 2013

Cara's feet always remembered the path to Lesser Lake. She could find it with her eyes closed in the dark if she wanted to, which was convenient because the moon had gone behind a cloud and she hadn't brought a flashlight. Everyone else was still back at the restaurant for the soft opening. Amy hadn't even noticed her sneaking out, which was a relief. She didn't want Amy to ask her where she was going.

She was not surprised to see him sitting on a blanket by the lakeshore, but she was surprised by the number of twinkling lights on the rocks. He didn't turn around at her approach, but she heard his typical greeting. "That had better be Cara sneaking up on me."

"Not sneaking, Matty. What's with all the candles?"

Matteo turned around and looked at her. "I thought you'd like it. I wanted to try and make it special for you."

She couldn't make herself smile at that. "Not necessary, but thanks for the thought. Should I go first?"

"Straight to business? I like it," Matteo joked, but the grin quickly faded from his face.

He had always been able to read her very well, so he knew this was hard for her. They both walked over to the edge of the water together.

"I saw a shooting star earlier," he told her, pointing above the pines. "Right there. Maybe it's a message."

"I almost hope not," she replied, and then realized how depressing she sounded. She put her backpack on the ground next to her and removed a film canister.

"You're starting with your mother?" he asked, and she nodded.

She leaned over and sprinkled the cremains into the lake. The moon came out then, nearly full, and it made the ashes shimmer on the surface of the water.

"I miss you, Mom," she said to the lake. "I really could have used your help this past year. I like to think you made me strong enough to survive anything, but there were times I wasn't sure. But I love you and miss you. Give me another good summer, please." She turned away as the words threatened to choke her.

Matteo hugged her and then he, too, spoke to her mother. "Cynthia, you were the mom that all of us kids wished we had. I think of you every time I eat a double-fudge brownie. I wish you had shared your recipe. Thank you for not killing me when I got Cara shipwrecked on Lonely Pines. You would be proud of your daughter if you could see her now."

After a few moments of respectful silence, Matteo ventured a question. "How many of those are left? It's been thirteen years."

"Only four. I spread some in Thailand in April, and I sent some with a friend to Italy. My mom would have liked that." In some ways, she was going to be glad when all the ashes were gone. She would have finished her duty, and maybe she would finally have some peace. At the same time though, this ritual meant a lot to her, and she was afraid when she ran out of ashes she would run out of the last tenuous connection to her mother.

The ritual of scattering ashes actually started with an idea from Cara's mom years earlier when she brought nine-year-old Cara to the edge of Lesser Lake at the start of Cara's first tourist season. "Your grandma believed that the spirits of the island reside in this lake," her mother explained. "So every year when I was a child, she and I came up here and asked them to give us another good summer. This is where your grandparent's ashes are scattered, so this is where we can talk to them and ask them to watch over us. It's hallowed ground."

The year Cara's mother died, she invited Matteo up to the lake to join her. She wasn't working there that summer. She had just come out to visit Uncle Paddy and get away from the oppressive sadness in her home. She wanted to follow her mother's tradition, but couldn't face dispersing the ashes herself, and her uncle couldn't bear to help. Matteo was like a brother to her, so it felt natural to invite him to come along. Afterwards, they never really planned it, but every summer when Cara came to the island, they consecrated the start of a new tourist season together. Cara always brought a small canister of her mother's ashes, and sometimes Matteo brought someone as well. They had said goodbye to one of his grandparents and a cousin. She never told anyone else about it though—their ritual was too personal.

"I have someone too." Matteo walked back to his picnic blanket and returned with a steel water bottle.

"Who's that?" Cara asked in surprise. She and Matteo spoke often, and he hadn't mentioned any losses.

"Jessica."

"Oh, Matteo, why didn't you tell me?"

"It happened in December, right after Phil's death so I didn't want to burden you. She had cancer." He suddenly started to cry, and Cara hugged him tightly. "She was sick, and I couldn't afford the treatments, and the doctor couldn't guarantee they'd do anything for her anyway. I took her for a last boat ride. We went out to Windward Pines, and she got to run around in the snow one last time. I took care of her myself. Dr. Ferrin gave me the medicine, so I was able to inject it and hold her as she died."

"Oh, sweetheart," Cara teared up as well. "She was the best. I'm so sorry." She could feel his heartbreak. She knew how much he cared about his dogs and how important they were to him.

It took him a few minutes before he calmed down enough to actually spread the ashes. They watched them swirl away.

"Jessica, I loved you so much. You were my favorite from the minute I got you. I don't know how I made it through the winter, and it's going to be a rough summer without you. I knew Berners didn't have long life spans, but the years we had together made the pain of losing you worth it."

Then it was Cara's turn. "Jessica, you were a good dog. You always took care of your family, and I'll never forget the time a skunk sprayed you and you were so embarrassed you hid in Matteo's bed. I gave you a treat for it, but I don't know if you understood why you got the reward."

That brought a smile to Matteo's face. "I forgot about that incident. Did I tell you Tristan and Martha got sprayed by skunks this spring? Maybe that was Jessica trying to get them treats."

They stood quietly, watching the ashes, and finally Matteo turned to her. "I'm sorry, I shouldn't act so upset over a dog when you've lost so much more than me. Are you ready to scatter Phil now?"

"He's not here." She stared out over the water to avoid looking at him.

"Oh. Oh, Cara, I'm so sorry. I misunderstood. I thought they cremated him. That's why I set it up so romantic for you here, so you could say a nice goodbye."

"I know, and I appreciate the gesture. Really, I do. And yes, he was cremated, and his parents gave me half his ashes. They wanted me to take them to Spain, where we met. They thought it would be sweet." She wouldn't turn her head, wouldn't make eye contact.

"What did you do with them?" Matteo finally asked, when the silence had been drawn out too long.

"I poured them in a dumpster in the back of an IHOP. He would have hated that." One of the things Cara always liked about Matteo was that he knew when to stop asking questions.

He stood quietly next to her and then reached out and took her hand. They stood together, side by side, for several minutes, silently watching the moonlight on the lake.

"Alright, enough of this. Let's get drunk." Cara released Matteo's hand and returned to her backpack where she had stashed a bottle of cheap tequila.

"That is the tradition." Matteo grinned, took the bottle from her, and took a swig. "Cheers, to your mom and Jessica. May they watch over us this summer."

She noticed he left off Phil's name, and was glad.

Chapter Eleven

Email from Amy O'Connell to Fabio Basile:

Sorry I missed our usual Skype time last night. We had the soft opening for the restaurant (it's like a practice to make sure the staff knows what they're doing), and the food was pretty good. You probably would have enjoyed it. I had the fish, which was fantastic. We get amazing fresh trout right out of Lake Superior. They catch it in the morning, and we cook it in the evening. (Ok, not we. I have nothing to do with any of it.) The other option, which Cara had, so of course she shared with me, was bison, which I always find interesting. It's tastier and more tender than beef. Have you ever tried it, or is it too 'American' for your tastes?

Half the business owners in town came up for the opening, and I may have gotten myself a little bit of side work doing some marketing for a couple of them. I've been in talks with the Chamber of Commerce for that new winter tourism initiative, plus I'm working on getting my favorite bar to let me design T-shirts. If I score the contract, I'll send you one.

Speaking of my favorite bar, after dinner that's where I went with that new guy I was telling you about, Tyrell. Except we didn't go immediately after dinner because it seriously took him an entire hour to get ready. Seriously. And he's not even one of those annoying metrosexual guys who gets manicures and puts on makeup. And he doesn't have that much hair, so how does it take him three times as long to get ready as it takes me? He changed his clothes like six times, and I finally got him to just wear this tight V-neck shirt that showed off his pecs (I thought it would be to his benefit). Then he put on some cologne—and right then Sam (that chef I already told you about) walked in. (They share a room.) And Sam started getting all upset because apparently molecules of scent might touch his precious clothes and cling to them and 'contaminate his palate' and make him make all the food in the dining room taste like cologne or something like that. It was a bit ridiculous, and after a really stupid argument, they came to an agreement that Ty would only spray his cologne on the front porch.

Incidentally, if I were Ty, I wouldn't have caved. But he is new here and he is stuck sharing a room with Sam all summer, so I guess he valued keeping the peace. Also, I guess he valued ending the discussion and (FINALLY!) making it down to the bar so he could try and flirt all night. He has these beautiful almost mournful looking dark eyes, and he used them to full effect. It'd be hard not to fall for him. I'll be honest; it was so adorable.

Cara didn't come out with us last night, and I don't know exactly where she went, but I do know she came back at 3:00 a.m., and I know that because that's the time I woke up and ended up holding her hair back for her as she vomited. I'm not even mad though because at least she was out having fun. I think it's been beneficial for her getting back here. She's starting to seem a little better. I mean, she's still on her whole I-feel-guilty-for-killing-my-fiancé thing, which I had hoped she'd get over by now (or at least move on from—I know she'll never really get over it. How can she? I can't either. I feel a little guilty too. Sigh.). She had all winter to think about it and heal, but obviously she didn't. Of course, working at an ice hotel in middle-of-nowhere Canada, which basically means sitting around freezing all the time in the dark, probably didn't help, but I thought our backpacking trip would. I know I felt better spending all those weeks on Thai beaches with a hot Italian. It's too bad you don't have a brother.

She's not the same person you met. Remember how you told me she seemed like the ghost of the person you imagined her to be? She's becoming a bit more human. Hell, last week I even saw her spontaneously smiling again, and it's been forever since that happened. I'd like to take credit for it, but I suspect it has more to do with the healthy living here—fresh air, plenty of exercise (no cars allowed, so we walk or ride bikes to get pretty much everywhere), and plus we're finally eating decent food again. I know I criticize Sam, but one good thing about him is that man can cook! This is the best we've eaten in a long time. It might be partly my fault. Before he got here, I was trying my hand at cooking, and Cara said she was not impressed at my attempts to pair Indian and Italian cuisine and she doesn't think my 'experimental' sauces go well on pasta (or anything else). But hey, it was worth a try (and yes, I know you told me the same thing, I wasn't listening to you either). Paddy never complained, but he also bought us pizza a couple of nights, so I guess maybe he didn't like it much himself.

One more rant about the chef though. Since I said complementary things about his cooking, I can also complain some, right? Did I tell you it's the same guy we had last summer; that supposed 'friend' who was the only one who didn't send Cara any condolences when Phil died? No calls, no emails, nothing, even though he and Cara used to be pretty close friends. I was so mad at him for that, so one night I sent him an email basically saying, 'What, you can't even call Cara? Just FYI, you're the biggest asshole I ever met.' And do you know what his response was? Something stupid like, 'Oh, why should I call, just because it was Thanksgiving? She doesn't want to talk to me anyway. But happy f-ing holidays to you both.' Seriously, that's what he said. I'll forward you what I wrote back so you can learn some new American swear words.

Anyway, he didn't respond, and neither of us heard from him after that. And then Paddy told us we needed a new chef and started interviewing people; then all the sudden this guy changes his mind and decides to come back. Don't get me wrong. I basically like him. He's fun to hang out with and he's delicious eye candy (don't be jealous though), but who doesn't at least express some sympathy when their friend's fiancé dies? A selfish jerk, that's who.

And ... speaking of selfish people, I'm going to be one right now and say that I wish you could come visit. First trip to the States? I know, I know. I stole enough of your time, making you extend your trip the way I did. And you have a lot going on, especially with your grandmother. But it would be so nice to see you again. I miss you.

After the inn opens tomorrow, I'm going to be on a regular schedule, and it should be easier for us to connect. I'll be at the desk from noon to nine most days, and we do have some slow periods in there. You can expect a lot of annoying emails when I'm bored.

Chapter Twelve

Whispering Pines, May 2013

Opening day. Cara woke up unnecessarily early in anticipation, even though it was her last opportunity to sleep in all summer. She usually worked the first shift and was up before sunrise. None of her morning tasks needed to be done today, when the first guests wouldn't check in until the afternoon. But still, it was important to try out waking on schedule. She had been following Amy's example of sleeping the morning away for far too long. Honestly, she probably should have shifted her sleep cycle days ago, but she had been having too much fun reconnecting with her island friends.

She could hear someone moving around in the staff kitchen. Strange, she hadn't expected anyone else to be up. Amy's arm still jutted out from the enormous pile of blankets on her bed, and she knew Ty wasn't an early riser. Could it be ... no. Sam didn't have to be up for work yet either. But maybe ...? Her heart beat a little bit faster, and she took the time to brush her hair and wash her face before she walked out of the room. There was Sam, standing at the stove in pajama pants and a T-shirt. He had on his wire-rim glasses, which she found so endearing, though he claimed he looked too nerdy in them and always switched to contact lenses.

"What are you doing up?" she asked quietly. He turned and saw her, and his smile made her warm inside.

"Old habits," he shrugged. His smile slowly faded as he pointed to a steaming mug of coffee sitting on the table. "Isn't this what we do? Or are things different now?"

It was a loaded question. Their mornings together had come to an abrupt end, and she had missed them. She hadn't been sure if they would resume this summer. She still had no idea how Sam felt, or what he wanted. She didn't know where they stood.

"Things don't have to be different. We've always been friends." That last word hung in the air between them as an offering from her.

She knew she lost her chance to have anything more, but they could be friends again, right? They could get back to that ease between them, their ability to talk about anything or sit relaxing in silence. That's what she wanted. Well, no, truth be told, part of her wanted more than that, but she'd settle for friendship. She wasn't sure if she was ready for anything else anyway.

"Friends." Sam seemed to be trying the word out in his mouth, tasting it. "Friends." Finally, he smiled again. "I can do that, Cara. I've missed you. Hungry?" he gestured to the pan. "I figured we're not serving down at the inn this morning, so I'd make you something here."

They ate in silence. She had no idea what to say or how to start a conversation. So much had happened since last summer, since last November even, and she didn't know how to start over with him. He'd been back for a week, and now, in their first moment alone together, all they'd been able to do is confirm their friendship. At least that was something.

"Hey, um, Cara," Sam said suddenly. He wasn't looking directly at her, his eyes remained fixed on the bottom of his tea mug. "I heard about Phil, and I just wanted to tell you I'm so very sorry for your loss. If you ever need to talk about it or anything, I'm here. I'm always here. I'll always be your friend."

His speech sounded rehearsed, and he didn't make eye contact at all, which made her wonder about his sincerity. And she didn't want to talk about Phil, not with him. *You know I'm the love of your life,* Phil had told her so many times. *We belong together. I can't live without you.*

"Why didn't you say anything before? Why didn't you call?" she asked before she could stop herself. She had received so many calls, so many emails in the months after Phil's death. Friends from college, friends from high school she hadn't seen in years, people she'd never met who knew her father and stepmother. It seemed like anybody even tangentially related to her life sent condolences, but not Sam. His number never showed on caller ID, and there was never a text or an email. Nothing. First, he'd ignored her when she sent the message asking if he still thought they belonged together, and then he'd ignored the terrible news, and she knew that it had reached him. His address was on every group email that went out.

The absence of a response still hurt. She knew he had been angry and felt rejected by her, but the least he could do for an old friend was reach out. He didn't have to still be in love with her, but she wished he still cared. It made her feel as though her connection to Sam had been permanently severed.

"Honestly?" Sam hesitated. There must have been something fascinating in his tea leaves, the way he was staring down into them. "Cara, I was really upset last summer, and I didn't react very well. You know that. And I guess I was being a little immature. I didn't want to hear about your stupid wedding, so I set up some filters on my email. I never got the news about Phil at all. I didn't even find out he died until Sato told me three days ago. I'm sorry."

Cara couldn't help herself. She laughed. It wasn't supposed to be funny, she was sure, but the idea of Sam being petty enough to filter her emails made her giggle. Relief washed over her. He hadn't been ignoring her; he was just being childish. All those months she had suffered from the bitter sting of rejection, but it was false. He'd never received her message, so maybe there was still a chance. He had come back, after all, when she knew more money and a better job awaited him elsewhere.

"When did you create the filters?" she asked. Had he done it while he was still here on the island? How long had he been mulling over their last conversation?

"October, I think. Maybe the beginning of November? I don't know. But it was poor timing, I guess."

Poor timing indeed. He looked embarrassed, and she couldn't help but laugh harder.

"I'm sorry." He sounded a bit defensive. "It's not funny. Look, I know I was being selfish and stupid. It's just, you know ... at the end of last summer things were so bad between us, and I overreacted. It's my fault. I was putting pressure on you, and I shouldn't have. I said things I shouldn't have said, and I acted like a jackass. I promise you, I'm going to be different now. I've moved on from my mistakes, and I really want to be your friend again. Can't we go back to the way we were, back when we were just friends, before I ruined everything?"

She did stop laughing then, and not only because of the aggrieved expression on his face. He wanted to reset the clock and go back to the way it was before he confessed his love. Was it because he didn't feel anything for her anymore? She supposed it didn't matter. She didn't deserve him anyway.

No one will ever love you like I do, Phil's voice whispered in her head, as though she needed the reminder.

Chapter Thirteen

Last summer: Whispering Pines, September 2012

The end of the season is near, and everything is getting ready to close down. There are fewer tourists on the island, especially since the school year has started and most families can only come on weekends.

Cara is sitting in the staff office using the computer. It is her day off, and she is idly shopping for her upcoming job. She will be helping Paddy close up the inn for the winter, then she will spend a few weeks with her family in Texas. Amy will be there too, otherwise she wouldn't even consider going and putting up with her stepmother. In December, she will head to Canada to work at an ice hotel for one of Paddy's old friends. The ice hotel, when built, will only be open for three months, making it the perfect winter position for her, timing-wise. She is dreading living in a place cold enough to maintain ice buildings. Right now, she is looking at thick coats and wondering how many layers she's going to need underneath them.

Her fiancé is still angry with her for taking the job. Phil lives in Chicago and expected her to spend the winter with him as she did last year. They've been arguing over it lately, fortunately just over the phone. The fights would be worse in person. Maybe he'll eventually see her reluctance to live with him this winter as a sign that they shouldn't get married? That's what she's been hoping, but she knows it won't be that easy.

She is about to add an enormous down parka to her online shopping cart when she hears a radio call from Sato. "Amy,

Cara, someone, can you hear me? We've got a situation up at Lesser Lake."

Amy is at the desk and she asks what is going on. There is worry in Sato's voice as he tells her that a child is missing. He has taken some of the inn guests up for a picnic and a frantic woman has come running up asking for help. The woman keeps insisting that she just turned her back for a minute and her son, a six-year-old, disappeared from the blanket where he was napping. The child is autistic and non-verbal, which will make the search much harder. On this chilly end-of-tourist-season day, the family were the only people at the lake.

Cara immediately springs into action. She directs Amy to call the sheriff's department and to start contacting potential volunteer searchers. Cara herself grabs a backpack, several extra radios, whistles, and some rain ponchos, so she can run up to meet with Sato and start getting things organized. She also takes a large flashlight, just in case. The inn is the closest business to Lesser Lake, just a half mile of well-used hiking trails away, so Cara arrives there about fifteen minutes after the call comes in.

Sato is already directing people to start a search. A group of other tourists fortuitously arrived soon after he made his radio call, and they, along with the inn guests, have volunteered to assist. Two small groups are walking slowly around the lake's perimeter in each direction looking for any evidence of the boy's passage. Cara hands Sato the backpack with supplies, but she pulls out a radio, a whistle, and the flashlight for herself. She shows it to him and tries to be discreet because the mother of the missing boy is standing right next to him and she doesn't want her to know what she's about to do.

"I'm going to go check the Blackhauer property real quick," she tells Sato, trying to sound casual.

He looks at the flashlight in her hand and nods, expression unchanged, but she can tell he has already thought of the property. He suggests she take two people with her. The Waverlys, a couple who stay with them at the inn every summer, immediately volunteer. Cara gives them each a whistle, and she leads them up the trail.

"What's the Blackhauer property?" the missing child's mother asks as they walk away.

Cara trusts that Sato will be careful not to alarm her.

The hike is short and easy, only a few minutes from the lake, though the path is partially overgrown. On the way, they look for any signs of a child. Cara tells them where they are going: an old farm that burned down over fifty years ago. According to island legend, Mr. Blackhauer set the fire himself for the insurance money while Mrs. Blackhauer was out and his children were at school. Unfortunately, he was unaware that his oldest boy had stayed home with the flu, and his wife, who he thought was running errands, had come back from the village with medicine for the child. They both died in the fire, and the property was abandoned. Nobody seems to own it now, and even the island children avoid it because of the rumors that it is haunted.

While the charred remains of the house are dangerous, the main reason Cara and Sato are both concerned is the old well. It's been boarded over, but the covering is almost flush with the ground, so the danger isn't apparent until it's almost too late. The makeshift lid, which is just splintery old two-by-fours, rots away every once in a while due to the harsh weather here. In the past, Paddy has told Cara that he occasionally hikes out and replaces them, and she knows he hasn't done it this year.

The well is still covered, and, although a piece of wood is broken, there isn't room for anyone to have fallen through.

Cara examines the splintered end anyway. No hairs, no threads. No reason to believe the boy is in the well. Cara lets out a breath she was not aware she was holding.

The three of them decide that the tourists will stay by the house for a little while, on the off chance the boy finds one of the numerous trails leading to it. The surrounding area is heavily forested state park, and there are few clearings, so hopefully the boy stumbles upon a path. If so, he will eventually come out of the woods either on the Blackhauer property, at Lesser Lake, or at one of the many trail access points on the road around the island. If he finds a trail, they can find him.

Cara updates Sato and then leaves the radio behind. By the time she makes it down to the lake, Deputy Saunders and Deputy Mills have arrived and taken over. She tells them that volunteers are at the Blackhauer property with a radio, and they decide that a team of people should stay there, patrolling the area so they don't have to keep checking the well.

The next thirty hours are intense. Cara manages to grab a little bit of sleep, but she mostly devotes her time to doing whatever she can to help out. They have set up a way station at the inn, and the restaurant has been turned into a regrouping area for volunteers. Sam makes batch after batch of hot soup, and is constantly filling thermoses and sending them up to the searchers near the lake. Some inn guests complain that the fine-dining experience they expected is not available, but Paddy thinks (and the staffers all agree) that it is better to commit their resources to finding little Donovan.

Margaux brings loaves of bread from the bakery and stops a moment to confide in Cara. "I'm worried about Sato," she says. "He's been going nonstop because he thinks it's his fault. He was supposed to take the guests up earlier, but he was the one who decided to delay their hike. He thinks if only he had left on time, the boy would have still been napping, and they would have seen him when he woke up."

It's not Sato's fault, of course. Cara—and probably everybody else—secretly blames the child's parents for leaving the boy alone. The mother even admitted that she hadn't just turned her back; rather, she and her husband snuck off into the woods for some alone time and were gone for at least twenty minutes. The parents are complete wrecks right now. They haven't slept at all. They're spending all their time up at the staging area by Lesser Lake. They need to be close so if the boy is found alive (which is becoming less and less likely with each passing moment), they can rush to him. There is a concern that if and when Donovan is located, he will try to evade his rescuers because he is uncomfortable with strangers and is unable to communicate.

Margaux offers to take over for Sam in the kitchen so that he can participate in the search. It is late afternoon, and the boy has been missing for over a day. Rain is coming down in a cold drizzle, dampening everyone's hopes and spirits.

Cara hikes up to the command center with Sam, and they are immediately assigned to relieve the volunteers at the Blackhauer property. That area has been staffed throughout the search, with Sato even spending the previous night there, constantly shining a searchlight into the woods around the edges of the clearing and hoping the boy would see it and follow the light to safety.

Cara and Sam walk around the clearing to keep warm during their vigil. Talk between them is strained. It's been like that a lot lately, and she misses the ease they used to have between them. It doesn't help that when he looks at her she feels a strange yearning and a sort of urgency in her jaw like she needs to grab him and kiss him and dissolve into him. It's not fair of her to think this way. It's not fair of her to imagine running her fingers through his dark curls and pulling him towards her, to imagine his hands touching her body, his lips . . . she can't. She can't think about these sorts of things at all. She is engaged to Phil, and Phil will never let her go.

"How's the wedding planning going?" Sam asks suddenly, and she is embarrassed because wedding planning has not been on her mind at all.

"Haven't done anything," she admits. The soft drizzle intensifies, and she shivers.

"My brother Nathan got married a few years ago. They told me about the engagement the day after he proposed, and by then Iris had already investigated several venues, picked the colors for her bridesmaid dresses, and had a list of questions for me about my ideas for catering."

Cara does not respond to this statement, so he continues.

"I guess what I'm trying to say is that you don't seem excited about getting married. Amy tells me you haven't set a date or anything. You've been engaged for six months. Don't you want to marry the guy?"

The question hangs in the air between them, almost tangibly, and Cara turns away. She can't bring herself to answer, at least not honestly. She walks to the edge of the property to stand under the branches of an enormous pine tree. Is it a whispering pine? She wonders, for the first time, if Whispering Pines Island is named after an actual pine species. Wow, her mind really must be trying to avoid his question.

Sam follows and stands far too close to her. It makes her breath catch in her throat. She can't be this close to him. She just can't.

"Seriously, why are you marrying him?" he asks. "He's not the right man for you. You know that as well as I do."

There is an intensity in his face that she has not seen before, and it scares her because it makes her pulse quicken and makes her feel warmer somehow, like a fire is kindling in her blood. She pushes back her hood and looks him right in the eyes. She's not sure what she's going to say. *I love him?* No, those are the wrong words. *He wouldn't let me say 'no'?* She can't admit that; she can't tell the truth about her relationship. Before she can formulate a response, a welcome call comes over the radio.

"We've got the boy! He's alive! We're bringing him back now! Volunteers, please return to the Inn."

Exuberant radio chatter follows as people all over the island express their relief.

"They found him!" Cara is so happy she forgets the tension in the air and hugs Sam, and he hugs her back tightly. He is so warm despite the rain, and she fits so perfectly in his arms, but she can't let herself think about that now. She can't think about the firmness of his body, and the great need that is rising within her, making her heart race and her nerve endings tingle.

She starts to step back, but somehow, his palms find her face, his fingers tangle in her damp hair, and his thumbs caress her cheeks so very gently. He brings his forehead down to hers and stares into her eyes. It is terrifying, this feeling, because he seems to be looking directly into her, past all her barriers, to everything she tries so hard to keep hidden. The intimacy of the moment makes her dizzy and she grasps at his chest, wrapping her hands in his jacket and holding him close. They stand unmoving maybe for a second, maybe a minute, maybe a hundred lifetimes.

"Oh, Cara, you know we belong together. I am so in love with you," he whispers in a voice so tender and soft it sounds like a prayer.

Slowly, he angles his face down and just before his lips can touch hers she pushes him away. The world is suddenly colder and emptier, and there is a strange sense of loss and longing deep in her heart.

"Cara, please," he says, but now he sounds like he's in pain, and she wants to slap him or cry or maybe do both.

"I'm engaged." The words catch in her throat, and she's not sure why she's telling him that, if it's meant to be a warning or regret. "We need to go back."

And she turns and races back down the trail, and he does not follow. A week later, Sam leaves on the ferry, and she doesn't know if she'll ever see him again. And Cara is left with a sick sense of emptiness and despair.

Chapter Fourteen

If I had the connectivity, I'd take you on a tour of the island and then you'd see what I've been talking about. But I can't, so I've attached some pics. Maybe I'll try and make a video later. (Oh, and maybe I can charge the village council for it, and they can use it in tourism promos. Good idea or bad idea?) I promise, you would love it here, even if it's not a fancy Mediterranean island like you're used to.

The first few pics are just some exterior shots of the inn. Beautiful, right? We painted the shutters and porch that bright blue color a couple of years ago. (Totally my idea no matter what Cara says.) This is my seventh summer working here. Cara's been here for ten—that's because she started in college. I did summer internships elsewhere and then I got hired on at a marketing firm in Dallas when I graduated. I thought it was my dream job. I mean, that's what I went to school for and there I was living in the big city (ok, you can laugh, it's no Milan or Naples, but it felt like the big city to me). I thought I had everything. And it turns out I didn't. My coworkers were all men, and they called me 'sweetie' and expected me to take all the notes in meetings. If I offered an idea, it was ignored. But if one of the men made the same suggestion thirty seconds later, it was suddenly brilliant. I tried to work harder. I asked for more responsibilities, and I was told there was more work for me on top of the desk rather than behind it. I was demoralized and depressed and miserable, and I felt like I couldn't tell anyone because when I got hired I made such a huge deal out of how amazing my life was going to be.

It was Cara that convinced me to quit there (after filing a human resources complaint and taking a severance package, of course) and come work with her at her uncle's inn for a few months while I got things sorted out. And you know, as soon as I stepped off the ferry I felt a lot better about everything. Like I had been thinking my life was in shambles, but it actually wasn't. Have you ever gone somewhere and realized that even though you didn't live there, you were home? That's how I felt.

I mean, it wasn't my first trip to the island. I'll never forget the first time I got to fly on a plane all by myself. I was ten and my parents let me come visit Cara and Aunt Cynthia for a couple of weeks. I remember being so jealous of her. We spent all our time riding bikes and running around the woods, and her friend Matteo tried to teach me how to kayak (and I had a horrible drowning scare and haven't gotten into one of those floating deathtraps since). It was the best life.

I also came out here with Cara during Christmas break our senior year of high school. Aunt Cynthia had been killed by a drunk driver that April, and Uncle Alan was still living in a rehab facility learning how to walk again. He was pretty checked out emotionally, so Cara lived with us. Paddy invited Cara out to spend the holidays with him, and she asked me to come along. I was shocked when my mother agreed to it, but I think mom understood the importance of letting me go. Cara's never been just my cousin, she's always been my best friend, and she needed me.

That was my only trip out here in the winter. It was so f-ing cold. Like really. Like you have to learn to snowshoe if you want to go anywhere, and you can't go outside with wet hair because it will turn to ice and snap off.

As a Texan, that was my first experience with a real actual winter. Our occasional ice storms were nothing compared to it. We had fun playing in the snow though, and Matteo took us sledding. And actually, the first time Cara and I ever got drunk was that Christmas with Matteo. We got super wasted and then tried to go sledding again. He broke his wrist in an accident that I may have caused, but we didn't want to tell anybody because we were so drunk (btw drinking age is 21 here, it's not like Italy where I assume they put Chianti in baby bottles). So for some reason, we thought if he stuck his arm in the snow it would help with the pain and swelling. Yeah, that was dumb. He got frostnip, and he's lucky it wasn't worse. But hey, that's what he gets for taking snow advice from a couple of Texas girls.

Back to the pictures though. I've included a view of the village that I took from the ferry, so you can actually see almost the whole thing. I love it, but it's kind of weird sometimes. See how tiny it is? And since it's so small, there's a lot of gossiping—people that live here know everything about everyone all the time, pretty much immediately. True story, one year I got way too drunk at the bar and took a rather embarrassing fall on my way out the door. The next day everybody I talked to teased me about hangover, asked if I broke my ankle, etc. Every damn person.

But it's nice that when I'm working I can call up any business and say, 'Hey, it's Amy. I'm trying to do whatever,' and they know me. And they're like, 'Amy! How are you? Did you hear about X, Y, and Z? But enough gossip, sure, I can help with whatever.' One year, we had the town square set up for the annual Fourth of July barbeque (one of my favorite events, btw), when, suddenly, the clouds rolled in, and the sky turned black. Someone shouted, 'to the community center.' And every single person there—not just the people working, but every single island resident—grabbed stuff and started moving it indoors. We had the entire event disassembled outside and reassembled inside in less than fifteen minutes. That's community spirit.

Wow, this email is getting way longer than I intended. Sorry about that. I just miss you so much and wish you were here. Also, I'm trying to distract you and cheer you up a bit. Your last message sounded so unhappy. I'm so sorry about your grandmother. I know it's trite, but at least you do get to spend these remaining days with her. I'd fly there in a heartbeat to help you if I could, but Cara needs me here. You know why. And something else, too. I think this is the last summer we'll be working together, and I think she feels it too. It's like it's finally time to settle down. That's what you told me, isn't it? You said I wasn't serious enough about anything. I am, and you know it.

I miss you.

Chapter Fifteen

From the Inn at Whispering Pines blog:

The weather forecast is calling for three damp, drizzly days. I know that's not what you look for when you're booking your Whispering Pines vacation, but don't worry, you'll still be able to enjoy your visit. Rainy days on Whispering Pines are made for relaxing and enjoying peaceful time with your loved ones.

For guests staying at the inn, if you don't want to venture out into the cold, you won't have to. We'll keep a roaring fire going for you in the lobby. The activity shelves in the lobby are full of board games and decks of cards, and we're happy to arrange gaming tournaments in our dining room (until 4:00 p.m., when we set up for dinner service). Chef Samuel has given me his personal guarantee that he will keep the lobby stocked with various flavors of popcorn, hot chocolate, and some coffee that was locally roasted by Sato. (If you've stayed here in the past ten years, you already know and love him, but don't you love him more now that he's providing us with coffee?)

My 9:00 a.m. yoga class will be moved to the ballroom, even if it isn't raining at that time. I know; I too prefer the peace of the grove, but I don't like getting rained on, and I don't want to get the mats all wet from the damp ground. If there's any interest, I'll be happy to add an afternoon yoga class as well. I'll put a sign-up sheet at the desk.

Our usual Wednesday night bonfire has been canceled due to the weather. But that just means we have to use our backup activity. So yes, Karaoke Madness is back! We've got the song list at the front desk, if you want to peruse the selections in advance. Soft drinks will be provided; beer and wine will be available at the cash bar. You don't have to have a good singing voice, just bring your enthusiasm and be ready to have some fun.

If karaoke isn't your thing, and you want to spend some time outside, the hot tubs are actually quite lovely in the rain. However, if there's lightning or thunder, they will be closed.

Outside of the inn, there are still plenty of things to do. Ask us at the desk for umbrellas and/or rain ponchos, and then get out and explore. Go out to the woods—the pine trees will protect you from most of the water, and there is something very peaceful about hiking through the forest with the sounds of raindrops falling gently around you.

Our electric carts have rain shields to keep you dry as well, so Tyrell and Sato will be happy to take you into the village for some shopping or dining. Stop in Darling's Chocolatiers and try their hot chocolate, or spend some time at Margaux's Corner Bakery and Coffee Shoppe for some fresh-baked treats. The pizza oven at Antonio's will keep you nice and warm, or pop into The Digs and have Timmy make you something special. Tell him Amy sent you, and maybe he'll put an extra shot in your drink (or maybe he'll call to yell at me about creating specials without his approval again; try it and we'll find out together).

Chapter Sixteen

The first major thunderstorm of the summer rolled in on a Wednesday evening. The inn was supposed to have a bonfire that night, but the backup activity, a karaoke party, was going on in the ballroom instead. Cara could hear an occasional burst of music over the pouring rain, whenever someone opened the ballroom doors. At one point, she heard an off-key rendering of an old Dolly Parton song and knew that Amy had convinced Tyrell to cover the front desk so she could participate.

Cara briefly thought about going down and joining them, but chose instead to watch the storm from the swing on the staff-house porch. From here, she could see the lightning over the trees, and there, in the distance, over the lake. She loved watching storms from here. It always took her back to her childhood, when things were so much simpler.

Her first experience with lake storms had occurred when she was nine and she and her mother came to live with Uncle Paddy. Her father, an oil engineer, had been sent to the Middle East; and her mother flatly refused to accompany him. A month after her dad left, Paddy called, crying, and told them that his partner had been diagnosed with pancreatic cancer. Her mom immediately packed their bags, and they flew up to help. Cara had been excited, though she knew that their stay was colored by tragedy. She had always loved her Uncle Robert, and he was wasting away. And Paddy, who had always been so friendly and cheerful, became a shadow of himself.

But getting to live on the island! It was magical. She was enrolled in the tiny schoolhouse where the grades were combined and there were only thirty students. After school, she was allowed to roam wherever she wanted, and the other kids were happy to show her all the secret spots among the pines and the best places to play without being bothered by adults.

One night she was awoken by her mother, gently touching her shoulder. "Mom?" she asked, and her first worry was that something bad had happened to Uncle Robert, but then she heard the thunder that seemed to shake the roof. How had she been sleeping through that?

"Come outside and watch the storm with me," her mom said. She made them both hot chocolate, and they sat on the porch swing wrapped in a blanket.

Cara was scared at first, but sitting there, leaning on her mother, she knew she was safe. "I love these storms," her mother told her, and they talked softly while the lightning flared above.

That became one of Cara's most treasured memories, one she called on when she was lonely. It had been nearly thirteen years, and the loss of her mother still hurt her every single day. If her mother had still been around, she often reflected bitterly, everything with Phil might have been different. Cara would have been smart enough not to fall so hard for him, or, maybe strong enough to leave when things first went bad. Maybe then Phil would still be alive and Cara wouldn't still be fighting all this crushing guilt.

It was getting cold outside, and Cara yawned. She was about to get up and go to bed when a flash of lightening revealed someone coming, running up the path in the rain. As the figure reached the porch, she recognized a completely sodden Sam.

"You know we have umbrellas at the reception desk. We wouldn't even make you put down a deposit to take one," she told him as he bent down to take off his soaking shoes. She tried not to stare at the way his wet T-shirt clung to his skin, and she definitely tried not to check out his white chef's pants, and she tried even harder to keep her eyes off anything outlined by the wet fabric of those pants.

"I know, I just didn't realize it was raining so hard. Why aren't you at the karaoke party?"

"I like watching the storm," she replied. "Plus, I heard Amy down there. If I go, she'll drag me up in front of everyone and make me sing 'I Will Survive'. Why aren't you?"

"I did the food for it and didn't feel the need to stick around. Paddy's working as bartender, so I wanted to get away before he came up with any creative ideas for me to whip up. Plus, haven't you heard me sing? I can't put the guests through that." He ran a hand through his hair, accidentally splashing droplets of water at her. "I need to go change out of these wet clothes before I freeze to death."

With that, he was gone, and she had to stay on the porch. She didn't want him to think she was following him inside. She sighed and wondered how long she would have to wait.

A few minutes later, Sam reappeared, hair still damp, but now dressed in a dry sweatshirt and jeans. He had a big wool blanket with him and two mugs. "You looked cold," he said and passed her one of them.

Hot chocolate, just like her mother used to make. She took a sip. Ok, not quite like her mother used to make. Her mother never added Bailey's.

"Scoot over," Sam suggested, and then he sat next to her and covered both of their laps with the blanket. "You don't mind if I join you, do you?" He spoke in the careful tone of someone who wanted to make sure he wasn't giving the wrong impression.

Cara wanted to cry. She wanted to tell him that bringing her hot chocolate and a blanket was the sweetest thing anyone had done for her in a really long time, but she couldn't bring herself to say those words, so she just nodded.

"Cheers," he tipped his cup against hers. "To the first storm of the season."

"How about cheers to avoiding having to sing to a bunch of strangers?" she suggested. His laugh rang out heartily. Oh, how she had missed that laugh.

"Alright, I'll drink to that. It's going to be a good summer, isn't it?" His fingers tapped against his mug. There was a particularly loud burst of thunder, and she felt his body jump. He brushed against her, and she didn't move away.

It was strange to sit here, thighs touching, yet still so uncertain of what to say. She tried to ignore the feelings his body stirred up in hers, though it was difficult. *Relax*, she told herself. She should be happy to have those feelings again. She had thought Phil had killed off any sexual thoughts.

"Don't take this the wrong way," Sam said, after a long and slightly awkward silence, "but I've missed you. I've missed this kind of thing. I know you're in a vulnerable place right now, so I don't want you to think that I'm making any moves on you or anything. It's just nice to be friends again."

"Yeah, I've missed you too," she admitted, though there was a twinge of regret at his use of the word friends. As always, Phil's voice whispered, *you'll never find someone who loves you as much as me, angel.*

Sam shifted and stretched his arm out along the back of the swing, and for a second she felt her body freeze. Damn Phil for making her react like this. Sam immediately apologized.

"Sorry, I was just trying to get comfortable. I didn't mean to freak you out," he said, and started to withdraw the arm.

"No, you're fine, I'm just jumpy" she said, and daringly leaned over to rest against him. She could do this; she trusted Sam. He would never hurt her. When his arm came around her shoulders and he hugged her to him, she felt safe and re-laxed, a feeling that had been foreign to her for a long time. *This is how I'm supposed to feel,* she reminded herself.

"Tell me about your winter job. How was Aspen?" she asked, and as he talked she closed her eyes and listened. The rhythm of his voice soothed her, and she drifted off to sleep, a sleep that was, for once, blissfully dreamless.

Chapter Seventeen

Email from Amy O'Connell to Fabio Basile:

Terrible storm last night, and you know what that means . . .
karaoke party. Don't worry, I didn't embarrass myself (too
much). I dedicated a song to you, but you'll have to guess
which one. Hint: It was something dirty. But get this, when I
was walking back to the house, I saw Cara all snuggled up on
the porch swing with that cook Sam. I know I've told you
about him. What do I do to stop this? She doesn't need Mr.
Grabby Hands all over her.

Email from Amy O'Connell to Fabio Basile:

I know she can make her own choices and I know I said she
needs to move on. I just want her to find a decent guy for a
change. In Sam's first summer here, he f-ed his way through
half the island. Surely she's got another option? Hey, why don't
you send your cousin out here for her? He seems nice, and
who cares if he can't speak English? You can come too, to
translate.

And to see me. I miss you.

Chapter Eighteen

Whispering Pines, June 2013

Cara was sitting in the staff office trying to update accounts on the computer and half listening to Amy at the reception desk arguing with Matteo about placement of his new brochures. "You can stick them over there with every other business," Amy kept telling him, but Matteo insisted that they needed to be placed directly behind the service bell. Cara was amused by their argument and starting to wonder if it was more flirtatious than anything else when it suddenly stopped.

"Holy shit. Incoming!" Matteo exclaimed, turning towards the windows.

At the same time Amy called out, "Hey, Cara, I thought we were full. We don't have anyone coming in today, do we? Was I supposed to send a pick-up to the ferry?"

Cara emerged from the office to see one of the pedicabs dropping off an astonishingly beautiful blond woman. They watched as she stepped down and the driver lifted out an expensive-looking rolling suitcase.

"Whoa, Amy, check her out," Matteo said approvingly. "I bet the boys fought over who got to give her a ride here. Hey, if you're full, she can stay with me. I hope she likes dogs."

"She's carrying a Birkin bag and dragging a Fendi that costs at least four grand. No way would a woman like that allow you or your muddy dogs near her," Amy replied. She had an eye for pricey luggage, refined while working at several rather exclusive resorts.

"And anyway, Matty, we only refer people to reputable establishments." Cara told him as he rushed to open the lobby door.

The blond entered, bringing with her a cloud of expensive perfume, and took her sunglasses off. "Do you have a room available?"

They didn't, of course. They were completely full now and for the next two weeks.

"I'm so sorry, we don't," Amy said. "But I'd be happy to call some of the other lodging in town and see if they have any vacancies." She was just being polite; she and Cara both knew it was a hollow offer. In June, everything on the island was booked. It was the busy season. Nobody came to Whispering Pines without reservations, unless they wanted to end up sleeping on a bench in the square.

The confidence on the woman's face evaporated, and she looked suddenly uncertain. "Hmmm ... I don't know. Maybe. Actually, there is something else you can help me with. I came out here to surprise my boyfriend."

"If you give me his name, I can call his room for you," Amy offered. "I should warn you though, most of our guests are out and about right now taking advantage of this beautiful weather."

Probably a mistress, then. At any rate, Cara decided Amy had it all under control and turned to go back into the office, but the next words stopped her.

"Oh, no, actually he's not a guest. He works here. It's hard though, since you don't have cell service and he's not allowed to use the inn phone or computer for personal communications. I don't know how any of you put up with being cut off from your friends and family like that. I know it's just for the summer, but we miss each other so much when he's here. So I thought, why not come out and surprise him?"

Matteo had lost interest the second the word 'boyfriend' came out of her mouth. *Tyrell?* he mouthed at Cara, who shook her head in response. She was completely confident this had nothing to do with Tyrell.

"Oh, what am I thinking? You must know him," the woman smiled prettily. "Samuel Vervaine? I'm his girlfriend, Lizbet."

Chapter Nineteen

Sam was proud of his staff. With the exception of the dishwasher, everyone had worked for him last year, and he had turned them into a solid team. They worked efficiently and neatly, and had similar tastes in music, which meant there wasn't any petty fighting over the stereo during prep or clean-up. As he looked around the bustling kitchen while they prepared for dinner service, he felt good. It seemed that for once everything in his life was moving along the way he wanted it to. He and Cara were getting closer, all of his culinary equipment was in good working order, and he had talked Sato into going out for a cold beer after work. Yes, this was going to be a good summer.

Or at least, that's what he was thinking up until the moment the door opened and Matteo and Cara walked in. Matteo's mouth twisted as he worked hard to suppress a grin, while Cara kept her lips tightly closed and her eyes held an inscrutable expression. Angry? Sad? Disappointed? He couldn't tell, but something strange was obviously going on.

"No idle hands in the kitchen," he told them, his standard greeting for any non-restaurant staff. "If you want to be in here, get to work. And actually Matteo, you can't come in anyway. You're not an employee and you're a walking health-code violation."

"Oh, I wouldn't want to work here," Matteo replied. "No way. Not unless you form a union and make Paddy give you some of your basic rights back. To be honest, I don't know why you aren't on strike right now." His loud voice carried and Sam's staff started looking to see what was going on, though he had them trained well enough that nobody stopped working.

"Hmmm. As management, I probably shouldn't condone all this talk of unions and strikes," Cara shook her head. "But at the same time, he is kinda right. This is a terribly abusive environment; it's worse than a prison, really, the way we cut our employees off from all contact with the outside world."

Sam looked from one to the other and then cautiously set down his knife. "What are you talking about?"

"Yeah, prisoners can at least make one phone call, right? But here in this god-awful place they don't let you use the phone or the computer at all. That's keeping you in isolation. Hell, in these modern times, it's probably considered torture." Matteo's tone seemed serious, but a glint of amusement sparkled in his eyes and his dimples were showing.

"But they do let us. You know there's a staff phone, you've called me before ... wait, why are you talking about this?" Sam's stomach began to sink. "Seriously, what's going on?"

"It is terrible. It forces people like, oh, I don't know, the chef's girlfriend, to travel all the way here unannounced to surprise him." Cara looked him right in the eyes, and Sam felt like the world was rushing away. So much for training—all the noise in the kitchen stopped.

"Girlfriend?" he asked carefully, hoping it was a joke that he still wasn't getting.

"Surely you remember her? We haven't kept you locked up that long have we?"

"I'd never forget a woman like her," Matteo interjected. "Tall, blond, sexy? Wow, is memory loss a symptom of PTSD? How long have they held you prisoner?" Matteo turned to the rest of the kitchen staff. "Lizbet is hot. She's in the lobby, if you guys want to go check her out. I'm guessing she's probably high maintenance, but with that body, she's worth it."

They're messing with me. This is just some weird prank, Sam assured himself. There was no possible way Lizbet could or would show up here.

He ended things with her, or rather, he had gotten her to end things with him. She was upset when he declined the sous chef job in Denver, and she became enraged when she found out that the reason he turned it down was to return to Whispering Pines, a dead-end temp job that was just stalling him out in his career and his life (her words, not his). She threw a plate at his head and screamed at him, and later, he apologized, but told her he was still going. *I'm sorry, I'm taking this job, it's important to me,* he insisted. And that was it. She had understood. She even drove him to the airport when his contract at the ski resort ended in April. He had said goodbye to her with a hug and a kiss on the cheek and walked away, and it was over.

But now he was cutting through the dining room to the lobby with Matteo—and Cara—and as soon as the door opened, his heart sank. It wasn't a prank. There was Lizbet, leaning against the reception desk and chatting cheerfully with Amy.

Crap, this was not going to go well. He glanced at Cara, who maintained an unreadable expression, which unnerved him. Was she amused? Angry? Jealous? Matteo's smirking presence only made things worse. Soon everyone in the village would be talking about this, and he had enough problems with his reputation as it was.

"Darling," Lizbet called in her faux-posh voice as she rushed over to embrace him. "I've missed you so much, and I thought I'd surprise you, so ta-dah! Here I am!"

She was wearing perfume, which made him cringe. He didn't need any of that clinging to his clothes, especially now, when he was trying to prep for the dinner service. He wished he had taken off his coat before leaving the kitchen. Now he was going to have to change to his spare.

From the corner of his eye, Sam watched Cara rejoin Amy at the desk, both pretending they weren't straining their ears, and Matteo studiously sorting brochures on the stand while acting as though he wasn't edging closer.

"Let's go outside so we can talk." Sam took Lizbet by the hand and rushed her out to the porch.

"You act like you aren't happy to see me." She stuck her lower lip out in a pout. "I traveled all the way here, and you have no idea what an ordeal I went through. The last plane I took was so small it didn't even have first class. I had to sit in coach, where they keep all the crying babies. And the driver I hired to bring me up from Duluth just would not stop talking. Ugh. Anyway, here I am." She looked around. "It is lovely, no wonder you wanted to come back."

"Why are you here, Liz?" he asked bluntly. "I don't understand." He was genuinely confused as to why she would travel all this way to see him. He would never go through so much hassle for an ex, ever. Clean breaks were always preferable. Unless . . . for a horrifying moment he entertained the notion that she might be here to announce a pregnancy. No, that couldn't have happened, right? He always used protection. He looked at her waistline and did some frantic mental calculations.

"Oh, Samuel." She reached for his arm. "I'm here because I love you and I miss you, and I got tired of being so cutoff from you. I know you're busy and don't have access to a phone, but I couldn't sit around waiting for you to come back like I did last summer. I thought I'd come out here and maybe we can rent a place together in that cute little village. I wouldn't mind staying here for a few months. And then we can go back to Aspen and figure out the rest of our lives."

"I ..." Sam didn't know what to say. He was relieved, of course, that she wasn't showing him ultrasound photos and tearfully announcing his imminent fatherhood, but still, what was he supposed to do? Lizbet stood there, looking up at him with a smile on her face. She again reached for him, and he was afraid she was about to kiss him.

"Samuel, you don't seem as happy to see me as I expected. Is something wrong?" Now she was beginning to look hurt.

Sam hated every second of this. In the kitchen, he was confident and in control, but he tended to avoid confrontation at all costs when it involved personal issues. It was a failing of his, and he knew it. He glanced away from Lizbet's confused face and realized that they were standing in front of one of the large lobby windows, and the woman he really liked—the one that he thought he was finally getting somewhere with—was watching him. That gave him strength. If he had to crush someone, it wouldn't be Cara. He took a deep breath, preparing himself for an argument.

"Lizbet, you can't be here. We broke up." He expected her to be angry, but instead she looked surprised.

"Broke up? Oh, Samuel, what are you talking about?"

"Remember?" Doubts started swirling in his mind. They had broken up, hadn't they? They must have, he couldn't have imagined everything. "When I told you I took this job, and you called me irresponsible and selfish? And then we agreed that I was irresponsible and selfish and didn't deserve you and I should leave you alone? Remember?" He left off the part about her throwing things at his head and screeching at him.

"That was a fight, not a breakup." Lizbet's eyes widened in shock. "Samuel, I love you. We were planning on moving in together. I thought ... I thought you loved me, too. Relationships don't just end over one little disagreement." She sounded devastated. Tears appeared in her eyes, and she quickly pulled out a tissue to dab them away before they could ruin her perfect makeup.

Sam collapsed into the nearest chair and put his face in his hands. He hated this, hated it so much. He hadn't meant to hurt her. He truly thought they had ended things. That's why he hadn't bothered calling her in the six weeks he'd been away. Why would he? They were over.

Lizbet knelt down beside him, putting her perfectly manicured hands on his knees. "Samuel, look at me. I know you. I know this conversation is hard for you and you run away when things get tough. I know that about you, and I accept it. There's something broken inside you, and I've always had a soft spot for broken things. You and I, we can work together. We can mend whatever is wrong with your heart. That's what people do when they're in love."

Sam finally looked up at her. "Liz, I genuinely don't know what's going on here. Our relationship is over. There's nothing in me that needs to be fixed. I'm fine, just confused. You can't show up at my workplace and pull me out of my kitchen and tell me we're still together. That's not how these things work." He felt absurdly proud of himself for managing to string words into coherent sentences. He was so bad at this. If it weren't for his fantasies involving a relationship with Cara, he probably would have caved. And then he would have to put up with Lizbet's dramas contaminating the peaceful life he had built here.

"Samuel!" Now she was upset. "I should have known you'd do something like this. There's a reason my friends all warned me about you. I thought I could make you better. Apparently, I can't. You're so selfish and I can't believe I traveled all the way here for you. You know what? I give up. I'm done trying. I'm not going to be the one to fix you. You aren't worth it, you heartless bastard."

She looked like she expected him to comfort her, to beg her to change her mind. He wasn't going to give her what she wanted, not this time.

"I'm not broken." Sam finally found the strength to be honest. "And I'm not heartless. I have a heart. It just doesn't belong to you. You've never been serious about me either, so I don't know where this is coming from. I think you're just lashing out because for the first time in your life, you're not getting your way." That last bit was probably not necessary, he realized immediately as he watched Lizbet's face changed from sadness to fury.

"Alright, Samuel Vervaine. That is it! I am done. Done. Completely and irrevocably done. You are nothing, you know that, nothing. You don't matter to me, you don't matter to anyone. Just stay hiding out here on your little island and pretend you're a real boy with real feelings. I know the truth, you horrible jerk. You are nothing but a worthless shell. We really are broken up this time, and you will never see me again. Oh, and I'm throwing out all the crap you left in my condo, including your stupid cookbooks."

She stormed into the lobby, which was not the way he expected her to go. After a moment, he got up, shook himself, and went the long way around the building to return to the kitchen. Lizbet was wrong about him. He wasn't broken, and he wasn't just a shell. He was fixing himself, just not for her.

Chapter Twenty

Matteo leaned on the reception desk. "You should make popcorn," he told Amy and Cara as they watched Sam and Lizbet talking on the porch. Apparently, they didn't realize they were right in front of a large window.

"What do you think they're saying?" Cara couldn't read lips, so she tried to analyze their body language. Lizbet kept taking steps toward Sam and reaching for him, and he kept brushing her off. He seemed annoyed, she seemed angry and confused.

"You know Sam avoids conflict. He's going to apologize for whatever she's mad about and then they're going to start making out in front of us. Even if he doesn't want to. Don't worry, I'll go spray them with the hose before I let them have sex out there. We'll end up with too many guest complaints." Amy was matter-of-fact in her assessment.

She's probably not far off, Cara thought. Sam was the kind of guy who avoided uncomfortable conversations. That's why, even last night, when they finally began to reconnect and rebuild their former closeness, she still didn't tell him how much she regretted the way they ended things last summer, or about the email she had sent him last fall. She didn't want to watch him squirm and avoid the subject and inevitably walk away, especially now that every other word out of his mouth was 'friend.' How many times had he told her he was so happy they were friends again? Too many.

Cara watched as Sam put his face in his hands and shook his head while Lizbet ... oh no, she was coming back to the lobby. Amy and Cara quickly picked up a stack of papers and pretended to be immersed in reading them.

Lizbet came back to the desk. She looked furious, and she held her jaw firmly set as though she was trying not to cry. "Excuse me. You offered to call around and find me a place to stay. Could you instead find out if there are tickets available for the next possible ferry and a hotel suite back on the mainland? I'm too tired to keep traveling today, and it looks like I'm heading back to Colorado."

"I would be happy to take care of that for you." Amy smiled sympathetically. "And I know it's none of my business, but after several years of working with Sam, I believe I am justified in saying that he's kind of a jerk sometimes. I'm truly sorry for whatever just happened."

When Amy finished booking Lizbet's reservations, Cara took pity on her. "Come on, I'll give you a ride to the docks. And I'll buy you a coffee. You look like you need a sympathetic ear, and it'll be awhile before the ferry leaves."

🌲 🌲 🌲 🌲 🌲

Margaux's coffee shop was crowded, but Cara managed to secure a table for two. "Here, second best coffee on the island." She offered a mug to Lizbet.

"A broken heart doesn't merit the best coffee?" Lizbet asked with a strained smile.

"That's back at the inn. Sorry about that." She studied Lizbet's face. The woman was quite attractive, she had to admit. She and Sam probably made a striking couple. Still, Lizbet did not seem like the kind of woman she would have expected Sam to be with—though all of Sam's stories about her did seem to highlight her drama queen tendencies and vanity.

"It's fine. It's nice of you to bring me here. I must confess, I'm feeling a little … confused right now." Lizbet ran a hand through her hair and sipped her coffee. "Hey, do you know

Samuel at all? I mean, I don't know if you mix with the kitchen help or not."

"I've worked with him for a few years," Cara admitted, deliberately underplaying their relationship.

"It's so odd, him acting like this. I'm … I don't want to sound bitchy, but I'm used to being the one in control in the relationship. Now all of the sudden, here he is, telling me that he's the one who wants to end things. It doesn't make any sense. It's not like him. And after I traveled all this way."

"Yeah, I'm sorry you went through all that. It can be difficult to get here." Cara tried to force herself to sound compassionate, but something about Lizbet rubbed her the wrong way.

"I should have listened to my friends. They warned me about slumming it with a guy like him." Lizbet stared into space as she spoke. "Everyone told me he wasn't good enough for me. Once when I invited him to a charity gala, you know what he said? He couldn't go with me because he was helping one of his buddies cater it. Can you imagine how awkward that made the event for me? All my friends saw him there, passing around trays of food like a waiter. I loved the man, I really did. But who can build a future with a temporary resort cook? That's why I used my connections to get him an offer in Denver. He needed to move up in the culinary world. He was going to be a sous chef at a five-star restaurant, and when he got promoted to head chef, then he'd have been actual marriage material. And I was willing to wait. I'm so dumb. I can't believe I wasted so much time on him. I could have done so much better."

"He's an executive chef here," Cara said in a stiff voice. She started to get a tad defensive. "I mean, it may only be a seasonal position, but our restaurant is very highly rated and always has excellent reviews. We're on every list of must visits in Minnesota."

"Oh, well, Minnesota." Lizbet waved a dismissive hand. Then she apparently realized where she was and to whom she was speaking. "I'm so sorry. I don't mean to be so judgmental. From what I saw of it, your inn is a beautiful property, and Samuel always said this is the best kitchen he had ever worked in."

"So why exactly were you dating Sam if you think he's so far beneath you?" She tried to phrase it lightly, but the question came out sharper than she intended.

"I sound terrible, don't I?" Lizbet had the grace to look embarrassed. "Look at me, talking about my boyfriend—I mean, ex-boyfriend—in such a horrible manner. The truth is, I never cared what my friends thought. I didn't need a man to buy me things and take me on exotic adventures. I have my own money. I can afford whatever I want. I loved him because I saw so much potential. He could have been so amazing. You probably don't know what it's like, but sometimes you meet a man, and the attraction is there and, oh my god, the passion, so you overlook his flaws. Like Sam's not one for communicating, or sharing emotions, and believe me, that man doesn't have a single romantic bone in his body. But I never minded, because it's the little things that matter, you know. He might not say the words, but he showed his love in other ways. He took care of me, he would repair things in my condo, and make me food, and he helped me throw the most marvelous dinner parties."

"The little things, yes," Cara murmured, hiding a smile as she pictured Sam making her coffee every morning.

"He's just a big clumsy puppy. He doesn't always know how he's supposed to behave, but he's eager to please. Plus, he's had a rough life. I shouldn't judge him so harshly. You know his parents died when he was a teenager, right? He never talks about it, but you know that affected him."

"I was not aware of that." Sam's parents weren't dead, were they? She could swear he told her they lived in California. Sam always said they had a terrible relationship, but surely he would have mentioned it if they died?

"It's a tragic story, so I'm not surprised he hasn't shared the details with his coworkers. Don't tell him I told you, but yes, they passed away when he was sixteen. It was a dreadful situation. He was at his junior prom having the time of his life, and his parents went out for the evening and ended up killed by a drunk driver running a red light. The worst part was he knew the drunk driver—it was a boy from his school who had been kicked out of the prom for smuggling in a flask. Poor Samuel had to change schools and go live with his older brother."

Cara felt a cold hand clench her heart. Her vision darkened for a second. That was her story, word for word. That was the accident that killed her mother and hospitalized her father. Had Sam stolen her personal tragedy? Why would anyone do such a thing? She kneaded her hands together, trying to force feeling back into her numb fingertips. She was going to have a few words to exchange with Sam when she got back to the inn.

Lizbet didn't seem to notice her discomfort.

"Perhaps I shouldn't have followed him here," she mused, indifferent to Cara's expression. "He would have come home in a few months, and I probably would have taken him back. It's just hard, you know, being with someone who is so closed off emotionally. And the inability to communicate while he's here, it's like the dark ages. I don't understand how your employees put up with it. Last summer he only managed to call me a few times, always collect from a payphone. I didn't even know those existed anymore."

"Ummm ..." Cara paused for a second to clear her head. She would deal with Sam later, but for now she needed to keep her focus on Lizbet, and maybe try to learn what other lies Sam had told. "I don't mean to upset you, but that's not quite true. We've got two staff phones, including one in our house. Plus, last year, the inn finally got Wi-Fi. The signal doesn't reach our living quarters, but we share an office behind the front desk with a computer that our employees can use anytime."

Lizbet's mouth dropped open in surprise. "You mean all that time, he could have called? He lied to me all last summer? He ... oh, he's an awful man. If I didn't have a ticket for the next ferry, I'd go back up there and stab him or something."

"I'm going to object to you stabbing our chef right before the dinner service, but I'm happy to drive you back up, if you want to yell at him some more, maybe slap him across the face." Cara smiled. "He certainly deserves it." *Or maybe I'll do that myself.*

"Does he ever talk about me?" Lizbet asked suddenly. "I'm just wondering if he ever cared at all. Did anyone out here even know that he had a girlfriend?"

"He did." Cara tried to decide how much to say, settling on, "He said you're a demon on the slopes."

"And between the sheets, probably. I know what's important to him. Is that it? He said I could ski?"

Cara hesitated. Sam hadn't had many good things to say about Lizbet. He never described their relationship as serious; rather, she was a ski friend with benefits. In fact, he'd even said he could never be committed to a woman who was such a picky eater. To him, a man whose life revolved around food, that was the greatest sin of all.

"He said you were generous, and kind, and you do a lot of volunteer work." That was true, and she was glad she remembered because it got Lizbet to produce a real smile.

"Thanks. And thanks for the coffee and for listening. I should head to the docks now, right? Hey, next time you see Sam, go ahead and slap him for me, as hard as you can, right across the face. And tell him I'll mail him his cookbooks. I won't really throw them out."

Chapter Twenty-One

"Quite an interesting scene yesterday," Cara commented to Sam as she sipped her coffee in the staff house kitchen.

"Yeah, that was weird." He cast his eyes down at the table and shook his head. He wished he could avoid this conversation, though he supposed it was inevitable. "I don't know why she did that. Came all the way here, I mean. What was she thinking?"

Sam had been embarrassed by Lizbet's appearance. It didn't help that his kitchen staff had felt the need to tease him about it. He didn't mind a little good-natured ribbing, but it got more annoying once he heard a rumor that Cara had been spotted at the coffee shop with Lizbet while she waited for the ferry. He wasn't sure he wanted to know what they talked about.

"I suspect she thought she was visiting her boyfriend," Cara suggested. She appeared to be enjoying his discomfort. "After all, they were madly in love and planning on moving in together. I think she heard wedding bells in her future."

"Yeah, well, I think we had different outlooks on our future," Sam muttered.

"Oh, I know, it's hard for an orphan like you to get close to people and express your emotions."

This snapped Sam to attention. He stopped staring down into his tea and looked at Cara. "An orphan?" he asked carefully, wondering exactly how much Lizbet had said.

"Yes, an orphan. Oh, Samuel, I do wish you'd told me about your heartbreaking past. I could have empathized. I mean, apparently your parents died the exact same way as my mother. Why didn't you confide in me? We are friends, aren't we?"

The way she pronounced 'friends' made it sound like the word had been dipped in acid.

"Shit," Sam swore. "Oh, shit. Please don't be mad. I can explain. Listen, I just told her that to get her off my back. I met her folks, and she wanted to meet mine, and she's not the kind of person who understands these things. She would have insisted on visiting them or something, and I broke off all contact with my parents for a reason. I couldn't let myself be drawn back in. I couldn't. So I sort of borrowed your story." Even talking about seeing his parents caused a sense of panic. He knew he shouldn't have lied to Lizbet, but it had been the only way he could think of to keep her from insisting on an introduction.

"You used my mother's death. That's the worst thing that ever happened to me, and you treated it like a joke because you didn't want your girlfriend to meet your actual living parents. Do you have any idea how that makes me feel?" The catch in her voice made him realize she wasn't angry, she was hurt, which was much worse.

"Oh no, oh Cara, I am so sorry. Honestly, I only used your story because it was one thing I could think of that made me genuinely sad. You're the best friend I've ever had, and so I thought about you and what you went through, and it's so heartbreakingly tragic. I knew it was the only thing that I could put enough emotion in to make it sound truthful. If I lied and said my parents died in a fire or something, she never would have believed me because I wouldn't have sounded sad telling it."

"Sam, you can't steal bits of other people's lives," she informed him. She was doing that awful thing where she didn't move a muscle, just stared straight into his eyes as though she could see deep down inside him to the smallest ugliest parts. It made him feel worthless and weak.

"Cara ..." He reached across the table and took her hand, relieved that she didn't immediately pull away. "You're right, I should have been honest with Lizbet about my parents. I just ... I've been working so hard at breaking free from my childhood. I knew if I had to introduce her to them, it would bring all that negativity back..." He trailed off, focused down at her hand in his. There had to be a way to explain.

"You know," he started over. "You're the one that set me on that path."

"What path? You're blaming me for you hijacking my past for your own benefit?"

"No, that's not what I mean. Don't you remember my first summer out here, when you and Paddy were trying to decide if you should promote me to executive chef, and you had a little chat with me about my behavior?"

A tiny smile finally cracked her lips. "We must remember that differently. I thought it was more of a lecture."

"Right, that's probably more accurate. Well, I took it to heart, and I took your advice and decided to take steps to improve my life. For me, a big part of that was leaving my past behind. I guess I went about it the wrong way in this case. I should have thought about how using your story would have made you feel, and I didn't. I really am truly sorry for that. Please forgive me?" He looked her in the eyes as he spoke, hoping she could see how deeply he meant everything he said.

"Oh, Sam," she sighed. "I'm sure I will forgive you eventually. For using my past, I mean. I'm not sure, though, I'm ever going to get over the fact that I had to take Lizbet out for coffee. No offense, but I found her a bit insufferable. I'm starting to think you have appalling taste in women."

"I don't know about that, Cara." He smiled, but cautiously. As much as he wanted to, he refrained from saying, *My taste has improved. I'm only interested in you.*

No, cheesy lines would have to wait for later, when she wouldn't think he was just flirting to get himself out of trouble. Someday soon, he hoped.

Chapter Twenty-Two

Three years earlier: Whispering Pines, September 2010

It is nearing the end of Sam's first season on Whispering Pines Island, and he's hoping to be invited back next year. His boss Geoffrey has been talking about retirement and refers to Sam as the "heir apparent" often enough that it doesn't seem to be a joke. Truthfully, he hopes it isn't—coming back as executive chef would be his dream job.

When Cara O'Connell asks him to meet with her in the owner's office, he agrees enthusiastically. Although he's seen her around, he doesn't know her very well. She's the inn's general manager, and while technically his supervisor, she doesn't spend any time in the kitchen. He's run into her out at the bar though, and they've chatted a little, but she's really not his type. She's a little too serious, a little too reserved. He prefers her cousin Amy, who is much more fun.

"Sam, have a seat." She sits down behind her uncle's desk. "We need to have a talk."

"Oh?" he asks, smiling because he's sure he knows the reason for the meeting.

"It's time for your performance evaluation," she says, but her smile doesn't quite reach her eyes. She consults paperwork in front of her. "Geoffrey says you're the best sous chef he's ever worked with. He says you are talented and creative, you have an excellent palate, and you are the neatest person he's ever seen in a kitchen. He believes you've never dropped a crumb, and you clean while you work, which impresses him more than it probably should. He seems to think that you should be hired on as his successor, if he retires."

Sam starts to feel the excitement building, but then he realizes Cara said *if.*

She continues with her assessment. "From what Paddy has seen, you have the cooking chops to pull it off. We've noticed that you follow food trends and are constantly looking for new ideas, and some of the meals you've created this summer have been really innovative. Paddy likes that a lot. He likes to be cutting edge. He wants to bring in larger crowds. As the executive chef, you'd have pretty free rein. That's the joy of a prix fixe restaurant—you can change things up all the time and do experiments. Plus, I guess this would be a good job for you since you could keep up your winter work in Aspen. You'd be salaried rather than hourly, and you could live in the staff house for free."

"That would be great," Sam tells her. "I'll take it! Really, I'm excited about it." He has never felt better than he has this past summer. Whispering Pines is a relaxed, laid-back community. It feels like home, not the home he grew up in but the home he has always been looking for. There's something in the air here that agrees with him. As an added benefit, the kitchen is amazing, and he can save a lot of money if he lives in staff housing. This summer he's been renting a bed in a hostel in the village that is full of seasonal workers, and it would be nice to be able to live in quieter accommodations in the future. He's getting a little old for sharing a bunkbed and keeping his things in a locker.

Cara shakes her head. "I haven't offered you the job, and I don't honestly know if we're going to or not."

His heart sinks. Why was she talking about the chef position like it was his for the taking if she isn't making an offer?

"Look, Sam, you're fantastic in the kitchen. You make delicious food. Your direct boss respects you. But here's the thing—you haven't figured out what it means to live in a small town. You aren't as well regarded among the locals, and that does matter to Paddy. As far as he's concerned, the residents and the other business owners are practically family. This is a tight-knit community, and you haven't been impressing them."

"I haven't? Have they tried my food?" Sam doesn't know what to say. His head is spinning. He thought things were going so well. Why wouldn't people like him? He's made friends down at the bar, he has friends at the gym, and his buddy Matteo is on the village council. That should count for something.

"It's not about your food, Sam. It's about your actions. I'm going to guess you've never lived in a tiny place like this before, so perhaps you didn't realize the main topic of conversation is whatever scandal happens to be going on, and you've been involved in a few of them. Like the situation with Olivia." She stops and watches his face. It takes him a little while to figure out who she is talking about.

"Olivia from the Village Hotel? What about her?"

"You know you got her fired, right?"

This is news to him. He knew she moved out of the hostel and someone said she went back to the mainland. Sam had assumed she quit. She didn't like her job, he remembers that much about her.

Cara continues. "And Bernie called up here all pissed off and demanded that Paddy fire you too. You can't have sex with the night clerk behind the desk without horrifying some hotel guests, you know. And Paddy wouldn't fire you because you didn't do it *here*. If he ever found out about you doing something like, oh, I don't know, banging some random woman in the restaurant kitchen, you would be either on the next ferry or swimming behind it."

"I would never do that," Sam promises solemnly, but his heart is racing and his mouth is suddenly dry. She stares at him without moving a muscle for what feels like a long time, but is probably only about fifteen seconds.

"Don't lie to me, Sam." Her voice is flat. "First, you'd be a terrible poker player because you have an obvious tell. Second, Amy walked in on you. She couldn't identify your partner, but she did say you have a very nice ass. And she checked twenty minutes later, and you were sanitizing the surface, so kudos to you on not leaving bodily fluids everywhere. She told me, not Paddy or Geoff, and that's why you still work here. Also, the cleaning up after yourself thing. That matters."

Sam is terribly embarrassed, but he knows enough to keep his mouth shut. Technically, Amy hadn't walked in on him, but he doesn't want to correct Cara. She doesn't need to know what really happened. Maybe he should quit right now, just walk out the door and never come back. That's what he's always done in the past.

But something keeps him seated in his chair, thinking. He's not sure why it happened, but when he stepped off the ferry on his first day on the island, he felt a sense of homecoming, which grew into an internal peace he has never experienced anyplace else. For the first time in his life, he feels like he belongs somewhere, and he can't imagine just walking away.

"How can I fix this?" he finally asks, and he can't quite bring himself to look at Cara. "I want to stay. I want to come back next year, and I want to take over for Geoff. What can I do? How can I show you that I can do this?"

"You need to start being concerned about other people. You need to think about how your actions affect others. Can I speak frankly to you? Not as your employer, but as a friend?"

He nods, still not quite meeting her eyes. They aren't friends, not yet at least, but he's willing to listen to her.

"Sam, I've seen you around here, and I see how you interact with others. You're a friendly guy, but it's all surface. You don't seem to connect on an emotional level, and you don't think about how your actions affect other people."

"That's not true," he protests. But it is, and he is surprised she is able to read him so clearly. She barely knows him.

"Work on it, Sam. Do some self-reflection. I think you're a good guy, really. I think there's a part of you that cares deeply about others. You cook for everybody; you like to share your food. I think that's your way of reaching out. What else do you have to offer? If Paddy gives you the job, you need to come back willing to actually be a real member of this community, to participate on a level other than just, well, sleeping with everyone."

She is right, and he knows it. He thinks about the therapist he started seeing in Aspen. He left after his first few sessions, but maybe that was a mistake. Maybe he should go back. He can do this; he can work on himself. He can be better.

"Cara," he assures her, hoping she can hear the truth in his voice. "I love this island, and I do want to be a part of it. I'll do whatever it takes to prove I deserve this job. Give me a chance and I promise I will show you. Please, tell your uncle I can do this."

She looks at him, unblinking, and he finally manages to meet her eyes, her unexpectedly and incredibly deep gold-flecked eyes. The contact is almost physical, and something powerful, some kind of an understanding passes between them. It throws him off balance, leaving him both unsettled and strangely energized.

After a moment, she appears to make a decision. "I'll talk to him. But you hold up your end of the bargain. Get yourself together."

He is still shaken from the unexpectedness of that strange connection, but he nods. "I will. I swear." He means it too. He will do anything to be able to come back here, to this peaceful place, where he can cook whatever he wants in a clean and well-stocked kitchen. It's his dream life, and he will prove he is worthy of it.

Chapter Twenty-Three

Whispering Pines, June 2013
Email from Amy O'Connell to Fabio Basile:

Thank you, thank you, thank you! I know you told me you make jewelry, and I know you showed me pictures, but I had no idea how exquisite it would be. I love the bracelet! I'm wearing it right now, and every time I look down at my wrist, it brings a smile to my face. Best birthday present ever! I also love the T-shirt. Cara was like, 'OMG, is that the same dirty old shirt he wore all through Southeast Asia?' and I was like, 'Ummm, yes, but he washed it, and I'm going to sleep in it every night.' It makes me feel closer to you. Thank you, thank you, thank you!

Oh, and I was briefly really impressed at your timing. I mean, you managed to send a gift that arrived exactly on my birthday? My parents can't even do that, and we live in the same time zone. But when I said something to Cara about it she got this weird expression on her face, and so I made her tell me the whole story. She said you contacted her weeks ago with the tracking number, and the gift actually arrived last week.

She told me she and Sato had been watching online, and on delivery day, Sato went down to his wife's bakery and waited for Donna, the mail carrier. He told Donna he wanted to accept the inn's mail down there, and she refused to give it to him, even though she knows him. So he explained he needed to intercept my present and promised he would give it back to her to deliver to the inn on my actual birthday, and she said legally, she couldn't do that. Federal law or something. So he rather annoyingly followed her on her whole route, and the second she set foot on the inn's property, he asked if he could have the mail. She wouldn't give it to him until they were on the front porch. So then he hid the package outside, brought in the rest of the stuff, and told me he just ran into Donna and here's today's mail.

Then Sato got distracted by a maintenance issue, and while he was dealing with that, a guest found the hidden package and turned it over to Tyrell, because I (luckily) happened to be away from the desk and he was covering for me. That's when Cara came in, super upset, and told Ty that Sato lost a special present sent to me from my Italian lover, and Ty pulled the box out and gave it to her. He was about one minute from giving it to me because he didn't know about the hide-the-mail scheme. So Cara stuffed it down her shirt and ran out the door and went to the bakery. But by then, the bakery was closed, and Margaux wasn't home, so Cara went all over the village looking for her, finally tracking her down at the pizza place.

So Margaux and Sato had my present, and they were holding on to it so it could be delivered on the right day. When my birthday came around, Margaux was supposed to give the box to Donna and have her bring it (I guess Donna agreed and decided it wasn't violating federal law to return a 'found' package to the addressee—I suspect cookies may have influenced her decision). But Margaux's been kind of hormonal and forgetful lately, and she forgot. She did eventually remember and called the inn. Paddy answered, and then he got Sam (because Sam is in pretty good shape and can run fast enough) and sent him sprinting the half mile to the village to get the package, and then Sam had to hurry back and intercept Donna. Somehow, he did it, catching her right before she got to our driveway, and so Donna brought the mail into the desk and gave it . . . to Tyrell.

See, the hole in their plan was that Paddy offers staff a paid day off on our birthdays. And nobody thought about that because this year I'm the only one with a summer birthday, so I'm the only one who gets to take advantage of it. So I wasn't even there for the delivery, and Cara could have just had Tyrell hide my gift in his room or something without all the drama. Anyway, thank you. I love you, and I love my beautiful new bracelet!

Email from Amy O'Connell to Fabio Basile:

Yes, the rest of my birthday was fabulous. Paddy got me a cake from Margaux's bakery. It was delicious, but I think I would have preferred if it didn't say, 'You're 29, Ha Ha Ha' on top. Sammy made some honey caramel ice-cream to go with it, proving he's not totally useless. It was some darn good ice-cream.

Tyrell gave me a headband that he knit himself. Yes, he knits. Apparently, he picked it up while recuperating from the loss of his leg. He was stuck in bed or a wheelchair for a long time (had to wait for some other injuries to heal before he could even get crutches, much less a prosthesis) and so he took up knitting and actually got really into it. He says it's a useful form of meditation and he can teach me, but I think I'll pass.

I'm going to tell you something you shouldn't mention to Cara. I was a little disappointed in the present she gave me.

It's a framed picture of you and me on our trip. Don't get me wrong, I love the pic. I didn't notice when she took it. We're sitting in a little beach café with the ocean in the background and we're holding hands and laughing (and of course you're wearing my new nightshirt). The reason I was disappointed was not the content, but the fact that she gave me a photo. I was kind of hoping for a sketch of you. She's amazingly talented at drawing people. She sees things others don't and she draws how people look on the inside (personality, not guts). I really wanted to see her impression of you, but she's still on her art hiatus, I guess. It's a shame.

Anyway, Cara and I ate my birthday dinner together at the inn in the dining room. Very fancy. Then afterward we went down to my favorite bar and had a couple of drinks with our local friends. Sato even came out, and he rarely does (his wife wakes up at 3:00 a.m. to start baking, so their bedtime is super early). Tim the bartender covered my tab, and he never lets me drink for free. Somehow, he must have known it was my birthday. Maybe Ty told him, or maybe he just noticed that I was wearing a sparkly pink boa and a glittery tiara with '29' on it, and he made a lucky guess. Who knows?

It was a wonderful celebration, but it would have been more wonderful if you could have been there. I miss you. I miss you every day.

Chapter Twenty-Four

Excerpt from The Inn at Whispering Pines blog:

Every year people ask for suggestions: What is there to do on Whispering Pines Island? How do I make the most out of my vacation experience? Let me help you out with that. I'm interviewing some of our long-term staffers over the next couple of weeks, because believe me, they know this island and they make full use of their time off. I'm starting with our talented chef, Samuel Vervaine.

Me: "Sammy, if you had a day off on our lovely island, what would you do? What would be your perfect day?"

Sam: "My perfect day? Well, I assume I'm staying here at the Inn at Whispering Pines, hopefully in the Lovers' Roost, our nicest room. My girlfriend and I would wake up early—"

Me: "Girlfriend? Who is this girlfriend? And don't roll your eyes at me."

Sam: "Amy, you asked about my perfect day. If it's a perfect day, then I have a girlfriend. This is my fantasy, so stop interrupting and stop making that face at me."

Me: Important takeaway from this: Ladies, Sam is straight and single.

Sam (clearing his throat): "So ... we'd wake up early and head down to breakfast. I guess I'm not the one running the omelet station on this day, but I'd probably hop back there and make our eggs anyway. After breakfast, we would walk into town and rent some kayaks from Matteo at Cap'n Rentals and pick up some pastries to go at Margaux's Corner Bakery and Coffee Shoppe. We'd paddle out to Windworn Pines Island, hike around a bit, have a small picnic, and then come back. We'd go out for a late lunch, either Chicago-style pizza at Antonio's, or fish and chips from Harbor Snax, depending on what we're craving."

Me: "That sounds lovely, though you should also consider the Village Diner. Have you had their burgers? But anyway, where to after lunch?"

Sam: "We'd walk around and explore all the art galleries and shops. I'd probably buy my girlfriend some unique jewelry ..."

Me: (OMG LADIES WHY IS THIS MAN SINGLE????)

Sam: "... Afterwards, we'd be tired, so back to the inn, where we'd schedule an in-room couple's massage from Ladli and Jay. I suppose we could have gone to their spa, Holistic Haven, but since they're willing to come to the inn, we'd take advantage of that service."

Me: "Sorry, I have to interrupt you here. Sam, this is a PG-rated website. Please, no post-massage, pre-dinner plans."

Sam (clearing his throat again): "Dinner, of course, is at the inn. Ordinarily, I'd be cooking the delicious prix fixe meal, but since this is my day off and I wholly trust my amazing kitchen staff, I'd be there just as a diner and wouldn't even peek in to check on them

Me: (Ha! Every single member of Sam's entire staff assures me this is a lie. Sam would probably insist that he and his date eat in the kitchen so he could supervise during his romantic meal.)

Sam: "After dinner, we'd take a box of wine out to the hot tub and look at the stars. Amy, I said box. I know the policies on glass in the pool areas, so stop looking at me like that. If it's a clear night, maybe we'd hike out to Paddy's telescope platform later for one of his stargazing talks. Then, well, back to the room, and you said you didn't want to hear about that."

Me: So there you have it folks, a perfect day, lots of fun island activities and dining experiences. And, of course, now that we all know Sam is single and has this romantic day planned, we're going to have to form a line. Behind me, please.

"How much of this is true?" Cara asked after reading over Amy's latest blog post.

Amy peeked out from the door of the staff office. "Does it matter? It's all marketing," she replied. "It's part of my employee interview series. Ty's will run in two weeks, right before PrideFest, and I'll include a sexy photo of him, if I can get him to take his shirt off. Sato's going to talk about family friendly stuff and the Fourth of July. I'm taking the new dad angle on that one. You're last. You're going to talk about Gallery Row before the big art festival in August."

"But are you actually conducting interviews?" Cara's eyes didn't leave the screen. Did Sam really say any of this? Really? This was so different than anything she would have expected from a man whose normal day consisted of work-gym-nap-work-drink-sleep. She always thought of him as more practical than romantic, so she couldn't quite imagine him planning anything like this, though it did make for a nice fantasy.

Just then the subject of the blogpost walked through the lobby and came around to go into the staff office.

"Amy, get off the computer. I gotta check a recipe issue," Sam said, but then he stopped, looking at Cara's screen. "Hey, is that my interview?"

Cara felt his hand on her shoulder as he leaned in to read the post. His face was so near to hers she could see the tiniest smudge of white flour on his cheek. She fought the urge to wipe it off. She tried not to stare at his lips and the adorable way he moved them as he read. It wasn't fair, having him so close, not after reading about this perfect date. She inhaled deeply, trying to clear her mind, but it didn't help. The smell of fresh herbs combined with the warmth of his hand triggered a surge of something running through her body. Desire, maybe? No, she couldn't allow that. Like he always said, they were just friends. There was no attraction left, at least not on his part.

She told herself to stop thinking about him, even though he was right there, right there touching her. Stop thinking about his face next to her, so kissably close. Stop imagining kayaking out to one of the other islands, stop imagining holding his hand in an art gallery, and especially stop trying to picture what he would look like rising from a massage table and re-moving the sheet . . . *Stop it, Cara! Just stop it!*

"This . . . is not exactly what I said," he told Amy.

Amy gave one of her dramatic sighs. "You said, and I quote, 'Amy, I don't care. Go kayaking, have some pizza, do the art gallery thing. Whatever. Write something about that.' So I did. I made you sound awesome, by the way. You should be thanking me. You might get laid from a post like this. Really."

He laughed. "Okay, fine. Thanks for making me sound awesome. I actually wouldn't mind spending a day like that with the right woman."

Was it Cara's imagination, or did Sam's fingers tighten on her shoulder as he said that? He stood up abruptly, taking his hand away, but the heat from his palm still lingered.

She skimmed through the post again, wondering why Amy would write something so flattering about someone she didn't even particularly like. A sneaking suspicion arose, and she clicked over to the inn calendar to verify it. "Amy, did you happen to check this week's reservations before you posted this?"

Amy grinned maliciously. "Of course I did. I told you, I know marketing."

"Excellent timing," Cara grinned back. Poor Sam. Amy must still be mad at him about Phil's funeral. She did tend to hold a grudge.

"Wait, what's the timing? What's so funny?" Sam called out. He had gone into the office but was evidently listening.

"Isn't there a staff meeting today? I guess you'll find out," Amy said, with an innocent expression on her face.

Cara laughed to herself. Sam should have known better than to get on Amy's bad side.

Chapter Twenty-Five

Sam hit the gym in the village for his usual workout, but he lost track of time and ended up late to the biweekly all-staff meeting. He tried to slip in the back unobtrusively, but everyone turned around when he entered, and most of them laughed. "What?" he asked.

"Nothing, Sam," Cara said from the front of the room. "We were just talking about Amy's recent blog post, and the schedule this week, and I mentioned that many of our rooms are booked for the annual Gabby Gals Mother and Daughter Weekend. For some reason, everyone thought of you."

Sam's stomach immediately dropped. It was the one weekend he dreaded most. The Gabby Gals were a group of women who had met in college some decades ago and now planned a yearly get together with each other and their offspring. They showed up every year for a loud, boisterous reunion, where they became cheerfully intoxicated and way too sociable for Sam's comfort.

"Now for those of you who are new this season," Cara continued, "especially those new *gentlemen*, you may experience an unexpected level of guest friendliness."

"In other words, hide your packages," someone up front—possibly one of the prep cooks—muttered loudly.

"We do not condone that sort of misbehavior, and I talked to the organizers about it again this year," Paddy announced. "But yes, be on the lookout for wandering hands."

"Excuse me, I have a question," Tyrell spoke up. "Why was everyone laughing about Sam? Fill me in on the joke." He looked to the back of the room. "Sorry, roomie. I need to know."

"It's like this, Ty." Cara tossed her hair and changed her voice to a falsetto. "Oh, Chef Sam, your arms are so strong from whipping all that cream. What else can you whip?"

Then Yadira, the grandmotherly woman who oversaw the housekeeping department jumped in. "Oh, Chef Sam, instead of a plate, I want to eat my meal off your abs."

Another one from Dina, who up until that very moment had been Sam's favorite waitress. "Oh my goodness, Chef Sam, this sausage is so amazing! Do you have a bigger one I can put in my mouth?"

"Okay, okay you've made your point." Sam's face was so red he felt hot. "This is the worst weekend of the summer. They harass the hell out of me every year. It's awful. And just a note to all my restaurant staff—anyone that makes a joke about it is volunteering to clean all the grease traps after dinner service tonight."

"Oh, Chef Sam, I've got a grease trap for you," Amy yelled, and shrugged when he glared at her. "What? I don't work for you. You can't make me do anything."

"I'd call it the best weekend," corrected Francisco, who was one of Sam's line cooks. "I don't mind the attention. Buncha drunk ladies. They all come from money too. Nothing wrong with a little sugar-mama action."

"Let me remind you then, of my no-consorting-with-guests policy," Paddy said. "Come on, people. These ladies come to relax, blow off some steam, and maybe blow ... sorry, I was caught up in the moment and was about to get inappropriate. Listen, if any of their behavior makes anyone uncomfortable, report it to me. I'll do what I can. You know I don't tolerate harassment of my staff."

After the meeting was finally over, Sam made his way to Cara. "So the timing on that blog post? I'm guessing Amy's mad at me about something. Is this because I wouldn't make my wait staff sing happy birthday to her last week? Anyway, the jokes on her. I'm taking the weekend off. It's a family emergency. I just heard about it, I swear. In fact, I need to go right now and buy my plane ticket to anywhere but here."

She looked amused. "Nice try. Orphans don't have family emergencies. Hide out in your kitchen. You'll be fine. I guarantee every female employee puts up with far worse almost every day of their lives."

"Thanks. Thanks a lot. Oh, and by the way,"—he lowered his voice to a husky whisper and leaned towards her—"I can whip more than cream."

He winked and walked away, sure that she was watching him, and hoping she was smiling. Despite the impending harassment, he actually felt good.

Chapter Twenty-Six

When Amy insisted on handling all of the event planning with the Gabby Gals, Cara was admittedly a bit relieved. She sometimes found it hard to deal with this crowd. Not the original Gabby Gals themselves—they were a fascinating group of women. Her problem was with the second and third generations. It bothered Cara to listen to women her age standing around the lobby complaining about being dragged on yet another vacation with their mothers. She would have given anything for that kind of opportunity, so she couldn't relate.

On Saturday morning, several frowning Gabby Gals confronted Cara at the desk. "Excuse me," said the eldest woman, who appeared to be in charge of group. "I cannot help but notice that it is breakfast time, and yet Chef Sam is not at the omelet station. Must we lodge a complaint?"

Her friends behind her giggled, and Cara fleetingly wondered if at 8:00 a.m. they were already drunk. Or maybe *still* drunk? With these ladies, she never knew.

"This is Chef Sam's morning off." She leaned in closer and dropped her voice conspiratorially. "But I'll let you in on a little secret. He went out jogging this morning. If you walk down the driveway to the main road and turn left, away from the village, he should be coming along soon. He left about a half hour ago. Oh, and he's not wearing a shirt." Amy would be so proud of her.

"Really?" There was a smattering of giggles from the small crowd and one particularly rowdy woman cheered.

"Oh yes. Believe me ladies, if I wasn't stuck behind this desk, I'd be down there myself." She said it to be friendly, but secretly, she meant it. She always liked to be in the staff house when Sam came back from a run. He would walk in shirtless, muscles glistening with sweat, and drink glasses of water in the kitchen while she pretended not to watch. He was an attractive man, far more so than Phil had been . . . she shouldn't have thought that. It just brought Phil's voice back into her head. *No one will ever love you the way I love you, angel.*

"Hmmm." The leader of the Gabby Gals paused, then nodded. "I've always liked you, Cara. I know we're not the easiest guests, but you go out of your way to take good care of us every year. So I think I'm going to help you now." Her demeanor suddenly changed from friendly and possibly intoxicated to querulous and rude. She raised her voice and called out in a demanding tone "This is ridiculous! Where is your boss, young lady? I demand to speak to the owner of this property!"

Truthfully, Cara was a part-owner herself, having inherited her mother's share years ago. But she wasn't going to argue, not with this crowd, and not since she suspected what they were about to do.

As luck would have it, Paddy was in his office with the door cracked open. He rarely worked this early, but he had an appointment in town and, for perhaps the first time this summer, he was out of bed before nine. He came right out to the desk. "Is something the matter, ladies?"

"Yes. I am appalled at the service we are receiving! We need the assistance of this young woman immediately, but she says she cannot leave this desk. You must find someone to cover for her so she can help us."

Paddy looked back and forth between the giggling faux-angry women and Cara, who professionally suppressed her smile. He volunteered to assist but was rebuffed.

"I'm not even going to try to figure out what's going on," Paddy told Cara. "You know these are valuable guests, so you had better see to their needs. I'll take over reception for you."

She led her gaggle of guests carefully down the driveway, holding the arm of one who appeared particularly tipsy. Briefly, she wondered whether mimosas were being served at breakfast again, though the woman's imbalance could have been due to age.

And, there he was, Sam, running towards them. She could tell the instant he noticed the group, he slowed a bit and shook his head. But he wasn't the type of man to be intimidated by a cheering crowd. He smiled broadly as he approached, and when he passed them he turned back and blew the ladies a kiss. The Gabby Gals cheered and laughed. Cara just smiled. He'd made eye contact with her as he blew the kiss, and she had to stop herself from pretending to catch it. He'd been different lately, relaxed and flirtatious. She was enjoying the change, but she wondered if she was quite ready for it.

Chapter Twenty-Seven

Email from Amy O'Connell to Fabio Basile:

It's reverse sexual harassment weekend! I love it!

Every year this group of old ladies and their middle-aged daughters comes out for four days, and they get completely wasted and harass all the men who work here. Ty just walked past the desk and whispered, "I'm not used to getting my ass grabbed by women," and Sato has been propositioned twice, both times by women old enough to be his mother. They like to rub his head, 'for luck' they say, and then ask when they'll be able to get lucky. Ewww. But every time the male staffers complain I'm like, "Oh, hi, welcome to my world." Seriously, as a semi-attractive young woman, I get catcalled and groped and old men make gross sexually suggestive remarks to me all the f-ing time. Don't get me wrong, it's not so bad here at the inn. But I've worked in a lot of places where the guests treat me like an object and ask questions like, "Are you included with the room?" I like seeing the reverse. (Not that I condone harassment; it shouldn't happen to anybody. I just like that it's the men who have to deal with it for once).

Have you ever heard the saying "revenge is a dish best served cold"? It's true. Remember how I've been mad at Sam for not expressing any condolences to Cara after Phil's death? I'm not mad anymore—because I've finally gotten my revenge. The leader of the Gabby Gals (that's what these old ladies call themselves) asked me to put together a few activities for them. I did the usual, a wine and cheese social, a dessert party (Sato's wife makes amazing cakes!!!!), and of course I couldn't let the weekend go by without culinary demonstrations. That's right. I made Sam do two different cooking demos, where the group gets to hang out in the kitchen and "help" and learn new techniques while Sam and one of his assistants make them lunch. I made sure that there was plenty of wine available, and I, of course, stayed to supervise, which meant keeping the drinks flowing and encouraging the women to be active participants in the cooking process. He had so many drunk women coming on to him and saying all kinds of obscene things. You'd think that a guy like him would be in heaven with something like that, but it actually made him extremely uncomfortable. Ha!

Email from Amy O'Connell to Fabio Basile:

No, I'm not condoning sexual harassment. Look at the situation this way: this guy, who previously acted like a selfish jerk and also happens to be very gropey with my cousin, ended up being groped himself. I've told you how he's always putting his hand on Cara's shoulder, or touching her arm, or accidentally-on-purpose bumping into her. He's not subtle about it either. Well, now he knows what it's like. Maybe he'll think twice before being so touchy-grabby-handsy with Cara.

Also, it was hilarious to watch.

And, side note, you missed a golden opportunity. 'Semi-attractive young woman'? You need to step up your game.

Email from Amy O'Connell to Fabio Basile:

You think I'm beautiful? Awwww, you're so sweet!

Ha, ha. I wasn't really fishing for compliments. It was a joke.

Chapter Twenty-Eight

Article from Midwest PRIDE Magazine, March 2013

It's not the biggest Pride Festival, but it may be the most remote. Whispering Pines Pride Festival is a three-day event culminating in a bike ride/parade around the island. Never heard of Whispering Pines? You aren't alone. It's the largest of the Piney Islands, an archipelago in Lake Superior, accessible only by boat or ferry. The resident population is tiny, with only about 150 people making their home there year-round, but during the summer months, hundreds, if not thousands, of daily visitors make the crossing to take advantage of the beautiful hiking trails, the unique art galleries and the delicious island cuisine.

WPPF has been a yearly event since 1986, when Padriac 'Paddy' Conaghan and his partner Robert Parreli decided to throw a party and see what would happen. That first year, PrideFest was attended by fewer than twenty people, all of whom were old friends of the couple. From those humble beginnings, the event has blossomed into an annual gathering of nearly two thousand people.

"Robert and I bought The Inn at Whispering Pines in 1983," Paddy told us from one of the many rocking chairs on the inn's front porch. "Back then it wasn't much, but he wanted to run a restaurant, and I wanted to run a hotel. This was our dream come true."

Paddy may say it wasn't much, but even in those early days, the inn had an excellent reputation as a surprisingly luxurious remote getaway. The property had been in Paddy's family for two generations, until it was sold in the 1970s. Fortunately for

Paddy and Robert, the Conaghan family had retained a right of first refusal if it ever came up for sale. With the help of Paddy's sister, they were able to snatch it back before it was officially on the market.

They purchased the inn as part of their escape plan—Paddy and Robert lived in New York in the early eighties, when their friends began to get sick and die. "It was the atmosphere in the city. That's what Robert told me," Paddy reflected. "He insisted we get out and away. There were too many funerals and too much fear." When they arrived to take over the inn and make their home on Whispering Pines, they were wary of the reception they might receive. At first, they acted as though their relationship was strictly business, even going so far as to pretend they were living in separate cottages on the Inn's property. That changed when they were paid a visit by Victor Breza, the grizzled old sailor who ran the island's ferry service and lived nearby in the island's only village.

"I'll never forget Victor showing up at our door," Paddy reminisced, smiling. "He was a big guy, tough looking, the type of man you would refer to as an old salt. He looked at the two of us and in this big gruff voice he said, 'Boys, I don't think you're just business partners. I think there's something else going on here.' Well, I looked at Robert, and he looked at me, and we both thought that this was it, we were about to get our asses kicked. But then Victor just kind of growled at us, 'And if anyone gives you any trouble, you just tell me. I'll take 'em to the mainland and won't bring 'em back.' That's when we knew we were safe here."

Over the years, several of Paddy and Robert's friends and contacts began buying up Whispering Pines homes and businesses, and soon the village became a thriving artist's community. A new section of the village, now called Gallery Row, was built up to provide studio and gallery space. As the demographics of the population transitioned from cold-tolerant retirees to younger progressive families, the infra-structure of the island changed as well. Now visitors have their choice of dining options, boutique shopping, spa services, and plenty of access to the natural beauty of the island's parks and trails.

Unfortunately, Robert missed out on most of the new developments, after losing a battle with pancreatic cancer in 1994. His partner Paddy has continued on, and still MCs Pride Fest every year. He hosts beautiful commitment ceremonies at his inn, and as same sex marriage becomes closer to legalization, is preparing to offer weddings as well.

This year's Pride Festival will take place June 28-30. If you wish to stay on the island, you'll need to make your reservations quickly. Aside from the inn, there is only one hotel and just a few bed and breakfasts. Camping is also available, and camping gear can be rented in the village. If you cannot find room on the island, numerous hotels in the town of Ferry's Landing on the mainland will be offering special rates. Victor Breza's daughter is the ferry master now, and she promises additional late-night runs for those who want to participate in festival activities but stay on the mainland.

Chapter Twenty-Nine

Whispering Pines, June 2013

"Can I hang out with you?" Sam came behind the reception desk without waiting for an answer. Cara didn't look busy anyway.

"No idle hands behind the desk. You'll have to work," she told him with a challenging smile.

He looked around the reception area. "Umm . . . what can I do? I'm not really qualified for anything. I mean, I guess I could sit here and look pretty. That's what you do, right?" He winced internally—that line was not as smooth as he intended. Fortunately, she seemed to be in a good mood, and did not take offense at the implication that she didn't actually work.

"I suppose you can do that. You'd have done a better job if you hadn't cut your hair though."

"Hey, it's growing back. The curls are starting to come out again, see?" He tipped his head to show her and was surprised when instead of just looking, she ran a hand through his hair.

"Getting there," she said with a smile.

For a second, he thought she might run her hand down his face as well, but she pulled it back suddenly, as though she realized what she was doing. Things were definitely improving between them. They just looked at each other for a moment, and Sam felt a foolish grin spreading across his face. He tried to think of something flirtatious to say but failed.

When the silence stretched out too long, Cara finally broke it. "Aren't you supposed to be at the gym right now? I thought this was the time you and Timmy devoted to getting all buff or whatever."

"Not during PrideFest week," he replied. "No way." He didn't expect the sudden incredulous look she gave him or the way she narrowed her eyes before she spoke.

"What exactly do you mean, Sam?" and then he realized his mistake. He was not particularly successful with words today.

"No, no, not because of the gay thing, I promise," he said, holding up his hands in supplication. "I mean, other than Paddy and Timmy I don't really know any gay people, but I like them just fine." He hadn't thought about the way it would come out. Truth be told, he was a little uncomfortable when the gym filled up with this week's visitors, but, though he had occasionally been hit on, a quick 'sorry, I'm straight' always put an end to that.

"Only Paddy and Tim, really? That's all?"

"Well, they're the ones I can think of off the top of my head. I'm sure I've known others. But I just mean I'm not homophobic or anything. The reason I can't go is because my workout partner won't let me. Timmy says I cramp his style."

"You cramp his style? He actually said that? Recently?"

"I guess not recently, but he says it every year. He's all, you know . . ." Sam deepened his voice in a poor imitation of Tim. "PrideFest week, man. The gays are coming, and I'm gonna get me some of that man candy.'"

It took Cara a couple of minutes to stop laughing. "Hold on, let me note the time." She scribbled something down on a piece of paper. "I'm going to have to go back to the security footage and pull that part where you talk about man candy. Amy's probably going to want to make it her new ringtone."

"The cameras record sound?" Sam felt an instant paranoia. He had always been aware of the cameras, of course, but until that moment he hadn't actually thought about the recordings.

"The terrified look on your face makes me want to go re-view the tapes from the kitchen," she said, raising an eyebrow and smiling. "Anything I should know about?"

"Ha, no," he tried to sound casual. But his mind was think-ing back to his conversation with Sato about Cara and worrying that it might be archived somewhere. If she hap-pened to watch it, would she be annoyed if she knew he was still interested in her? He'd been ramping up his flirting, test-ing the waters, and she had seemed receptive. She certainly smiled a lot, and she'd often reached out to touch his arm while he was talking. That was a good sign, right?

"Hey, um, speaking of the kitchen," he changed the subject. "We had a disaster last night that only you can fix."

"Nice try. Just like Paddy already told you, we're repairing that freezer, not replacing it."

"No, not that. Though—no pressure—I did leave printouts of some specs and cost estimates on his desk for you two to go over. I was actually talking about your picture, the one hang-ing by the kitchen door. It fell and the glass in the frame broke, and then it got spilled on. I need you to draw another one."

The picture in question was a sketch Cara had done of him a couple of years ago. Standing over the prep table, a cartoon version of Chef Sam held a knife with a dismembered hand in front of him. The caption underneath proclaimed: *No idle hands in my kitchen . . . or else!* It was his absolute favorite art-work, partly because of how special it made him feel knowing that she had taken the time and effort to capture his image so perfectly.

Was he mistaken, or did a look of sadness flit across her face?

"Oh, that." She turned away from him and started sorting through a stack of papers. "I don't draw anymore, Sam. You'll have to come up with something else."

"But I don't want anything else. You're the artist in residence, aren't you?" Though, when he thought about it, he hadn't seen any new work of hers this summer. When was the last time he'd even seen her with a sketchbook? Two summers ago when they'd often spent their entire day off together up at Lesser Lake? Maybe.

"Use those." Without looking directly at him, Cara pointed towards some photo albums on a shelf beneath the desk. "Amy's been digitizing them for Paddy. Maybe you can find something there, a staff picture or something."

"Cara ..." Something about the sorrow in her eyes made him want to reach out to her, to comfort her. Why didn't she draw anymore? There had to be a reason. But before he could do or say anything, the lobby doors opened and a family entered.

Cara greeted them, and he sat back and flipped through the nearest album. The photos were almost a decade old, but there was Cara, with short hair and shorter shorts. Nice. He turned a few more pages. Apparently, Matteo used to work at the inn, and apparently, he had a bowl haircut. Poor guy. But why were he and Cara always standing so close together? Sam studied the pictures intently, trying to see what they might have been like back then.

Chapter Thirty

"Welcome back to Whispering Pines," Cara greeted the guests walking through the lobby doors. She was relieved when they arrived, cutting off a conversation with Sam she didn't wish to have. The smile she turned towards the incoming guests was genuine—PrideFest week was one of her favorite times on the island. Most of the families staying at the inn had been coming there for years, and she had gotten to know many of them pretty well. This particular group, the Anderson-Samora family, had vacationed here every summer for nearly a decade.

"Cara, so good to see you," one of the men said with a grin. "Come over here and give us some hugs." She walked around the desk to oblige, and then spent the next several minutes squatting down and chatting with their six-year-old daughter, Destiny, who was proud to show off her nail polish.

"I look forward to this week every year," she told them as she returned to the desk to swipe their credit card and give them their keys. "It's like a family reunion. Don't forget we have a wine and cheese social in the ballroom tonight. Paddy says he has a Pinot Grigio that you're going to love. Destiny, if you want to skip the social, Amy said you can hang out at the desk with some of the other kids. She'll teach you all how to make friendship bracelets."

The child looked to her fathers for permission then nodded with excitement.

"Oh, believe me, this is our favorite week too," Eric Anderson told her. "Though I do wish it was scheduled for later this summer, like maybe after the first of August." He waved his left hand at her, showing off a ring.

"Engaged? Congratulations! Oh, I'm so happy for you." Cara beamed at him.

Engagements seemed to be the theme this weekend. Same-sex marriage had been signed into Minnesota law and would be legal in August. In anticipation of that, many of their returning guests were walking around with fancy jewelry, and there were at least three proposals planned in the restaurant. Amy usually took care of helping with those. She made sure they took place at different seatings, so nobody's thunder was stolen, and she made arrangements for a photographer (most often disguised as a busboy) to capture the moment on film.

"By the way, Gentlemen," Cara added, "I don't want you to think I'm only saying this to sell you something, but you did hear we're going to be open on weekends this winter, right? Imagine how beautiful your wedding photos would be with a snowy backdrop."

"Oh, that would be lovely." Rodrigo nudged Eric. "See, honey, I told you we could have the wedding here. Did you have your ceremony here, Cara?"

"Me? No." She glanced down at her ring-less hand. This was one of the hardest parts of her job. She gave them a professional smile. "I didn't get married after all."

"Oh, that's so sad," both men said simultaneously, and then they looked at each other and laughed.

"Did he cheat on you?" Eric asked.

Rodrigo elbowed him in the ribs. "You can't ask such things."

"Actually, he passed away in November," Cara admitted, which was always the quickest way to shut down questioning.

Embarrassed, they offered the usual condolences, just like everybody else. This was the third time this week she'd been asked about her engagement. That was the problem with friendly recurring guests—they remembered details she wanted to forget. *We belong together, Cara,* Phil's voice whispered in her head. *You can't get rid of me.*

After the family took their keys and went off to their room, she put her head down on the desk and sighed. Last summer had been just as bad. Everyone who saw the diamond on her hand wanted to talk about it. She repeated the story of how Phil proposed so many times it almost started to sound nice. Nobody ever interpreted his words the way he meant them, when he told her he couldn't live without her and that he'd never let her go. *You're mine now,* he said when he slipped the ring on her finger, and how could she say anything when there were so many people staring and such a warning in his eyes?

"You okay?"

The hand on her shoulder made her jump. She had been so focused on not letting herself think about Phil's death that she completely forgot Sam was hanging out behind the desk. She looked up into his concerned face, but she couldn't meet his eyes, not when Phil was still on her mind.

"You're still here looking pretty? It's not working, you haven't gotten a single phone number yet," she told him jokingly, trying to lighten the mood.

"I got distracted by these albums. Do you know if you go far enough back, Sato actually has hair? You can flip through and watch it recede." He studied her face, searching. "Are you sure you're okay? It must be difficult getting asked about Phil."

She tried to shrug it off. "It's no big deal. It just seems to come up a lot more right now because I've known most of this week's guests for a long time. They're like family, or distant relatives at least."

"I can tell it's bothering you," Sam said. "C'mon, Cara, I'm your friend. You can talk to me."

She shook her head. "I'd rather not talk about it. Give me that photo album. There's a hilarious picture of Matteo from when we were kids. He had a mullet long after they were popular."

She didn't want to discuss Phil with guests, and she certainly didn't want to discuss how she felt about his death with Sam. How would he feel if he knew the truth? What would he think of her if he knew that all of her tears had been not due to sorrow but relief?

Chapter Thirty-One

Whispering Pines, July 2013
Email from Amy O'Connell to Fabio Basile:

You will not believe the morning we've had! It's cold and damp and rainy, so I had to move my 9:00 a.m. yoga class indoors to the ballroom, but nobody showed up. I didn't want to walk back up to the staff house, and I didn't feel like doing yoga by myself, so I grabbed some breakfast and decided to hang out with Cara behind the reception desk.

While I was sitting there, I saw two scruffy looking guys come up on the porch and take off their backpacks—big camping packs with sleeping bags, so we knew they were coming from one of the campgrounds. They left their packs outside and came sauntering through the lobby straight into the dining room, like they belonged there. They helped themselves to massive plates of food and multiple cups of coffee. They even had Sam make them some omelets. Right after he made them, he came out and asked if we'd seen the guys because, although he's kind of dumb, even he was able to tell they didn't belong.

When they finished their breakfast, they walked out and headed straight for the door. So Cara very politely called them to the desk and asked them to pay for their meals. "We thought it was included with the room," one of them smirked. She told them, yes, it was . . . for guests of the inn. But as they were not guests of the inn, they needed to pay $19.95 each, and she was happy to take a credit card. First, they tried to flirt a little and get her to let them have the meal for free because "nobody's going to know." But when she told them no, they got mean. Seriously, oh my god, these guys turned into such rude low-lifes, and they laughed at Cara and said, and I quote, "You stupid bitch, we're not paying for anything, and there's nothing you can do about it." And they just walked out laughing because, clearly, those idiots thought they got away with something.

Cara was on the phone with Vivian down at the ferry before the lobby door even shut. Meanwhile, I was on the computer pulling stills from our security cameras. These jackasses had no idea who they were messing with.

Here's what happened when they reached the ferry docks (according to Viv): They tried to buy two passages back to the mainland, and Viv told them that it would be $75. They got really pissy because the fare is only $8 each way. Then Viv says, "Well, yes, it's $8 each, so $16 for that. But you also owe another $40 for the breakfasts you stole from the inn. Plus, I charge a convenience fee of $19 for collecting the money on your behalf and transmitting it to them." She said they started yelling nonsense about how they hadn't stolen anything and she'd mixed them up with someone else, so she showed them the picture I emailed her. Then one of them (probably the same one who said it to Cara) said, "Nice try, you stupid bitch. Here's the money for the ferry, and that's all we're paying," and he threw some cash down on the counter.

Vivian didn't touch the money. She just looked at them and said, "Well, if that's the way you want it." And then she waved Johnny over—he's the deputy who lives on the island full time. "Deputy Mills," she called, "these are the young men who stole from the inn and were verbally abusive to the employees. Cara said she wants to file charges."

This is the point when Sam and I pulled up in one of the inn's carts. I had changed into my inn polo shirt, which was exactly what Cara was wearing at the desk, so they thought I was her. Sam's a big guy, at least six two (that's almost 1.9 meters, for your metric brain), and he has really broad shoulders. When he's cooking he wears a bandana tied around his head like a pirate, and he still wore that, but he had taken off his chef's coat, so he was in a tight T-shirt that showed off his muscles. He looked tough and mean. I jumped out of the cart and shouted, "That's them right there!" and pointed dramatically (you know how I am). Sam got out slowly and kind of flexed his muscles and said, "Hey Deputy Mills, it looks like these guys are gonna resist arrest. Need some help subduing them?" And then, I kid you not, he cracked his knuckles.

Johnny looked at them and put his hand on his metal crowd-whacking thingee (that I had never until that very moment noticed he carried!!), looked at Sam and kind of nodded and said, "Yeah, that sounds like how this is about to go down." Then Vivian got into it and said in a completely deadpan voice, "Oh no, my security cameras appear to be on the fritz again," and reached back and turned off the TV monitors. (Incidentally, the cameras were still recording. She sent us a copy, and we've all watched the video like ten times.)

I swear, these obnoxious crapheads who thought they were so tough not five minutes earlier suddenly turned into sniveling little babies who acted so apologetic about the 'misunderstanding' and said of course they were going to pay. Then Vivian interjected, "It's nice you've had a change of heart, but I believe you called both me and the manager of the inn stupid bitches. I think you owe us some apologies."

The one guy turned to me and said, "I'm so very sorry. You're not a stupid bitch. I shouldn't have called you that." I told him he was apologizing to the wrong person and that he had said it to my cousin. Then Sam totally exploded. "What? What did you call Cara?" And even though he is usually quite passive, he started moving toward the guy like he was going to break his face, and Johnny actually had to step in front of him and hold him back. I thought the stupid thief was going to wet himself. Vivian made him write an apology note to Cara. (It's now hanging up in the staff office, next to a picture of the guy looking terrified—Vivian's security camera is amazingly high quality). I collected the money for the breakfast in cash, so they couldn't do a credit card chargeback, and made them give Sam a tip for making their omelets. (He doesn't usually get tips, but I thought it was important in this case.) And then Viv let them buy their tickets, and they left to sit quietly in the boarding area and think about what they'd done. Vivian told me she was going to make one of her sons keep an eye on them during the voyage, and that he'd be obvious and intimidating about it. (Her boys are huge. Even Sam looks small next to them.)

Awesome, right? We islanders stick together.

Email from Amy O'Connell to Fabio Basile:

Nightstick. Thank you. How did you know that word and I didn't?

Chapter Thirty-Two

"Why are you up so early?" Cara seemed surprised to see him in the staff kitchen.

"I was making you coffee," he replied, offering her a mug. "I'm always up this early, remember?"

"Well, yes, but it's the Fourth of July. I thought one of your line cooks was covering breakfast for you since you'll be working the barbecue all day." She accepted the coffee and smiled as she sipped it. "I expected you to sleep in."

"If I slept in, who would make your coffee? Or this?" He set a plate in front of her, and she looked down at it and clapped her hands in delight.

"You made me an American flag pancake?"

"Of course. It's a holiday." The happiness on her face gave him courage. Today was the day. He was finally going to do it.

He sat down at the table across from her and took a deep breath. "Hey, I was thinking," he began, trying to sound casual. Was it too soon? Why did she make him have all these doubts? "Are you going to watch the fireworks tonight?"

She nodded, and he took that as both affirmation and encouragement to continue. "I was thinking, um, I'm done at the barbecue around eight thirty, and sunset is at nine o'clock, so I guess the fireworks show starts after that. Do you maybe want to watch them together?" There, he'd done it. He'd asked her out.

She looked surprised, then bit her lip and smiled. "Yeah, I'd like that. That'd be fun. I'll be on desk duty since Amy's going to be running the main event, so I'll come down there when I lock up. Paddy told me to close it all down at nine, since everyone's going to be watching the show."

"Perfect, I'll wait for you." He grinned and then, embarrassed, looked down at his tea. He didn't want to seem too excited, but he was. Finally, this was going to happen. A date. Their first date.

🌲 🌲 🌲 🌲 🌲

True to his word, Sam did wait for her. All day, he waited, thinking of nothing but his evening plans. The fireworks were always spectacular, so they'd be a fitting backdrop when he made his move. He had everything he needed: he had brought a picnic blanket and a good bottle of wine—not the cheap five-dollar-a-glass house red Cara usually drank at The Digs. He knew exactly where to take her, a semi-secluded spot with a great view of the lake.

In his imagination, nobody else would find that particular location, so they would have complete privacy. He would spread out the blanket and pour her some wine (*shit, he forgot glasses! Okay, they'd share the bottle. At least he remembered a corkscrew*), and he would sit with his arm around her. They would toast to something, maybe the fact that they were finally together? *Cara, my feelings have never changed. I'm still in love with you,* he would say, and as fireworks exploded overhead, she would smile and tell him she felt the same way, and he would finally really kiss her, firmly and deeply, and maybe afterward they'd make their way back to the staff house before their roommates got home, so they could spend some time exploring the physical side of their new relationship. Not that he expected *that* right away, but he was certainly willing if she was. That was his fantasy.

The reality, though, was very different.

In reality, he stood behind a hot grill all day, sweating and making small talk with countless tourists. Putting up with the public was why he preferred working in the kitchen, nobody in there was likely to give him unsolicited advice on his meat. He stopped counting the number of balding middle-aged men who offered to come back there and show him, 'how it's supposed to be done.' *Amazing how many grilling experts managed to make their way to this barbecue*, he thought. But despite it all, he kept a smile on his face and a friendly tone throughout, because no matter how annoyed he got, this evening promised to be the best evening of his life.

Finally, food service ended. He packed everything away, and Tyrell came with a cart to take the supplies and equipment back to the inn. Sam walked over to a bench at the edge of the square and waited for Cara. He sat waiting for her long after sunset, long after the fireworks started.

Chapter Thirty-Three

Cara was almost finished with her shift. She was planning on changing clothes before meeting with Sam, wearing something a little nicer, maybe even putting on makeup, just in case. She wasn't entirely sure if they were going on a date or watching the fireworks as friends. She had done a little scouting earlier, asking her other coworkers their plans to find out if it was intended to be a group thing. But Tyrell was meeting Tim and watching from the bar, and Sato was going to enjoy the evening with his wife, so it seemed that it really would be just her and Sam.

It was exciting, but she felt a little nervous, too. She had fantasized about Sam sometimes (many times, if she was honest), and she wondered how the reality would measure up. Would he make a move right away? Should she? Would they even watch the fireworks? She knew a secluded place they could go for privacy and a great view of the lake—but was she reading too much into this? He kept harping on being friends, but he had gotten up early today when he didn't have to, just to make her breakfast and ask her out (on a date, right?). And was she really ready to date again?

But that's when the night was ruined. One of the guests, Mrs. Severson, came into the lobby carrying a miserable-looking toddler. "My son is sick," she said. "I need you to watch him for me so I can go to the fireworks."

Cara smiled as politely and professionally as possible. "I'm sorry, I can't do that. Would you like me to call the medical center for you?"

"I don't need a doctor," Mrs. Severson snapped. "I need a babysitter. The rest of my family has already gone to the show, and I'm not going to miss it."

"I'm afraid the inn doesn't offer babysitting services," Cara replied. Was this woman serious? Babysit her sick child for her? The boy's eyes were bright with fever, and he looked like he belonged snuggled up in a bed.

"Well, you should. This is ridiculously bad customer service. We came for the fireworks show. We come every year, and I'm not missing it!" Mrs. Severson's voice increased in volume, and her son started to cry. She shushed him angrily.

"Again, I'm sorry, but we cannot provide staff to care for a sick child. You'll have to either stay with him or take him to the show."

"Aren't you listening? I can't take him with me. He's sick! He's burning with fever! You want him to get worse? He needs to stay here, and like I said, I'm not missing the show."

Cara took a deep breath. "Mrs. Severson, as I told you, we do not provide babysitting services. If you leave your child here, I am required by law to call the police and child protective services. You may either stay with your child, or you may take him with you, but that's it. Like I said though, if you need medical care, I can call someone for you. And if you need medicine, I can call down to the drugstore. They'd be happy to help you. They usually close at nine, but I'm sure they can stay open a few extra minutes, or I can ask them to reopen for you after the show."

The guest narrowed her eyes and stared at Cara. "Look, lady, I know you're just sitting here. Everyone else is down by the lake. You have nothing else to do. I don't understand why you're ruining my vacation. I know the owner. I'm going to file a complaint, and you'll be fired."

"Oh, which owner do you know?" Cara inquired politely. "My uncle, or me? Because I don't know you, but I do know I'm not going to fire myself for enforcing our policy or the law. And no, I'm not staying up here. I'm going to be locking up the lobby and heading down to the show as well." She realized her mistake immediately, but it was too late to take the words back.

"You think so?" Mrs. Severson walked over to the nearest chair and sat down, still holding her whimpering child. "You can't lock up while I'm in here. And I'm not leaving until you agree to watch my son." She glared at Cara over the boy's head.

"That's your choice, Mrs. Severson." Cara kept up her polite façade but inwardly seethed. She picked up her radio and tried to make a call. She knew Sam didn't have one. Tyrell did, but he had already left to meet Tim, and the radios didn't get a signal inside the bar. Amy was busy coordinating the event and was unreachable. Damn it.

She looked at the charger behind her. Three of the five other radios were there. She cursed under her breath and tried Tyrell again. She imagined Sam waiting for her in the square and wondered who she could call to let him know how trapped she was, but everyone was at the lake. A few minutes later she heard the first of the fireworks. She was missing the show. She was missing her date, and there was nothing she could do about it.

She opened up a file on the computer and made a note on the Severson's profile: DO NOT ACCEPT RESERVATIONS. BANNED.

As the sound of the final fireworks faded, Mrs. Severson finally got up from her seat. "Well," she said, in the same nasty tone as earlier, "I guess you've learned a lesson about customer service."

Cara gave her a very professional smile. "I guess I did. By the way, Mrs. Severson, do you like camping?"

"I don't see what that has to do with anything, but no, I don't camp."

"Well, that's a shame," Cara said, still using her politest tone. "Because I know you and your family always spend the Fourth of July on Whispering Pines, but unfortunately for you, the Village Hotel and all the Bed and Breakfasts share the same blacklist as us. And now that you're on it for abuse of staff, you won't be able to book a room at any of our island lodging facilities. Have a good night, Mrs. Severson."

Cara maintained her professional smile while Mrs. Severson screamed at her, and she even kept it as the woman stormed out. Finally, she was done. If she hurried, maybe she could make it into town and find Sam.

Though why hadn't he come looking for her? She was an hour late for their meeting, surely he would think to return to the inn. That's when she realized the truth— he hadn't asked her on a date at all. He was probably down there with a large group of friends, and she had completely misread the situation. She should have known better than to get her hopes up.

Chapter Thirty-Four

Maybe she had been confused as to where they were supposed to meet? Sam said he would wait for her, but maybe he wasn't specific enough? When the fireworks started he went down to the lakeside park where everyone was gathered. He worked his way from one end of the crowd to the other but couldn't find Cara. Three people told him they saw her, but two of them also pointed out Amy up on the stage by the water, so perhaps they weren't reliable sources.

When the show ended and people started to disperse, he continued standing there, feeling stupid with his bottle of wine and blanket. At least he had the presence of mind to put them in a backpack, so he didn't look like a complete reject, holding an unopened bottle and staring forlornly at the crowd.

And now he didn't quite know what to do. Should he be mad at her? He was, a little bit, but he was more hurt and disappointed. Maybe she wasn't ready to date yet and he shouldn't have asked her out? Maybe when he asked she hadn't realized it was meant to be a date, and when she finally figured it out she decided not to go? How should he play this off?

He eventually wandered down to The Digs looking for Tyrell, but Tyrell had already left to drive guests back to the inn from the fireworks show. Then he tried to sit at the bar by himself, but nothing was working out for him that night. It was so busy there were no stools available, and Tim didn't even bother to ask what he wanted, just handed him a beer and walked away. He had planned to order something a bit stronger, but apparently, he couldn't. He stood there, alone, feeling out of sorts, when a trio of women at a table invited him to join them, so he did.

"You're that guy from the barbecue," one of them said. "We all liked your meat." The trio burst into giggles.

Sam smiled as though he hadn't heard that joke before. They were drunk and friendly, and leaving the island the following day, which made them the ideal people to talk to.

"You know," he told them conversationally, "I don't understand women. I got stood up tonight." It was the perfect opening line. Hell, if he had known the effect of a line like that, he would have been using it years ago back when he did try to pick up women in bars. That wasn't his goal now, of course. He just wanted some advice, and who better to ask than women who were not in any way connected to the situation? They'd provide him the unbiased feminine perspective he needed.

Unfortunately, the advice they gave him wasn't necessarily what he was hoping for. He laid everything out, how he was in love with a coworker, and how he came back to the island when he found out she was single only to learn her fiancé had died, and she kept using the term 'friend' as a defensive weapon. And when he finally built up the courage to ask her out, she stood him up.

"Oh dear," the blondest one said. "That's not good. You've heard the phrase 'she's just not that into you,' right? I hate to tell you, but it applies."

"Look," the darker-blond woman to Sam's right said, placing a hand on his arm. "If she wanted to show up, she would have. Every single person on the island was at the show. I think she had second thoughts. She probably just didn't know how to say no when you asked her out."

"Yeah," blondest agreed. "She's a coworker, so she probably felt pressured to accept. If she's been saying you're just friends all summer, that means she's not interested."

A hand suddenly caressed Sam's knee under the table. It belonged to the third woman, an extremely attractive brunette who kept making uncomfortable eye contact with him. It seemed like she moved closer every time he blinked.

"I had a boyfriend die once," she told him somberly. "It was awful and tragic and took me months to get over. I can't say I don't sometimes think of him even now, and that was four years ago. If your friend lost a fiancé recently, I'd guess she's still in mourning. She may have said yes to you fully intending to go on the date, but later started feeling guilty, like she was betraying his memory. I know that happened to me. She's not ready for you yet. You have to give her more time."

He hated to admit it, but the brunette actually made sense. Now he needed to figure out what to do. Apologize? Ignore it and pretend it never happened? Wait for her to say something? How fortunate that he had a crowd of intoxicated advisers to help.

"Be romantic and tell her you'll wait for her to be ready. All women love a man who is willing to wait for them," advised darker-blond, who had admittedly also spent ten minutes waxing rhapsodic about her obsession with rom-coms, especially those with British actors playing male leads.

"No, that won't work. Put her on the defensive," suggested blondest, who appeared to possess a psychologically manipulative streak. "Tell her you're sorry if she misinterpreted things, but you were just asking her if she wanted to watch the fireworks as friends. Maybe all your other friends were busy or something, or say you felt bad because you thought she might be alone. Make it all about her reading too much into it. That way, you save face."

"I think the best thing is for you to move on. She doesn't want you. Surely you can find someone else." The brunette's hand moved up his leg, and he grabbed her wrist to stop her from publicly groping him. "Look, Sam, she still needs time. I was like that too. But I'm ready now."

🌲 🌲 🌲 🌲 🌲

Sam came back to the staff house very late, still considering what to say. By the time his alarm went off the next morning, he wasn't ready, and he couldn't bring himself to face Cara yet. He deliberately stayed in bed until he heard her leave the house, then he jumped up, showered, and rushed down to the kitchen to start work. He knew he was being petty and silly, but despite having hashed the situation out with a group of strangers, he still hadn't come up with the right words.

Cara was helping Sato set out the pastries when Sam arrived in the dining room. She said good morning to him, and to his ears it sounded a bit tentative.

"Listen," he said. "About last night . . ." He was about to ask her what had happened when he looked at her face and realized that asking her out had been a huge mistake. The dark circles under her eyes and the wariness of her expression showed him how selfish he'd been. He'd taken things too far. He'd thought that she was receptive to his flirting, but he'd completely misread the situation. She was still in mourning for her lost fiancé, so of course she wasn't ready to date yet. What kind of an asshole was he?

"I'm so sorry if you took it the wrong way," he continued. "When I asked you to watch the fireworks with me, I didn't mean as a date." Would this work? Would this help the situation?

She stared straight at him for what felt like far too long. "Then I guess it doesn't matter that I didn't make it." Her smile was thin and forced.

"I'm ... we're friends, Cara," he said, hoping that she believed him. He needed her to think that he wasn't putting pressure on her, wasn't trying to make a move when he shouldn't.

"Of course. We've always been friends, haven't we?" She took a doughnut from the table and walked off to the reception desk. He watched her go, still uncertain whether he had made things better or worse.

Chapter Thirty-Five

Email from Amy O'Connell to Fabio Basile:

You would have loved the fireworks show last night! Best one yet! Don't worry, I'm not going to try to send you a bunch of crappy blurry phone pictures. You'll just have to imagine what it would have been like, watching bursts of colors exploding over the lake, gold and white and purple. It was better than the one you and I went to at that hotel—though to be honest, I was so focused on what you were doing to me that I don't know if there was a real fireworks show or if it only happened in my head. Did your face turn an adorable shade of red when you read that last sentence?

Oh, and get this: I went to the bar afterwards to look for Cara or any of my other coworkers (or really any local willing to have a drink with me), and Mr. Gropey McGroperface was sitting at a table with a group of women, and at least one of them had her hands all over him. I made sure to mention it to Cara when I got back. (I didn't stay at the bar long, too many tourists, and some drunk guy grabbed my ass, and I elbowed him as hard as I could and left.) And then this morning she tells me she doesn't think he came home last night; he showed up late to work this morning and they usually walk down together, but he wasn't there. See, I told you he was a dog.

Email from Amy O'Connell to Fabio Basile:

Keep up with the gossip, please! Yes, Gropey McGroperface and Mr. Grabby Hands are the same person.

I hope we finally get a chance to Skype later. I haven't seen your face in a week and I may be going through withdrawal.

Chapter Thirty-Six

"Man, why are you always late? You miss the good stuff," Sato said when Sam snuck in to the biweekly staff meeting.

The room was loud, with everyone talking at once. Paddy stood in front holding a piece of paper and trying to calm the staff down.

"I was at the gym. What's going on?" Sam slid into a chair beside Sato.

"It's ridiculous," Sato replied. "The Seversons' lawyer sent a letter threatening to sue us. They're demanding an apology from Cara, a stupidly huge amount of money, and guaranteed reservations every Fourth of July week for the next ten years. Can you believe that sense of entitlement?" Sato looked amused.

Sam tried to ask what he was talking about, but Paddy shouted for silence.

Amy stood up as soon as the room was quiet. "I don't care about the rest of it, but y'all know she's not apologizing to those lunatics, right?"

"Amy, sit," Paddy admonished. "And you're right. Nobody's apologizing for anything. My lawyer is sending their lawyer a very polite response, which will include a copy of the security tape and a notice warning them that if they continue threatening us, the video itself will be released. I'm sure Mrs. Severson will enjoy what the Internet has to say about her parenting. And Amy, I'm going to need you to respond—politely—to the negative reviews they've posted online."

"Seriously, what happened?" whispered Sam when Paddy moved on to some discussion of housekeeping that Sam had no interest in hearing.

"Jesus, man, how do you miss these things?" Sato whispered back. He filled Sam in on an argument between Cara and Mrs. Severson, ending with, "After the fireworks, the crazy lady even went and got her husband. They both came back to the lobby and started screaming at Cara and knocking over furniture. We had to call Deputy Mills and evict the whole family at eleven at night. It was awesome, and the entire debacle is on tape. I can't believe they think they can sue."

Sam sat back, stunned. That was why Cara stood him up? So it had nothing to do with him moving too fast? He thought about how he told her it wasn't a date, and his stomach sank as he realized how badly he had messed up.

"Oh, I know why you didn't know," Sato continued. "Wasn't that the same night you hooked up with some tourist at The Digs?"

"What? I didn't ..." Sam's voice trailed off. He *had* been drinking with some tourists, but when the bar closed, he'd come home alone. His roommate could vouch for him, right? No, Tyrell hadn't come back that night.

"Amy saw you, Tim saw you, and I saw you, and you were late to work the next day, so nice try." Sato laughed at him. "I knew all that crap you were saying at the beginning of the summer wouldn't last, Mr. Ready-for-a-Relationship."

Chapter Thirty-Seven

After the staff meeting, Cara went into Paddy's office and locked the door behind her. She leaned against it for a moment to prepare herself. Some of her weekly therapy sessions were more difficult than others, and she was in a bad place emotionally right now. Sometimes talking to Dr. Iddings helped, but other times hearing her soft Texas drawl sent her back through time and she regressed into an angry teenager trying to process her mother's death and her father's injuries. "My job is to help you move forward," the doctor told her back then. "Someday, you won't need me anymore."

That second part was a lie. Sure, for years Cara had thought she was fine, but she couldn't have been or she never would have fallen into such a terrible relationship with Phil. After his death, she'd resumed long-distance phone therapy. "I'll always be available to help you," Dr. Iddings had promised, but the cynical part of Cara knew that meant as long as she kept paying for the sessions.

As always before picking up the phone, Cara turned over all the pictures on her uncle's desk. Everyone in the photos was gone now, her grandparents, her Uncle Robert, her beloved mother. All long dead, but she could still feel their eyes on her, feel the judgement in their stares. No, she couldn't face her family when she talked about her issues. She was too ashamed.

Dr. Iddings began today's session as she always did, asking Cara what she was doing to take care of herself. As always, Cara assured her that she was eating well, pretended she was not drinking too much, and slightly exaggerated how much yoga she was doing because the lie seemed to impress her therapist.

The preliminaries over, Cara could finally move on to what she really wanted to talk about. "A year ago today, I picked Phil up at the ferry. He came out to see me. I told you what happened on that visit, right?"

"You did, yes. How are you feeling about the anniversary of his trip?"

"Conflicted. I only saw him twice after that, and so the guilty part of me wants to look back with nostalgia. But I can't just forget everything he did to me either. I'm trying to focus on the good memories, but they're fleeting."

"How are the memories of that visit affecting your life right now?"

"Well, I'm having those nightmares again. The ones where Phil is on top of me, I'm suffocating, and he tells me he will never let me go. Last night, I made so much noise I woke Amy up, and she sleeps like a rock."

While it was true that Amy possessed the ability to sleep through anything—alarm clocks, fire alarms, and on one terrifying occasion, a semi-truck crashing through the wall of the apartment beneath her—somehow, she always sensed when Cara needed her. There had been many nights when Cara woke sweating and shaking and crying from a terrible nightmare about Phil, and Amy climbed into bed with her and held her until she fell back asleep.

Unfortunately, talking about the nightmares with Dr. Iddings didn't help. She offered Cara a prescription for a sleep aid, but Cara wasn't interested in pills. She wanted something more new-agey, positive-thinking training or meditation advice, that sort of thing. Some kind of activity she could do to block the bad dreams. Truthfully, she was afraid that medication might make her sleep too deeply, so deeply she wouldn't be able to wake up before dream-Phil hurt her worse.

The therapy session got even more depressing when Dr. Iddings asked her what else was going on in her life right now, and she felt obligated to talk about the date that didn't happen and how her heart had been ripped out once again.

"I was supposed to go on a date last Thursday, and it didn't work out." Saying those words still stung quite a bit. She'd spent the entire fireworks show in the inn's lobby, glaring at her recalcitrant guest and wondering when Sam would finally come up to look for her. He must have known that if she didn't make it to meet him, she would still be at work. The inn was only a half-mile walk from the village, it would have taken him less than ten minutes. All he needed to do, if he cared at all, was come back and check. But instead, he went out drinking at The Digs and left with some tourist. A brunette with huge boobs, according to Amy's description, though Sato said they weren't that big. It didn't matter; he had evidently chosen someone else, someone he didn't even know, over her. And worse, afterwards, he told her he hadn't intended to ask her on a date, as if he thought she couldn't tell when he was lying.

"Was this date with someone you actually liked, or is this someone your cousin set you up with?" Dr. Iddings already knew about Amy's desperation to get Cara back in the saddle again. Sometimes, Amy seemed to be making Cara's love life her own personal mission. Sometimes, Amy just needed to back the hell off.

"It was with the chef, the one I mentioned before," Cara mumbled, embarrassed. She had previously confided that she liked the guy, and that, in fact, she had been having some pretty interesting sexual dreams about him (something else she feared would be affected by sleep medication). "I thought I was ready to try dating again and that we could build something special together, and I was wrong. So now I have to re-think everything. Is this because of Phil? Am I ever going to be able to move on? And will there ever be anyone who actually loves me again?"

"Cara, what do you think?" the doctor asked, using that an-noying therapist trick of answering a question with a question.

"I think I'm unlovable and that I will be single for the rest of my life. I think it's my fault Phil is dead, and my penalty will be a lifetime alone." Even as she said the words, she knew she was being overly dramatic. It sounded like something Amy would say, if Amy ever actually cared what other people thought about her. Amy would have moved on by now. Hell, Amy would have hooked up with someone at her dead fiancé's funeral just to prove that she could.

"Cara, you know that will only be true if you make it hap-pen. If you isolate yourself and choose to focus on your past, you won't be able to move on in the future. What did Amy think about your date?"

The question surprised her. "Don't you always tell me not to worry about other people's opinions? What difference does it make what Amy thinks?"

"It doesn't matter what she thinks as much as it matters that you haven't talked to Amy about this at all, have you? Look at the situation this way—Amy is your closest friend and fami-ly member. You've always been deeply connected. You've always told each other everything, but you've avoided sharing some of the worst things that happened to you. You never told her the truth about Phil, which prevents you from telling her the truth about your problems now."

"I didn't tell Amy about the date because she doesn't think the chef is a good guy for me. She calls him Mr. Grabby Hands and thinks he just uses women. And you know I can't tell her about Phil. You know that. She'd look at me differently. She'd ... she wouldn't understand." It was bad enough that Amy was there at the end, even without her knowing all the details that led up to it. She never wanted Amy to find out the real story. Cara couldn't handle the contempt she'd see in her cousin's eyes if she found out the truth.

The call concluded soon after that, and Cara stayed in her uncle's office afterwards for as long as she could reasonably get away with. Amy was right outside the door, and Cara never liked seeing her after these sessions. Her cousin always read her emotions too well. She knew when Cara was stressed and upset, and Cara didn't want her to see that today. Not on the anniversary of Phil's last visit. Not when she already knew she was in for a long night of terrible dreams.

She needed to get away from the inn for a while. Maybe she needed a trip to The Digs. Or, better yet, maybe she needed to call Matteo and kill a bottle of tequila with him. Drowning her problems sometimes helped.

Chapter Thirty-Eight

Last summer: Whispering Pines, July 2012

People seem to think Cara should be excited that Phillip is coming to see her. She's maintained the mask of their relationship for so long that it's now in her nature to smile and say, *yes, it's wonderful that my fiancé is visiting.* Nobody can hear her inner voice screaming.

She's a little bit resentful that he's coming here, that he'll be encroaching on her territory, especially when she's not sure which version of Phil will arrive. He's never come to Whispering Pines, not once in their nearly two-year relationship, not even during the first year when they were genuinely happy. Having him here interrupts her life and disrupts her routine. Summer is for spending time with her uncle, hanging out with Amy, and drinking coffee with Sam—things she doesn't want to share with her fiancé.

Amy would call that a red flag, she thinks to herself, though Amy doesn't know the half of it. Her cousin has never been a fan of Phil, even without knowing the truth about him. If Cara were ever brave enough to tell her, Amy would go nuclear on him. That might be nice to watch, though the fallout would be devastating.

Phil sounded happy and optimistic on the phone earlier this week, so she hopes he can maintain his good mood. When she left in the beginning of May, he was so angry. For some reason, he thought their engagement meant she would give up working on the island and find a permanent job in Chicago. When the small boutique hotel she worked at over the winter came up for sale, Phil was furious she declined to purchase it.

He pointed out that if she sold her interest in the Inn at Whispering Pines she'd easily be able to use the proceeds as a down payment, and then she could live with him all of the time. But she'd never sell her share of the inn, and not just because she doesn't want to tie herself to Phil and the greater-Chicago area.

He's picked a terrible time to visit. It's early July, which is always busy. At least she was able to talk him out of coming last week for the fourth. She would barely have had any time to spend with him then. (Though maybe that would have been for the best?) The inn is fully booked right now, at the height of tourist season, but she doesn't want to stay there with Phil anyway. Does she want Yadira making the bed for her and seeing condoms in the trash? Does she want to see Sam cooking them breakfast? Well, that second one, yes. She loves seeing Sam in the morning. Her feelings for him are not strictly platonic, but she won't act on them, no matter how much she sometimes wants to. She knows better.

Cara uses one of the inn carts to pick Phil up from the ferry and takes him to the Sunrise Point Campground. Phil is not happy to find out that they are camping, though she swears she told him about it.

"Don't you own the place? I can't understand why you can't get us a room. Just kick somebody out," he complains.

"I only own one-third of the inn, so I'd only be able to get one-third of a room," she jokes. But he doesn't laugh, so she tries another tactic. "Phil, I thought you would like camping. Remember how much fun we always had when we camped near Lake Michigan? Don't you think it's romantic?"

And it could have been romantic. She has a very nice campsite prepared, one with an unobstructed view of the lake. She's rented an enormous tent and comfortable air mattress from Cap'n Rentals, which Sam helped her set up this morning. (Later, she will discover he pounded the stakes into the ground so hard that she can't pull them out. She will end up paying Matteo for the damage when she gives up in frustration and cuts the ties.)

This morning, she and Sam lay down on the mattress to test whether it was comfortable for two people, and for a second when she looked at him she wondered ... no, she can't think about that now. She can't think about how Sam propped himself up on his arm and looked down at her with a smile that made her heart twist in her chest, and how she felt electricity between them, and how she just wanted to grab him and feel her skin melt into his. She can't think about the way his eyes seemed to glow and his face softened, and how for a moment—just one moment—she thought he might kiss her. She would never let that happen though.

After showing Phil the tent and listening to his grudging approval, they drop off his suitcase and head back to the inn. They have to return the cart, but she's going to take some staff bikes for them to use for the duration of the trip. Phil loves riding bicycles, so she hopes it will help him enjoy the visit.

He's already met Paddy a few times, and of course he knows her cousin. Unfortunately, as they walk into the lobby to get the keys to the bike shed, Sam is standing behind the reception desk talking to Amy, and she has to introduce him.

There's a strange tenseness in the air as the two men shake hands. She can see Phil trying to squeeze Sam's hand hard, in some kind of power play. She's been carefully vague about Sam, referring to him only as an employee and housemate, never letting on that they speak regularly during the off season, so she can't imagine Phil would have any reason to be jealous. She walks around the desk and enters the staff office to retrieve the keys. When she comes out, Amy is making small talk with Phil about his visit, and Phil is being his usual charming self. He can turn that façade on so easily. He doesn't even like Amy—he thinks she's a bad influence on Cara—but nobody would be able to tell.

"Want me to come to the shed with you so you don't have to walk all the way back here to return those?" Sam asks, touching her arm. She freezes and hopes Phil doesn't notice.

"I'll bring them back, but thanks anyway," she tells Sam, keeping her tone professional.

Later that afternoon, after she's taken Phil on a tour and they've ridden the loop of the island, they stop to enjoy a snack in a grassy area overlooking the lake. The weather is perfect, and the visit is going much better than she expected. They sit on the ground, and she leans back against him. He wraps his arms around her, and for a second, one foolish second, she relaxes.

And then his fingers dig painfully into her skin.

"What's going on with you and that guy?" he asks, squeezing just enough to hurt but probably not quite hard enough to leave bruises. He's careful like that.

His hostile tone makes her wary. Has he been thinking about this for the entire outing? She thought they were having fun.

"Sam? Nothing," she says, but somehow that makes him angrier.

"So you knew exactly what guy I was talking about? I saw how you are with him. I saw how he puts his hands on you, like he has the right." Phil's voice is rough with anger, and she is glad they are in a public place, glad that they are surrounded by other couples and family groups. He is subtly hurting her, but he won't do anything worse in front of people. He would never do anything to harm his image.

She tries to protest that there is nothing going on. She would never cheat on Phil, ever. She still remembers that dinner party they hosted back in April, when one of Phil's friends asked how Phil could handle having Cara go away for months at a time. "Aren't you worried she's going to cheat on you?" the friend had asked, and it was clear that he was just teasing.

"Oh, I'm not worried at all," Phil had replied, continuing to cut his steak. "She knows if she cheats on me, I'll kill her." He grinned at them, and then looked down at the knife in his hand, and held it up, slashing the air in a joking manner. Everybody laughed. Mild-mannered Phil, sweet Phil who captures spiders and takes them outside instead of smashing them, gentle Phil would never lay a hand on anyone. Cara is the only one who can sense the truth behind the words, the threat in his eyes.

That threat is lurking again, and Cara has to defend herself. "I promise, he's just one of my employees, that's all. And he doesn't put his hands on me."

This is all a lie. It almost feels like a betrayal of her friendship with Sam to say it so dismissively, as though he is just a minor figure in her life. He's far more than just an employee, and she knows his hands very well, the weight and comforting warmth of them as he rests one on her shoulder whenever he's talking to her at the computer. She knows how well she fits against his body when he puts his arm around her, which he does sometimes (but she tells herself it's friendly, never romantic). She knows his legs too, how he stretches them under the table as they have their morning beverages. Inevitably their legs touch, and he won't do what most people do and reflexively move away at contact. No, he sips his tea, smiles at her, and lets his calf rest against hers. She never moves either.

But she can't say any of this to Phil. She can't tell him that those moments with Sam are the only time she can relax and feel like herself again, just like she can't tell Sam that he is her escape fantasy. She knows exactly what would happen if Phil ever knew any of it, and she doesn't think she'd survive his re-action.

For the first evening of his visit, she has reservations at the inn for dinner. It wasn't her first choice, but Phil insists, and she can't come up with a reasonable excuse not to go there. They get ready for dinner and bike back to the inn. Phil is pleasant enough. He even jokes around with her, and that gives Cara hope that they can make it through the meal with-out any issues.

"Sam said to give you the best table," says Dina as she seats them right next to the kitchen door.

Cara laughs at this. She and Sam have had this argument many times. He insists that if you can see into the kitchen, you have the best seat in the house, while she always tells him that all of the non-chefs in the world disagree.

"Best table, really?" Phil looks at the kitchen door and smirks.

He maintains an unpleasant attitude throughout the meal. He has the aggressive need to point out the flaws in every-thing. He complains that the tablecloth is dirty, though Cara can't see the faint stain he claims exists. The chairs are uncom-fortable and probably cause back problems. He feels a breeze and doesn't like it—are they sitting under an air vent? The kitchen is too loud and destroys the ambiance. The appetizer course is unappealing and barely edible. (Cara disagrees and eats his share as well.) When the entrées arrive, Phil hardly glances at his before he pronounces it burnt and sends it back.

Dina looks at Cara, one eyebrow raised. Cara shrugs and shakes her head. She doesn't know what to do. Phil is in one of his moods.

A minute later Sam is next to their table in his chef coat and the red bandana he uses to keep his hair back while cook-ing. For some reason, he appears amused rather than angry. A glint of humor sparkles in his blue eyes as he says, "I heard we had a customer complaint, and somehow, I just knew it came from you."

Cara is embarrassed and can't meet his eyes.

Phil is simmering with barely controlled fury. "You knew it came from me because you deliberately burned my food."

Sam laughs as though it's a joke. "Sure thing, champ. I burned your meal on purpose because you're eating with my boss and I wanted to get fired. It was an act of self-sabotage." He winks. "Wait till you see what I did to your dessert."

Other diners who have been surreptitiously watching the confrontation lose interest and turn back to their own meals. Sam has successfully converted the situation into a jest between friends rather than a legitimate grievance. This may make it better from a business perspective, but Cara can tell by Phil's expression that he's making it worse for her.

"This is ridiculous! You can't talk to me that way! I expect a new plate. We should get our entire meal comped," Phil snaps, looking around the room as if searching for agreement. His face is getting red, and Cara worries what will come next. He doesn't usually act out in front of other people. New behaviors from him scare her.

"It's okay, Phil," Cara intervenes, but gently. "Our meal is comped anyway, except the tip, and I'm covering that. Everything's fine, Sam will fix it, right?" She finally looks up at Sam and notices that, while he still appears amused, a wrinkle of concern creases his forehead. "Sam, could you bring Phil a new entrée? Please?"

Sam claps a cheerful hand down on her shoulder. "Sure, boss. Anything for you and your culinary connoisseur here." His fingers tighten, squeezing her gently, and he returns to his kitchen.

A new plate comes out for Phil, and Cara doesn't tell him that she's pretty sure it's the exact same one. They finish the meal without speaking, and Phil refuses dessert.

They ride back to the campground, still without speaking. His silence makes her nervous, and she desperately tries to think of where else they can go so she doesn't have to be alone with him. She suggests going out for a drink in the village, but Phil insists on going back to camp. She pedals as slowly as she can to delay the inevitable.

Once they are inside the tent, Phil lets loose his fury, though he's discreet enough to whisper so other campers can't overhear. "How dare you treat me like that in public? You embarrassed me! Was that supposed to be funny, letting the chef mock me like that? I'm your fiancé. You need to show me more respect."

"You were making a scene. That's where I work. The waitress, the cooks, everyone could hear you. They're not just my employees, they're my friends." She keeps her voice calm, trying to placate him.

"Oh, since you're friends with the chef, I have to eat bad food? What else do you do with him?"

"What the hell do you mean?" Her irritation is starting to show, and that's not good for her. She knows she shouldn't rise to his bait. She should let him calm down before things get worse, but she is getting angry too, and sometimes she can't help but snap back. She should be able to control herself better by now.

"I'm saying I think you're fucking the chef. You're supposed to be mine. Should I just go kill myself now so you can dance on my grave?" He is glaring at her, anger writ large across his face. This is a dangerous moment, and she needs to be careful.

"Phil, can you please calm down? I love you. Just you, I promise, okay?" She reaches for his shoulder to soothe him, but he bats her hand away and then hits her hard across the face. She isn't expecting it, not yet at least, and she falls backward to the air mattress.

Phil follows her down, climbs on top of her, and puts his hand on her throat. He doesn't squeeze, doesn't choke her yet. But the threat is there, and she is afraid to move. She forces herself to remain calm, to breathe slowly, to avoid provoking a worse reaction. There are two ways this can go.

"You and me, Cara. We belong together. I love you. You're my angel. You have to stop making me hurt you." His other hand begins fumbling with her pants, pulling at the waistband.

She waits patiently, reassuring herself that his right hand is the one on her throat. He is never able to tear her pants off with his left. He gives up and briefly tightens the fingers of his right hand, and she lets out a strangled gasp. The sound she makes is enough to change things. He stops and stares at his hand as though he doesn't know why it's there, loosens his grip, and starts to cry. He lies against her, weeping, apologizing, and begging for forgiveness, and she finds herself once again comforting him and hating herself.

The next day Cara leaves Phil sleeping. She bikes to the staff house to wash up because, while she could shower at the campgrounds, her bathroom is much nicer and she wants to clean the feeling of last night away before work. Paddy had offered her time off for Phil's visit, but she turned him down. That was probably a good decision.

Midmorning, Phil shows up with a box, a smile, and an apology. This is his usual behavior. "I'm sorry we fought last night. I don't want to ruin my vacation out here by having you mad at me. You know how much I love you, right? I can't live without you Cara, I just can't."

She opens the box to discover her favorite candies. "How did you know I would like these?" She is genuinely surprised he would remember. She's not surprised, however, that he brought a gift; this is what he does. He thinks he can buy her goodwill. It's not the gifts that keep her in the relationship though. It's the fear of what will happen when she's finally strong enough to leave.

"I didn't, but I went to Darling Chocolatiers and the woman at the counter said she knew you and you'd like them." He is beaming, proud of himself for doing something right, and she needs to smile and be grateful and appease his ego. That's how this works. If she can keep him happy, he won't hurt her, and he won't hurt himself.

"Hey, chocolates." Sam walks by the desk on his way to Paddy's office with a stack of binders. It is a menu planning day, so he and Paddy are going to be drinking whiskey together for a while. He peeks in the box. "Oh, marzipan. I know those are your favorites, but who can eat that crap?" He turns to Phil, his voice friendly as though last night's scene in the restaurant never happened. "I keep telling her there are way better options, but why would she listen to me? I'm just a guy who devotes my life to good food." He takes one from the box anyway, pops it into his mouth, makes a face, and saunters into the office.

Cara watches him go, and when she turns back, Phil's face is clouded with rage. "Really, Cara? Really?"

Cara knows she will be walking on eggshells for the rest of his stay. Fortunately, a guest approaches with a question, and she spends her shift focused on working and managing things. Phil passes the time sitting in a lobby chair, purportedly reading a book, but actually just staring at Cara. She is relieved that when Sam comes out of his meeting, Phil happens to have gone to the bathroom, and he misses seeing Sam stop to chat and put an arm around her shoulders to give her a half-hug.

"Don't worry about last night," Sam says. "Your boyfriend was just showing off. Not sure why he thought you'd be impressed though. He should know you better than that." He grins at her, and, for the first time since Phil's arrival, she feels a tiny thread of happiness.

Somehow, though, the rest of the day is fine. Phil is different, more like the man he was early in their relationship when they were happy and he didn't have his savage mood swings. After work, she takes him to a late lunch in the village and then for a hike up to Lesser Lake. They go out for pizza and beer and watch the sunset over Lake Superior. He suggests hitting the local bar, but Cara has realized she can't take him to The Digs. She is good friends with the bartender, who happens to be a man, and she doesn't want another episode of Phil's jealousy. If she tells Phil the bartender is gay, he won't believe her and will accuse her of lying to cover up an affair. Plus, she knows that Sam and Sato have their darts league tonight, and she definitely doesn't want Phil and Sam to run into each other when alcohol and sharp projectiles are involved.

Even though she's never imagined Phil getting into a physical altercation (other than with her, which doesn't count because other than one awful time when he ended up cracking one of her ribs, she has never fought back), she does worry he might start something with Sam. That might be nice though, because Sam is big and tough—she's seen him working out, she is fully aware of how muscular he is (oh, and how lovely those muscles are), and he could probably beat the crap out of Phil. She would enjoy watching that, but she'd pay dearly for it later.

That night, in the tent, they have consensual sex for the first time in months. He is attentive and sweet, and it reminds her of how much she once cared for him, and what does it matter if she is maybe imagining that she was with someone else? Does it matter that she pictures a pair of bright blue eyes looking down on her? And does it matter that she pretends a different voice is whispering endearments in her ear rather than Phil's voice telling her he's sorry for accusing her of cheating, that it's obvious she wasn't since she is 'too tight to have been getting it regularly'? And afterwards, as they lay entwined in each other's arms, does it matter if she hopes it's the last time she will have to do that?

Cara wakes up the next morning when something heavy thumps down hard on the mattress next to her. She checks to see what it is, and there lies Phil, fully dressed and collapsed on top of the covers with his body twisted in an awkward position. For a second, she thinks he is just messing around but then she finds a piece of paper that had been placed next to her. With shaking fingers, she picks it up and reads:

Please remember me as I was yesterday, my angel. Always remember our perfect love.

Fearing the worst, or perhaps the best, she reaches out and rolls him over. He is still alive, but fabric, which she will later discover was torn from the bottom of a t-shirt, is wrapped tightly around his neck and twisted into a knot in the back. She can see where he had held it securely until he passed out. Fortunately for him, the noose has loosened enough that he did not, in fact, strangle himself. Cara isn't sure if she is supposed to be happy or sad about that.

Damn you Phil, she thinks. For a brief moment she considers tightening it back up, and waking up in an hour, but the moment passes and she unties the cloth from his neck. *Damn you, Phil.*

Chapter Thirty-Nine

Want to hear the latest ridiculous guest story? You know you do.

So this afternoon, Cara is at the reception desk while I was working on some marketing stuff (wrote up three blog posts for the inn to share over the next week). This angry guest—and since I can't say his real name for privacy reasons, we'll call him Mr. Jackass—comes up and he is furious. He tells Cara that a very expensive necklace has been stolen from his room. Keep in mind, we do have safes in the room, so guests can lock up their valuables. Also, keep in mind this is a remote island, and there is literally never any need for fancy jewelry.

Cara is her usual calm professional self. I've never even seen her raise her voice to a guest. She starts asking him about it, and he describes a gold-and-diamond necklace worth many thousands of dollars (probably an exaggeration). I could tell she thought he was going to accuse the housekeeping staff, but then he says, "And you and I both know who's responsible for this." Cara very nicely told him that she has never had problems with any of our employees and we will do a thorough investigation. That's not enough for Mr. Jackass though. He accuses Tyrell, of all people, even though Tyrell wasn't even at the inn this afternoon—he was leading a bunch of people on a hike.

I wish you could have seen her. Cara always has the sweetest face, so people think they can walk all over her, but she was just like, "Oh, no, we have the utmost trust in Mr. Waters. He came highly recommended, and we have never had any complaints about him." Waters, is, obviously, Ty's last name, and you can tell Cara is holding back her fury when she talks like that. Well, Mr. Jackass seems to be one of those coming-out-of-the-closet racists, and he starts talking about how, "Well, you know how *those people* are," and she said, "Look, we are aware that this is Minnesota, and Mr. Waters revealed in his interview that he is a Packers fan, but we chose to overlook that particular flaw because of his many good qualities." She said it so innocently and so calmly, it was awesome. Mr. Jackass' face turned a little redder—see, she was going to force him to say what he was implying.

So then Mr. Jackass is all, "I don't care what football team he cheers for, even though the Vikings are better"—Minnesotans have to get that in—"but come on, you know what I'm talking about. You know, *people like him.*" So Cara takes in a sharp breath like she's suddenly offended and she says, "Mr. Jackass! Really! I don't care what your political beliefs are, we do not disparage our disabled veterans here. Mr. Waters gave his leg in service to our country."

Now Mr. Jackass is on the spot. Tyrell wears pants when he's working, so you don't necessarily notice that one of his legs is metal. And Mr. Jackass probably didn't know Ty was a vet because why would he? But since Cara's informed him of that, he needs to respond.

"I didn't realize he was a vet, and of course I'm thankful for his service," Mr. Jackass says carefully, "but it doesn't change the fact that my wife's necklace was stolen from our room, which means it has to have been someone who works here who took it. Some stereotypes exist for a reason, and he's the only one who is . . . you know." But notice he still can't bring himself to say 'black.' So then Cara, still maintaining a look of professional confusion says, "Oh. I know what you're getting at, Mr. Jackass, and I must inform you that this is 2013, and we don't discriminate against homosexuals in our hiring choices. I also feel compelled to inform you that my beloved uncle, who has owned this property for nearly thirty years, is gay himself. This island has always been welcoming to the LGBT community. And I have never heard any stereotypes about gays being jewel thieves."

So now Mr. Jackass is starting to get pissed. There are several other guests in the lobby, and they're all listening, and so far it sounds like he hates Packer fans, the military, people with disabilities, and gays. (He's right to hate one of those groups—GO COWBOYS!). Well, meanwhile, as all this is going on, I'm sitting there in the staff office eavesdropping while updating social media, and guess what appears on our Facebook page? A selfie, posted by Mr. Jackass' daughter, taken in their room right then at that very moment, and it says, "Just chillin' with my chocolates @WhisperingPinesInn @DarlingChocolatiers #familyvacay," and it's her sitting on the bed, wearing one of our robes and THE MISSING NECKLACE! That's right, his teenage daughter had it the whole time. So I printed out the image, walked over and said, "Excuse me, sir, I think I've figured out who took your necklace. Would you like me to call Deputy Mills and have him come up here and arrest the guilty party?" I held the picture so Cara could see it and he couldn't.
Cara then says, "Thank you, Amy. Yes, we have a zero-tolerance policy for theft on our property. This person should be prosecuted to the fullest extent of the law. Given what you said about the value of the necklace, this is a felony case. Don't

worry, we do have a holding cell on the island, and they'll be transferred to jail on the mainland in the morning."

Mr. Jackass puffs up real big, all proud of himself, and announces loudly to everyone in the lobby. "Good, I'm glad you've found the thief. This is supposed to be a safe family- friendly place. Maybe you'll be more careful in your hiring decisions next time. And I do expect some sort of compensation for my troubles."

Cara's not as loud as him, but her voice carries pretty well. "Fortunately, sir, we've discovered it wasn't hotel staff who stole your jewelry, it was a guest of the inn. That guest will, of course, be permanently banned from the property. Here, do you recognize this woman?" and she hands him the printout, where I've put a bright red arrow pointing to the necklace on his own daughter.

What do you think, Fabio? Did he apologize for accusing Tyrell? Did we all laugh about how he learned a valuable lesson about discrimination and making assumptions? Or did he slink away in embarrassment with Cara calling after him, "Wait, do you still want me to call the police on your daughter?" Yeah, it was the second one.

Don't worry, the story doesn't end there. Just about every guest who witnessed the interaction slipped Ty a tip throughout the course of the night. He had no idea why all the sudden people were giving him money and telling him 'good job,' but he sure was happy about it. He made like $200 bucks, and he spent some of it on cookies for all the desk staff, which I will never turn down. Do you see why I love this place?

Chapter Forty

It was Phil again, chasing her, appearing not as he was in life but in death, his face cherry-red, his eyes open and unseeing. That Phil, dead Phil, reaching for her, hands stretching towards her throat. And she tried to escape, tried to run, but her body was too slow to move, and his hand crept toward her and she couldn't scream ... and a loud ringing jolted Cara awake.

She took a deep breath to calm herself down enough to answer the phone. It was a noise complaint, of course. Nobody else would call her at one thirty in the morning. She felt a surge of annoyance. Usually, Paddy handled all of the late-night calls, but he had a cold and had asked her to transfer the phones to the staff house rather than to him.

She looked across the room at Amy, who hadn't even moved when the phone rang. Her cousin's ability to sleep through anything aroused a brief surge of resentment, an unjustified reaction that probably stemmed from the lingering effects of her nightmare. She couldn't blame Amy. If Cara had four younger siblings, she probably would have developed the same skills. And it didn't matter. The caller was complaining about what was most likely a drunken bachelor party, and Amy wasn't the right person to help her break it up. For this, she needed Tyrell.

But when she knocked softly on the door to the men's bedroom and opened it, she saw Ty's bed was made and empty. Damn it, he must be out for the night. Sam was home though, and he was, fortunately for Cara's peace of mind, alone in his bed. He sat up, fumbling for his glasses.

"What's going on?" he asked.

"Sorry, I was looking for Ty." She made sure to only look at his face and not at his shirtless torso. "We've got a bachelor-party situation going on at the inn."

"Oh. I don't think Ty's here," he mumbled. "But if you give me a second to get dressed, I'll come help you."

By the time he stumbled, blinking, into the living room, Cara had already pulled a jacket over her pajamas, put her shoes on, and tied her hair back in a ponytail. She waited by the door, somewhat agitated. She hadn't yet shaken off the fear and anxiety of her nightmare. All she really wanted to do was curl up in bed and cry herself back to sleep.

"I hate bachelor parties," she said as they ran down the path to the inn. "It's almost two in the morning. Timmy must have kicked them out of the bar, so they're continuing here."

"Are you sure it's not just a regular noise complaint?" Sam asked.

"Positive. This morning a group of men asked Sato where they could get a stripper. I guarantee it's them."

They could hear the party as soon as they entered the building. Cara marched down the hall, right to the door with the noise and pounded on it loudly. No surprise, it was the same guys from earlier.

"We didn't order room service, but I'll take it." The man who opened the door reached for Cara's arm to pull her into the room. She stepped back out of his fumbling grasp and bumped into Sam.

"You don't get to touch her," Sam warned. He tried to step in front of Cara, but she put up her hand and blocked him. She wanted to prove she could stand up to an aggressive man in the way she wished she could have stood up to Phil.

"That is ENOUGH," she told the drunk in a furious voice. "Where's Zackary? I want to talk to the groom, now!"

"You don't need a groom when the best man is here." The intoxicated jerk in the doorway tried to grab Cara again.

Sam reached right over her this time and pushed his arm away. For a moment, Cara was concerned there would be a fight, but she elbowed Sam back. He took the hint and stayed behind her, glaring with his arms crossed. She was going to handle this.

"Alright, let me tell you something, *best man*." Her tone made the title an insult. "Tomorrow is supposed to be Katrina and Zackary's wedding. I've known Katrina for a decade, and she has always wanted to get married in our gazebo. Always. This is her dream wedding. If you touch me one more time, you'll be explaining to her why the best man is in jail and missing the ceremony. And if there is one more noise complaint about this or any other room in the inn tonight, you, *best man*, will be explaining to Katrina why her wedding got canceled."

"You can't do that!" he argued. "You can't cancel the wedding!"

"Oh, I can." Her voice was deadly serious. "If your groom over there is capable of rational thought, he'll pull out his copy of the contract and show you. I'll probably give Katrina a partial refund out of the goodness of my heart, but you're all going to have a mad scramble tomorrow to find a new place for the ceremony and reception. The diner might be available to cater on short notice, if Katrina doesn't mind eating French fries in her four-thousand-dollar dress. Of course, she might also decide Zackary isn't worth the trouble."

"You . . . you can't do that," the best man repeated, but his voice took on a desperate note.

The groom, who had been lolling on a chair, looking nearly unconscious, staggered over to them. "No, no, she'll kill me," he slurred. He swayed, barely able to stay upright.

"Oh, I can do that. This is my inn. I can do whatever the hell I want when some drunken assholes wake up my guests and then try to assault me on my property." Cara and the best man stared at each other, unblinking, for at least thirty seconds before he broke.

"We'll stop," he said. "I promise."

🌲 🌲 🌲 🌲 🌲

After Cara made sure the attendees dispersed to their own rooms, she and Sam went down the hall to the lobby. "We need to hang out for a few minutes, to make sure they don't recongregate elsewhere. We're lucky that was a room party. Those are much easier to break up than when they sneak into the hot tub."

Sam let out a deep breath. "That was intense, Cara. I thought I might have to hit that guy or something."

Cara laughed as she collapsed onto a couch. "You would have won that fight. You'd just need to step out of the way when he took a swing, and he'd go crashing to the ground. They were all pretty drunk."

"Would you really do that? Cancel the wedding, I mean?" He sat next to her, close enough that his sleeve brushed against hers.

"What? No, of course not. I love Katrina's family. They've come out here every summer for like twenty years. I'm not going to alienate our recurring guests. But he thought I would, and that's what mattered. Thanks for coming with me by the way."

"I'm glad I did. I was impressed." Maybe it was the late hour, or maybe it was the abrupt awakening, but something about Sam seemed less inhibited than usual. He leaned toward her and said in a low voice, "I've gotta tell you Cara, the way you stood up to that guy, it was kind of hot. No, not kind of. It was hot."

She looked at him speculatively and saw something in his eyes she hadn't seen in a long time. "Oh yeah?" she asked, and her voice held a challenging note. "You think that was hot?"

He swallowed. "Yeah, yeah I think so." His face was suddenly so close to hers, so very close.

Her heart started racing, and she swallowed back the sudden fear. *Sam is not Phil,* she reminded herself, *and this is what I want.* She could do this, she could move on with her life. All she had to do was lean forward a couple more inches . . .

A door opened, and one of the groomsmen came into the lobby. "Hey," he said, and Sam abruptly withdrew. "Sorry to bother you, but I need to ask you a favor. Can you not mention any of this to the bride? She's . . . well, she's not very forgiving."

"If I don't hear any more complaints, Katrina will never find out about any of this," she assured the groomsman, and he flashed a smile and thanked her before stumbling off. She turned to Sam, but he was leaning back against the couch and looking away, one hand on his mouth. Well, that ended that possibility. She sighed and rose to her feet.

"Come on Sam, let's go home. We both have to be up in three hours."

They walked back to their house in silence, but when they arrived, Sam put his hand on the door and stopped her from entering. "Wait. Before you go back to bed, there's something I want to tell you. This probably isn't the time or place, and maybe you don't care at all, but I just want to make sure you know: I didn't hook up with a tourist after the fireworks. I know there's a rumor going around, but it's not true. I promise."

"Why . . . why are you telling me this?" She looked up at his face, and he looked away. She wasn't sure if the redness of his cheeks came from the porchlight or embarrassment. Either way, this changed things, just a little. She already knew he'd been lying when he claimed he hadn't asked her on a date, and she had assumed it was because he'd gone home with a tourist and was trying to make himself look like less of a jerk.

"Because I care what you think of me. That's all. Anyway, it's late, and, like you said, we both have to get up in a couple hours. You're definitely going to need your coffee." He opened the door and gestured her in first. "Good night."

"Good night, Sam." When she returned to her bed, she couldn't fall back asleep. She was wondering about possibilities, and what she would be able to handle. *You're mine, angel,* Phil whispered, and she concentrated very hard on shutting him up.

Chapter Forty-One

Cara stood off to the side of the ballroom watching the wedding reception and making sure things were running smoothly. So far, everything was perfect. The best man had come up to her twice to apologize for his behavior and make sure she wasn't going to say anything to the bride about the bachelor party altercation. She noticed he wasn't drinking alcohol, and there appeared to be some animosity between him and the groom. Good, maybe he'd learned a lesson.

She didn't notice Sam's approach, but when a hand gently touched her back she recognized it immediately. His breath was warm in her ear as he tipped his head towards hers and asked how the reception was going.

"It's been great," she answered, leaning back against him a little and smiling. The music was loud and the guests were drinking heavily, so he had to stay close to hear her. She didn't mind. "You done in the kitchen?"

"Almost. I have to go back and make sure the caterers get everything cleaned up. I'm so glad Paddy decided to outsource the bigger weddings this summer. By the way, I set aside a few plates to bring up to the staff house later. Did you try any of their crab puffs? Better than mine, I think. I should ask where they source their crab meat."

"I think it came from a can," she told him, and enjoyed the disgust that flitted across his face. She tried to come up with something else to say so he would stay there, his body up against hers and his hand so warm on her back. "Did you see the best man tonight?"

"Nope. Is he harassing you again? I'd be happy to punch his face for you," he offered.

She laughed and shoved him gently with her body. "I think the groom took care of that. Look closely at his left eye, if you get the chance. He's wearing make-up, and apparently nobody taught him how to blend the edges."

"I imagine it takes skills to hide a bruise," Sam said. "He probably needs practice."

"It's not so difficult," she replied, and immediately regretted the slip. She really needed to be more careful. "So, um, what do you think of the music?"

"Not bad for a cover band. Are they local?" He didn't seem to notice her abrupt conversational shift.

"Some of them. You didn't recognize Everett?"

Sam squinted at the band before spotting the younger of the ferry brothers on the drums. "I guess I've never seen him without a hat."

They stood watching for a moment. Sam's hand had moved up to her shoulder, and she found herself resting against him. *Friends can stand like this*, she imagined him saying.

"You ever think about getting married?" he asked her suddenly. Her face must have shown her surprise because he immediately started stammering. "I don't mean to me or anything. I just meant in general, that's all."

"You mean other than when I was engaged?" Bad enough the best man's shoddy make-up job had already made her think about Phil. Talking about her engagement would ruin the rest of her good mood. The ghost of the ring tightened on her finger. She gritted her teeth and forced the memory away.

"Ahhh . . . sorry, yeah, I wasn't thinking about that. I didn't mean to bring it up. I know you're still in mourning. I, well . . . I look at things like this and it makes me feel a little lonely. You know, they've got all their family and friends celebrating together and everybody looks so happy."

Cara was mildly surprised to see how serious he looked staring out at the crowd. "I never actually planned my wedding," she admitted. "But if I ever do get married, I want something small. Just Uncle Paddy and my dad, and I guess his wife, if she has to tag along. And Amy's family, of course. So my five cousins, but then the boy twins would want to bring their wives and kids—okay, my imaginary wedding is getting out of hand already."

"I don't even have that much," Sam reflected. "But it wouldn't matter. The only thing I would care about would be marrying the love of my life."

He looked down at her, and her heart fluttered wildly. She did her best to stop it. He couldn't be talking about her. "So you do have a romantic side?"

"Of course. I just don't let it out much. Hey, I actually like this song." He tilted his head toward the band and hummed along for a second. The melody was slow and dreamy, and his hand moved slightly as he swayed. His hip bumped against hers. "Dance with me?" he asked in an unexpectedly husky voice.

She looked up into his eyes. There was something in them, the same burning light she had seen before. Her breath caught in her throat, and the flutter in her chest started again. Was this it? Was he finally moving past his 'just friends' thing and actually interested in her again? Last night it had seemed like they missed an opportunity, but there was nothing to stop them now. *Just do it! Seize the moment.* She wasn't sure if the advice was for him or her.

"I'm supposed to be working, but I suppose one dance won't hurt." She turned her body so they faced each other, and he started to draw her to him.

As soon as their bodies touched, Amy arrived like a bucket of ice water. "Hey, Cara, there's an issue with some random people trying to crash the open bar. We need you. What are y'all doing anyway?"

Cara sighed. She felt the abrupt release of Sam's hand and the cold space it suddenly left behind. "I'll take care of it," she said, looking at Sam with regret.

"Yeah, I gotta get back to the kitchen anyway." He shrugged and walked off. She watched him go for a second before sighing and getting back to work. She shouldn't have tried to dance with him anyway. It was unprofessional, and on his end, probably meaningless.

Chapter Forty-Two

One year earlier: Chicago, March 2012

Cara lies curled up under the blankets. She hasn't been able to move from the bed. Everything aches. At least she's not crying anymore; her tears have finally run out. The last words Phil said are pounding in her head: *You turn me into an animal Cara. I hate that you do this to me.* He slammed the door when he left, and she pulled the comforter over her head and wondered how she had let this happen.

She needs to get up; she knows this. She needs to get up and do ... something. But what? She knows she's not supposed to shower because that washes away evidence, but then what evidence does she need, really? He's her boyfriend, and they live together. It's not like any charges would be filed, even if anybody believed her. And she knows they wouldn't. That's the problem with Phil: his mask is too perfect. He's too perfect.

Cara finally manages to crawl out of bed. She wraps a blanket around herself and staggers to the living room. Her purse is still on the floor where she dropped it when she came home from work. She wishes she had been more careful, that she had sensed Phil's mood more clearly. She wishes she hadn't come to Chicago at all.

Her phone is still there. Good, she was afraid he might have taken it when he left. They don't have a landline, so he would have cut off her ability to communicate with anyone. But who could she call anyway?

Amy is too far away, asleep on the other side of the world right now. And what could she do? She'd tell Cara to walk away, and she wouldn't understand why that's not always an option.

She looks at Matteo's number. Geographically, he's her closest friend, but he may as well be a million miles away. She could call, and he would be angry, and he would swear he'd be coming to kill Phil, and maybe he'd even make it as far as Duluth before the panic attacks overwhelmed him and he had to return to the island. She can't burden him with the knowledge of her circumstances when there is nothing he is able to do. And she can't risk the embarrassment that he might tell her uncle. She never wants him to know the truth. How could he ever look at her the same way if he did?

That leaves Sam. They became so close over the summer, and she often wondered if things were different, if she hadn't been with Phil, if maybe something would have happened between them. But if she calls him now and he finds out how damaged she is, he'll lose all respect for her. She fantasizes sometimes about him rescuing her, a knight in shining armor, but that's not reasonable. He'd probably ask what she did to deserve it, what did she do to make Phil so mad, what was wrong with her anyway?

The phone rings in her hand and the name Veronica shows on the display. That's Sam, that's the pseudonym she came up with to keep Phil from getting angry at how often she talks to another man. It shouldn't be a big deal, she should be allowed to have her own friends. Phil has a lot of female friends—and all the single ones that Cara has met have told her half-seriously that if she's ever tired of him, they're willing to take her place. They have no idea what they're asking for.

She doesn't answer the phone. What would she say? *I'm hurt, I'm broken, please help.* No. She can't say anything. She can't tell anyone. It stops ringing and a minute later she gets a text.

Tonight I'm cooking for a celebrity party so exclusive that I have to sign a nondisclosure agreement! In the big leagues now!

Even though it hurts, she is still able to smile for him. But she doesn't reply right away. She doesn't want him to know she's standing there with the phone in her hand. She doesn't want to explain why she didn't answer.

She finally does shower, with the hot water turned up as high as she can stand. Her skin is turning red from the heat, but she doesn't feel clean. And to think, this hadn't started out as such a bad day. Things with Phil had been calm for a month, a full month of no fights, of no anger, of Phil maintaining the illusion of having changed. And then she came back from an early shift at work to find him in the house, all the lights out, sitting quietly in the dark in front of a roaring fire.

At first, she thought he was putting together something romantic. With all the ice and snow on the ground outside, it would be pleasant to spend the afternoon by the fireplace, maybe with a bottle of wine. But then he turned and looked at her, and she knew it was the other Phil in control.

And then she saw what was in the fire.

"Are those my sketchbooks?" she asked, horrified.

"Is this what you think of me?" Not everything from her books was burning. Phil held out a picture she had drawn of him, of rage-Phillip, his face contorted and monstrous, his fists larger than life. She tried to approach carefully, tried to calm him down, all the while surprised at his utter hypocrisy.

"If I'm like this, it's because of you! You do this to me!" he finally yelled, and that was it. She stands in the shower under the scalding water and tries to scrub away those memories. He burned her books, he burned her pencils, and he tried to destroy her. She looks down at her fresh bruises and thinks about her life outside of Phil. She thinks about Whispering Pines Island. And she makes a decision.

She is going to leave him this time. It really is over. She can find somewhere else to stay for the next two months, while she finishes her job here. And then she's going back home to her safe little island, to her friends, to her real life. She doesn't know where he went today, or when he's coming back, but that's alright. Now that she has a plan, she is confident again. She can wait until he leaves for work Monday morning. It is her day off, so she will have a guaranteed nine safe hours, and it won't take her long to pack. She doesn't own anything, just some clothes, a few pictures, and ... she doesn't have her sketchbooks anymore. That's fine, it's less to deal with. She's free.

The water heater eventually runs out, and she steps out of the now-cold shower. Her plan makes her feel stronger. She will survive this relationship, and she won't let him do this to her ever again.

When her phone rings, she hopes it's Sam calling again. Maybe she'll explain to him that nondisclosure agreements mean maybe he shouldn't tell people the party exists, and he'll laugh, that great roaring laugh that always brings a smile to her face, and it will help her forget, just for a little while. But the voice on the other end is not Sam, it is a woman, a nurse, and she says there's been an accident. Cara's first emotion is elation. She really is free! Phil is dead, and she is free.

"What happened? Is he okay?" she asks, but already her heart is singing.

"He's going to be fine. The airbags saved him. He's asking for you."

And just like that, she is trapped again.

Cara takes Phil's old car, the one he lends her when she is in town. He bought himself a new Subaru last year, so that must be what he wrecked. She makes one stop on the way, at a drugstore where she pays cash for Plan B and swallows the pill in the bathroom.

🌲 🌲 🌲 🌲 🌲

Phil has been charming and wonderful ever since he came home from the hospital. He cleans the house, he cooks the meals, he tells her she's beautiful. Cara wants to believe he's actually changed, that the accident knocked some sense back into him, but she's not that stupid. This is just one of the good periods. His rage will be back.

But it doesn't matter. She knows how to leave. In two months, her job here will end, and she will move back to Whispering Pines. When she gets there, she will cut off all contact. She will block him on email and on all her online accounts. She won't answer the staff phone, ever. Her housemates can do that. She imagines that after Phil hears Sam's voice telling him she's unavailable enough times, he'll take the hint. And she'll block him from the island as well. All she has to do is give his picture to Vivian, and Phil will never be allowed to board the ferry. Sure, he can try to hire a boat, but even if he does, Cara will be safe at the inn. She lives in a house with two men, plus she shares a room with two other women, so he'll never get her alone. She will finally be able to break free. She knows he won't make another attempt at suicide—he needs her to be around for that. If he can't reach her, he won't do it because it won't work as a manipulation tool.

So it's all going to be fine. She just has to make it through the next couple of months, which should be easy because Phil is acting like the man she fell in love with, and she can handle being with that version of him. As long as she's careful and doesn't make him angry, everything will be fine, and she will be able to escape.

But no, nothing in Cara's life works out as it should.

It is one week after the accident, and they are going out to eat. When they arrive at the restaurant, there is a sign outside, *Closed for a Private Event.* "That's okay," she tells him, "we can go somewhere else," but Phil says he'll pop in and ask. He comes out a minute later with a hostess.

"I'm so sorry," the woman says. "This should have been taken down. We were only closed at lunch." She takes them in and seats them. The restaurant is half full, surprisingly so since all of those people must have walked past the same sign. But Cara doesn't think too much about it. She should have, maybe she could have avoided what was to come.

Dinner is pleasant enough, though Phil seems nervous. They are seated in a corner near the stage, where a string quartet is performing. She can't see what's going on in the rest of the room, but Phil keeps looking past her shoulder and nodding to himself. That too, should have been a warning.

When Phil excuses himself to the restroom, she sips her wine and smiles as she thinks about her countdown. Eight weeks to go.

"Hello, everyone." Phil's voice on the microphone surprises her.

She turns and sees him standing on the small stage. The quartet has stopped playing, and the entire room is looking at him. She scans their faces. Phil's colleagues from the office. Phil's running group. Phil's triathlon team. Phil's co-volunteers from the various community events he participates in. Both of Phil's parents, who can barely stand to be in the same room as each other. Oh no. Cara's heart starts racing. This is not good.

"I want to thank you all for being here tonight. Just a week ago, I was in the hospital, again. You all know me and my perpetual bad luck. Or at least, it may seem like bad luck, but the truth is, I always have an angel watching over me. You've all met her. She's right over there." He points at Cara, and people clap.

She flushes and wishes she could run from the room, run away right now without looking back.

"Have you all heard the story of how we met?" Phil continues. "I was in Spain, admiring the architecture and paying absolutely no attention to my surroundings, and I stepped off the curb right in the path of a bus. Suddenly, this beautiful woman throws me to the ground, and the bus passes by. I didn't know if she was real, or if I just imagined her, but then I was fortunate enough to meet her the very next night. And that's when I learned that not only was she beautiful with extremely fast reflexes, but she was also sweet and smart, and, best of all, was about to move to Chicago for six months. It was fate.

"She saved my life a second time, too. Remember last year when I was hospitalized with the flu? I nearly died on the floor of my kitchen. I passed out from being so sick and dehydrated. That was before Cara and I were living together, and we didn't have plans to see each other in the next couple of days, yet somehow, she still knew to stop by for a visit. She found me and called the ambulance, and I spent almost a week in the hospital. I learned two things that day. The first was, obviously, get a flu shot, and the second was that I truly could not live without this woman." He pauses to wipe a tear from his eye.

Cara grits her teeth to keep from screaming. He's selling his lies so well. He may have told everyone it was the flu, but he actually overdosed and spent three days under observation in the hospital's mental health unit. And Cara went to his house because he texted her an apology and a goodbye, because he said he couldn't live with what he had done to her. That was his first suicide attempt.

"And last week, she did it again. Usually, she drives my new Outback, because it's safer, and I take the old Civic. For some reason, when she went to work last Saturday, she took the Civic. She must have known somehow, what would happen. I was waiting for a call about a purchase I had made, something I was desperate to pick up before she got home. Well, I got the call, and it was later than I would have liked, so I got into the Outback, and on my way there, I'll admit it, I was speeding a little—like I said, I wanted to finish my errand before she came home—and I hit black ice. I lost control of the car. It spun, and I crashed into a tree. At the hospital, they told me the only reason I survived was because of all the safety features. Had I been in my ten-year-old Civic, I would have been dead. But as you see, it wasn't luck that saved me from my carelessness, it was my angel."

This is all a lie, a complete and total fabrication. Cara drove the Outback to work that day. Phil took it after she got home. He is twisting the story, as though everything he did to her that afternoon hadn't happened.

"While my car was spinning, all I could think about was Cara's face, and how terrified I was that I might never be able to see her again, never be able to tell her how much I love her, never be able to . . ." He trails off and covers his eyes for a moment to regain composure.

He is a convincing actor. The audience appears to be holding their collective breath, even Cara, though for a different reason.

He is finally able to continue. "I never wanted to leave her like that and I'm so glad I didn't have to. Now, I suppose you're all wondering what was important enough to make me drive like a maniac. You see, I was on my way to pick this up." He reaches into his pocket and pulls out a ring box.

He's woven his trap so well, and she is firmly snared. He calls her up to the stage. Her feet are made of lead. She stumbles as she walks and she's crying, and everyone is misinterpreting her reaction.

Phil drops to one knee in front of her. "Cara, I love you. I truly cannot live without you. I'm asking you to love me for the rest of my life. I want to marry you, and hear you vow to love, honor, and *save* me till death do us part. Please, Cara, my angel, save my life again and say you'll marry me."

And what can she say, here in this room, surrounded by all the people who don't know the real Phil? Here, in front of his mother, in front of his coworkers and friends? She continues to cry, she can't help it.

Phil stands back up to embrace her. His breath is hot in her ear. "Don't embarrass me, Cara." His tone is dangerously close to his abusive alter ego. She knows what will happen if she refuses, and she's not sure she'll survive.

So she lets him slide the ring on her finger. And her escape plan melts away.

Chapter Forty-Three

Whispering Pines Island, July 2013
Email from Amy O'Connell to Fabio Basile:

OMG, Mr. Grabby Hands was at it again! He was putting the moves on Cara at a freaking wedding. First off, what a conniving jerk. You know her fiancé literally just died, so going after her at a wedding is low and secondly OMG! Why can't he keep his hands to himself? I actually went over and interrupted them to rescue her. You know Matteo, that guy that runs the rental shop? He and one of his buddies were trying to crash the wedding, wearing tuxedos and everything. The couple hired a bartender from the mainland, so Matteo totally thought they could get away with sneaking in. I guess he heard it was open bar. So I pointed them out to Cara, and it was so f-ing funny. She went over there and grabbed him by the ear and dragged him out. She was way more pissed than I expected.

Email from Amy O'Connell to Fabio Basile:

I don't speak British English. Pissed means angry, not drunk. I meant she was mad.

Obviously, yes, I could have handled the wedding crashing idiots myself, but it provided an excuse to rescue my cousin, so why wouldn't I use it? I also made sure Sam slunk back to his kitchen alone while Cara was busy.

And yes, I know, she's an adult and she can handle herself, but look at the situation: it was a freaking wedding. How much more vulnerable can a near-widow be? At this time last year, she was supposed to be planning her own wedding. (Not that I thought she'd go through with it. I didn't really see Phil as a viable long-term option for her.)

Hell, I feel vulnerable and kind of lonely at weddings, too, and I've never even been close to being engaged. Don't get me wrong. I love my lifestyle, and I have no regrets about the decisions I've made. But sometimes I look at happy couples and wonder when I'm going to have that. You know I love you madly, but you're also on the other side of the world right now, and we don't know what's going to happen for us.

Don't you get the same way? Weren't you just telling me how lonely you felt at your friend's wedding when everyone around you was all coupled up and you were alone? It's like they're all moving forward into the future, and you're standing still.

Email from Amy O'Connell to Fabio Basile:

My last email was kind of a downer, so let's change it up. Funny story time. You're going to appreciate this one. Remember I told you Cara got really mad at Matteo for trying to crash that wedding over the weekend? I still don't know why she was that upset over it. It's not the first time he's tried that kind of thing, but she was, and I guess she decided she needed to get revenge on him.

So today, Cara and I were having an early dinner at the reception desk, and who should walk in but Matteo? He's all dressed up in nice pants and a button-down shirt and he strolls over to the desk like he belongs there.

Then he asks us to call up to one of our guest rooms. "Could you tell Emma Smith I'm in the lobby?" he asks us. (I changed the last name for privacy reasons.) The 'Smith' family have a reunion going in our inn this week. Cara's just like, "Why, did she book a tour with you?" and Matteo's like, "Umm, no, can't you tell from my outfit we have a date? I'm taking her out. There aren't any rules about inn guests having to sleep here, are there?" Pretty f-ing sleazy, if you ask me. But Cara gave him her up-to-no-good smile and said, "No problem."

So, then Cara picks up the phone, but before she dials, she says, "Just so you know, I'm going to call her parents' room first." And, of course, Matteo asks why, and she says, "Well, if some thirty-year-old man came to pick up my fourteen-year-old daughter, I'd sure want to know about it." You know in cartoons when someone runs so fast their legs spin in circles and there's a dust cloud at their feet? I'm pretty sure that's what happened. I'm not even sure if Matteo opened the lobby door or teleported straight through. FYI, Emma is the oldest of the Smith girls, and we don't know her age, but we do know she's a college graduate, so early twenties at least.

It was hilarious.

Chapter Forty-Four

Cara was lying on her yoga mat in the grove, relaxed and half-asleep when she heard footsteps crunching through pine needles on the approach through the woods. She assumed it was Amy, since her cousin was the one who was supposed to meet her there fifteen minutes ago. Then she realized the tread was too heavy, especially when the person stumbled and swore in a masculine voice.

"Sam?" she sat up in surprise.

"Hey. I heard you were out here." He smiled, and it felt a little bit like the sun came out from behind a cloud. Oh, the things she wanted to do with that man, if the specter of Phil wasn't always hanging over her head.

"Yeah, Amy and I are going to do some yoga. She wants to try out a new thing for her class, and I'm her guinea pig. How was your trip to the mainland?"

"Got everything I needed." Without asking, he sat down on the mat next to her. "And I brought you a present." He handed her his backpack.

"Thanks, but I already have a dirty old backpack," she told him, and he made a face.

"Yeah, I didn't have wrapping paper. Look inside."

She started to, but hesitated. "It's not a duck, is it?"

Sam's laughter rang out loudly. "Why would I bring you a duck?"

"You said you were going to the farmer's market to meet with your new duck dealer, so why wouldn't you bring back a duck?"

"First of all, he's a duck supplier, not a duck dealer. And I did bring back a duck, but it's in the kitchen and I'm cooking it for all of us tonight. The guy does this interesting dry-brining method. He says he can give us a pretty good deal, but I want to test it out first, see how I like it. I thought I'd . . ." He trailed off as he realized she had been joking. "Fine, Cara. Very funny. Just open the bag."

She didn't expect the contents to make her feel a sudden onslaught of grief, but they did. He had brought her a sketchbook, a pack of colored pencils, and a set of her favorite drawing pencils. "Sam, what is this?"

"Has it really been that long?" he teased. "Cara, you don't recognize paper and pencils? You used to draw, remember?"

She sighed deeply, still trying to process this. Even after Phil's death she hadn't been able to bring herself to sketch. "Sam, these are Tombow Mono pencils. How did you know those were my favorites? But I never worked with color . . . and I don't sketch anymore."

The art supplies were causing such a swirl of emotions. Pain and grief warred with a tiny kernel of pleasure. How did Sam know her so well? Did he know how seeing art supplies would make her feel? She tentatively touched the pencils with just one finger. Could she really let herself enjoy drawing again?

"You used to, and it made you happy, so I thought maybe . . ." Sam paused for a second before starting over. "I know you've been going through a lot, and you've been kinda low. The colored pencils are to help pull you back up. You remember last summer, when I started experimenting with octopuses . . . octopussies . . . octopusseses?"

She laughed and patted his arm. "*Octopi*, Sam, it's octopi. And yes, but mostly what I remember is the lecture Paddy gave you about keeping costs down and to stop buying weird imported ingredients to play with."

"Yeah. That was not a pleasant conversation. But anyway, I was experimenting with the *octopi* because I was in a food rut. I was feeling uncreative, like I'd lost my inspiration. Whenever that happens, I go buy an unfamiliar ingredient or learn a new technique. I play with it until I get my mojo back. I know you gave up on your art, but I think you miss it, and maybe you just don't know how to start again. And I got you the colored ones because you don't usually use them. They're your rut-breaker. The woman at the store was super helpful, and she recommended this kind. She gave me her number, so I guess you can call if you have any questions about them."

"Uh huh, sure that's why she gave it to you," Cara muttered. Sam was one of those people who received excellent service everywhere he went, and he never seemed to realize it wasn't normal. Nor was it normal for salespeople to slip their phone numbers to customers so often. "Sam . . ." She looked up, unsure of how to express how deeply moved she was by his gift. When she met his eyes, they had taken on that glow again.

"I just want to make you happy, Cara," he told her. The intensity of his stare made her heart race.

She felt her breath catch in her chest. Sam's gaze flicked from her eyes to her lips and back again. This was it! This was their moment!

Phil's voice tried to intrude. *Maybe I should just kill myself so you can dance on my grave.* She forced it into silence. *Not today, Phil.* She would not let his voice overpower her again.

She started to lean in for the kiss. But then, damn it, another, louder voice stopped her.

"What are y'all doing?" Amy's voice cut through. She somehow always managed to show up at exactly the wrong time.

Sam suddenly blushed and stood up. "Just showing Cara something. Umm, I'll just take this back down to the house for you. Have fun yoga-ing." He picked up the backpack and walked away.

🌲 🌲 🌲 🌲 🌲

When Sam had gotten far enough down the path to be out of earshot, Cara turned to Amy. "You are such a cockblock."

"Are you kidding?" Amy shook her head. "Yuck. You're welcome. Hey, you ready to begin?" She spread her yoga mat on the ground.

"What do you mean 'you're welcome'? Sam was about to kiss me. You couldn't hang back just five more minutes?"

Amy squinted at her. "You're joking right? Gross, Cara. I know I said you need to get laid, but you can do a lot better."

"What's wrong with Sam? Even you said you wouldn't mind giving him a try. Summer of Sam, remember?"

"I was making a hilarious joke, not a real suggestion. You can't be seriously considering doing anything with him. He's a philanderer. And you, well, you're past the point in your life where you play around with guys like that. You want someone more stable, and you know it."

Cara hesitated. In some ways, Amy was right. But then again, Amy didn't understand Sam the way she did. Sam wasn't some foolish playboy, he was serious and stable, and he made her feel safe. She reminded herself what her therapist had said. *If you can't talk to your own cousin, why not? What are you so afraid to hear?*

"You don't know him like I do," Cara said. "And to be honest, I think we've both been kind of into each other for a long time. But he's been hesitating to make a move on me, and I . . . I still have Phil's voice in my head stopping me from making a move on him. But just now, he brought me a present, and I thought he was about to kiss me when you walked up."

"Oh, Cara, come on. No. He's not into you. He just sees you as a challenge. He's a predator, and you're his prey."

"Last summer he told me he was in love with me." At the shocked expression on Amy's face, Cara went on to finally tell her about that moment in the rain. Even thinking about it made her pulse quicken and heat rise in her cheeks, but Amy didn't respond the way she'd hoped.

"Are you kidding me? Let me get this straight: Last summer, when you were engaged to someone else, Sam tried to get with you. When you rejected him, he stopped speaking to you and totally quit his job, and dropped off the face of the earth. All of that petty stupid bullshit was because you wouldn't cheat on your fiancé? Yeah, he sounds like a real winner. And might I remind you that he had a girlfriend, too? Remember, you met her, since he didn't break up with her this summer either."

Cara had deliberately put all of those details out of her mind. "Look, Amy, I didn't necessarily expect you to understand."

"He tried to get you to cheat with him, what's to understand? And now, what, he's buying you stuff? Is that his seduction attempt? Is he tired of the tourists already?"

"It's not like that," Cara protested. "Maybe you'd get it if you'd ever been in a real relationship."

"I've been in real relationships!"

"Your Italian puppy doesn't count!"

"What I have with Fabio is more real than anything you've ever had with anyone, and I don't care that you can't see it."

"And I don't understand what your problem is with Sam. He's not a bad guy. He's very sweet and caring, and easy to talk to, and he makes me coffee every morning. You're always telling me it's time to move on from Phil, so why are you stopping me?"

Amy took a deep breath. "Because I slept with him, ok? I slept with him, and he never even mentioned it to me again. He's a user, Cara, and you deserve better."

Cara was floored by this revelation. When? When could this have happened? And then she realized exactly what Amy was talking about. "That first summer, when you said you walked in on him in the kitchen?"

"Yeah, I didn't exactly walk in on him. I was kind of an active participant."

"Amy! Why didn't you tell me?"

"I didn't want to get fired. You caught me erasing the security tape, so I had to say something. I mean, once I knew Paddy wasn't going to find out about it and fire us both, I thought about telling you. But since nothing else happened between us, I figured it didn't matter. I'm sorry I didn't say anything before."

A mix of jealousy and anger warred within Cara. She couldn't hold it in.

"How many names have you checked off your islanders list? You have quite a collection. Sam, Matteo, who else? Is there something you want to admit about Sato? Or the ferry brothers? Do you hang out by the docks and pick up fishermen?"

"Don't get nasty, Cara. You can't slut-shame me. I've known you forever. Your number is way higher than mine. Look, I'm sorry you found out this way. I should have told you before. The fact is, you deserve better, and we both know it. There are millions of men in this world; you deserve a good one."

"We're done here." Cara didn't bother rolling up her yoga mat. She bundled it in her arms and strode off down the path. Amy had just destroyed the fragile hope she'd been building up.

I told you so, whispered Phil's voice. You'll never find anyone to love you like I do.

Chapter Forty-Five

Email from Amy O'Connell to Fabio Basile:

I'm done. I am so f-ing done. I'm done dealing with my stupid cousin and her stupid bullshit. You know I've done everything I can to help her get through this terrible depression she's been in since Phil died.

Well, we got into an argument today because she's being stupid, and I won't tell you exactly what she said to me, but she was rude and nasty. Maybe I said some awful things back, but mostly I was dropping truth bombs, and she was responding with hate.

And now I'm regretting it. She's all worked up about our argument, and she's not speaking to me. She's acting all mopey and hurt, too. I feel bad, because she's still so f-ing fragile about everything. I know, I know. She's grieving, and I have to give her time. But how much time does a person need? How do I fix this?

Email from Amy O'Connell to Fabio Basile:

YES I ALREADY APOLOGIZED!!!! Really, you think that's great advice, just tell her I'm sorry? Like I didn't think of that?

Email from Amy O'Connell to Fabio Basile:

All good now. Cara and I went down to The Digs with Ty and got hammered and cried and hugged and made up. Now I'm hungover, but that's ok. I wasn't the one who had to get up at five o'clock this morning.

Chapter Forty-Six

Whispering Pines, August 2013

Sam couldn't quite figure out what to do about Cara. Sometimes, she seemed so open to his advances, and sometimes so distant and cold. Last week, in the grove, she had been so close to kissing him; he was sure of it. But then afterwards, she'd been standoffish and careful, as though she was worried he would overstep his bounds. He needed time to have a long, private talk with her and tell her how he felt. If he could just find the right words, he was sure she'd be receptive.

The best plan he could come up with involved food, of course. The stars had aligned tonight—Sam and Cara were both off work, Ty would be at the desk, and, earlier, Amy mentioned she was going to a small party at Matteo's. Since the two of them would have the house to themselves, Sam would cook Cara a meal he knew she'd love, they'd open up a good bottle of wine, and then they'd have the kind of intimate conversation that two people can share when they're full of food and drink and sitting on a cozy couch together listening to the rain outside. He'd confess that he still had feelings for her, and tell her he was willing to wait until she was ready to date someone again. Ideally, she would say something like, "But Sam, I'm ready now," then they would make out for a while. Ideally.

Of course, Sam's plans never seemed to work out. When he went down to raid the restaurant kitchen for supplies, Amy was doing the same thing.

"I thought you stuck to sandwiches on your days off," she said. "Are you actually cooking tonight? What are you making?"

"Chicken and dumplings," he told her and added, "The weather is so cool and drizzly it put me in the mood for comfort food." He opened the fridge to pull out the bird he'd roasted earlier in the day and then realized she was staring at him.

She gave him a suspicious and appraising look. "You're making Cara's favorite meal."

"Am I? I didn't know." He tried to sound casual and returned her stare, willing her to drop her gaze first. She didn't. Her eyes bored into him until he turned away uncomfortably, then she took her armful of leftovers and walked out. Hopefully, she was on her way to Matteo's.

When he got back to the staff house, Cara was sitting on the couch reading a book. "I brought supplies for making dinner," he announced, holding up the bag. He still needed to get the wine from his room. Maybe he'd pour her a glass and she'd come sit on the kitchen counter and watch him cook?

God, she looked sexy tonight. He imagined walking over to her, taking her book and throwing it across the room, pulling her to her feet and . . . no, he wouldn't do that, of course, he's not a monster. He would mark her page and set the book down gently, pull her to her feet, and say something suave like 'let's stop ignoring this attraction between us.' And he'd kiss her, and she would jump into his arms and wrap her legs around his waist, and they'd just start going at it. The first time would be rough and fast and urgent. And when they finished, he'd lift her from the floor (because, obviously, that's where they'd end up) and carry her off to his bed, where they would do it again, slower this time, and he'd finally be able to act on a few of his fantasies.

Something of his thoughts must have shown on his face or elsewhere because Cara's cheeks turned pink and she bit her lower lip. He started to take a step towards her—maybe they could eat dinner afterwards instead? If he could just ... and then his careful plans were shattered. Amy came out of the bedroom door, holding the cordless phone.

"Oh, hey, is there enough for three? It's raining, so Matteo moved the party indoors, and you know I'm allergic to dogs. *Of all kinds.* So I guess I'm staying in tonight." She stared Sam directly in the eyes as she spoke, and he knew she changed her plans on purpose.

Damn it, Amy.

"Yeah, that's fine, there's enough," he told her, trying to hide his annoyance. Was it his imagination, or did Cara look disappointed too? Was she, perhaps, also regretting her cousin's presence?

Of course, Amy wasn't the only problem. Sam barely started cooking when the front door opened.

"What are you doing here? Who's covering the desk?" he heard Amy ask in surprise.

"Oh, Sato and I traded shifts so he can go with Margaux to a doctor's appointment on the mainland tomorrow morning," Tyrell replied. "And since that means getting up at five, I figured I'd avoid The Digs tonight so I can go to bed early. I thought about going into town for dinner though. What are you guys up to?"

"Sam's cooking for us," Cara told him. "Hey, Sam, Ty's here too. Is that okay? Do we need to go scavenging in the restaurant kitchen again?"

Sam stepped into the living room. "I've got plenty of food for everyone." He could swear Amy muttered something about how she should have gone to Matteo's after all, but he wasn't certain.

"This will be fun." Cara sounded cautiously optimistic. "Nice cozy night staying in. This is the first time we've all spent an evening together since before we opened, isn't it?"

"We can make it fun." That came from Amy. "But I think we'll need some drinks."

"In that case, I can contribute something interesting." Ty went into the bedroom he shared with Sam and emerged a few minutes later on crutches and carrying a bottle. "Here, Sam, can we do anything with this? Tim was experimenting with infusions and he made this for me—it's pepper vodka. The flavor is a bit strong. Do we have any mixers?"

"Mixers? Y'all know we always start with shots, right?" Amy followed him into the kitchen and started rummaging for shot glasses.

Sam shook his head, resigned. This night was definitely not going according to plan. At least he hadn't opened the good wine yet. He could save it for another occasion. Someday he and Cara would find some time to be alone.

Later, after dinner—which, in Sam's professional opinion, should never have been paired with pepper vodka, no matter what it was mixed with—they moved back to the living room. Ty sprawled across one end of the couch with Amy at the other end. Cara curled up on the only armchair, so Sam casually seated himself at her feet.

"There's still room on the couch," Amy offered rather sharply.

"I'm fine," Sam said.

Behind him, Cara let out a long sigh. He wasn't sure what that sound meant, but he hoped it was directed at Amy.

"Now what?" Sam asked everyone. His plans might have been ruined, but he was still enjoying himself. He was still spending time hanging out with Cara after all.

"Hopefully, now we drink something else." Cara tipped her glass and studied the contents. "No offense Ty, but this vodka is kinda gross."

Ty laughed. "Why do you think Tim gave it to me? He couldn't serve it in his bar, but he figured we could make use of it. Not all of his infusions work. I think I have some brandy in my room, and there's some Bailey's in the cupboard. That's all I got."

"I didn't picture you as a brandy drinker," Sam told him. "You seem more like a craft beer kind of guy."

Ty shrugged. "I'm a man of mystery. And I like a snifter of brandy on a cold night."

"Ohhhh, you know what brandy goes well in?" Amy said. "Coffee. It's like a cheap knock-off version of a *caffè corretto*. We have decaf, don't we, Sam?"

"Amy likes her coffee like she likes her men," Cara teased.

"Please don't say black," Ty begged.

"No, weak and Italian."

"Not funny." Amy glared at her, and Sam sensed an argument brewing. He stood up abruptly.

"Make a pot of decaf and add alcohol. No problem, that's exactly what I went to culinary school for."

When he returned a few minutes later with mugs and a bottle, he was gratified that not only did Cara still sit in the chair, she had shifted position to let a leg dangle in front of it. When he sat back down, he found his arm resting against her calf, and she didn't withdraw it. He grinned up at her and thought he saw her cheeks flush. So, it was intentional. That was a good sign.

Amy flashed him a dirty look, then she surveyed the room and smiled. "Anyone up for truth or dare?"

Cara immediately started laughing. "No, no, no! Guys, say no. Amy plays competitively and she comes up with the worst dares. Unless you want to end up running naked through the inn, you'd better say no."

"Why don't we bring back truth or chores?" Sam suggested. They invented the game last summer when someone (Sam always suspected Amy) had failed to put a lid on the blender and did not cleanup the resulting smoothie explosion before it turned into a hard paste. The game continued for several rounds, with Amy asking increasingly raunchy questions, until Sato finally gave up and cleaned the mess.

"Yes! I love that game." Amy turned to Ty. "Here are the rules: we go around the room asking whatever we want, and if you refuse to answer, you have to do some cleaning. Sound fair?"

Ty nodded.

"Alright, let's go clockwise." Amy rubbed her hands together with glee. "Cara, you start. Ask Tyrell anything."

"Anything?" Cara grinned wickedly and raised an eyebrow at her cousin. Sam sensed the look that passed between them and experienced a moment's pity for Ty. "This is going to be awesome. Okay, Ty, there is something Amy and I are just dying to know. If you don't want to wash the dinner dishes, tell the truth—how's Timmy . . . in bed?" Sam almost choked on his drink.

"What the hell, Cara?" Sam immediately felt the need to defend his roommate, who appeared rather annoyed.

"That's not a fair question," Ty protested. He glared at the other end of the couch. "Amy, I've told you a thousand times, I don't discuss my sex life."

Amy shrugged. "Cara's the one who asked, not me. And there are an awful lot of dishes . . ."

"Wait, what? You and Timmy? Really?" Sam couldn't contain his surprise. He knew Tim was gay, but Ty? And when had this happened? "Oh, wait a minute. That time Tim brought your sweatshirt to the gym for me to give back to you . . . you didn't leave it at the bar, did you? You left it in his apartment."

"You seriously didn't know?" Tyrell looked amused. "So why exactly do you think I go to The Digs every single night?"

"I don't know, I thought maybe you were an alcoholic . . . I'm sorry, Ty." What else had he been missing?

"Ignore Sam. He's an idiot. Let's get back to the game. You have to give us a little bit. Some hint, please. Stop me when I get to it." Amy held her hands a couple of inches apart and slowly began to spread them further. "Seriously, stop me. Okay, this is getting ridiculous. Now I don't believe you." Her hands were a foot apart when she gave up.

"No, it's fine, he doesn't need to answer. I withdraw the question," Cara said over Amy's protests. "That wasn't fair to ask. Obviously, Timmy is fantastic in bed, otherwise Ty wouldn't keep going back for more. New question: Are you in love?"

"I will answer that one. Yes, yes I am, and yes we are." Ty beamed with joy. "He's the most amazing man I've ever met, and I can't believe that I am this lucky."

"I knew it!" Cara told him. "Congratulations! You know, after my uncle interviewed you, he told me that if you took the job, I had to drag you down to The Digs and introduce you to Timmy. He said you guys would be perfect together. Cheers!" She raised her mug.

"To true love," Amy added, and they all drank to Ty and Tim. Then she brought them back to the game. "Ty, you get to ask me something now."

"Alright, and since we're asking sex questions: Amy, truth or wash all the sheets, did you once hook up with Matteo? Because he claims you did, and I don't believe him."

"Really? That's your question? Ugh." Amy looked a little embarrassed. "It was like four years ago, and it was just like one time, and it was fun. But if I had known he would bring it up every single year, I might not have done it. I guess I was the best he ever had, so that's why he has to keep bragging."

"One time?" Cara repeated, a skeptical note in her voice.

"I said it was like one time," Amy replied, somewhat crossly.

"Uh-huh, right. Well, to be fair, I did warn you," Cara said. "Matty always did like to talk."

"Yeah, well I wanted to see if he lived up to all the hype, which, by the way, he did. When are you going to give him a tumble? I think you're the last holdout among island women. You're single now. You may as well get it over with."

"Very funny. You know that's never going to happen. Matteo and I have been friends for twenty years. I love him dearly. But if anything was going to happen between us, it would have happened a long time ago. There's an expiration date on those kinds of things."

The cousins stared at each other for a moment, and Sam thought he sensed more animosity brewing. He was more concerned with Cara's words than the atmosphere though. Was there really an expiration date on chances? Had his already passed? Bad enough the summer was nearly at an end, now he had to worry about this too?

Amy was the one who broke eye contact and looked around. "My turn. Sammy, truth or clean the entire staff-house kitchen, which I suspect you'll do anyway. Why did you cut your hair before coming here this summer?"

"What? Amy, that's the dumbest question I ever heard," Cara told her. "You're usually much better at this."

"Don't worry. This is only the beginning. I have a whole plan of escalating Sam's embarrassment. Well, Sammy, what's your answer?" Amy narrowed her eyes at Sam. "And don't lie. I'll know if you lie."

Sam stared back at her and did, briefly, think about lying. Finally, he took a deep breath. "Because back in April me and a bunch of friends from work frosted our tips. We were going to one of those throwback parties dressed as a nineties boy band. The guys with straight hair looked fine, but it was awful on me, I ended up with this fluffy bleached halo. I didn't realize it would be permanent. How the hell did you know?"

Everybody laughed at him, and he felt slightly ridiculous, though not as ridiculous as he had looked for a couple of days. Lizbet had been so mad at him when she saw his hair, she'd screamed in exasperation and immediately scheduled him an appointment with her hairdresser.

"You're not on Facebook, but I'm apparently a friend-of-a-friend of one of your coworkers, and he posted pictures. My friend commented, so it showed up in my newsfeed. I totally jumped in with the mockery when I recognized you—you looked pretty stupid. Beware the power of social media, Sammy. Even if you avoid it, it gets you."

"What?" Cara sounded scandalized. "Amy, if you saw that in April, you and I were together. How could you not tell me? No offense Sam, but I could have used the laugh."

"I was saving it for a funny surprise when he got off the ferry. I didn't expect him to cut his stupid hair off. But if you remind me later, I'll print the screenshot I took and hang it up in the office for everybody's amusement."

"Yeah, thanks, Amy." Sam ran a hand through his regrowing curls. "It's my turn to ask Cara now, right?" There were so many questions in his mind. Cara, are you ready to move on yet? Cara, the other day in the grove, were you about to kiss me? Cara, can we ditch these guys and go make out now?

"Hold that thought. Bathroom break." Amy jumped up and left the room.

"Good idea. I'll be back, too." Tyrell got up and crutched his way into the men's bedroom, leaving Sam and Cara behind.

"Got a question?" Cara looked down at him with those eyes that always made him weak.

"Can I ask a serious one?"

"Sure."

"I know you don't like to talk about it, and I know you've been avoiding the issue, but Cara, how did Phil die?" He only asked because he thought talking about it might help her move on, that getting things in the open and discussing it might let him take some of the burden. She looked so sad sometimes, and he wanted to help. But the way she responded, pulling her leg away from his touch, and the tears that suddenly formed in her eyes showed that he'd made a terrible mistake.

"That's really what you want to know?" Her voice was tight with either anger or pain. He couldn't tell, and that made him feel even worse.

"I just ... I thought it might help you to talk about it, I didn't mean to upset you ..."

Amy came back at that moment, and she immediately assessed the scene. "What the hell did you do Sam? I was gone for like two minutes."

"He asked his question, that's all." Cara stood up. "Sam, he killed himself. I broke up with him, and he committed suicide. And it's my fault. I could have stopped him, and I didn't. I left him to die. Game's over. I'm going to bed."

"Yeah, me too." Amy waited until Cara passed her. "Hey, awesome job, Sammy. Thanks for ruining the evening." She flipped him off as she followed Cara into their room and slammed the door behind her.

Tyrell had watched from the other doorway. "Man, that was messed up. You shouldn't have asked about that."

"Did you know he killed himself?" Sam replied defensively. "Because I didn't. How was I supposed to know it was a bad question? I was trying to help."

Tyrell just shook his head. "Young, healthy guy drops dead and nobody talks about why? Of course it was a suicide. What did you expect?"

Chapter Forty-Seven

Last fall: Midland, Texas, November 2012

Cara sits at the bar, waiting. It is Thanksgiving weekend, and Phil's plane arrived an hour ago. She made up an excuse not to pick him up at the airport, but promised she'd meet him at his hotel. He had expected to stay with her at her dad's house, but she told him she thought they'd have more fun someplace else. Early in their relationship, they used to do this on their numerous weekend trips: she'd go to the hotel bar, he'd come in and pretend to pick her up for the first time, and then they'd go up to the room and have amazing sex. She knows that's what he's expecting today.

But that's not her plan.

She's perched on a bar stool drinking a glass of water. She's already tipped the bartender way too much money to keep an eye on her. "I'm breaking up with my fiancé," she explained, "and I don't know how he's going to take it." This is it. She really is going to do it this time. She is strong. She is ready.

She had wanted to end the relationship when she stopped by Chicago on her way to Texas from Whispering Pines, but Amy was with her and the timing didn't seem right. Phil had been on his best behavior the whole weekend, and they actually had fun. She was afraid to crack that mood in front of her cousin. It doesn't matter though. She's thought about it for a long time and she's ready. She even emailed Sam to tell him she'd be single soon, and that he was right, they belonged together. She's positive he's going to call, and that gives her the strength to stand up to Phil.

Amy told her she was being cruel making Phil fly all the way out here on a holiday weekend just to get dumped, and Cara knows she's right. However, she thinks doing it in person is important. That way she can return the engagement ring, and she'll be able to deal with his reaction immediately. If she broke up with him over the phone, she would live in fear that he would show up at her door to either try and win her back or destroy her—she's not sure which.

She looks at her phone. Still nothing from Sam, but it's coming. He might not have spoken to her for the past couple of months, but there's no way he'll ignore her message. She's giving him what they both want. Maybe she can go visit him in Aspen before she heads to her job in Canada? She can imagine Sam teaching her how to ski, smiling at her over a candlelit meal, making love to her in front of a roaring fire.

Phil arrives, and she can't tell by his expression which version is in control. He tries to kiss her, but she turns her head. "Oh, is that the game we're playing?" he asks. "Let's not. I'm tired. I just want to fuck you and go to sleep. Come on." He holds out his hand like he's going to lead her from the room.

"Actually, Phil, we need to talk." She tries to use a firm tone. There's something in his eyes, something dangerous that is making her resolve crumble. She glances at her phone. Nothing yet.

"Women always want to talk," Phil complains, but he sits and orders a drink.

The bartender meets Cara's eye, and when Phil is not looking he mouths, 'you can do it' at her. He's right, she can. Tipping him well was a good idea.

"Look, Phil, it's about us." Cara launches into her speech, the one she practiced over and over with Amy until she felt confident. "I don't think we should get married. In fact, I don't think we should be in a relationship. You and I do not belong together. I'm not happy, and I don't want to be with you anymore." She takes off her engagement ring and slides it over to him. He leaves it on the bar.

"Very funny, angel. Put your ring back on. I told you, I'm tired and I'm not in the mood for games. Let's go up to my room now, and I'll show you we do belong together." He puts his hand on top of hers. To anyone else the gesture might appear sweet, but Cara can feel anger pulsing under the surface of his skin.

"Phil, our relationship hasn't been good for a very long time. I don't like the way you treat me, and I'm not going to put up with it anymore. It's over." She tries to keep from shaking. She doesn't want him to see her fear.

"There's nothing wrong with our relationship," he corrects her. "We're in love, and we're getting married. Sure, we fight sometimes, but so does every other couple. Imagine how boring our lives would be if we didn't fight and make up." His left hand is still on hers, but he moves his right hand under the bar to her leg. His fingers dig into her thigh muscle, and she pulls away.

"You don't get to touch me ever again. I said it's over." She stands up and puts her phone (still no messages—what's going on?) into her purse.

Phil grabs her by the wrist to stop her from leaving. He's changing tactics now. There are tears in his eyes. "You can't do this to me, you're my angel! You know I can't live without you. I just can't." He tightens his grip and tries to pull her back toward him.

The bartender appears. "I think you need to leave the young lady alone."

Phil looks back and forth between the two of them. "Oh, is that how it is? You're fucking this guy? Did you really think cheating on me was a good idea?" His tone turns threatening.

"No, Phil, I'm not. I've never cheated. This isn't about someone else. This is about what's best for me." She wrenches her wrist out of his grasp and steps out of reach.

"Really?" he looks at the bartender, who has picked up the phone. "I know you're lying when you say there's no one else. You have no other reason to pull this kind of bullshit. I warned you what would happen if you cheated on me."

"Hey, man, that's enough," the bartender interrupts. "We're not sleeping together, and I think she's made it pretty clear she doesn't want you either. You better get out of here. I've already called security."

"I guess that's it then." Phil smiles and is suddenly transformed back into his charming original self. "You know, Cara, this is a tragedy. We could have been so happy together, but you had to ruin everything. Don't worry, I'm sure you'll never have to see me again." He picks up the ring, drops it into his shirt pocket, and walks away.

"Wait for security to arrive," the bartender suggests to Cara. "I don't trust that guy. I want you to have an escort to your car."

Cara makes it back to her father's house safely, relieved. The break up went better than she had expected, although she's not naive enough to think Phil is done with her. She doesn't want to park in the driveway where Phil might see the car and know she's home, but the garage is occupied by her stepmother's Lexus and the sunfire-yellow 1967 Sting Ray that her father recently finished restoring. It's a midlife crisis kind of vehicle, Cara privately thinks, but he's also got a midlife crisis kind of wife. Cara's not a fan of her stepmother, a woman only five years older than Cara herself.

She's glad they aren't home, because she isn't ready to talk to them about her broken engagement yet. At the O'Connell family Thanksgiving dinner, her stepmother had asked far too many questions about her upcoming wedding and why it wasn't scheduled, not because she cared about Cara's happiness, but because the selfish witch wanted to shop for a mother-of-the-bride dress. *Spring or summer, I need to get the right seasonal color,* she kept saying, and Cara worked hard to keep herself from screaming. So yes, it's best she doesn't have to deal with that woman right now. However, she can't stay home alone.

It's not safe.

She checks her phone. Still no response from Sam. Maybe he doesn't check his email very often? He must be at work and hasn't seen her message. He will though. She's sure it's only a matter of time. Maybe she should call him?

Her phone goes off in her hand, a text from Amy. *You single yet?*

Yep. I'm coming over. Open a bottle.

Amy is home for the holiday as well, staying at her parent's house around the corner. Cara takes the long way, cutting through the backyard and then circling around the block, in case Phil decides to come talk to her. She doesn't want him to spot her outside where she'd be alone and vulnerable.

The cousins sit on the floor of Amy's childhood bedroom and share a bottle of wine. "You know I didn't like Phil anyway," Amy tells her. "I mean yeah, when we first met him he was fine. A little dorky, but fine. But I didn't like the way he kept calling the inn and asking about you."

This is the first Cara has heard about that. She asks Amy what she means and is surprised. "Oh, didn't I ever tell you? He used to call the front desk sometimes during my shift and ask how you were doing, who you were hanging out with, that sort of thing. He acted like he and I were such good friends, and really I thought he was just being creepy."

"What did you tell him?"

Amy cackled. "I told him that every day when you got off work you drank a fifth of vodka and passed out on the floor. And I told him you had started smoking crack with the crazy old man who runs the lighthouse. And you shaved your head and got a dragon tattoo on your scalp. You know, your usual activities."

"I love you, Amy."

"Everybody does. I'm the best."

They're halfway through the first bottle when Cara's phone dings. She recognizes Phil's special text tone, so it's not the message she's been hoping for.

"Phil? Don't read it," Amy advises.

"Don't worry, I wasn't going to." They continue to drink. Phil texts again fifteen minutes later. He's probably getting angry that she hasn't responded. She wonders if she should, but she changes her mind before her hand touches her phone. She knows Phil. She knows what he's doing, and she knows he needs an audience. She won't give him that. She is free. Someone else can save him this time.

When the wine is gone and Cara is starting to think about going home, she decides to read the texts.

The first one scares her:

I can't live without you, Cara. I just can't do it. Come downstairs. I'm in your garage.

The next one is worse:

My angel, I thought you'd come. You've made your choice, and I've made mine. I hope you can live with it. I'm sorry.

She and Amy sprint down the street and open the garage. The Sting Ray is running, and Phil is unmoving in the front seat. Amy immediately calls for an ambulance, and Cara momentarily freezes. She needs to shut off the engine, but she worries that if she enters she'll be overcome by the fumes ... and a dark voice deep inside her whispers that she should wait. Has it been long enough? Was he successful this time? And, if not, does she have to rescue him again?

Cara can't let herself think like this, and she rationalizes that opening the big garage door would have let in enough fresh air to let her safely approach. She runs inside the garage, yanks open the car door and turns off the ignition. Bile rises up in her throat as she looks at Phil's slumped body, his red face, his glassy and unseeing eyes. He did it. He really went through with it this time. She can't breathe, and she doesn't know if it's because of the foul air or the overwhelming emotions of both guilt and relief that are cascading over her.

Moving carefully to avoid touching him, she plucks Phil's phone from his lap. There is one last text message on the screen that he did not send. *Bitch. You made me do this.* She deletes it.

Amy hangs up and then comes over and embraces her. "The police are on their way. Let's wait for them on the porch."

Before she can lead Cara away, Cara reaches into Phil's shirt pocket, retrieves her engagement ring, and slips it back on her finger. Amy doesn't ask any questions.

Chapter Forty-Eight

Whispering Pines, August 2013
Email from Amy O'Connell to Fabio Basile:

Sometimes, I feel like I live in an f-ing soap opera. Seriously, what's going on around here?

Remember that fight I got into with Cara last week? Well, I didn't tell you this, but part it was because she said she kinda had a thing for Sam. WTF? Apparently, last summer he tried to get with her, and she turned him down. (Hello! She was engaged!) He's supposedly stepped up his game and started buying her presents. I don't know what, but I'm sure it was something stupid. Probably a heart necklace or a stuffed animal or a scented candle because that's the kind of crap most idiots think all girls like.

So now, for some reason, she likes this guy, and he once again proved what a jerk he is. Last Sunday night, we were all sitting around the staff house playing a game, and he took advantage of the moment to force Cara to talk about Phil's death. I don't know what his end goal was, but she cried herself to sleep. See what I mean when I say she needs to stay away from him? She doesn't need anyone dredging that crap up.

She's been in a pretty pissed off mood for days because of it, too. Not that I want to complain about her, but we do share a room, and she's been slamming things around and she knocked your picture off my nightstand. (Don't worry, the glass in the frame didn't break.)

That asshole chef has really gotten to her. I think next time he goes to the farmer's market on the mainland, I'm going to call down to the ferry and arrange an overboard accident.

Email from Amy O'Connell to Fabio Basile:

Ok, seriously, that was a joke. The ferry brothers have never thrown anyone overboard on purpose except for maybe one time a couple of years ago, and that was not at my instigation. And I wouldn't tell them to do it to our chef—who would handle the dinner service?

And also, you, sir, are taking the wrong side in this argument. I know I said she needs to get over Phil and under someone else, but I meant . . . someone else.

Email from Amy O'Connell to Fabio Basile:

Look, I've always been on Team Cara. Always. She's always been my best friend. I told you what it was like growing up, right? How my brothers were twins, and my sisters were twins, and I was the only singleton? I didn't feel so lonely when Cara was around—she was my other half. And yes, I was jealous sometimes. She spent two years in Venezuela and had a best friend down there (and also, she became super pretentious and when she came to visit for Christmas she kept doing this thing where she'd say stuff in Spanish and then be all, '*oh, Amy, I'm so sorry. I forgot you're monolingual. I'm just so used to speaking Spanish all the time.*' Plus, she spent a couple of years here on the island and became best friends with Matteo. I was admittedly a teensy-weensy bit jealous, but over the location, not the friendship. I can share, really. That's not the issue here.

My problem is she's just come out of long relationship that was serious enough she was willing to get engaged, and her fiancé committed suicide right after she dumped him. She blames herself, and she probably always will. She feels sad and guilty, and that makes her vulnerable. And when she's vulnerable, she needs someone to look out for her best interests. Hello, that's my job.

Email from Amy O'Connell to Fabio Basile:

That's my point. Your exact description of her: 'quiet and sweet'. That's not Cara. The real Cara is opinionated and feisty and adventurous. She's exactly like me, but with less dramatic flair. I can only take credit for half of the crazy things we've done. The other half has been all her.

She used to travel and make art and have dreams. Now she gets up, goes to work, and goes to bed (or goes to Matteo's and gets blackout drunk, which is also not like her). She works all the time, and even when she isn't on the clock, she hangs out behind the reception desk with me (and yes, does more work). I feel like she's trying to hide out. She's trying to fill her days with something meaningless so she doesn't have to think about anything real.

It is true though, that she's getting a little better since we've been back here. I saw her with some pencils the other day, so I think she's drawing again. I'm happy she's finally reached a place in her healing process that she can find her art. It's fantastic that she's finally back to doing something she loves, but her recovery is fragile. I don't want some jackass to cause her to have setbacks.

I want to see her be herself again, the way she used to be, before she ever met that monster Phil. And the way to get Cara back isn't through letting her retreat into her depressed self anymore, and it certainly isn't through losing her to some stupid chef who will bang anyone with a pulse. She deserves better.

Chapter Forty-Nine

"Did you see this name on the reservation list?" Cara asked, pointing.

Amy shrugged. "Yeah, so? I don't know them. Do you?"

"I think it could be Sam's parents. Vervaine isn't that common of a name, is it?" Cara tried to remember if Sam ever told her his parents' first names, but she couldn't think of them. But why would they come here? Sam said they didn't speak anymore, though he also told people they were dead, so who knew the truth?

"Really? I always assumed his father would've been named Samuel. Isn't he a junior?" Amy sounded mildly interested, but only mildly. She was busy trying to set the typeface for the next night's menu and complaining that it didn't look right.

"No."

"Well, he acts like it. Dang it, now the spacing is off. Why can't you let me buy some new software?"

"Acts like a junior? I have no idea what that means."

Amy sighed. "Authorize the purchase of a new graphic design program, and I'll explain."

"Seriously, Amy?"

"It means he acts like someone who grew up in the shadow of someone else, and he is perceived to have a number of shortcomings. He is always trying to prove himself and get people to like him. A perpetual junior. I'm surprised you haven't noticed."

Cara thought for a moment. "Are you taking psychology classes somewhere? Because that's a rather apt description. I always thought of it as little brother syndrome, but you're right, it works for juniors. But I don't think he is one anyway."

"Here, I'll settle this." Amy grabbed one of the radios. "Desk to Sam. Sammy, you out there?"

His voice came back answering in the affirmative.

"Sam, are your parents named Samuel and Samuela?"

"Ummm . . . what? No. Is Samuela even a real name?"

"You should have said Samantha," Cara told her, laughing.

Amy rolled her eyes. "Yeah, that would have been better." She hit the radio button again. "How about William and Linda?"

"I'm in the middle of inventorying the freezers, Amy. Stop harassing me." Sam sounded annoyed. "Yes, those are their names. Leave me alone."

Amy turned to Cara. "How long do you give him? Five minutes?"

"Two."

Cara was right. It only took two minutes before Sam was back on the radio. "Hey, Amy, wait, what's going on? How did you know their names? Seriously, how'd you guess?"

"They'll be here tomorrow, Sammy. On the eleven o'clock ferry. Want to pick them up?"

🌲 🌲 🌲 🌲 🌲

Sam felt ill. He lay awake listening to his roommate's soft breathing and wishing he were anywhere but here. His parents were coming. His parents were coming here, to his quiet island. He would have to introduce them to his friends and see the pity or contempt in his friends' eyes. This wasn't supposed to happen. When he cut off all contact, he meant for the severance to be permanent.

After the awful, terrifying, nauseating radio call from Amy, Sam had rushed back to the staff house to phone his brother. "Our parents are coming here. Why are they coming?" he shouted as soon as Nathan answered.

"Sam?" Nathan asked, as if anyone else would call with that question, that fear. "Is that you, bro?"

"Of course it's me! I just found out Mom and Dad have reservations at my inn. They're going to be here tomorrow! Did you know about this?"

"No, no way. If I had known, I would've warned you and maybe sent you a plane ticket out of there. Sorry, I don't know why they're coming. I haven't talked to them in a couple of months. Last time they visited us, Mom told Iris it's a shame she hasn't lost the baby weight yet and she needs to start taking better care of herself if she wants to keep her husband. Then she bought her a membership in some diet club. Like, really? Iris laughed it off because she knows how Mom is, but I was pretty offended by it."

"That sounds like something Mom would do."

"Yeah, and Dad was worse. He told me I need to discipline my children harder because Elliot spilled juice on the table. Apparently, I was supposed to paddle him. He's two; kids make messes. I told him I'm not raising my sons the way he raised us, and he said I was weak and nobody would ever respect me."

"Oh, yes, respect," Sam said bitterly. "That's what we feel for them. I don't know why you still talk to them, Nate. The best day of my life was the day I realized I could cut them out of it."

"College funds," Nathan sounded resigned. "With three kids, we really need the money, and they keep dangling it over our heads."

So that was it, his brother didn't know either, and somehow, that made Sam more nervous. He had the brief sick and hopeful thought that maybe they were coming because they were dying, and they tracked him down to tell him in person.

Sorry for the way we've treated you. We both have stage 4 cancer and will be dead in six weeks.

Or maybe it was an unlucky coincidence? They happened to be vacationing in the area and had no idea he was here? If that were the case, he could hide in his kitchen, have one of his line cooks cover the omelet bar at breakfast, and avoid them entirely. He wished that were a real possibility.

Chapter Fifty

"So, Sam, I guess the zombie apocalypse starts today," Cara said.

"What?" Sam asked, startled out of his reverie. He had been staring at the wall, thinking about stress and dread and would his parents recognize him if he slapped on an enormous fake mustache and spoke with an accent?

"This is the day your folks rise from the dead," she reminded him. "I'm so glad my mom was cremated, so I don't have to worry about her showing up."

"That's not funny, Cara. I'd rather deal with zombies. I don't know why they're coming here." He knew she was just trying to lighten things up, but nothing could help. A cloud of doom hung over his head. Too bad it was sunny outside. He wished it was stormy and raining to match his mood, especially around the time his parents would be on the ferry. His mother hated getting wet.

"It won't be that terrible, will it?" She reached out to take his hand. That was an unexpected bright spot. Cara's touch could make a lot of things better. He squeezed her fingers gently and ran his thumb over her knuckles. How was her skin so soft?

Holding her hand made him confident enough to open up, just a little. "I told you I cut off contact with them a while ago, and I had good reason to do so." He paused to collect his thoughts. How much was he willing to admit? He always avoided talking about his parents, both because he didn't like stirring up those memories and because he didn't need sympathy. But something about the way Cara looked at him, like she was actually interested, like she actually cared, made him want to say more. "They're toxic. Wait till you hear what they think of me: I dropped out of college, so I'm an uneducated failure. I don't have a permanent residence, so I'm no more than a homeless bum. I'm not married and have no children because nobody will ever love me. I'm a loser who will never amount to anything, and they wasted too many resources raising me."

"That sounds awful, Sam. You know, that may be what they think, but that's not what anyone here thinks. You are an amazing man, a wonderful chef, and you have a great life. Everyone here on the island loves you. Really." She looked him right in the eyes as she spoke, and for a brief moment the knot in his stomach untied.

"Everyone?" Sam raised an eyebrow and tried very hard not to smile. She blushed and looked away. Now he let himself grin. At least the day started off on a high note.

🌲 🌲 🌲 🌲 🌲

Sam drove the nicest electric cart down to the ferry, Sato by his side. He was so nervous his hands were sweating, and he kept wiping them on his pants. He didn't know what to expect when they arrived, how they would react to seeing him. Had they changed? Based on his conversation with Nathan, he was sure they hadn't, but he couldn't help but hope.

"You excited to see your folks, man?" Sato asked.

Sam shook his head. "Nope." He parked the cart and stood up to watch the ferry arrive at the dock. He shaded his eyes with his hand, scanning the passengers.

"Really? My mom's visiting this fall for like two months to help out, and I can't wait. They're your parents. You should be excited."

"I have a feeling you and I had very different parents," Sam replied.

He spotted them in the debarking crowd, looking exactly the same as they always had. His father still stood firm and tall, with broad shoulders, in excellent shape despite his age. He had been in the military and maintained a strict physical regimen throughout his life. His mother still dressed elegantly and kept her gray hair perfectly styled. She was always concerned about looks, presentation, and portraying herself as better than anyone else.

The Vervaines were among the last off the ferry. Sam straightened his spine and clenched his jaw as they approached. He told himself he was prepared, but his stomach was churning, and he wished he could pass out now and wake up after they left.

"Samuel, you're here!" His mother hugged him briefly. "You look well, though you desperately need a haircut."

Even though the hug was quick, he could already smell her perfume clinging to his clothes. That hadn't changed either. She still wore the same scent. It smelled of rotting flowers, and fear, and shame.

"Son." His father nodded at him and extended a hand. His handshake was crushing, as always.

"Mother, good to see you. Father, good to see you too, sir." His voice sounded stiff and formal to his own ears. Seeing his parents made his heart beat faster and triggered his fight or flight response. How soon would the blow strike?

"They have you picking up passengers? I thought you were supposed to be some kind of cook, not a servant. This is really what you've chosen to do with your life? Well, I suppose it's easy though, working in some tiny hotel in the middle of nowhere. Definitely don't need a degree for that." Boom, there it was.

Sam dug his fingernails into his palm, trying to calm himself. *Breathe.* "Father, I don't normally pick up guests, but when

I heard that you were coming, I offered to do so as a courtesy, so that I could greet you." The lie twisted awkwardly in his mouth.

His father stared at him for a moment then shook his head. "You knew we were coming? This hotel gives out guest information to anyone who asks? That sounds like a privacy violation. I suppose they gave you my credit card information as well?"

Sam gritted his teeth. *I will survive this visit.* "No, Father, they noticed your name and asked me if we were related. Our last name isn't exactly common."

"You do still use the last name then? No time for the family, but you'll keep the family name? That's fine, I can't stop you." He snapped his fingers at Sato. "You, load up our bags, carefully. Do not damage them." Without another word, William Vervaine got into the electric cart.

Sato raised an eyebrow at Sam but made a show of smoothly and gently placing the suitcases in the back.

Linda Vervaine was more polite than her husband, but not by much. She sat primly on the edge of her seat as though afraid she would get dirty. "Well, this is quaint. No cars? What an interesting place you've chosen, Samuel. Of course, you always were a rebel. Nothing we did could make you happy, but I'm sure you're doing just fine here in your little corner of nowhere."

"I'm so glad you came to visit." Sam managed to get the lie out in a pleasant tone. His parents, here. It was like a dark cloud descended on his peaceful island home. He caught a look from Sato. *I get it now*, that look seemed to say, and he nodded.

🌲 🌲 🌲 🌲 🌲

Sam took his parents to the inn's lobby and held the doors for them. He saw Cara behind the desk speaking into her radio, and when he glanced back at the cart, Sato winked. Sam took a long slow breath and followed them in. Having them here made him feel like a little kid again, always worried that he might do the wrong thing. Would he ever be able to overcome the deep conditioning of his childhood?

Cara greeted them politely. "Welcome! You must be Mr. and Mrs. Vervaine. We are so pleased to have you staying with us. Chef Samuel has become such a respected member of our island community, so it is a great honor to meet his family." She was laying it on a bit thick, and Sam was pretty sure his father was smirking as she spoke.

Cara went on, giving them information about the inn and the island, and made suggestions as to where they could go for lunch. "And one of our staff members will always be available for transportation to and from the village. Now, I do hate to do this to you, Chef, I know today is your day off, but Mr. Conaghan has requested a meeting with you. The village council is working on the plans for an upcoming festival, and they'd like your professional input. Again, I'm so sorry about pulling you away from your parents like this. It shouldn't take too long."

"No, that's fine," Linda answered for them all. "I'm just glad my son is important somewhere. We wouldn't want to take you away from your ... work. We'll meet up later? I'm sure you'd love to show us around, but I need some time to refresh." Somehow, she made it sound like she was speaking of something distasteful.

After saying his goodbyes to his parents, Sam walked around the desk to Paddy's office. He could feel Cara's eyes on him.

Paddy was seated inside with a serious expression on his face. "Come in and close the door." As soon as he did, Paddy poured a glass of whiskey. "I know it's early, but Sato suggested you might need this. He also suggested we call a doctor to remove that stick up your dad's ass, but don't worry, he did it over a private channel. Nobody else heard."

Chapter Fifty-One

When Cara's shift ended, she went looking for Sam. She had sent his parents into town, encouraging them to eat lunch at Margaux's bakery. Poor Tyrell had transported them, and they treated him with the same finger-snapping scorn as they did Sato.

She knew exactly where to find him. There was a spot up by Lesser Lake near where she and Matteo always scattered ashes. On Mondays, their mutual day off, she and Sam used to hike up there and lay down on a table-sized rock and stare at the clouds. Sam would always bring a picnic, and they'd hang out and relax. He often called it the most peaceful spot on the island.

Even from a distance she recognized him standing on the large flat rock, throwing stones into the water. There was something so sad about his pose, about the slump of his shoulders interrupted by the sudden fury of each throw that made her want to hug him.

"Mind if I join you?"

He glanced at her, and the sadness on his face wrenched her heart. He reached down to the rock pile he had gathered, grabbed another one, and threw it far out over the lake.

"How did you find me?"

"I know you, Sam. Where else would you be? Remember how many times we came up here, so I could teach you how to skip stones?" She picked one up from his pile and threw it, counting five skips before it sank in the lake.

He almost smiled. "I thought I taught you." He picked up a rock and tossed it as well, counting four skips as it skimmed over the lake's surface. "That would have been more impressive if I had beaten you. So why are you here? Please don't tell me my parents want to talk to me."

"No, don't worry. They're gone for a while. Tyrell took them into town to get something to eat. Your father called him boy, and your mother clutched her purse like this." She imitated holding a purse tightly to her chest with a horrified expression. "And they sat in the very back row of the cart as far from him as possible."

Ty had rolled his eyes at her before departing, and she left a cookie on the desk for him with an apologetic note. She knew he wouldn't blame Sam for his parents, but he still shouldn't have to put up with that kind of treatment.

"Yeah, that sounds like them." Sam looked embarrassed. "I'll talk to Ty about it later." He skipped another rock, then another. Cara waited patiently, thinking that he was steeling himself to speak. Finally, though, she got tired of waiting and put her hand on his arm.

"Stop. Sit and talk to me. I want to know what's going on with you." She sat down, and, after a moment, he dropped down next to her.

"Nothing's going on with me. I'm fine."

"You're clearly not. Sam, please. I think I might understand." She gave him time to respond. He stared out over the lake for a few minutes before sighing deeply.

"I didn't want my parents to come here. It stirs up too many old memories. You may have noticed, they're not good people."

"I definitely noticed." It was time to be blunt with him. "Sam, they abused you, didn't they?" The look in his eyes gave her the answer. It was something she had suspected for a long time, actually. There was something about the way he avoided conflict, something about his lack of self-esteem, despite his good looks and career skills, and something about the way he lied to protect himself about trivial issues. All of those were potential signs of a terrible childhood.

"You are the first person that ever guessed that," he said. He closed his eyes and took a deep breath. "Yes, yes they did. Me and my brother both. In fact, my earliest memories are of Nathan trying to protect me from our father. We used to have this pole in the basement, and he made us hold it as he beat us. And if we cried, he'd hit harder.

"Nobody ever believed us though. Nathan even made the mistake of filing a CPS report, and they came and interviewed our parents. I couldn't stand up straight for a week after that. But nothing was ever done, nobody ever protected us."

"That's why you ran away when you were sixteen, wasn't it?" She had heard that story before, of him getting on a bus and showing up at his brother's college apartment, of spending the next two years finishing high school while sleeping on a couch and working as a dishwasher. She had assumed he was just a rebellious teen seeking freedom, not someone desperately trying to escape an untenable situation.

"Yep. I came home on my sixteenth birthday, and my dad ordered me to the basement. And I refused to go. I told him I was a man, and I wasn't going to let him hit me ever again." He kept his eyes focused on some distant point.

"What happened?" Cara asked when the silence stretched too long.

"He showed me that I wasn't. It was the only time he ever hit me in the face. I snuck out that night to go to my brother's, and Nathan didn't even recognize me when he answered the door. He wanted to take me to the hospital, but I wouldn't let him. So he called my parents and threatened to call the police. They ended up signing papers to emancipate me."

"At least they did that."

"It was to protect my father; it had nothing to do with me. It was the first time we had real evidence against them. I don't know why I'm telling you all this."

"It's because they're here and they're stirring up all these memories. I understand."

"Seeing them makes me feel like a terrified child again. I just want to hide under my bed until they're gone. I fucking hate myself."

He sounded so bitter and hurt that Cara wanted to cry for him. Instead, she put her arm around his shoulders, leaned in close and said, "Sam, you are stronger than you know."

"What?"

"That's what my therapist always tells me. You are stronger than you know, look what you've survived."

"Cara, no offense, but I don't think you talking to a shrink about your ex's death is quite the same thing. Crap, I'm sorry, that came out harsher than I meant. I just mean it's a different issue."

"Yeah, well, I'm not actually talking to my therapist about that. I'm working through healing from all the times he hit me."

"Phil hit you?" Sam's eyes widened incredulously, and his face quickly shifted to fury. "I'm going to kill him."

"I think he took care of that for you," she told him, a weak attempt at a joke. But he didn't laugh. He looked at her, and she felt something shift. It was time; it was time to talk to someone about what Phil had done to her. It was time to stop keeping his secrets.

"The first time he hurt me," she began slowly, "we had just had an argument, our first real disagreement ever. He back-handed me across the face so hard it left a bruise. He was immediately so sorry. He cried. He begged me to forgive him. He swore it would never happen again. And for some reason, I believed him. I think I was just too shocked by the situation. You know, up until that point he had been perfect, always so kind and so caring, and so concerned about my needs. I guess I just wanted to believe it was an accident, a one-time thing.

"It was right before I came back to the island for the summer, and I didn't see him for a couple of months. You know how busy it gets here, but he called almost every day; and he was always so sweet and he kept sending me flowers and gifts. It made it easy to dismiss the hit as an isolated event, a mistake.

"Then, that fall, I said something he didn't like, and he slammed my head into the wall. 'That's it', I said, 'I'm leaving. You can't treat me like this.' And he apologized and told me he loved me, but I did it. I left. I wasn't going to be one of those women that puts up with domestic violence. I knew better, or at least, I told myself I did. But that night he overdosed. So I came back to him. I thought I was saving him. I didn't want him to hit me, but I didn't want him to die either. I thought I loved him, I really did.

"I always felt on edge, waiting for him to change. Everything would be okay—great, even—and it would seem like he was getting better, like everything was going to go back to the way it was before. But still, I had to be so careful of what I said to him. A lot of our relationship was long distance, and if I didn't call at the exact right time, he would decide that I must be leaving him and he'd either threaten to commit suicide or he would do some generous romantic gesture, sending me flowers, candy, whatever. I never knew which Phil he would be. And when we were together, sometimes he would be so sweet, and sometimes so possessive and angry. Even last summer, when he came out here, on the night he acted like such a jackass in the restaurant, he hit me later and put his hand on my throat and . . ." She paused to wipe her eyes. This was so painful to say out loud.

"That was our pattern. First, he'd attack me, then I'd try to leave, and the next thing I know, he's in the hospital. Once he drove his car into a tree because of me, but he walked away without a scratch, thanks to all the airbags. When he proposed, he made it huge and dramatic and very public, so I would look like a horrible person if I turned him down. And I knew if I said no he would have killed himself. He even said so. I spent months thinking about how to break off the engagement but still keep him alive. I knew the man I fell in love with was still inside him, somewhere, and that man deserved to live. I guess I just thought that if he got help, if I could make him stay alive long enough to, I don't know, get therapy, then the real Phil would come back. In my darkest moments, I even resigned myself to actually going through with it and marrying him because I didn't want him to kill himself. I honestly believed I could somehow save him."

Cara finished the story with her head down—she didn't want to see his reaction. When she finally looked up, there was a tear running down his cheek. He hugged her and she pressed her face into his chest. His embrace felt so warm, so solid, and so safe.

"Cara, we used to talk all the time, and I had no idea you were going through that. All those phone calls, and you never said anything. Why? Why didn't you tell me? I could have helped you. I could have done . . . I don't know what, but something."

She pulled back so she could meet his eyes. "Why didn't you tell anyone about your father? Some secrets are so shameful we have to keep them."

They studied each other's faces for a long quiet moment. She had never seen him so open, so vulnerable. This was Sam stripped down to his essence, the part of him he kept hidden from the world.

"Oh, Cara." He reached out a hand as though he was about to smooth her hair, but then his jaw tightened and something changed in his eyes, and he stopped himself. The openness closed off again, and he turned back to regular Sam. He took a deep breath. "You know what, I gotta go. It's cardio day." With that, he abruptly jumped up and took off running.

Cara sat alone in shock. Instead of bringing them closer, apparently, confiding their darkest, most painful secrets drove them further apart. How could he literally run away from her after that?

She started throwing the rest of Sam's rock pile into the lake. Each stone represented someone who had hurt her. She cast them as far from her as she could. Phil. Sam. Phil. Sam. Phil, Phil, damn Phil. Would she ever escape the poisonous taint of that relationship?

Chapter Fifty-Two

Sam came around a curve in the trail too fast and not only did he startle a group of tourists, but he also scared away the wild turkey they were taking selfies with. Running on the road was preferable, but the nearest path to it would take him past Lesser Lake, and he was afraid Cara might still be there. He couldn't face her right now.

He kept going, feet pounding, trying to see if he could run faster than his thoughts, further than his anger. The rage churned inside of him, directed at so many people. His parents, for showing up here and destroying his peace; Phil for being an abusive asshole; and Cara, oh, Cara, he was so angry at her for having chosen Phil over him.

He met the guy last summer and hated him on sight. Some small part of him had actually wanted to like Phil, so he could honestly say that a better man won, that Cara had found the kind of partner she deserved. But Phil acted so possessive. Sam saw how he looked at Cara; how carefully he watched her; how he sized up all the men in the room. And when they were introduced, Phil did that ridiculous alpha-male handshake thing, asserting dominance through crushing. Too bad for him Sam worked as a professional chef. He squeezed back until he saw Phil wince and then just a little longer for effect before grinning and releasing his hand. Now, when he thought back on it, all he could think about was Phil's same hand on Cara's vulnerable throat. He wished he could travel back in time and kill the bastard while he had the chance.

Listening to Cara describe the abuse she suffered had triggered a desire to comfort her. When he held her, he wanted to whisper in her ear that he would protect her forever, exactly the response the broken-child version of himself had always craved. For a moment, seeing his own old wounds reflected in her eyes connected them, deepened their bond, and showed him he had finally found someone he could share the ugliness of his past with, someone who understood.

But that only lasted for a moment.

Because then he realized that their experiences were so very different. Sam had been a child, a child who always lived with violence and knew no other way. His life seemed normal to him; not good, but normal. He didn't know other kids didn't have whipping posts in their houses, that they weren't terrified of their parents. And if he had known, it didn't matter; he was just a kid. He couldn't escape. He couldn't pack his things and move. He couldn't change his number and start over in a new city. He couldn't run away until he was sixteen and even then his survival depended on his older brother.

Cara's situation was completely different. She was abused as an adult. Hell, she didn't even live in the same state as Phil for part of the year. How hard would it have been to leave him? If she really wanted to, she could have dumped him easily. And why did she care so much if Phil killed himself? Why was she still grieving for that monster? Shouldn't she have been relieved by his death?

His footsteps stirred up pine needles on the trail, sending their scent into the air, and reminding him of how last year he had stood under a tree in these very woods and confessed his love. He told the only woman he ever cared about exactly how he felt, and what did she do? Reminded him about her engagement and ran away. Knowing he loved her, knowing he was the kind of man who would never hurt her, knowing he could protect her, she still chose Phil. She chose the man who beat her. She chose to stay with the man who abused her.

What did that say about her? And what did that say about how she felt about Sam? Maybe what his father had told him his entire life was true. Maybe Sam was worthless after all. He was clearly worth less than Phil, less than a manipulative girlfriend-beating monster.

He ran until he couldn't breathe and then he ran some more. But he still couldn't escape the vicious cycle of his thoughts. She still wasn't choosing him.

Chapter Fifty-Three

It was bad luck that his parents arrived on a Tuesday. On Tuesdays, his restaurant only opened for breakfast, and he had the rest of the day off. He delayed as long as he could, but he finally mustered a level of either courage or resignation sufficient to face them.

They begrudgingly agreed to Sam's suggestion of dinner at the Village Diner. He was confident they'd find something on the menu they were willing to eat, and he guaranteed the food would be delicious—two of his cooks worked at the diner when they weren't working for him.

"First a coffee shop, now a diner? How quaint," his mother commented, and he knew she didn't mean it as a compliment.

As soon as they walked in, they were welcomed by Wayne, the diner's owner and Sam's occasional rival. The two of them engaged in friendly competitions at town events, and every time Sam entered the building, Wayne would accuse him of spying. 'You can eat here, but only if you aren't facing the kitchen,' or 'you can eat here, but don't talk to my employees; and you can't write anything down.' It was all in fun. If they ran into each other at the bar, they'd take turns buying rounds of drinks and spend hours talking about spice combinations and debating the best way to cook fresh fish.

This time though, Wayne skipped all the usual jokes and greeted Sam with a hearty clap on the back. "Chef Vervaine, so wonderful to see you. Please sit anywhere. I've been developing a new sauce recipe I'd love to get your opinion on."

"Sure, I can do that." Sam tried not to sound suspicious. After he and his parents sat at a table (and then moved to a different one because the one Sam chose wasn't good enough),

Tim approached them. Sam could tell by the cheerful look on his face that he had not yet spoken to his boyfriend.

"Hey, Chef Vervaine, it's so great to run into you." Tim shook Sam's hand enthusiastically. He turned to Sam's parents. "This guy is amazing. We're so lucky to have him here on our island. If I were picking a last meal, he would be the one I'd beg to prepare it." As he walked away, he looked back and winked at Sam and mouthed the words *Cara called*.

"Well, Samuel, now I know why you come back here every year," William Vervaine remarked. "At first, I thought it was for those attractive twins who work the front desk."

"William, that's not appropriate," Linda interrupted with a warning tone.

"I know that, but he doesn't. You know our Samuel doesn't think with his brain. But that's not the reason at all, at least not entirely. He's here because this is his tiny worthless little pond, and he likes being the big fish in it."

"We're in Lake Superior. It's the biggest pond in North America." Where did that come from? Sam had never talked back to his father before. He felt slightly nauseous.

His father sighed deeply. "That's an idiom, Samuel. I wish you had gone to college. I'm aware of the size of the actual lake. What I'm saying is that you like being here because you like the way these hicks out here treat you."

Arguing with his father always proved fruitless. In Sam's entire life, he had never won an argument with the man, even about established and easily proven facts. He took a deep breath. "I understood what you meant. And I'm actually here because I enjoy the work. I like running my own kitchen, I'm successful, and it pays well."

"To be fair, it's not your kitchen. It belongs to that Irishman who owns the inn," Linda corrected. "And I don't understand why you can't do the same thing somewhere else. Somewhere less . . . remote."

"If this place is so remote, how did you find it? I never told you I lived here." Sam was rather impressed with himself. He never spoke like that to his parents. If he were a child, he'd be bleeding already.

"We know how to use the Internet, Samuel," his father said. "You might not use computers the way the rest of the civilized world does, but you still come up on searches. Someone wrote a terrible article about the things you like to do here, which apparently involves getting massages and having intercourse, so everyone knows you're still living like a homeless gigolo. I suppose we should be grateful you're employed, at least temporarily."

"I don't think that's quite what Amy's post said," Sam informed him. There was a moment of complete silence while his father stared at him, and, as always, Sam dropped his gaze first.

"It appears you haven't changed at all. You're still so disrespectful."

"If I'm so disrespectful, why are you here? You clearly have no interest in visiting this island, so why come at all?" Did they just come here to torment him? He hadn't seen them in years, why would they travel all the way across the country just to harass him? It didn't make any sense.

"I had a conference in Duluth, of all places," William replied. "Since we were forced to fly all the way out to the middle of nowhere, we decided we'd travel a little farther and see what our youngest son traded his future for. Well, we've seen it."

That explained everything. Sam didn't want to admit it, even to himself, but there had been a tiny kernel of hope that they came to visit because they felt sorry for the way they had treated him, or maybe even because they missed him and were interested in his life. But, of course, his hope was unfounded. His parents had not changed. They never would.

Chapter Fifty-Four

Cara was still awake when Amy entered their room. She listened to her cousin brush her teeth and a few minutes later climb into bed. "Amy?" she asked hesitantly. "Can I talk to you for a minute?"

"You're still up? Yeah, we can talk, unless it's work related. I'm off the clock."

"No, it's not that. I want to tell you the truth about Phil. There are some things I never told you ..." And it all spilled out—the violence, the fear, the manipulation. Somehow, having talked about it earlier, the words came easier this time. She had barely gotten started when Amy crossed the room, sat down on her mattress and held her tight.

Tears splashed from Amy's eyes on to Cara's face. "Oh, Cara, Cara, Cara, why didn't you tell me before? I could have done something, I could have helped you."

"You were so far away when most of it was happening, and I thought I could handle it. And then when it continued, I guess I was just embarrassed and I didn't think you'd understand," Cara said. "I thought I was saving him ..."

Amy cupped Cara's cheek with her hand. "Look at me. You're my cousin. I don't need to understand in order to support you. I would have sent you a ticket to join me, or no, better, I would have flown back and killed Phil."

"Good thing he did it on his own," Cara said.

"Yeah, that was lucky for him. Believe me, it would have hurt a lot more the way I would have done it," Amy replied, and somehow, that brought a smile to Cara's face.

They slept curled up together in Cara's bed that night, the way they used to when they were small children. The next morning, Cara woke up cold because Amy stole all the blankets and wrapped herself up tightly in them. Some things never changed.

🌲 🌲 🌲 🌲 🌲

When Cara walked out into the staff house kitchen, she was mildly surprised to see Sam there before her. After his abrupt departure from their conversation, she was afraid he was going to avoid her like he had last summer. She was even more surprised at the smell filling the room and the amount of food on the counter.

"I prepared a special breakfast for you," he said. "Remember that diner in Albuquerque you and Amy always talk about? The one you always went to in college?"

"The one we'd stumble into drunk because greasy eggs and spicy chilies are the best hangover prevention? Yeah, I remember. I still fantasize about it." When her mother died, her dreams of going far away for school died as well because she didn't want to leave her father alone. The University of New Mexico was a compromise; she got to move out of state, but stayed close enough to come home for visits easily. Amy gave up her admission to UCLA to come with her, and they later both agreed they had made the right decision.

"That's the one. I've replicated your favorite dish. Corn tortillas, hash browns, fried eggs, *carne adovaba*, and of course, chile sauce. You like green, Amy likes red, right? I put some in the fridge for her."

"Are you kidding me?" Cara was shocked. "How did you even remember all those details? And *adovaba* takes hours. How long have you been up?" She watched as he started frying eggs. There were already two plates on the counter piled high with the rest of the meal. This was so absurd it almost frightened her.

"I remember everything you tell me, especially if it involves food. Besides, the meat isn't difficult. It only takes four hours, and most of that is just letting it simmer." Sam crackled with an intense energy. "Luckily, I had all the spices. It was something I planned to try eventually anyway. This morning seemed like as good a time as any."

"Sam, this is crazy; you know that, right? Were you up all night?" She started to get genuinely concerned. Their conversation yesterday made her worry he was going to be depressed throughout his parents visit, but instead he seemed almost manic.

"Yeah, but, I couldn't sleep anyway, so I thought I'd use my time productively and make something different. A nice big meal. I'll leave a note for the others to check the refrigerator. The hash browns won't be great reheated, but I'm sure they won't mind. I'm not doing their eggs though. I don't think they'd hold until they're awake."

"Sam, stop. Seriously, what's wrong with you?"

He turned from the stove to look at her. "I stayed up all last night thinking about my parents and the things I want to say to them. They have no right to show up here after all this time, and they have no right to judge me for what I'm doing. They come here, they insult me, they talk down to my friends—"

"Sam, please listen to me." Cara walked over to him and put her hands flat on his chest and felt the racing of his heart. "Your parents don't matter. In fact, they don't even deserve the title. They are nothing more than rude inn guests, and we get those all the time. Who cares? They're just passing through, and you will never have to see them again. I already put them on the blacklist, so they aren't welcome here. They are nothing. Don't let their presence hurt you."

They stood together, staring into each other's eyes, and for a tiny moment she saw a look of tender sadness. He was remembering everything they shared yesterday, she just knew it. Did he regret running away? Could she forgive him if he did?

Sam placed his hands over hers and swallowed audibly. "You're so right. And you were right yesterday. I'm stronger than I know. I can face them today. I've been thinking about it all night, and I'm ready. Now sit, I'll bring you your plate."

Cara smiled as she took her seat at the kitchen table. She was still feeling a bit thrown off by his running away, but perhaps making her a thoughtful breakfast was his first step toward apologizing.

Chapter Fifty-Five

Sam waited patiently at the omelet station. His parents were always early risers, and they would definitely come to breakfast. He wished he could avoid them, but he reminded himself of what Cara told him. Her last words before work had been a promise: *Don't worry, I won't fire you if you tell them off.* He was ready. He could handle this. They were just rude guests.

"Good morning, Samuel," his father greeted him.

Sam said the same and started counting in his head, one, two, three . . .

And then it came: "I didn't expect to see you out here. I thought you said you were a chef, not a caterer. I'm surprised your boss doesn't make you wear one of those oversized white hats like you see in the cartoons."

"Those hats are actually called *toques*," Sam informed him, smiling politely and pretending his father was merely a rude customer and not the man who tormented him all his life. He put his hand on his chest where Cara's had rested earlier and drew strength from the memory of that contact. "And this isn't catering. I'm the executive chef, this is my restaurant, and this is a service I like to provide. Here on Whispering Pines, we find that our visitors appreciate the personal touch." He managed to meet his father's eyes, and held his gaze. His father's fingers twitched, and Sam knew he was imagining holding a switch.

His mother's hands twitched too, and he knew she was imagining rearranging his station. He kept everything neat and orderly, but she was a perfectionist, and she held to the firm belief that her way was the only way. Growing up, she kept their house perfectly spotless and organized, never a single item out of place. Neither dust nor dirt nor clutter was permitted on any surface, ever. He and his brother were raised knowing that anything left anywhere outside of their bedrooms overnight would be thrown away. Once, in middle school, he had spent days working on a model for his science class. Without thinking about it, he left the project on the kitchen table while the glue dried, and the next morning, he found it smashed to pieces in the trashcan, and she reminded him he should have known better than to leave clutter in her clean house.

"Most restaurants that we go to give us menus, and there are waiters who bring the food to your table. I suppose we're not used to how they do things in quaint rural places like this." Linda got the words out in a pleasant enough manner, but Sam could hear the acid behind them. How much longer did they plan to stay here?

"Well, some people can't handle trying new things. Different is scary, especially after you reach a certain age. If you'd like to take a seat, I'll ask my colleague Sato to bring you some food." He maintained a calm, professional tone and stood as still as possible so they wouldn't see him shaking. He had never talked back to his parents like this in his life, and it was terrifying and empowering at the same time. Amazingly, they did sit at a table, and Sato did take them plates of food, which of course, they rejected. They finally walked out, having nothing but coffee and croissants.

After breakfast service, he went straight to Cara at the reception desk. "I stood up to my parents and their passive-aggressive bullshit," he told her. He was inordinately proud of himself. His whole body felt charged with a powerful energy. He could do anything!

"That explains a lot," she replied. "They just came down here, complaining about how disrespectful my staff is. They've canceled the rest of their reservation and are leaving on the next ferry. They didn't even object when I charged them a cancellation fee. I think you've won the battle."

"First time I've won anything," he said. He needed to call Nathan and tell him about this. His brother would be extremely impressed. This was the first success either brother achieved throughout the very long war.

"You should celebrate."

"*We* should celebrate," he corrected her. "You helped. Listen, about yesterday ..." He was going to ask her about the weird way people treated him at the diner.

"Yesterday when I confided my darkest secret in you, and you got up and ran away?" she asked, and from the look on her face he realized he had really screwed up. Oh, no. He honestly hadn't thought about how it might have appeared from her perspective.

"Ummm, yeah, about that," he said slowly. He glanced around to make sure the lobby was empty. "I didn't react well, did I? I don't always know what to say, and I was kind of angry and sometimes when I don't know how to deal with things I run away."

She didn't say anything, just folded her arms and looked across the desk at him. She seemed to be waiting for something, and he couldn't figure out what—and then it hit him. He was such an idiot. He owed her a real apology.

"Cara, I'm sorry. I'm really, truly sorry. I think I got caught up in my own stress, and I didn't know what to say to you. My reaction was stupid. You're my best friend, and I want to be there for you, and I am so, so sorry that I wasn't."

That sounded good to him, true and heartfelt. But she still didn't smile.

"Sam, you keep saying you want to be my friend, but you ran away. You can't do that, literally or figuratively. Friends take care of each other."

He could see she was still hurting, and he felt a pang in his chest. He knew this was an important moment, and he needed to man up. Fortunately, he was still buzzing from the high of standing up to his parents, and it made him strong enough to be completely honest.

"You're right. I'm selfish, Cara. I didn't think about you and how you would feel. All I could think about was how mad I was at my parents and at Phil. Running away from you was probably the worst thing I have ever done, and I am sorry. I swear to you Cara, next time you need me, I will be there. Next time you confide in me, I will stay and listen until you're finished talking. I . . . I really do care about you." *And I love you*, he wanted to add, but this was not the appropriate time for that.

They looked at each other for a long moment, and then he saw a change in her eyes, a relaxation. She had forgiven him, he hoped.

"Work on it, Sam," she told him. And her smile, though tentative, was real.

"I will," he promised. "Oh, but while we're on the subject of yesterday, what exactly did you tell people about my folks that made them treat me like some kind of celebrity?"

Cara laughed. "That was awesome, right? I called Wayne and told him your parents were terrible snobs who acted as though they were horribly embarrassed by having their son work as a cook on this godforsaken island. Wayne was like, 'What? Have they tried his food? It's magic!' Then he made me promise not to tell you he said that. I thought maybe if they saw you as a respected member of this community they might be a little impressed. So, no?"

"My dad said it was obvious I like being a big fish in a small pond and these hicks don't know what they're talking about."

"That's unreasonably harsh."

"It's better than his original theory."

"Oh?"

"Yeah, that I stick around for the hot twins who work the desk here."

"But there aren't any . . . oh. Well, that cements it. Your dad is an irredeemable asshole."

"True, but he might be half right." Sam winked at her and walked away, feeling proud of himself. He hoped Cara interpreted his remark the way he wanted.

Chapter Fifty-Six

Email from Amy O'Connell to Fabio Basile:

I can't stop crying.

Last night I had an extraordinarily disturbing conversation with Cara. She told me Phil used to beat her (and it goes without saying that you will never repeat this to anyone, right? You know I trust you.). He used to hit her, actually hit her, not just playing around, and she never told me about it.

My cousin, my very best friend in the whole world, was being abused, and I had no idea. None. I knew about how he would threaten suicide to keep her from leaving him, but I didn't know he physically abused her too. She told me some horrifying stories she's kept hidden from me.

I'm devastated.

Why didn't she tell me before? Didn't she trust me? I could have helped her. I could have gotten her out. I could have murdered Phil for her.

I could have done something. Anything.

And this awful revelation has made me realize something else: that night when Phil killed himself, he tried to kill her too. He thought she was home, and he texted her asking her to come downstairs, but he knew she wouldn't. She would stay upstairs, hiding from him, and that's exactly what he wanted. He thought she'd die there.

See, I wondered why he didn't do the thing where people connect a hose to the exhaust pipe and put it directly in the vehicle. But he didn't do that because he was trying to fill the house too. I told you the police wouldn't let us in there until the air was cleared, right? Cara's old bedroom is above the garage. If she had been in her room, if she was hiding or sleeping in there, she would have died too. The engine would have kept running until the car ran out of gas, and it would have poisoned her. I thought he was just trying to make it take longer, you know, expecting Cara to show up and save him. I knew he was suicidal; I didn't know he was murderous too.

My cousin could have died.

I wish you were here. I kind of need a shoulder to lean on right now.

Email from Amy O'Connell to Fabio Basile:

Stop telling me your English is terrible when you can write such beautiful things! You always know what to say. I love you.

Chapter Fifty-Seven

"Sam, I have a favor to ask." Cara came into the kitchen while Sam was starting to prep food for dinner.

"If you want to talk to me, grab a knife and help," he told her. "No idle hands in my kitchen." He knew she wouldn't do it. Actually, no, he knew he'd stop her if she tried. She chopped an onion for him once. It took her at least fifteen minutes and the pieces were all different sizes. The resulting debris had gone straight into the compost.

She laughed at him, grabbed a towel, and slowly wiped a corner of the prep table. "Will this do? Anyway, a favor. Do you think tomorrow morning you can whip up a couple of nice lunches? I have a . . . lunch meeting with someone."

"Maybe. Depends. Is it a date?" He tried to sound like he was joking, but it was a serious question. Things had been slightly awkward between them lately, despite his apology for running away. He was worried that she no longer trusted him, and he had lost any chances with her.

"No." She looked down at the invisible spot she was scrubbing on the table. "It's Phil's mom. She called and said she's coming out and would like to meet with me. She'll be on the one o'clock ferry. I don't know what she wants to talk about, but I thought it best not to take her down to the diner or anything. I'd rather meet with her here on my territory, so to speak."

"Phil's mom? Why? Does she know what he used to do to you?" Sam felt a sense of protective anger rising up in him. How dare that woman come here? Hadn't Cara been through enough?

"I don't think so. I never told her. I haven't talked to her since his funeral, when she blamed me for his death, so I don't know why she's coming."

He watched her for a moment, uncomfortable with the situation. He could cook for them, but he didn't think it was a good idea. Cara shouldn't be forced to have any contact with Phil's family at all. However, if he refused, Phil's mom would still be here, but somewhere else, somewhere Sam couldn't keep an eye on things.

She must have noticed his hesitation. "Nothing fancy, Sam. Just something I can throw in the microwave when she gets here. I'm not asking you to give up your time off for me."

The utter horribleness of that statement snapped him out of his discomfort. "Absolutely not! Cara, I will not make something for you to microwave. You know that's not the kind of food I cook. And I don't trust you to use a microwave properly."

"I know how to microwave food, Sam."

"No you don't! You put everything in for three minutes, regardless of what it is. Cup of water? Three minutes. Frozen burrito? Three minutes. Leftovers that I clearly labeled 'microwave for sixty seconds'? Three freaking minutes."

"Microwaves have sensors. It doesn't matter how much time you set it for. The computer adjusts the heat levels accordingly."

Sam had to take a deep breath and count to ten before he could respond to that. "Microwaves do not have computers in them!" He had to stop himself from permanently banishing her from his kitchen. "Oh my god, Cara, you're worse than Amy, and I once saw her microwave a piece of raw chicken!"

"Hey, with ketchup that chicken didn't taste half bad."

He stared at her for a second, unable to formulate a response. In the past, he had expressed an appreciation that the

O'Connell cousins would eat anything, but there should be limits. Then he noticed the quirk of her lips as she suppressed a grin. He shook his head ruefully.

"Cara, you're making me ill, and I refuse to discuss this anymore. I'll cook the two of you something fresh and delicious, and I'll even serve you. But tell Paddy so I can get overtime." He was kidding about the overtime, of course, and he could tell she knew it.

"Thanks, Sam," she said, and she looked at him a long moment. It seemed like she was on the verge of saying something else, but the words didn't come. That was okay. He was patient.

Chapter Fifty-Eight

"You're nervous, aren't you?" Amy asked from behind the reception desk. She had agreed to work an hour early so Cara could join Elaine, though she also demanded that Cara buy her pizza for dinner, so she wasn't being totally altruistic.

"Of course." Cara had neither seen nor spoken to the woman who would have been her mother-in-law since her fiancé's funeral, and she still had no idea why Elaine wanted to talk to her. What if she asked what Cara did with Phil's ashes?

"I can tell. You're wearing a hole in the lobby carpet with all that pacing. Did you hear Sato on the radio? He picked her up."

In fact, Cara had not noticed the radio call. She was lost in her own head. If she had married Phil, having Elaine for a mother-in-law would have made it almost bearable. She loved Elaine, and they used to get along so well. When Cara had lived in Chicago, they lunched together weekly. It was almost like having a real mother again.

Without Phil though, what kind of relationship could they have? Yesterday's phone call had been the first time she spoke with Elaine Holloway since the awful day of the funeral when Cara was supposed to eulogize Phil, but instead Amy did. Afterwards, everyone offered their condolences to Amy as though she had been the fiancée. Cara just couldn't handle it. She couldn't handle the pain, or the guilt, or the truly terrible, awful sense of relief.

"Does she know what a monster her son was?" Amy interrupted her musings.

Cara leaned against the desk and rested her head on her hand. "I never told her. And I doubt he ever admitted to anything. It would have messed up his perfect image." She started to go through some of the worst incidents in her mind, wondering if she had ever given Elaine cause to suspect what Phil had been doing to her.

"Hey, they're here." Amy snapped her fingers, breaking her out of her reverie. "Be strong. You can do it, Cara."

When Elaine walked into the lobby and removed her sunglasses, Cara was a bit shocked to see how much she had aged in nine months. Phil's mother had always taken care of herself so well, but gray streaks showed in her hair now, and sorrow carved deep lines in her face.

She still smiled though, when she saw Cara, and hugged her just as tightly as always. "Oh, my darling girl, I've missed you so much!"

The greeting made Cara feel a little better. If Elaine was starting out with a hug, it must mean she didn't intend an acrimonious meeting.

After a brief tour of the rest of the property, Cara led her to the dining room. "Our chef has offered to make us lunch today," she said as she gestured towards a table already set with ice tea and salads. "We're normally closed at this time, but since you came all this way, I wanted to treat you to a nice meal."

True to his word, Sam arrived to serve them pan seared whitefish in a wine sauce over angel hair pasta. "Your meals, ladies," he said, and bowed with a flourish. "There's going to be dessert as well, so ring the bell when you're ready."

"The bell?" Cara glanced down at the table. "Oh, Sam, that belongs on the reception desk. Amy's going to kill you."

"No, she won't. I made dessert for her, too." Sam winked and returned to the kitchen. Cara watched him walk away with a faint smile on her face. He really was trying hard to be there for her.

"I see you've moved on already," Elaine murmured, with a hint of sadness in her voice.

"What? Are you talking about Sam? We're not together."

"Really? Maybe not yet, but I saw how you looked at each other. It's fine, Cara, truly it is. You're an amazing young woman. You deserve happiness."

They ate in silence for a moment. Cara collected her thoughts and said, "Can I ask you—"

Elaine stopped her. "You must be wondering why I called after all this time. I owe you an apology. Lots of apologies, actually. There were some things I wasn't honest with you about." She paused and dabbed at her eyes with her napkin. "Cara, darling, I love you. You're the daughter I always wanted, and so I hid some things from you because I didn't want to lose you. Oh, my sweetheart, I know you think I blamed you for Phil's death, but I don't anymore."

"Anymore? But you did though." Cara knew that from the funeral. That was expected. It was, after all, Cara's fault. She didn't like to dig too deeply into the emotions of that terrible night, but she had made the decision to ignore the texts, pretending that as long as she didn't respond, he wouldn't do anything, lying to herself that he required a witness.

"Of course I did, you ended the engagement. But what he did afterward, that wasn't your fault."

Cara's heart stopped. "You knew I broke up with him?"

"He left me a voicemail. I've listened to it a thousand times, just to hear his voice again. He said you called off the wedding, he didn't deserve to live anymore, and he was sorry. I had gone to bed early that night, and my phone was in my purse, so I didn't get his message until it was too late. I've been beating myself up over that for months."

"Elaine, I . . ." Cara didn't know what to say, what kind of apology would work. She'd pretended they were still engaged and had begged the police officers not to tell Phil's parents the reason that they'd fought. She was trying to protect herself, to deflect the blame. Perhaps that was the wrong decision.

"No, Cara, it's alright." Elaine sighed heavily. "I need to be honest: I always knew Phillip would make you a widow; I just hoped you would have a baby first. I'm so very sorry. I thought if I told you about his suicidal tendencies you might leave him. Please forgive me, he was my only child, and I wanted to be a grandmother so badly."

"His suicidal tendencies?" she repeated in disbelief. Elaine knew about them? Every time he ended up in the hospital, Phil begged her not to tell his mother the real reason. He wanted to protect her, he said, and Cara always went along with it because it was too painful to tell the truth.

"Oh, Cara, I'm so sorry I never told you. It must have been quite a shock, him doing what he did. He'd tried before, and he always insisted that you not know. Do you remember that awful car accident? I hate to tell you this, darling, I truly do, but that was a suicide attempt. He hit the tree on purpose. He didn't want me to tell you, and I didn't want to burden you with that knowledge."

"I knew," she told Elaine quietly. "I also knew when he was in for an overdose and told you it was the flu."

"He told *you* it was the flu . . . oh, no." They both realized they had been played. "Oh, Cara, you knew all along. I thought I was protecting you. I was afraid you'd blame yourself, but it was something inside of him, some terrible darkness that was always there."

Then Elaine began to talk, weaving a story of Phil's teenage years, and his first suicide attempt at age thirteen when his mother wouldn't let him go to a co-ed sleepover and he swallowed a bottle of pills.

"After that, it was like I became his hostage. He always held his death over my head. You won't buy me a PlayStation game? I might as well kill myself. You won't let me go on Spring Break with my friends? Then I should just die. He made several attempts. When he was nineteen, he tried carbon monoxide in the garage because a girlfriend dumped him. I still remember the doctor telling us that the reason he failed was because newer cars have catalytic converters and don't put out as much carbon monoxide as the older models. Phil must have overheard and remembered."

This new revelation stunned Cara. Not the use of the same manipulation tactics as a teenager, she should have suspected as much. No, the fact that he committed suicide in her father's classic car, knowing full well it would work. She had assumed it was another of his carefully calculated but inevitably non-lethal manipulations, and she'd as good as murdered him by not responding to his texts in time. But no. He knew. There were two cars in the garage that night, and he intentionally chose the one most likely to kill him. Was it possible his death wasn't entirely her fault?

"I got him help, of course," Elaine continued. "Therapists, psychologists, medication. The thing was, Phil acted so charming, and seemed happy and well-adjusted. He fooled a lot of people into thinking he was fine, but he made at least four attempts on his own life in high school alone, and I don't know how many later. I never knew if he seriously wanted to die or if he only latched on to it as a method of getting what he wanted. I think he enjoyed the attention and the worry that he caused. You know, Cara, when he found you, I had such hopes . . ."

"We met because I stopped him from stepping in front of a bus. Was that a suicide attempt? Did he step off the curb on purpose?" As the realization dawned on her, she felt foolish. Had she really fallen for his tricks even before they knew each other? Had their whole relationship been based on him tricking her into saving him over and over again?

"I never wanted to admit it, but I think so," Elaine confessed. "He broke up with a long-term girlfriend before the trip and told her he probably wasn't coming back. I hoped it meant he planned to move to Spain, but I suspect he decided to go out in a dramatic way, and you stopped him."

"I guess all I did was delay him," Cara said slowly. She bought Phil two more years of life. Was it worth it? Was it worth the price she paid? Was it worth the suffering she'd been through ever since?

"Cara, honey, I want you to forgive yourself," Elaine told her, and her voice sounded firmer, stronger than it had been. "His suicide was not your fault. I'm sorry, I'm so sorry I've let you shoulder any of the blame."

"I understand," Cara said, wiping tears from her eyes. "And I'm working on it, I promise." Even though her heart broke for Elaine, she herself felt suddenly free. Phil's death was not her fault. He knew exactly what he was doing and merely followed through with the threats he had made for years. The cloud of guilt that had hung over her for so long started to dissipate, and she already felt lighter, happier.

"Good." Elaine blinked a few times and managed to compose herself. "Now ring the bell and have your gentleman friend bring us our desserts. Do you think he could fetch us some martinis as well? I have something else to talk to you about, and you may want a drink."

Cara rang the bell though she didn't need to. She could see the kitchen door was propped open, and Sam was pretending to work but was actually keeping an eye on them. That was sweet, but not necessary. Elaine was nothing like her son.

Chapter Fifty-Nine

Long after Elaine left, Cara still felt weak with shock. She kept pulling out the envelope, looking at the contents, and closing the flap again. It still looked real.

"I didn't think life insurance paid out on suicides," she had thoughtlessly said when Elaine first gave her the paperwork.

"All policies are different. He purchased it through his employer, and the suicide payout prohibition was only in effect the first twenty-four months. There was some back-and-forth about Phil's mental health problems, but they dug up his original application, and he did disclose his depression, so it was valid. You were listed as the beneficiary." Elaine smiled sadly at her. "I know nothing can make up for losing your fiancé, and all the plans for your future that the two of you made, but I hope it helps a little bit."

After driving Elaine back down to the ferry and hugging her good-bye with a promise to stay in touch, Cara hurried back to talk to Amy. She wanted her cousin to verify that she wasn't imagining things. She handed Amy the letter from the insurance agency, without explanation, and watched her eyes widen in surprise as she skimmed it.

"Does this seem legit?" Cara asked, showing her the check.

"Wow, that's a lot of zeros! You just tripled your life savings." Amy examined the document carefully. "Yep, definitely real. Congratulations! What are you going to do now, Ms. Moneybags?"

"I don't know," Cara replied slowly. "Can I keep this? Do I really deserve it? It's blood money."

"Cara, don't be a dumbass. Phil was a terrible abusive monster. Consider this his apology for everything you put up with. Most domestic violence survivors get nothing."

"Maybe I'll give it to a shelter or something," Cara mused.

"Remember five seconds ago when I said 'don't be a dumbass'? Donate some if it will make you feel better, but keep most of it. Think of it like the proceeds from a lawsuit. Like what if you sued him for assaulting you? This is what he would have had to pay. It's your money. I hate to say it like this, but you kinda earned it."

"Perhaps you're right." The money could be life changing. And he did owe her something. She bought him two years of life with her blood and pain. This was the least he could do to make up for it.

"I'm always right. So I vote you take a big chunk of that cash and take your favorite cousin on a trip this spring, maybe Australia? And with the rest, you can finally buy that investment property you and Matteo have been talking about forever. See, it's a win for everyone."

"That would be one way of turning Phil's death into something positive. But I don't know if Nikki wants to go to Australia with me." She ducked away as Amy tried to hit her shoulder.

"Not funny, Cara. But I'll forgive you if you buy everybody drinks tonight. I'm off at nine, and Ty's off anyway, so call Matteo and we can all get wasted on your tab. We can even invite Sam."

Chapter Sixty

Sam tried to make it to The Digs, he really did. When Cara came into the kitchen with a smile on her face and invited him to join the rest of the housemates for drinks after work, he agreed enthusiastically. There was something about the way she looked at him, something in her eyes that made him think that this might be a very good night for them.

But this was the night the big walk-in freezer finally died. He'd been having problems with it all summer, and Sato had repaired it a few times with the hope that the compressor would last to the end of the season, but no such luck. Almost immediately after he sent all his kitchen staff home and started to walk out the door himself—his hand was actually on the light switch—he heard the alarm. *Not tonight, please, not tonight.* He checked, hoping for an alarm malfunction rather than a freezer malfunction. *Damn it.*

Paddy was at the desk, so he let him know, but with everyone else off, Sam was the only one available to figure out how to fit everything into the smaller reach-in freezer, which was already somewhat full. It took two hours of swearing and rearranging, which included a trip into town with a cartload of frozen meat to put in borrowed space in Wayne's walk-in. In retrospect, he should have stopped in The Digs after dropping the goods off at the diner, but he was in a hurry to get back and finish his task.

After he finally salvaged everything, he hurried to the staff house to change into clean clothes. He'd be able to make it down to the bar for at least one drink, maybe two. But when he entered the house, he encountered Amy.

"Back already?" he asked, disappointedly looking past her

at the closed bedroom door. Nothing ever worked out in his favor. He'd missed Cara entirely; she must be asleep. He hoped she wasn't, that she might hear him talking to her cousin and come out of the room.

Amy glanced at the door then back at him. "Yeah, it's late, and I have to make a call. You missed out on a fun time. Even Sato came out tonight, though I'm kind of mad at him."

"You're always mad at somebody. What'd he do to you?" Amy held grudges over the silliest things.

"He won't let me throw Margaux a baby shower. Apparently, her best friend and her mom get to do it, but I had a lot of ideas, and you know I'd do a better job than them."

He laughed at that. "Doesn't she need to be pregnant first? You've got time to change his mind."

Amy blinked at him. "Are you kidding me? My goodness Sam, you might be the dumbest person I've ever met. Have you seen Margaux lately?"

Had he? Yes, just last week in fact. She had gained quite a bit of weight since getting married, but Sato was getting awfully round himself. He'd chalked it up to the combination of marital happiness and living in a bakery . . . oh.

"I guess I forgot," he said carefully. "Of course she's pregnant." He would have to say something congratulatory to Sato tomorrow morning.

"I don't know how you even function as a human being, Sam. Seriously. You probably need instructions in how to put your pants on—it's one leg at a time, by the way. Well, I'm going down to use the computer, good night!"

With that Amy left Sam alone to stare at the women's bedroom door. Still closed. Oh well, he'd talk to Cara in the morning and apologize, and maybe suggest going out for drinks, just the two of them, to make up for missing the gathering. That might even be better.

Chapter Sixty-One

Cara could hear men's voices arguing.

"I could carry her back to the inn, but it's pouring rain and I really don't want to."

"Nooooo, baby don't go!"

"Clearly, you have your own drunk to deal with. I'll take her."

"You can't carry her that far."

"Are you doubting my strength? Well, you're right, but I can at least get her back to my place."

"Baby, I'm so druuuuunk!"

The voices came into focus. She opened her eyes to see six men standing over her. No, three. No, six. No, definitely just three.

"I'm fine." She waved a hand up at them. "Don't worry about me, I can just sleep here."

"She can't stay in my bar." Tim ignored her and directed his attention to Matteo. "Maybe she can walk?"

"Seriously, I'll take her. It's not the first time I've had to do this. She doesn't weigh much. And you should catch him."

There was a crashing sound followed by giggling as Tyrell hit the floor.

"Baby, my leg fell off."

Tim sighed deeply. "Love, you didn't have your leg on, remember? Okay, I can't handle both of them. Matteo, you deal with her."

Matteo lifted her in his arms and carried her out of the bar. The swaying sensation made her sick, and she had to struggle to make him set her down so she could throw up in the road.

The rain was coming down so hard it washed away immediately, and she turned her face to the sky, trying to drink it in.

"Come on, climb up." Matteo made her ride on his back the rest of the way to his house, only letting her down when he had to stop and fumble for his keys. "I hate having to lock my doors. Summer sucks."

She stumbled through the living room to the bedroom where she collapsed, and two of his dogs jumped on her. She giggled helplessly as they started licking her face.

"Off, damn it." Matteo grabbed them by their collars to pull them back before shooing them out and firmly shutting the door. "My poor babies will get alcohol poisoning from licking you. Here, change out of those wet clothes." He tossed her a T-shirt and sweatpants, then turned his back.

"I stay over here often enough you should keep pajamas in my size," she complained, but she was grateful for the clothing and the towel he gave her for her hair.

"I've got shirts in your size over in my shop, but you have to pay for those. Give me your clothes. I'll toss them in the dryer." He left the room and came back a few minutes later in dry sweats and carrying a large glass of water and a bucket.

"I'm rich now. I can buy your entire inventory." She drank the water and attempted to place the glass on his nightstand, but dropped it on the floor, almost falling over as she tried to pick it up.

"True. I'll write you an invoice. But I want you to give me cash so you can't cancel the check when you sober up."

"Funny, Matty. You're always so funny." Her voice sounded slurred and distant, even in her own ears. She was drunk, and she was annoyed. Sam was supposed to come with them tonight. He should have been the one to carry her home, not old Matty. "You seem sober. That's not fair. Why are you sober?"

"Because I'm smarter than you. And because I stopped drinking when I saw you wouldn't. Here, let me help you." He tucked her into his bed before climbing in on the other side. "I worry about you sometimes, Cara. You drink too much. You really need to stop."

"I did stop, remember? Tim cut me off."

"Not soon enough. Please don't get into any more drinking contests with Tyrell. Neither of you can handle it, though at least he's a happy drunk."

"I was going to stop when Sam arrived. Why didn't he show up? Doesn't he love me anymore?" If she hadn't been so intoxicated, she never would have said that out loud.

"Sam? Why would he love you? Wait, sorry, that came out wrong."

"No, you're right. He doesn't care. Why would anyone love me?" Tears of self-pity stung her eyes. Briefly, earlier, when she found out she was not responsible for Phil's death after all, she had thought she had been set free. But what difference did it make, if the one she wanted wasn't interested?

"I love you, Cara. I always have. You know that." Matteo reached over and brushed her hair out of her eyes. "You're not going to be alone forever, I promise. A lifetime alone is my destiny, not yours."

"Don't say that Matty. Someday, your prince will come."

"I'd rather have a princess, please."

"Maybe you can go find her. You made it to Phil's funeral after all. I never did ask you how you managed it." She was getting drowsy, and her head was still spinning.

"I don't think any woman, princess or not, would want me in the state I was in at the funeral. I took a ton of Prozac, and Margaux held my hand the whole time. The whole experience was horrible, and I don't plan on going through it again. But you know I'd do anything for you."

"I do, and I love you for it."

"Yeah, I know. Now shut up and go to sleep. You can babble more in the morning. And please, if you need to vomit again, use the bucket."

"You're better than I deserve."

"I know. Now seriously Cara, I have a busy day tomorrow. Be quiet."

Chapter Sixty-Two

She didn't show up in the kitchen the next morning. Sam made her coffee—stronger than usual to combat her probable hangover—and watched it cool on the table. He finally knocked softly on her bedroom door in case she had overslept. But when he quietly peeked in, he saw Cara's bed was completely empty. Hadn't she come back last night?

He looked for her in the lobby after the breakfast service, but she wasn't there either. "What happened to Cara?" he asked in surprise when he discovered Paddy sitting behind the reception desk. His boss rarely worked mornings, claiming sleeping late as the benefit of being in charge.

"I'm sure she'll turn up soon enough," Paddy replied. "Matteo called me last night and said she crashed at his place. She'll stumble in any minute now, hungover as hell and covered in dog hair. I told him to let her sleep as long as she needs, but you know Cara, she's going to be mad that he didn't wake her at sunrise. Did you need something, Sam?"

"Oh, no, I was coming over to check on her since she wasn't around to help set up breakfast this morning. I should have guessed she stayed out," he said, but he was lying. He had assumed Cara was already in bed when he got home, or he would have met up with her at the bar. He silently cursed himself. It was a mistake not going down to The Digs. If she ended up at Matteo's, who knows what might have happened?

"Hang on, that's probably her now." Paddy answered the inn's phone. "Hello? ... We have caller ID. Don't you lecture me on how to answer the phone at my own inn ... You and Matteo did what? Are you serious?"

Sam had started to walk away, but stopped, blatantly eavesdropping.

"No, no, I'm happy for you both, that sounds great. Have you thought this through though? . . . Yeah, but a commitment like that . . . No, that's not what I meant. I love Matteo like a son, and I'm sure he'll be an excellent partner for you, and I'm thrilled to welcome him into the lodging family. But this timing makes me worry that you're moving too fast . . . Ha, yeah, that makes sense, since you'll both be here this winter . . . Yeah, okay. Congratulations, and I'll see you when you get back, which better be before Amy comes on shift. I'm not working with her. You know she'll spend the whole time nagging me about marketing schemes and new software and whatever else she wants me to waste money on."

Sam did what he does best: avoided a difficult situation. He walked away before Paddy hung up the phone so he wouldn't have to discuss what he thought he overheard.

🌲 🌲 🌲 🌲 🌲

Sam went for a run on the road around the island to try and work his thoughts out. Paddy's half of the call kept playing in his head. How had this happened? After everything they'd been through, after all the conversations, after all the talks, after all the shared looks and the moments verging on physical connection, how could she choose Matteo? It had to be a misunderstanding, right? The flirtatious way her eyes met his, the way she touched his arm when she invited him out for a drink last night. He couldn't have misconstrued that, could he?

He just about convinced himself that he had, in fact, misinterpreted Paddy's conversation, when he encountered Sato wiping down an electric cart outside the shed. Sam walked over to congratulate him on his impending fatherhood, slightly embarrassed that he hadn't noticed before.

"Hey, Sato," he started, but he was interrupted.

"Did you hear about Cara and Matteo?" Sato asked cheerfully.

Sam swore under his breath. It must be true, if word had spread throughout the village so quickly. "Yeah, I heard Paddy on the phone. How did you hear already?"

"I was dropping off some tourists and ran into Cara. She was walking a couple of Matty's dogs, Tristan and Beverly, maybe? I can't keep their names straight. The corgi and the husky."

"Martha is the husky," Sam corrected automatically. He felt ill. "How was Cara? Did she seem . . . did she seem happy?"

"More hungover than happy." Sato laughed. "But yeah, I guess. I'm just glad she finally jumped on the opportunity. She's been hesitating for far too long. But that visit from Phil's mom really changed things." Sato seemed oblivious to the sound of Sam's heart breaking.

"Maybe it was Matteo who did the jumping," Sam muttered. It figured that Matteo would take advantage while Cara was vulnerable from dealing with her ex's mother.

"No, I doubt it." Sato looked thoughtful for a moment. "No, I'm sure it was mostly Cara. It wasn't a sudden thing. She told me she wanted to do it last summer, but the timing was bad. But you're right. Matteo's always been interested. He'd brought it up several times, too."

"They discussed it with you before?" Sam could hardly form the words. He tried to look like he was just tired from his run and not desperately trying to hold himself together. He felt betrayed, by both Cara and Sato. How could Sato have listened to him confess his love for Cara back in May and not have warned him that she was in love with someone else?

Sato shrugged. "A few times. I told them it was a big commitment, but . . . oh, just a sec." He answered a brief radio call. "Sorry, got to get back to the lobby."

He waved as he walked away, leaving Sam to process this devastating new information. Cara had once again chosen another man.

Chapter Sixty-Three

"Matteo, give me the mouse!" Cara tried to reach past him to take it, but he pulled it away.

"No, I'm controlling the zoom." He held it out of her reach, continuing to use the mouse wheel to scroll in. They were sitting in the staff office examining satellite pictures of the Blackhauer property. Actually, no, the former Blackhauer property. They hadn't come up with a good name for their new purchase yet.

"Stop it, Matty! You're focusing on the wrong place. I want to see the access points so we can see where to connect to the island road."

"Well, I want to see the old fireplace. I'm going to take a big sledgehammer up there and knock it down."

"I wanted to do that part!"

"You can't lift my sledgehammer."

"Neither can you. You don't even own one."

"Sorry, am I interrupting something?" Sam's voice cut them off. She hadn't seen him in days. For the past three mornings, she'd come into the kitchen at her usual time to find a cup of coffee cooling on the counter for her but no Sam in sight, and no explanation. He didn't enter the lobby while she worked, and if he was home, he stayed in his room with the door shut.

"Where have you been, Sam?" Cara asked. She suspected he was upset with her for some reason, and was doing his usual avoidance. Did he blame her for not replacing the freezer sooner? He was a bit obsessed with how he ran his kitchen, but it seemed like a strange thing to be so bothered about, especially since her uncle was the one who made the final decision, not her.

"I just needed the computer for a minute." He dodged her question. "Though I am wondering why Matteo is here. I thought this office was for staff only."

"Easy, buddy. We're working," Matteo said. "And I'm a former employee, so I have lifetime privileges. Plus, this computer is much faster than mine."

"Shouldn't you be working in your shop?" Sam folded his arms. "You know what, it doesn't matter. I'll come back later. Have fun."

"What was that all about?" Matteo asked after Sam stalked away.

"I have no idea. He's been weird lately," Cara replied. The whole encounter was confusing, but she'd been too busy to try and track Sam down to discuss anything. She and Matteo had made several trips to the mainland to sign the paperwork for their new property, and she'd spent every free moment pouring over regulations. They'd have to start clearing the land this fall, as much as possible, before the snows came. Hopefully, they'd be able to find an architect to help draw up plans over the winter, so they could break ground in spring.

"He's jealous. I recognize the signs."

"Jealous of what?" Then it hit her: she had accepted the insurance money. Sam probably saw that as her taking a bribe to keep silent about Phil's abuse, and maybe he didn't understand that it wasn't a payoff, but an apology. And she was going to do a lot of good with it. Some of it was going to a domestic violence shelter, just as her cousin suggested. And some of it was going to help the island economy.

When she and Matteo built their eco-friendly tiny cabins, they were going to use all local labor. Sato and Tim had both already expressed an interest in helping clear the trees, and they could donate some of the wood to families who relied on wood-burning stoves to heat their homes. When the property was up and running, they'd have to hire help too. It was a win for the island. Why couldn't Sam see that?

"Never mind, I get it," Cara said. "I'll find him later and straighten things out. Too bad he's going back to Aspen soon. We could have used his help." Too bad he's going back to Aspen at all, she added privately. Sam had never once asked about the possibility of staying on over the winter. If he did, they'd hire him in a heartbeat.

Chapter Sixty-Four

After work, Sam made his way to The Digs. He had resolved to drink his emotions away. He couldn't shake the image in his head of Cara and Matteo sitting so close together in the office, of the way they were flirting and teasing each other, and the way Matteo held the mouse in his extended arm, forcing her to reach over him . . . it broke his heart.

Sam was working on his fourth drink and finally feeling a little bit buzzed when Timmy came over to chat with him. Of all the conversation topics in the world, he had to bring up the one thing Sam did not want to talk about.

"Hey, you hear what Cara and Matteo are doing together?" Timmy asked as he took away Sam's glass and poured another.

"Yeah," Sam grunted, kind of hoping Tim would take the hint and walk away. He really wasn't in the mood to discuss Cara's recent actions.

"Crazy, right? But it's a good idea, too," Tim continued, ignoring Sam's discomfort.

"How is that a good idea? Cara and Matteo? Ridiculous. That guy is so irresponsible . . ."

"Whoa, careful. No, he isn't," Tim held up a hand warningly. "You only know summer Matteo. His whole laid-back-charming-idiot vibe is an act he puts on for the tourists. Marketing, you know. He's actually quite smart. He's finishing up a second master's degree, and he pretty much spends the off-season reading. Also, he knows this island well and he has mad business skills. I think they'll do great. You've seen what he's done with his rental shop."

"Well, I still think Cara could do better," Sam muttered into his glass.

Tim shrugged. "Maybe. She did talk to Sato about it before too, but with him starting the coffee roasting company and expanding the bakery, he's stretched awfully thin. Plus, timing-wise, I think he's going to be busy with other things this winter."

Sam knew that, while Tim was usually up on all the local gossip, he was dead wrong here. "Sato's married," he pointed out, rather drunkenly.

"That doesn't mean he can't identify a wise investment when he sees one. And I think it's wonderful they're finally turning the Blackhauer property into something worthwhile."

"The Blackhauer property?" Sam repeated dumbly.

"What land did you think they bought? Most of the rest of the area is all state park, so there's not much else available to build on, and someone should get some use out of it. Remind me to ask Cara who they're using to draw up the partnership paperwork. I have something I need to talk to a decent attorney about too."

"They bought the Blackhauer property?" Sam's alcohol-addled brain tried to process this new information. Why would they buy that? Were they going to construct their dream house and live happily ever after?

"Sam, I'm cutting you off. You're obviously too drunk. You know they did. That's all anybody is talking about. Hell, in the spring when they start building their little eco-village or whatever they're calling it, I hope they hire Tyrell to do some of the construction. He's handy with tools."

"Eco-village?" Sam started to feel like a parrot. He couldn't seem to make his mind function other than to repeat what Timmy had just said.

"Yeah, eco-village, tiny rental houses, whatever. I heard Matteo is campaigning to call it Cap'n's Acres, though I doubt that'll stick. It doesn't really matter what they finally name it.

It will be good to be able to sleep more visitors. We've been getting busier every year. Though I do hope nobody else tries to open a bar. I've got ideas for expansion, but I'm not looking for competition."

Sam let Tim's words wash over him as he sat in stunned silence. Cara went into business with Matteo? It wasn't romantic? Damn it, Sam had screwed things up again.

Chapter Sixty-Five

Whispering Pines, September 2013

The night air was chilly, so after the usual Wednesday night bonfire ended, Tyrell offered to rebuild it for a small gathering. Sam reflected on how pleasant it was to be out like this, sitting around a fire, surrounded by the noises of the forest and a few good friends. Well, maybe not friends, exactly, not after Sam had embarrassed himself by avoiding Cara and Matteo for days because of a minor misunderstanding.

"I brought the makings for s'mores," he told them, handing out marshmallows and roasting sticks. It was his way of apologizing without actually saying the words.

"These look funny," Amy complained, but she took several anyway.

"Hey, don't judge. It was my first time making them. And I brought whiskey, too." He pulled the bottle from his backpack and passed it around.

"I don't like whiskey," Cara said through a cough after taking a swig.

"I know," Sam told her with a grin. "I've got something special for you." He tried to hand her a bottle of rum.

"Gotta pour one out first." Matteo grabbed the rum before Cara could touch it and poured a little on the ground. "That's for our fallen comrade, Sato. May he rest in marital bliss."

Everyone laughed and Amy threw a pebble at him. "Stop wasting good alcohol! And this is a staff party. You don't work with us! Go home."

Matteo ignored her and sat on the log next to Cara, handing her the bottle. Sam hid his annoyance—he had been planning on sitting there once he finished organizing the s'mores. If Cara and Matteo weren't together, Matteo had better start backing off. Sam was running out of summer.

"I'm going to miss this in a couple of weeks," Matteo said suddenly. "I hate the end of the season."

While it wasn't fall on the calendar yet, it felt that way. The leaves were turning, and the tourist trade was drying up. There were even openings in Sam's restaurant this coming weekend, when all the tables were normally fully booked.

"Me too," Amy admitted. "I feel like Whispering Pines is my home. I can't wait to get back to traveling, but this is the place I miss when I'm gone. Though I might think differently if I'd ever spent a winter here."

"Where are you going this year?" Sam asked her. He hadn't heard anyone's plans yet. He only knew his own; he had a plane ticket to Aspen, leaving in just over two weeks. It was hard to believe that the season was almost over, and he still hadn't been able to tell Cara how he truly felt.

"I don't know exactly," Amy said slowly. "I wanted to take a trip to Italy, but I haven't really been invited. I have a job offer from my old boss in Thailand. He's opening a new resort in December and wants me to help out, so I might take it. They like me there. But that's not for another couple of months."

"Do you really need an invitation?" Sam asked curiously. He'd only left the country once, on a ski trip with Lizbet, and she had made all the arrangements. He wasn't clear on the procedures for acquiring a visa.

"I don't need one. I want one," Amy said, twisting her silver bracelet around on her wrist. "It'd be nice to be sure I'm welcome, you know?"

"Actually, I do know." He looked across the flames at Cara as he spoke, but she was talking to Matteo in a low voice, and he was pretty sure she wasn't listening.

"What do you do during the winter, Matteo?" Ty asked as he added more sticks to the fire.

"You mean besides clearing my new land? I've got a few hundred bikes to clean and fix up, and I maintain property for some of the summer people," Matteo replied. "Plus, I work out, I read a lot of books, and like everybody else, I grow a huge beard."

Cara started laughing "I had forgotten you guys do that. Tyrell, did Timmy tell you about it? The men on the island stop shaving on Halloween. Nobody's allowed to shave until what, April first? And then they do a big facial hair removal party at the bar. I've only seen pictures, but I think it gets hilariously ridiculous. My Uncle Robert used to grow an enormous bushy black beard. He looked kind of terrifying."

"I remember that," Amy said. "Cara, remember that year he and Paddy came to visit you for Christmas, and we told my little sisters he was a werewolf? Nikki was so scared she peed herself."

"Oh." Ty was quiet for a moment. "I guess I'm going to have a hard time fitting in then. I can't grow facial hair at all."

"Does that mean what I think it means?" Cara asked.

"Yeah, it means he lacks hair follicles in his face," Amy explained, and Cara shoved her backward off the log. Amy threw a handful of pine needles at her as she got up, and both women laughed.

Ty's grin was wide and happy. "That too. But it also means I'm staying here. Tim asked me to move in with him. Paddy said he might have some hourly work for me this winter, if the inn hosts any weddings or anything, and I've got my disability checks, so I can make it through."

"Are you gonna marry him?" Amy grabbed Ty's left hand to check for a ring.

He pulled it away. "Shut up, Amy. You're starting to sound like my mother."

"Notice he didn't actually answer the question," Cara pointed out. "We should talk dates so you can have the wedding at the inn, Ty. And I'm glad you'll be here this winter, so I have someone fun to hang out with."

"Ahem," Matteo cleared his throat loudly. "I'm here too. Have you already forgotten me?"

"She said someone fun," Amy informed him. "You don't count."

"I'm ignoring you," Matteo said. "Ty, be warned. Winters are tough. If you stay here, Timmy's going to make you go ice fishing. And he's going to try to talk you into joining his bandy team."

"I've never heard of that. What is it?"

"It's when you drill a hole in the ice and drop in a fishing line," Amy offered helpfully.

"It's a different version of hockey that they play out here." Cara rolled her eyes at her cousin. "Amy, you are the least helpful person I've ever met."

Sam watched them joking and bantering with each other. If they had another gathering a month from now, only Sam and Amy would be gone. A deep sadness welled up inside him. This had not been the summer he hoped for, and it was mostly his fault.

Chapter Sixty-Six

The bonfire and the supply of alcohol were both dwindling when Cara rose to her feet. "Sorry guys, it's late, and I have to be up early. I'm tired. I'm going home."

Matteo immediately jumped up and offered to walk her back.

Sam swore under his breath. "Matteo, you stay. I have to get up early tomorrow too, so I was going to leave anyway."

"I don't need an escort," Cara said as they set off. "I've walked this trail a hundred thousand times. I'm positive I can find the staff house on my own."

"It's not that. I wake up at the same time you do, remember? Or rather before you do, since I'm the one who makes you coffee."

The pine forest was dark around them, and once they came around a curve, the firelight disappeared, and they were limited to the faint moonlight that made it through the trees. Neither had brought a flashlight.

"You make me coffee and then you disappear," she pointed out.

"Not this morning," he reminded her.

"This morning when you made your bumbling apology because you thought I was sleeping with Matteo? Why would you care anyway?" That last question sounded like a challenge.

"It wasn't bumbling, I just . . ." He couldn't finish his sentence because he tripped over a rock and almost fell. To stop himself, he reached out blindly and accidentally grabbed Cara's hand.

Even though she seemed annoyed, she didn't pull away. It seemed only natural to hold on and continue holding on to her. Walking with her, alone in the moonlight, slightly tipsy ... perhaps this would be his best opportunity to finally say what he needed to say. *Time is almost up, stop being a coward. What's the worst that can happen?*

When they were nearly back to the house, he stopped walking, tugging on Cara's hand to halt her next step.

She turned back, confused. "Did you trip again, Sam?"

"No, I'm not that clumsy. I just ... before we get back, I have something I need to say." He took a deep breath, and reached out to gently touch her face. She didn't pull away, and that gave him hope. "I am so sorry about everything. I'm sorry about Phil, and I'm sorry I acted so weird about you and Matteo. I ... there has been so much I've wanted to say to you, and I haven't been able to. I'm not good at these kinds of things. But I need you to know ..." He cupped her cheek with his hand.

She stared deeply into his eyes. The moonlight reflecting from the gold glints in her irises was almost too much to handle. She was too beautiful; she made him too nervous.

"Oh, Cara ..." He hesitated for just an instant too long. *I am so in love with you,* he was about to say. *I am so in love with you, and we belong together* and then he would kiss her and afterwards she would tell him she loved him too ...

The loud snapping of a branch and the sound of running feet interrupted them. They jumped apart almost guiltily just as Amy came barreling down the trail. Damn it, Amy. Her timing was always impeccable.

"Every damn time," Cara muttered, which mirrored Sam's thoughts exactly.

"Oh good, I caught you." Amy stopped right in between Cara and Sam. "Cara, do you have your keys on you? I need to go down to the office and make a call. I've decided to be proactive and get myself that invitation I've been waiting for."

"My keys are in the bedroom. And it's midnight."

"Not in Italy." Amy grinned. "Oh well. I guess I have to stop by the staff house after all. I'll walk the rest of the way back with you. Come on." She linked arms with her cousin and dragged her down the path. Cara glanced back once at Sam, and even though it was too dark to read the look in her eyes, he was sure they held regret.

Chapter Sixty-Seven

The sound of Sam's door opening woke him up. Like in a dream, he saw a long-haired figure slip through the doorway and come closer to him. Without his glasses, he couldn't make out the numbers on the clock, but no light came through the windows, and Tyrell still slept soundly in his bunk across the room. "Sam?" the woman whispered, and he recognized Cara.

"What's going on?" he asked, sitting up and looking groggily over at his roommate.

She put a finger to her lips. "Shhhh. I'm doing something daring and reckless. Scoot over." And she pulled back his blanket and got into his bed.

"Something reckless?" he whispered, his mouth dry. She smelled of campfire, and faintly, as her head neared his he caught an underlying whiff of her strawberry shampoo. Was this really happening? He had wanted her in his bed for years, but he never expected it to happen like this.

"Am I being too daring? Do you want me to go?" She asked in a husky whisper.

He reached out and touched her face and was surprised to find tears. "What's wrong?" he asked.

"It's nothing. Don't worry about it. Just kiss me."

She didn't need to tell him twice. She tasted of whiskey and smoke, and her skin felt so soft under his hands. Was this really happening? He rolled on top of her, kissed her deeply ... and felt nothing. She lay still under him, barely responding.

"Are you okay? This is too soon, isn't it?" He should have known. What the hell was wrong with him?

"It's not too soon. I'm single, you're single, we're consenting adults. Let's just get this over with. Put on a condom and fuck me already." Her fierce whisper made him want to obey, but the words were not the ones he had hoped to hear.

"Get this over with? Are you kidding?" As much as he loved her assertiveness—it was exactly as he'd imagined—this was not how he wanted to do it. He wanted her to want him just as badly as he wanted her. "Look, maybe this isn't the right time for this. We're both kinda drunk, and you're crying. Your ex was an asshole; I'm not."

"Sammy, I'm so heartbroken," she said, then began sobbing helplessly. He glanced over his shoulder at the other bed to make sure Ty wasn't waking up and then wrapped his arms around her.

"I'm sorry for what he put you through, I really am. But you should know I've been in love with you for years. I promise, I'll be here to support you as you're going through this, and I'll take care of you."

"Stop," she said, but she nestled up against his chest and allowed him to comfort her.

"Shhh, go to sleep. We can talk more in the morning. Just know that I love you, okay?" He kissed the top of her head and held her, and she eventually drifted off to sleep. *This is it. It's not starting out as I hoped, but I'm finally going to get everything I've ever wanted,* he thought to himself before he too sank into sleep.

🌲 🌲 🌲 🌲 🌲

The telephone ringing in the living room woke him up with a start. He heard running footsteps and someone answered the phone. Who would be calling at this hour? He reached over and held his alarm clock close to his face so he could read the time. 6:15. Ooops. They had both overslept. *They* had. A slow smile crossed his face and he looked over. It wasn't a dream.

Cara was still there, though she had stolen the entire blanket and burrowed so deeply that only part of one arm showed.

A soft knock on the bedroom door startled him. "Sam!" Amy whispered from outside. He put on his glasses and stumbled to the door, carefully opening it only partway so that she couldn't see past him to the sleeping figure on his bed. He didn't think Cara would want anyone to know yet.

Cara was the one knocking on his door. No.

Was he dreaming?

It was Cara.

This couldn't be real.

It was Cara. It was real.

"Sam, we overslept. We're really late. Sato just called with the bakery delivery. I'll run and unlock the kitchen for him and then I'll come back and shower. You need to hurry up and get down to the restaurant."

"Cara, I . . ." His words trailed off. He suddenly felt very, very ill.

"No time to deal with a hangover, Sam. We've got some birdwatchers who will be at breakfast early." She started to go, but turned back and added, "Hey, I've been thinking a lot about our conversation last night. Can we talk later? Maybe after my shift?"

He could only nod. He closed the door, went over to his bed, and pulled back the blanket. Damn it, Amy.

Chapter Sixty-Eight

As soon as he served the last omelet, Sam packed up his station, wheeled the cart back to the kitchen, and asked Sato to take over for a bit so he could talk to Cara. He needed to reach her before Amy.

"Something wrong, man?" Sato asked, starting to put away food and sort the dishes.

"Last night Amy and I kind of ... well, we, um ..." Sam tried to explain, but Sato interrupted him with a laugh.

"You hooked up with Amy last night? Is that why she canceled her yoga class this morning? Too sore? I assumed she was hungover, but I guess not."

"She's already been down to the inn? Shit." If Amy cancelled her yoga class, she had to have talked to her cousin. Sam was too late.

"I knew it. All that talk of 'I only want Cara,' and 'Oh, I'm reformed. I'm a nice guy now.' I knew it." Sato's continued laughter started to get annoying.

"Don't gloat. It was an accident," Sam insisted, but that only made Sato laugh harder.

"An accident, right. What, did you trip and fall into her? Man, you messed up," Sato told him.

Sam did mess up. He was fully aware of that. His only excuse was that he couldn't see well, but he suspected Cara wouldn't buy it. "Nothing much happened, we just made out a little. And honestly, I didn't know it was her."

"What, did you think she was Cara? Yeah, you should inform Cara that even after all these years you can't tell her and her cousin apart. Women love to hear those kinds of things."

"It was dark. I didn't have my glasses! She was just a blur with hair."

"Oh, that's flattering. Tell her that. You know they don't sound alike either."

"She was whispering! What the hell am I going to do?"

"Well, for one thing, be more observant. For another, keep me posted on the situation. Margaux's gonna love this twist." "That's not helpful. Quit acting like you're enjoying this! I'm going to go find Amy and do some damage control."

He left the kitchen in a hurry, cut through the dining room, and stopped in the doorway. Crap! He should have talked to Cara before breakfast. He should have told those stupid bird watchers to cook their own omelets. There were a thousand things he should have done, but he was too late. Amy was at the reception desk, and, though he couldn't see Cara's face, he could tell by her posture that she was not happy. Damn it, Amy.

Chapter Sixty-Nine

"You didn't make it home last night," Cara commented when Amy came into the lobby.

"I'm canceling yoga. People can stretch without me." Amy removed the sign from the desk. "Oh, looks like nobody signed up anyway. This must be my lucky day." She collapsed on the floor behind the reception desk.

"What's wrong with you? This is not your usual hangover behavior." Her cousin preferred to exercise hangovers away, something Cara could never understand.

"You want to hear about my night? I found out that Fabio is cheating on me. We broke up, so I went and hooked up with Sam. Petty revenge, I guess."

"That's a joke, right?" Amy didn't look like she was lying, but how could that be true?

"I wish. Can you believe it? I mean I know long distance relationships are tough, but I'd rather he dumped me than cheat on me."

"I meant the other part." Cara must have heard wrong. She and Sam were meeting to talk later, a talk she'd deliberately scheduled for a time when her cousin couldn't interrupt them. He wouldn't have hooked up with Amy last night, would he? After the way he looked at Cara, the way he'd been flirting, the way he'd opened up to her? No, it couldn't have happened.

"What, Sam? Yeah, you know me. I like to burn bridges and I wanted to make myself feel better. I thought about Matteo, but I didn't want to go all the way into town and deal with his stupid dogs. It wasn't a big deal. Although Sam did tell me he was in love with me. Can you believe he pulled out such a lame line?"

"No. No, I can't." Amy's words stabbed her in the heart.

"It was kinda funny actually. I mean, obviously he didn't mean it. I guarantee a guy like Sam says the same thing to every girl he manages to get in his bed. It's part of his charm." She deepened her voice. "'Oh baby, I love you, I want you, I need you.' Then the next day it's all, 'Oh baby, you gotta go before my roommate wakes up. I'll call you, I promise. Oh wait, I can't. I'm not allowed to use the phone.' C'mon, you know his type."

"I guess I just thought he was different." Cara replayed every interaction she ever had with Sam in her mind. All this time she thought they were growing closer. All this time she thought they were building a strong bond, and maybe she meant something to him. Obviously, she didn't. Amy was right all along. He only wanted one thing and he'd take that wherever he could get it.

"Players gonna play, right? But I don't want to talk about that, I'm embarrassed. Why do I do such stupid things? And what the hell happened with Fabio? I thought we were soulmates." Amy leaned against the wall and closed her eyes. Tears ran down her face, and Cara was torn between the desire to comfort her and the desire to punch her.

"Cara, what am I going to do? I went to call him and tell him that I wasn't going to wait around for an invitation any longer. I was coming to Italy so we can be together, and he was out cheating. I can't even scream at him or slap him or anything. He's gone." Amy began sobbing, great heart-wrenching sobs, and Cara forced herself to put aside her own feelings. Her best friend needed her.

"Stand up, Amy," She pulled her cousin to her feet and hugged her tightly. "I'll help you come up with revenge on Fabio later. For now, go back to bed, curl up, and I'll have Sato run down and pick you up some chocolate cake. Okay?"

Amy tearfully nodded and left. Cara watched her go, then turned around to see Sam watching them from the dining room door. Their eyes met, and she shook her head and turned away. He was the last person she wanted to talk to right now. He'd betrayed her trust. He'd tricked her. Or maybe it was her fault. She had read him wrong, just as she had read Phil wrong.

Maybe she should thank her cousin for showing her the truth.

Chapter Seventy

Email from Amy O'Connell to Fabio Basile:

Really? That's what you choose to focus on? Really? Please, tell me more about American women. I'd love to hear it. Jackass.

Email from Amy O'Connell to Fabio Basile:

You've never done anything spontaneous in your life, but let me quote you from our last Skype: "I'm about to do something daring and reckless." And you were with a crowd of women. And I saw one of them wrap a very lovely arm around you and pour a shot into your mouth. And it couldn't have been later than what, 9:00 a.m. for you? So don't pull this holier-than-thou crap. You want to do something daring and reckless? Well, have fun. But you can't stop me from doing the same.

Email from Amy O'Connell to Fabio Basile:

"You weren't supposed to see that." Seriously, that's your explanation? Oh, ok then. I guess I'll just forget about it. Please, have a fabulous time day-drinking with a bunch of drunk girls. Sounds lovely. I'll just pretend I'm blind. Or maybe, when you're out cheating on me, DON'T ANSWER YOUR PHONE! This is on you.

Email from Amy O'Connell to Fabio Basile:

Fine. If that's the way you want to end things, fine. Have a great amazing life without me. I'm sure it will be wonderful. I'm sure you'll get everything you deserve.

Chapter Seventy-One

"You need to help me kill Tyrell," Amy muttered.

Cara looked up from her plate. "He just brought us food. I think we should keep him a bit longer."

"But he also just walked through the lobby whistling. How dare he be in a good mood when my life sucks? If you won't let me kill him, can we at least punish him?"

"Maybe." Cara thought about it. Not about actually punishing Tyrell, obviously. He didn't even know anything was wrong. But the O'Connell cousins needed to do something to change things up. They had both lost something—Cara, the hope for a relationship, and Amy an actual relationship. "I have an idea. I'll give you tomorrow night off. Paddy will cover for you, if we tell him about Fabio. We can go to the mainland. Find a club or something?"

"Or go see a movie? I think I've had too much to drink lately. That would be fun." Amy smiled wanly. Her eyes were still red. Cara knew she'd been sneaking to the bathroom to cry on and off all day.

"And we'll try a new restaurant. What's the opposite of Italian? You need the least Italian evening possible."

"Brazilian, I think. Or at least, that's what a certain soccer fan I used to like would say. But we're not going to find a Brazilian restaurant in this part of Minnesota, or even a Brazilian man."

"We could road trip to Duluth, find a Brazilian stripper and sleep in the inn's van," Cara suggested. They had done two of those three things in the past. "Let me check with Paddy and make sure he'll cover the desk." She knocked on Paddy's office door, but although she knew he was in there, he didn't answer.

"He's probably on the phone," Amy shrugged. "Wait till he comes out. Meanwhile, I'm going online and finding us the best male strip club in Duluth."

Cara laughed. "That's probably the first time that sentence has ever been uttered. Make sure it has a safe parking lot for the van so we can get wasted."

A few minutes later, the door to the office opened and Paddy came out, but he didn't acknowledge Cara's greeting. He walked past them into the lobby where he stood staring at the empty fireplace.

"That's weird," Amy said.

When Paddy turned back toward the desk, Cara noticed something different about his face. One side was sagging, as if he was a slowly melting wax version of himself. "Uncle Paddy, are you okay?"

He appeared confused. "Cynthia? What are you doing here?" His voice came out slow and slurred.

"Is he drunk?" Amy whispered, but then Paddy's leg seemed to give out and he slowly toppled over sideways. "What the hell?"

Cara rushed to her uncle's side while Amy grabbed the radio and called Tyrell to come assist immediately.

"I think he's having a stroke," Cara called out. She and Amy had attended numerous first aid trainings, and she recognized the signs. Paddy was a little young for it, but that was what killed his father in his early sixties. "Amy, check the dining room, see if Dina is working tonight." One of the local EMTs moonlighted as a waitress, and fortunately, she was there.

After a quick assessment, Dina confirmed their suspicions. "Cara, you're right. It's probably a stroke. We need to get him to a hospital immediately. Time is the most important thing here."

"What should we do? Does he need a helicopter evacuation?" Amy had a look of fear on her face that Cara was sure she matched.

"Actually, it'll be faster if you can take him in a speedboat. I can call ahead and have an ambulance waiting at the mainland docks. I'll notify the hospital too, so they can get him a CT scan immediately."

Chapter Seventy-Two

Sam missed all the drama, since it occurred during the middle of the dinner service. At some point, he noticed one of his waitresses had skipped out, but it was near the end of the season and their six thirty seating wasn't busy anyway. He assumed she had gotten sick or something and handed off her tables. He planned to have a private word with her later about checking with him first.

After he sent the last plate out, Amy walked in with a serious expression on her face. "Leftover dessert?" he offered, but she shook her head.

"I just wanted to update y'all," she gestured for the kitchen staff to gather around. "I heard from Cara. They made it to the hospital. Dina was right. It was a stroke. We're super lucky she was here. She said time is of the essence in stroke treatment."

His stomach dropped. "Wait, Cara had a stroke?"

Amy responded with a glare. "Sam, what is wrong with your brain? Paddy did. He collapsed right out there in front of your dining room doors. We pulled your waitress to treat him and take him in. How do you not know about that?"

The truth was he had been too caught up in his own thoughts to notice anything going on around him. Although he normally maintained a tight focus while working, on this particular evening he had been distracted by how he would deal with the fallout from last night's disaster, so much so that he wasn't paying attention to anything else.

He turned to his line cook and told him to supervise the rest of the cleanup. "Which hospital? I'm going to help."

"Ummm ... you know you aren't a doctor, right Sammy? There's nothing you can do, and anyway, you know the ferry schedule. There are no more runs to the mainland tonight. Finish what you're doing here. Cara's taking care of Paddy, and I'm sure she has it under control."

"I'm not going for Paddy. I'm going for Cara. Someone needs to take care of her."

"And you think you're the right person for that job? I'm doing it. That's why I'm staying here running this place. I'm taking care of her by doing everything so she doesn't have to worry."

"Technically, isn't this your shift anyway?" he asked, and immediately regretted it.

"This is not the time to argue with me, Sammy," she told him in a dangerously angry voice.

Amy was not someone he liked to cross, but for Cara's sake, he would.

"I'm not arguing with you, I'm ignoring you. You may be in charge of the inn, but you're in my kitchen, and I make the decisions here. I'm going, and you can't stop me. Francisco, the kitchen's yours." Sam hurried out before Amy could say anything.

Amy had been right about the ferry though, so Sam grabbed the staff phone, desperate to find a ride across the lake. Tim couldn't leave the bar, Sato didn't pick up, and he was getting really frustrated. He made one last call.

"Are you kidding man?" Matteo answered on the sixth ring, sounding annoyed. "I just got back from taking Cara and Paddy over there. You're gonna have to refuel my boat. But yeah, fine, I'll do it. Meet me at my launch."

Chapter Seventy-Three

The nursing station gave Sam the room number, and he raced down the hall. He stopped in the doorway to take in the scene—he hadn't quite come up with what he needed to say yet. There was Paddy on the bed, pale and hooked up to several machines and IVs, either asleep or unconscious. Cara sat in a chair next to him, with her head in her hands, her hair curtained around her face. She looked up when he said her name.

"What are you doing here?" She sounded weary, and she wouldn't make eye contact. Still angry, probably. He silently cursed Amy.

"I came to help you."

"Sam, you're the last person I need help from right now. Go away." She covered her face with her hands again, so he crossed the room and knelt on the floor in front of her.

"Look at me, please, Cara. I'm begging you."

She did, and her expression did not give him hope.

"Cara, I'm sorry, about everything."

The pain in her eyes was so heartbreaking, he couldn't say anything else. He just reached out, wrapped his arms around her waist, and hugged her. After a moment, her arms came around him too and he felt her start to cry. He held her tightly and let her tears flow.

When she stopped and pulled away, her eyes were red, but her expression had become stoic. "It's time for you to go, Sam. There's nothing you can do here. Paddy is going to be okay."

"I'm not here for Paddy. I'm here for you." He reached towards her face slowly, touching her cheek, her hair. He wanted to kiss her, kiss her softly and finally tell her how he felt, but she pushed his hand away.

"Sam, stop it! I don't need you in my life. Amy is my best friend. We talk. I know about last night. I know what you said to her. I know what you guys did. If it hadn't already been perfectly clear that you and I are always and forever just friends, you telling Amy that you're in love with her clinched it. You're an opportunist, Sam. Please, please just go home."

"No, Cara, you don't get it. Everything I said to Amy I said because I thought she was you."

"Do you think I'm stupid? You've known us for years. We don't look that alike, Sam."

"You do in the dark when I don't have glasses on and she used your shampoo."

"My shampoo?"

"You always smell like strawberries, she smells like citrus. But she came into my bed smelling like you and whispering and . . . believe me Cara, everything I said to her was meant for you." He paused, took a deep breath, then plunged ahead with it. It was time to be truthful. "Please listen to me. I am so in love with you, and I have been for years. I came back here for you, only for you. All summer you've been breaking my heart, and now it's almost over and I've really screwed things up. I've been working up the nerve to tell you how I feel, but I'm running out of time and it seems like every time I thought we were getting close, something happened, and I'm tired of being interrupted. I want you Cara, I . . ."

But he was interrupted again. She stopped him with a kiss, and it was everything he had wanted it to be. He rose up, pulled her body to him, tangled one hand in her hair and pressed the other into the small of her back. The kiss went on forever and fire ran through his veins, and he knew there was nothing he wanted more than this moment . . .

. . . and then Paddy coughed politely, bringing them both back down.

Chapter Seventy-Four

Cara looked down at Sam's hand entwined in hers. Paddy had shooed them out of his room so they could talk privately. There was nowhere to go in the hospital, but they found a bench outside that was at least far enough from the building that the lights were dimmer and they could speak without being overheard. Cara sat sideways across his lap, holding his hand and tracing the scars.

"Burns, all of them. I didn't used to be very good with ovens," he explained.

She laughed. His other hand, running up and down her back, sent shivers of excitement through her. "You spent most of the summer saying you wanted to be friends," she told him. "How was I to know you wanted anything different?"

He chuckled and shook his head ruefully. "And all summer I thought you were keeping me at an arm's length, always using the word 'friend' as a defense."

"Sam." She put her hands on each side of his face and pulled him in for another kiss. "If we had communicated better, we could have been doing this all summer long."

He hugged her body closer to him. "I know. I'll regret that for the rest of my life."

"You know it's September. The season is over. You're heading back to Colorado soon."

He started to kiss her neck, scraping his teeth lightly over her skin. His voice was muffled. "Come with me."

"What? To Aspen? You don't mean that!" She felt goosebumps. His breath was hot in her ear.

"I do. Come with me. I know people. I'll help you find a job. We can rent a tiny overpriced apartment and spend all winter doing this." His hand roamed over her body, setting fire to whatever he touched.

"Don't you think you're getting ahead of yourself? We haven't even gone on a date yet, and you want me to move in with you? That's moving a little fast, isn't it?"

"Cara, we've lived together for years. The only difference is that we'd be sharing a bed. That's not moving too fast. That's just practical."

"You know I can't. I'm staying here." One of his hands slipped under her jacket and up the back of her shirt, making every nerve come alive along the passages of his fingertips. It was hard to talk, hard to answer him, hard to think about anything but his hands on her flesh and the heat and desperate need building up inside her.

"You never said what's happening with the restaurant." He had moved his other hand to the inside of her thighs, and it was driving her crazy, making her regret not wearing a skirt.

"It'll be open on weekends, same as the inn. We'll see if it works out."

"You'll need a chef." He started kissing her neck again.

"Yeah, Paddy's been looking. Wayne said he might do it until we find someone else." Her back arched involuntarily. Everything he was doing felt so right.

"That hack? Forget it. I'll do it."

That stopped everything. She shoved his hands away and pulled back. He stared at her, and she couldn't catch her breath. "What do you mean you'll do it?"

His eyes burned with passion and promise. "I'll stay here. Hire me. Can this be my job interview?"

He brought his face back to hers and she lost herself.

🌲 🌲 🌲 🌲 🌲

They eventually returned to the hospital after Sam abruptly shoved Cara off his lap and informed her they needed to either stop immediately or find someplace much more private. Unfortunately, there weren't any private places.

Cara thought wistfully of the inn's van, safely parked at the docks. If only Sam had borrowed the van instead of taking a cab, they would have found their private space, and she wouldn't have had to sit there with frustrated desires, patiently waiting as Sam focused on taking slow breaths and thinking unsexy thoughts.

When they got back to Paddy's hospital room, they were stopped by a nurse.

"It's past visiting hours. We only allow one family member to stay overnight."

"I live on Whispering Pines Island, what am I supposed to do?" Sam protested, fingers squeezing Cara's hand.

The nurse was unmoved. "There's a cafeteria downstairs and a waiting room down the hall. Sorry, it's hospital policy."

Sam turned to Cara. "You'll be okay?"

His smile made her feel warm. "Of course, I'll be fine. I'll come find you in the morning." One more kiss, quicker this time, and she watched him walk away.

Cara entered Paddy's room and was glad to see him awake. She quickly crossed to him and gave him a hug, mindful of the wires and tubes connecting him to machines.

"Don't cry," Paddy told her, and it wasn't until that moment she realized that she was, again. There had been too many tears shed today.

"Paddy, you scared me so much earlier. I don't want to lose you." She wiped the tears away and tried to smile for him.

"Oh, don't worry. I've got a few years left in me. You're not getting your hands on my share of the inn yet," he promised. "The doctor says I'll be fine. They're keeping me in a couple of days for observation, and I may have to make some lifestyle changes, but Robert's got to wait for me a bit longer. I might have another stroke though, or maybe a heart attack, if you don't fill me in on what the hell is going on with you and Sam." He smiled as he said it, so Cara knew he wasn't upset. That came as a relief; she had worried what her uncle might think.

"I don't know," she said, blushing. "We've both liked each other for a while, but nothing really happened between us until tonight. He came to support me when he heard about your stroke. And, here's some good news. We can stop looking for a winter chef. Sam took the job."

"Wonderful, I'm glad that it's finally happened. I hired him for you, you know."

Chapter Seventy-Five

Cara found Sam the next morning. He was sleeping on a bench in a corner of the waiting room in what looked like a terribly uncomfortable position, though he had somehow managed to find a pillow and blanket. She wasn't used to seeing him asleep. He looked much younger and more vulnerable than she'd expected. Tentatively, she reached out to wake him.

He blinked sleepily and then smiled. "It wasn't a dream, was it?"

She tried to kiss him on the cheek, but he turned, caught her with his lips, and kept her there for a while.

Finally, they went to the cafeteria where she could get a mediocre cup of coffee, and he found a tea he was willing to tolerate. He stretched his legs as soon as they sat down, and from the way he grinned at her, she knew he was resting them against her calves on purpose. He took her free hand and began stroking her fingers.

"I'm so glad I can finally do this," he said. "You have no idea how long I've been waiting for you."

"Maybe I do. But let's talk about that," Cara said. "What do you want from me? What are you looking for?" Now that the drama of the previous night was over, she needed to know where they stood. She had to make sure that any promises he made last night weren't just in the heat of the moment.

"Well . . ." His grin showed all his teeth. "I want everything." He leaned in closer and dropped his voice. "I want to see you naked. I want to taste every inch of your body. I want to be inside of you, I want . . ."

She stopped him. "Yeah, thanks, we're in public, and I already know all of that. There's more to a relationship besides sex, you know." She watched his face. This was one of the things she was concerned about. Admittedly, since their make out session the night before, she already planned to sleep with him no matter how he answered, but she did need to know if she could expect anything more from him. "Seriously, Sam. What are you looking for from me?"

"I told you I want everything. I want to wake up with you and make you coffee every morning. I want to be able to put my arms around you and kiss you whenever I want—"

She interrupted again. "You can't while we're at work. It's unprofessional."

"I can when there aren't any guests around."

She stuck her tongue out at him, and he laughed.

But then he continued more seriously. "Cara, you remember the night when we sat on the porch and watched the storm, and you fell asleep against me? I want that comforting feeling of having you with me, of being together. I want to be the one you turn to when there's a problem. Next time some crazy person starts throwing things at you in the lobby, I want to be the one to tackle them. If someone hurts you, I want to be there not only to comfort you, but to help you plot your revenge. Oh, and I want to teach you how to cook so you never have to eat anything your cousin makes ever again. That's probably the most important."

"Only some of that is in any way romantic, Sam." She had watched him carefully as he spoke, and she knew every word came from the heart.

"Maybe I'm not romantic, but I am practical. I thought you'd appreciate that about me." He brought her hand to her mouth and kissed her fingertips. "There, I just made a romantic gesture. But what about you? What are you looking for from me?"

She looked away for a minute, considering. When she turned back to him, she gave him a wicked smile. "You mean besides finding out if you're truly as good in bed as rumored?"

He rubbed his leg against hers and nodded.

"Sam, I've felt something between us for a long time. I'm really attracted to you, you should know that. And I feel so safe and comfortable with you. But I want to be clear that I'm someone who is looking for a long-term thing. I want a real relationship, not a fling. That means you have to be open with me. And you have to promise not to walk—or run—away when things are tough."

"I'm done running. You'll see," he said, and she told him she was ready to give him a chance. He took the opportunity to lean across the table and kiss her, almost knocking over his tea in the process.

"Well, let's talk about other things. Paddy's going to be in here for another couple of days, so we need to discuss logistics." Cara turned the conversation to a subject she had been worrying about.

"Oh, I thought about logistics all night," Sam assured her. "I was thinking I should buy condoms at the drugstore here, so people on the island don't gossip too much."

"Sam!" Cara pretended to be scandalized, but she had already thought the same thing.

"Kidding! Well, not really. But yes, other logistics. I'm going to need to fly out to my brother's house in Nevada to pick up all my winter stuff, and I think I should also get some snowshoes or cross-country skis, especially since I'll miss the real ski season. I did talk to one of the nurses last night though, and she assured me there's some good downhill nearby, so we'll have to get you some skis so I can teach you. We can take some mid-week trips. And I guess I need to call my boss in Aspen and let him know I'm not coming back. Also, I have to go over everything with Paddy. I have no idea what the food situation is in winter, but I imagine I need to fully stock the freezers with meat, and I need to figure out root vegetable storage in the kitchen. I want to stick to fresh ingredients as much as possible, so I'll start working on some new winter squash recipes, since I think that's what I'll have the most access to, and—what? Why are you looking at me like that?"

"It's adorable how you've already turned so much of your focus onto winter food. Really. But I meant logistics for today. We need to go back to the inn, so I can grab some stuff for Paddy and come back. Amy's got things handled, and Tyrell's happy with the overtime, so they don't need me, and I want to be here for my uncle. You have to get back to the kitchen. Sato and Francisco covered breakfast this morning, but you've got a busy dinner shift."

Chapter Seventy-Six

It was a two-mile trip from the hospital to the dock, and Cara had insisted on walking. Sam didn't mind. It gave him plenty of time to hold her hand.

They made one stop on the way back at a drugstore to pick up a few necessary items. While Sam was paying for his purchases, Cara walked up and dropped a bottle of citrusy shampoo on the counter. "For Amy, so there are no more mistakes," she said, giving Sam a pointed look.

He took that to mean that while he was forgiven, he was perhaps not entirely trusted. Fair enough. He supposed he hadn't proved himself yet. He had messed up so many times over the summer that he knew he had to earn her trust.

The weather was perfect for a long walk—sunny, but not too warm. As Sam held Cara's hand, he reflected on how good it felt and how right it was to actually be able to touch her, to occasionally kiss her cheek, to sometimes pull her into an alley and press her up against the wall and kiss her deeply.

"You think we can get ourselves a room at the inn tonight?" he asked hopefully, after one such make out session.

"Don't you think you're moving too fast?" she teased. "We haven't even been on a date yet, and you want to get a hotel room together?"

"What are you talking about? Last night I took you to a park bench for our first date, and let me remind you that you kissed me first. Then, this morning I bought you oversalted food that I didn't cook, so obviously that was our second date. We're currently on date three, a romantic walk. On date four, I'll take you on a lovely boat ride to a beautiful island. So nobody's going to judge you if you put out tonight. It will be our fifth date, after all."

She laughed, but then it was her turn to pull him into an alley and kiss him, and he felt a surge of excitement through his whole body. "Alright, tonight. Date number five. I'll get us a room, if you bring drinks and dessert," she offered.

They made it to the docks, and he kissed her again as they waited to board. He could do this now, he could do this whenever he wanted, or at least, whenever she would let him. She planned to return to the hospital later this afternoon, but she promised she'd be on the last ferry back to the island, arriving right around the time his shift ended. This was going to be the best night of his life.

He glanced toward the ferry and saw Everett and Duncan looking at him. Everett grinned and gave him a thumbs-up, while Duncan frowned and shook his head. "Ummm ... I think word is going to get out about us," he warned Cara. "Both the ferry brothers just saw us."

"I don't care. Let them tell everybody. Besides, I called Amy last night, so that means half the village probably knows."

"Well, if they already know, I'll give them something else to talk about." He went in for another kiss but missed. She had turned away, distracted.

"Hang on. Is that who I think it is?" She squinted at a man buying passage at the ticket window.

"I don't know. I don't recognize him," Sam started to say, but Cara was already walking away. He watched her approach the man and grab him by the arm, spinning him around. Based on the anger in Cara's voice, Sam felt a moment's sympathy for the stranger.

"Hey! I thought it was you! What the hell are you doing here?"

Chapter Seventy-Seven

Email from Amy O'Connell to Amanda O'Connell and Nicole O'Connell:

Dear Mandi and Nikki,

I'm going to kill you bitches. Both of you, you're dead.

Seriously.

When a man shows up at our parents' house and says he's flown all the way over there from Italy to ask dad for permission to marry me, you need to tell me immediately! YOU SHOULD HAVE CALLED!!!!!

And what you certainly shouldn't have done was taken him out and gotten him drunk. Fabio says you told him it was tradition that he had to buy you both shots all night, and all your friends too. Yeah, that's not a tradition. He also said you, Nikki, tried to get him to tattoo my name on his ass. You have no right to look at his ass, talk about his ass, or do what he says you did and pull down his pants to show him where on his ass you wanted the tattoo.

And Mandi, seriously, did you see me when I Skyped him at the bar? Did you see me on his phone when you wrapped your arm around his neck and poured a shot half into his mouth and half all over his shirt? Because I saw you, but not enough of you to recognize my own baby sister (nice manicure, btw).

All I saw was my boyfriend out getting drunk with some random tramp. You should have said something!

You're fully aware I broke up with Fabio over that incident! And I know you both know that because I emailed you the next day and told you I was single again because my dumbass boyfriend decided to go out and cheat on me. Nikki, you responded with, 'too bad, better luck next time,' and Mandi, I believe you told me it was expected because, 'Italians are skeezy.' I don't even think that's a real word.

I was devastated and heartbroken, and I blame the two of you.

Email from Amy O'Connell to Amanda O'Connell and Nicole O'Connell:

What is wrong with you? Of course I said yes! You saw Fabio, he's gorgeous. And he's funny and smart and he makes me jewelry, and he likes to travel and he gets my sense of humor and he's the most perfect man I've ever met, and I've known from the first time he kissed me that I was going to spend the rest of my life with him.

And no, neither of you is going to be maid of honor. I'm going to ask Cara because she would never let me suffer for two days thinking my relationship was over due to a misunderstanding. (Yes, I'm obviously still mad at both of you.)

But since you asked for the story, here you go:

I think I told you Paddy had a stroke. (He's going to be fine.) Cara went to the hospital on the mainland with him; and on her way back, who does she run into buying tickets at the ferry office but Fabio? At first, she was like, 'That can't be him. Not only did he and Amy break up, but that loser is in Italy.' But then he turned and saw her, waved with this big grin on his face, and she started yelling at him (see, one of my relatives is supportive!). Well, then he told her the truth about the situation, so she called my coworker and told him to take over the inn desk for me and make me come down to the ferry and pick her up. She didn't call me directly to ask for a ride because she didn't want to give anything away.

For many reasons, I didn't want to (you may already know our cousin is in a new relationship with a guy I don't entirely approve of, so that was part of it). So I was pissed, but I drove down to the docks anyway. And I'm just standing there, leaning against a post, and thinking of all the awful things I'd like to do to Fabio and his new lover (Ahem, Mandi.), when I heard someone speaking with an Italian accent. At first, I thought I only imagined it because nobody sounds like that out here, but then I recognized Fabio's voice.

Incidentally, he later said he was again struck by my beauty when he saw me and he knew instantly and absolutely that coming here was the right decision—super flattering and romantic, right? I got me a good man!

But anyway, I was pretty mad at first and told him I didn't even want to talk to him. At the same time, my heart was just racing and all I could think was, oh my god, did he seriously fly halfway around the world for me? Really, for me? But is this enough to make me forgive him for cheating? You know my college boyfriend cheated on me, and I think cheaters are the lowest of the low, so obviously I was angry. But then he explained how he had researched American traditions for proposing, and he made me a ring with a diamond in it—yes, he made the ring himself (he showed you when he was in Texas, right? It's stunning!!!!) and went to ask Dad in person. Then, he admitted he had been out drinking with 'the little twins' to celebrate, and told me all about what you girls did, and how he wasn't cheating but he couldn't defend himself to me because it would ruin the surprise, and he said he loves 'to do surprises on people.'

So even though I had dumped him, he didn't care, and he was here because he wanted nothing more than to spend the rest of his life with me.

Yeah, I cried. So did Cara (she watched the whole thing). Then I brought Fabio up to the inn, and we celebrated.

Y'all need to get passports. I'm thinking we'll get married in Italy. I've already scouted out a few places, and Fabio's family has connections—we may be able to do it at a vineyard. I don't know what color your bridesmaid dresses will be. It depends on if we have it this fall or next spring. I'll keep you posted. And I'll send you links to potential dresses for me. Maybe we can convince Mom to take us all dress shopping in New York?

OMG I'M GETTING MARRIED!!!!!!!!

Chapter Seventy-Eight

"Do you have a key for me?" Sam asked at the reception desk, trying not to sound impatient. He had rushed through the dinner cleanup as fast as his innate discomfort with messes would allow. It was time—he was off work for the night, and Cara was waiting for him.

"Depends. Do you have something for me?" Amy responded pertly. She was in a much better mood than she had been earlier.

"Amy, be nice to the man." Fabio's heavily accented voice came from the staff office.

Sam wasn't sure if that was appropriate, having Amy's boyfriend—no, fiancé, apparently—hanging out with her behind the desk, but nobody else seemed to mind. "I brought you both dessert." He set a covered plate down. He had been balancing two of them—the other, of course, was for Cara. He'd packed up her favorite vanilla panna cotta with berries, along with the bottle of wine he'd been saving all summer.

"This is leftover cake from yesterday," Amy complained, lifting the lid. "You're getting nothing from me."

"I like cake," Fabio told her mildly as he came out to stand behind her, and she turned and kissed him on the cheek.

"Oh, fine. Here, Sam. Cara left you a key. I don't think she's in the room right now though; I don't know where she went. She said for you to wait for her, but don't be too upset if she changes her mind and doesn't show up. Room 24." She slid the key across the desk to him, but he didn't pick it up right away.

"Why wouldn't she show up?" He hadn't even thought about that possibility. Last night had been so full of promise, and he spent the entire day fantasizing about what this night would bring. All of those fantasies entailed Cara being in the room waiting for him.

"Maybe she came to her senses? I don't know. But if she doesn't show, you'll probably be leaving for Aspen soon, right?"

"Yeah, I guess." He took the key, and feeling unsettled, started down the hall, but Fabio called him back.

"Samuel, wait. Amy has something she needs to say to you, don't you, *mio amore?*"

Amy shook her head, but, after a flurry of angry whispering in Italian, she finally rolled her eyes and said, "*Fine.* Sam, give me that key back. She's in 16."

🌲 🌲 🌲 🌲 🌲

It was the moment of truth. He put the key in the lock, turned the knob and . . . yes! She was there. Cara had folded back the comforter and was reclining on the sheets. She had changed out of the jeans and T-shirt he saw her in earlier into leggings and a soft-looking sweater. He took a moment to admire her as his eyes traveled up her body to her face and . . . she was asleep!

He had no idea what to do. He let the door swing closed behind him, but it didn't slam, so it wasn't loud enough to wake her. Neither did the sound of the plate being set ungently down on the room's table, nor the unnecessarily loud noises he made taking the wine bottle out of his backpack and thunking it onto the table.

Had they been in a relationship longer, he would have slipped off his shoes and climbed into bed next to her, wrapped his arms around her, and fallen asleep himself. But that would be too presumptuous right now, when they've never been in a bed together before, and he didn't even know if she still wanted him. Amy did say she might have changed her mind.

He unpacked his bag, put his toothbrush in the bathroom and then considered what to do. He couldn't sit on the bed, he hadn't earned that right yet. Should he leave? And why was he so nervous? He had known Cara for years. He thought of her as his closest friend, but this change in their relationship made him so unsure of himself.

He finally gave up and sat down on a chair to wait. And he didn't mean to do it, but it had been a long day. He hadn't slept well the night before so, just like Cara, he fell asleep.

Chapter Seventy-Nine

Another nightmare, Phil, again. I told you what would happen if you cheated on me. I think you're fucking the chef. He reached for her, and Cara tried to run. You're dead, Phil. It's not cheating if you're dead, but of course he didn't agree, and he was so much faster than her. As his hands wrapped around her throat, there was a loud crash followed by swearing . . . and then strong hands, real hands grabbing her.

"Wake up, Cara, wake up. You're having a nightmare."

And then she was awake, and Sam was holding her in his arms, comforting her. It took a moment to come into the reality of the situation. Sam was here, not Phil, and she was safe. She took a few deep breaths and her heart rate gradually slowed. *Safe. I'm safe.*

"When did you get here? What time is it?" She couldn't believe she had fallen asleep. Well, no, she could believe it. She had been exhausted, but she had been really anticipating their 'fifth date' plans. It was a good thing she had already bribed Tyrell to take her shift tomorrow—this was going to be a late night.

"I don't know," Sam said. "I fell asleep too. Oh, no, I hope it wasn't too long. I brought you *panna cotta*, and it shouldn't be sitting at room temperature. It's supposed to be eaten chilled." He climbed out of the bed and almost tripped over a chair, which he had apparently knocked over in his earlier haste.

"Sam, it's fine. I can eat it anyway."

"No, you can't. Damn it, I promised you dessert, and now it's ruined. I can run down to the kitchen and get another one . . ."

He looked so disappointed she almost laughed at him. After her nightmare about Phil and the complications of that relationship, it was refreshing to be with a man who was so focused on such inconsequential things.

"Really, Sam, you brought wine, and do I see berries? I think we'll be fine. I'm just glad you came."

"Me too. I almost didn't." Second thoughts already? Had he planned to run, again? He must have realized what it sounded like because he explained, "Amy tried to give me the wrong key. But Fabio stopped her. I think I like that guy."

"So do I. But I like you better." She crossed the room and kissed him, and he kissed her back so deeply she could feel it in her toes. When they finally broke apart, her lips were tingling. "How about you pour me a glass of wine?"

He did, and one for himself. "To us," he said, looking in her eyes and making the toast. But unfortunately, looking into her eyes meant he wasn't quite watching what he was doing, and he sloshed wine on her sweater.

"I can't believe I did that. This evening is not going as I'd hoped. But don't worry, I can get the stain out before it sets. Quick, take your top off."

"Subtle, Sam, really subtle."

"No seriously, I just need some salt and hot water. Do we have salt in here?"

"Why would we keep salt in the rooms? It's fine."

"The wine stain . . ."

"Seriously, it's okay. I borrowed this sweater from Amy anyway."

"Oh, well in that case . . ." He pretended to pour the rest of his glass on her, and laughing, she ducked away.

"Here, you really want to remove the stain?" She slowly took the sweater off and tossed it at him. He caught it but didn't move. She could feel his eyes travel over her body, and her pulse quickened. That was pure desire she was seeing.

"Nice. Black lace bra? Really nice. Not what I would have expected, but very nice. Can I see what you've got under it?" His voice had gotten husky and he dropped the sweater on the floor, the spilled wine all but forgotten. That was okay. Her cousin owed her anyway.

"What did you expect?" she asked as he pulled her toward himself.

"I don't know, beige, maybe?" His hands slid down to her waist, and she felt goosebumps and a flash of annoyance.

"Beige? What?"

"The way you dress, with those polo shirts all the time, I just thought that's the kind of thing worn with beige bras."

"You mean my uniform? You know that's not how I always dress. I can't believe that in your wildest fantasies you picture me wearing a beige bra."

"No," he corrected her, his breath hot in her ear. "In my wildest fantasies, you're taking a beige bra off."

She felt his hands reach behind her toward the clasp, and she pushed him away. Much as she wanted to do this, there was a conversation they had to have first. "Not so fast, Sam. This isn't a fair situation. Take off your shirt."

He complied with alacrity and reached for her again.

"Nope, still not fair. I've seen you shirtless before. Maybe you should take your pants off?"

He certainly had no problem doing so, and swiftly too. He was still wearing his clothes from work, and those pants were designed to come off quickly in case of fire or spills of boiling liquids. He had once told her he could strip in less than five seconds in the kitchen, and he proved those skills came in handy here as well.

"Hmmmm . . . white boxer briefs, not what I expected," she teased, taking a moment to look him up and down. He was well-built, that was for sure. Well-built and rather turned on.

"It's easier to bleach the stains out of white," he told her.

"Gross, Sam, that's disgusting. I don't want to hear about that!"

"What? Oh, shit, no," he said, with a panicked look on his face. "I mean, not shit. That's not what I meant. It's for spills in the kitchen, and since my pants are white I wear white underwear. I swear, it's not what it sounds like."

"Even so, maybe you should take them off too."

"Really? Already? Wow, I like fifth-date Cara."

Cara waited until he was completely naked. She took the opportunity to take a good long look—a hard look, she thought to herself, and inwardly giggled. But she knew better than to laugh out loud. Men never liked that. "Very nice, Chef Vervaine."

"Your turn." He smiled a wicked smile and reached for her again. But that would have to wait.

"Just a minute. We need to talk."

He looked down at himself. "I'm naked in a hotel room with a beautiful woman. Clearly, talking is the last thing on my mind right now."

"I can see that, but I have something I need to say first." She picked up her glass and finished the wine in one large gulp.

"Hey, don't chug it. That's an expensive wine. You're supposed to savor it," Sam protested.

She poured herself another glass for strength. "We need to talk, Sam," she told him again. "Please sit down."

He did, seating himself on the edge of the bed and pulling a pillow over his lap. Good, that covered up the distractions.

"Do I have to be naked for this?" he asked.

"Yes. That's how I can guarantee you won't run away immediately. Call it insurance." Using her foot, she kicked his pants and briefs out of his reach. "There's something I need to say. It's about Phil. He and I . . . well, we had sex . . ." She was interrupted by a snort of laughter.

"I know that Cara! You're thirty, I'm not expecting a virgin!"

"I'm twenty-nine, you jerk!"

"Really? But I thought you were older than Amy and she just turned twenty-nine."

"Do you understand how calendars work, Sam? I'm only two months older than her." She shook her head and took another swallow of wine. He was distracting her, and she needed to focus on what she had to say—the painful secret she had been carrying around for so long. "Sam, can we please be serious? I need to tell you something. When Phil and I had sex, it wasn't . . . it wasn't always consensual." It took a moment, but she could see the instant when understanding hit his eyes.

"Are you kidding me, Cara?" Sam's voice sounded incredulous.

Cara closed her eyes, waited for his inevitable departure. He was going to walk away, she just knew it. She was too damaged for him. It was her fault anyway, for staying with Phil for so long, for not leaving him when the monster first emerged, for not letting him die sooner. She had bought him two more years of life, but at what cost to her?

She heard Sam get up, but she kept her eyes closed so she didn't have to watch him leave. Suddenly, though, he was there, strong arms wrapped around her, hugging her very tightly.

"I am so sorry, Cara. I wish that son of a bitch wasn't already dead, so I could murder him. But first I'd castrate him

and make him eat his own dick—and I would cook it very badly, no salt or anything."

That was a sweet offer, sweet, but kind of gross, and in
spite of herself, in spite of the seriousness of the conversation,
she giggled.

"Cara, I mean it, I'd kill him and happily serve time. Nobody should get away with doing that to you, nobody."

"It's a little late for that sentiment," she told him. "And the
reason I'm saying something now is because as much as I
want to move forward with you, I'm frightened."

She hadn't wanted to say anything, afraid she'd hurt his
feelings, but it was true. Earlier, when they had been walking
from the hospital to the docks, he had pulled her into an alley,
shoved her up against the wall and kissed her. At first, it was
fine, exhilarating even, but then her body clenched with fear
when she had the sudden realization that she was utterly help-
less. He had seven inches and at least eighty pounds on her,
and his weight pressing against her reminded her that no
matter what she did, she'd never be able to fight him off; she
would always be at his mercy. She tried to manage her fear,
she even pulled him into an alley later herself just to prove she
had some measure of control, but it didn't help. He was always
going to have the physical power.

He looked wounded. "Cara, you know I'd never hurt you.
Well, not intentionally. I mean, I am kind of clumsy. And if
you ever try to take me dancing, I might break your toes. But
I'd never hurt you on purpose. And we don't have to do anything tonight. You can probably tell I really want to have sex
with you. Really badly. It's all I've been thinking about all day,
but I'd never force you. If you don't want to, we won't. End of
story. I have a safe word, and it's stop. That's all you have to
say. Just say stop and I will, I promise. I love you!"

"See, that's part of the problem, you saying you love me." She forced herself to continue speaking, even though it was difficult, even though he was holding her and he was naked. She could feel her heart pounding and half of her just wanted to push him down on the bed and take him for a ride. "Phil told me he loved me on our third date. He said he was so in love with me, he'd never felt that way about anyone before. It made me feel so special, so good. And what I didn't recognize at the time is that it was typical abuser's behavior. They come on so strong in the beginning, and they convince you they love you and they kind of magic you into falling in love with them. It's part of the trap. And I know that now, so it scares me to hear you tell me you love me, because I know—"

"Cara, you're wrong," he interrupted her. "Look at me. Listen to me. I'm not Phil, and I never will be. He may have told you he loved you on the third date, but even though I'm only saying it now, I've loved you for a long time. I realized it years ago, when you were sick and I made you all that soup . . ."

"You made gallons of it, Sam. It's all we ate in the staff house for two weeks." She found herself crying again. It seemed that's all she had been doing for days.

"Yes, because I was in love with you. But it wasn't just a passing thing, and I'm not trying to manipulate you or trick you. I fell in love with you when I got to know you. When I first met you, I thought you were kind of, well, not dull exactly, but not my type at all. But after weeks of living with you and having breakfast with you and going on all those hikes and talking behind the reception desk, I saw you for who you really are, and you shook me to my core. You're an amazing woman, beautiful and smart, and perfect. I'll never quite feel like I deserve you."

"But Sam, now you're putting me on a pedestal. That's just as bad."

"No, I'm not. Maybe I shouldn't have said perfect. I know your faults. You cry too easily, and you're kind of a perfectionist, and you don't know how to cook, and Cara, you wear shoes in the house. Do you know how much dirt that tracks in? So you're not perfect, but you're wonderful. And it took me time to realize it. But once I did, there was no turning back. Even when you rejected me last summer, it didn't change how I felt. I love you, for real, but I can wait longer for you, I mean it. I'm already telling everyone you're my girlfriend, and I so badly want to have sex with you. Well, I'm not actually telling people that last part. But if I'm being honest, that's all I thought about all day. No pressure though. I'll wait until you're ready, I promise."

She stared at him for a long moment, looking into his eyes until she felt weak. "When did you learn to start saying the right things? You might need to have a little bit of patience with me sometimes, but I am ready. I'm ready for you, and I'm ready for this."

And she kissed him until they fell over onto the bed, and the fear was gone. Her body was on fire, and she discovered that not only had Sam learned the right words to say, he also knew the right things to do.

Epilogue

Cara wakes up and stretches, and immediately notices something different—Sam is gone. She reaches out to his side of the bed and discovers cold sheets. He's been gone for a while then. Good. He's an infuriatingly annoying man, and it's best that he's not here. There's a limit to how much of him she can put up with, and she's already reached it.

The light coming in through the window is soft and grey—it's snowing again. If the weather forecast is correct, there's going to be another six inches on the ground by the afternoon. She is glad she doesn't have to go to the inn today; she doesn't want to cross-country ski, and she can't use a snowmobile anymore.

She gets out of bed slowly and carefully, but she doesn't even make it all the way down the stairs before Sam comes running. Ugh. So he's still home. He's the last person she wants to deal with.

"Cara, what are you doing? Go back to bed." He reaches for her, and she pushes his hand away.

She doesn't want to be touched by anybody, especially him. Everything about him annoys her.

"Leave me alone, Sam. I hate you," she tells him, and instead of being hurt, he laughs. That annoys her even more. She wishes there were some sort of weapon handy as she sits down heavily on the bottom stair.

"I know you do. That's why I called Elaine and told her I'm bringing the kids over today."

"I like the kids. It's you I can't stand."

"I know." If anything, his grin gets even bigger. She'd like to smack it right off his face, but she can't because Cindy and

Robbie come running out of the kitchen and she doesn't want to hit their dad in front of them. Not that she'd ever hit him, but the urge is strong, especially when he keeps looking at her with that obnoxious smile.

"Mommy, we were making you breakfast in bed," Cindy shouts excitedly. "Daddy let me do the eggs all by myself." She is wearing the little apron Sam gave her for Christmas last year. Her curly hair is messy. Sam never remembers to comb it properly.

"Then we go to Grandma's," Robbie yells with glee. "I bringing my cars!" He is clutching his favorite toys in a bag in his fists. He has Sam's eyes, and they are filled with excitement.

"Why are you taking them to Elaine's?" she asks crossly. It's a Tuesday, so the inn is closed, making it their family time. They're supposed to spend the day together. Leave it to Sam to selfishly change their plans without discussing it with her first.

"Because Paddy is watching Violetta while Fabio and Amy are at his immigration appointment in St. Paul, and he can't handle all three of the kids. And because I'm taking you to the mainland."

"I don't want to go to the mainland," she informs him. "I don't want to go anywhere with you."

"Tough." He is so infuriatingly happy. "I've been through this with you twice already, Cara Vervaine. The first sign of labor is you start to hate me. You're past thirty-six weeks. That's full term for twins. I think they're coming out soon. I already called your doctor, and she agreed. I've got your hospital bag packed, and immediately after you eat breakfast, we're dropping the kids off and heading to the docks."

"I hate you, Sam," she tells him again, but they both know she doesn't mean it. She feels a sudden rush and looks down. "And damn it, you're right. My water just broke."

ABOUT THE AUTHOR

Sara LaFontain is usually in Tucson, but you can find her more easily at www.saralafontain.com or www.facebook.com/saralafontainauthor

Read the entire Whispering Pines Island Series:

Whispering Pines Island #2
No Longer Yours

She's the sunny new teacher. He's the village curmudgeon. Is man's best friend the key to happily ever after?

Cherry Waites never thought her idyllic marriage of ten years would end with divorce papers. Humiliated to finally discover her husband's year-long affair, she accepts a teaching position on a secluded island and hopes for a better life. But her new beginning hits a rocky start when she trips over a grump's beloved dog.

Matteo Capen prefers the company of canines to people. Paranoid his isolated haven will become overcrowded, the self-proclaimed bachelor shares some choice words with the clumsy new schoolteacher he mistakes for a tourist. But when his dogs take a liking to her, the ice in his heart begins to melt.

Though Cherry's eternal optimism rubs Matteo the wrong way, he gallantly steps in when her online dating attempts end in disaster. And as the winter storm season approaches, Cherry wonders if her future might offer another chance.

Can two lonely souls overcome their baggage and risk love?

Read on for a sample

No Longer Yours

Chapter One

Parsons, Ohio, February 2014

Cherry Dryden's dreams are about to come true: she is ovulating. The test confirmed it this morning, giving her a smiley face in the little plastic window. The next forty-eight hours will be the optimum time to finally conceive a baby. What a shame that Gary had to coach his team's early practice this morning, she reflects as she stares at the stick. We could've gotten started now. I could be pregnant by breakfast.

She texts Gary before work: *It's a happy face! Baby time!*

He responds: *Girl, Imma knock you up!*

This is exciting, she thinks, as she floats her way through the school day. They've talked about children for so long, and now, finally, it's time. Just two months ago, at Christmas, he gifted her a box of digital ovulation tests.

"Does this mean what I think it does?" she asked, heart in her throat.

"We've been together over thirteen years. That's long enough to be sure, isn't it?" he responded, and that night she threw away her birth control pills.

After having The Talk, the rest of holiday break was full of research as they studied conception methods. She started taking folic acid and hard-to-swallow prenatal vitamins. She choked down fish oil capsules, even though the smell made her gag. She made a chart, took her temperature daily, and began using the ovulation tests, and now, finally, they can move forward with their plans.

This really is the best of all possible times to have a baby. They are in excellent shape financially, they've paid off the last of their student loans (early, too!), they own a comfortable house in a good neighborhood, and depending on when the baby is born, she could maybe take a whole semester off to stay at home with it. They are ready!

Gary sends her messages throughout the day. He has to judge projects at the elementary school science fair, but he'll be home as quickly as he can. He is just as excited as she is. He texts again: *Sex + Wine + Sex + Dessert + Sex?*

Last alcohol for nine months, I'll get an expensive bottle, she responds, adding a winky emoji for good measure.

Finally, school lets out, and after taking about an hour to finish grading papers and to stop in the theatre and assist with the drama club's rehearsal, she is ready to head home. There will be time to swing by the store and pick up wine, and something fancy for dinner. Steak? Gary always likes that.

As she walks out to her car, she notices a man leaning on the vehicle parked next to hers. She doesn't know much about cars, but she can identify that one. It's a Jaguar XF, Gary's dream car. He has fantasized about getting one for a long time, but that's way out of their price range. He'll be jealous she saw one at the school. The man looks up, directly at her, and straightens. Oh, darn it. That means he's waiting for her. He must be a parent.

"Cherry Dryden?" he asks as she gets close. Using her first name, that's unusual. She tries to think of whose father he might be. "Cherry, I don't know if you remember me, my name is Tyler Rivera. I'm Megan Rivera's husband."

"Oh, yes, of course. I met you at the holiday party," Cherry replies. She should have recognized him from his television commercials as well—Tyler Rivera, owner of every car dealership in town. No wonder he has a Jaguar. They had chatted briefly while waiting in line at the buffet. She stands a bit awkwardly, balancing her cardigan and a stack of papers in one hand while trying to get her keychain out of her purse with the other.

To be polite, she asks, "How are things going?" The elementary and middle schools share a staff parking lot; he must be waiting for his wife.

"Well, not great. Megan and I are getting a divorce." He seems nervous, shifting from foot to foot and looking at her as if he's anticipating a reaction.

"Oh, I'm so sorry to hear that," she says. She has no idea why he's telling her this. She doesn't know him or his wife very well. Megan teaches second grade, like Gary. She finds her keys and holds them in her hand, ready to go, hoping he hurries up.

"Yes, it's a terrible shame," he says, and she fears he's about to launch into a story. For as long as she can remember, complete strangers have liked to confide in her. Gary complains every time they go shopping because she can't make it out the door without a cashier or fellow shopper wanting to share all their problems with her. But she doesn't want to listen to Tyler's tragic tale of divorce, she wants to buy wine and go home and take her shoes off and make love to her husband in a position beneficial to conception. She uses the key fob to unlock her door, hoping that the sound will signal to him that it's time to go.

But Tyler ignores the hint and continues. "The worst part is that Megan has decided to ruin two marriages. I've got some photos here that my attorney is going to use as exhibits in court. They're not pretty. I brought you copies though, because I thought you might want them."

"That's sweet of you to think of me, but we don't cover civics in the sixth grade, so I don't really have a use for legal exhibits." She forces a friendly smile, but this is rapidly becoming awkward. She had talked to him for what, ten minutes, over two months ago? She didn't think they were establishing a friendship, and he knows she's married. Did he think she was flirting before?

She suddenly understands. That's what this is. He's telling her about his divorce because he's going to ask her out. Oh, Gary is going to laugh about this later.

"You're misunderstanding me. These photos aren't appropriate for your classroom." He slips his finger under the flap of the large envelope in his hands.

"Look, Tyler, I'm sorry," she is about to let him down gently, to apologize and politely state that she hadn't meant to lead him on, but then she catches her first glimpse of the photos he is showing her. She drops everything that was in her arms. There is a roaring sound in her ears and her vision starts to blacken. She reaches out to steady herself. Tyler grabs her and stands there uncomfortably for a minute, with one hand supporting her and the other holding a color photo of her husband, her Gary, laying back in a bed naked. It's not an obscene picture though—Megan's head makes sure of that.

Chapter Two

Ferry's Landing, Minnesota, August 2014

"Long-term parking," Cherry read the sign out loud. She'd been talking to herself for most of the journey in a desperate attempt to combat the loneliness. When she left her parents' home in Madrid, Ohio yesterday morning, she told herself she was full of hope and optimism as if saying it enough times would make it true. She was starting over and she was doing it on her own. This was a sign of independence. She didn't need Gary, she didn't need anyone. Her new life started now. The mantras all rang hollow.

On the first night of the drive, she stopped in the Wisconsin Dells and stayed in a resort. Some of her former colleagues had told her the vacation town would be a good stopping point, since she 'deserved to have a little fun.' But as she sat in the resort bar sipping an overly sweet cocktail and looking at the children playing in the indoor waterpark, she couldn't help but feel resentful. Happy families everywhere, and she was completely alone. She was supposed to be pregnant by now, she was supposed to be preparing for her own family, and it wasn't fair that her entire planned future had been ripped away. When she finally went back to her room, she laid down on the far-too-empty queen bed and cried.

But she was improving now, right? She'd eaten a big breakfast, and driven the rest of the way, with her music cranked up and singing as loudly and tunelessly as she could. Well, the tuneless part was unintentional. But loud?

Heck yes. Gary always used to tease her about her singing, saying what a shame it was that someone who loved to sing so much had such a flat voice.

"Lucky you, Gary. You don't have to listen to me anymore," she told his invisible presence. And she rolled down her window and sang along to the songs she knew and made up words for the ones she didn't. It made her feel better, or at least chased some of the sadness away.

And now here she was, in the small town of Ferry's Landing, gateway to the Piney Islands. They liked their descriptive names in this part of the country, apparently. As she drove down to the lakefront, she tried to keep an eye out for stores she might need but hadn't spied much that would be of use to her before she reached her destination. The docks were lively, filled with larger crowds than she would have expected, but then she remembered it was still tourist season.

She followed the signs and found her reserved space. "Here I am, C-22," she announced to herself. She pulled in next to a van with *The Inn at Whispering Pines* painted on the side.

"Hello van, I guess we're neighbors now." As soon as the words left her mouth, she felt silly. She'd progressed from talking to herself to talking to inanimate objects; she needed to stop before she embarrassed herself.

There wasn't much to unload from her trunk. Very few things had come out of the marriage with her. She'd made Gary buy out her share of all their furniture and household goods. Better to walk away with a check than to have to sanitize everything Megan's naked body may have touched, and Megan had been everywhere. They had even done it in her home, turning the house she and Gary had bought and decorated and loved into a tawdry lover's nest while she was on a girls' weekend in Windsor with Katie. How could Gary betray her so completely? And worse, why did he let her find out such details from the local news?

No, she had wanted nothing from their broken home. She took her clothes, and her personal items, those few things that were untainted in her memories. She ordered brand new sheets and towels, untouched by her husband's lover, and shipped them all directly to her new address, which was a furnished apartment. She wasn't ready to deal with the hassle of trying to buy furniture and decorate and make friends and learn a new town and start a new job and ... she was too overwhelmed for a moment to move. Her future weighed down upon her, heavy and lonely and harsh.

When she was ready, when she managed to breathe again, and clear the tears that threatened to overflow from her eyes, she took her two suitcases and purse and dragged them to the ferry's ticket office. She took a deep breath to prepare herself and got a nose full of the rather unappealing scents of diesel fumes and fish. These were the smells of her home now, she supposed. At least it smelled better than sex and betrayal.

"You look familiar," the woman behind the ticket window said.

"Oh, no, this is my first time here. I just took a job teaching on Whispering Pines Island," Cherry explained.

"Ah, that's why! You've changed your hair. I'm Vivian Ryan, from the village council."

"Yes! I recognize you from my video interview! I'm so excited to be here and start working." She tried to sound much more cheerful than she felt as she put a hand to her head, slightly embarrassed. Her hair was starting to grow back from her spontaneous and misguided attempt at a pixie cut. Gary preferred long hair, so somehow she thought chopping hers off would show him that she was moving on. Unfortunately, short hair did not flatter her face, and she didn't like what she saw when she looked in the mirror. But she wouldn't have liked her reflection anyway, even without the terrible haircut. All she could see when she looked at herself was a broken woman.

"Welcome, we're so glad you took the job. All four of my boys attended that school, and my granddaughter is there now. I help out by teaching a course on island history in the spring. You'll find a lot of us volunteer there, it keeps us busy." Vivian's weathered face cracked into a friendly, open smile. "We were expecting you yesterday. I hope you didn't have any problems on the trip."

The effusive greeting lifted her spirits, at least a little bit. She smiled in relief. "I decided to break the drive into two days. I'm so happy to get here though. I've been looking forward to this for months!" As she said it, she realized the truth in the words. Despite her misgivings, starting over was exciting, and a welcome respite from the gossip and tears back home. No, not home, not anymore.

Vivian handed her a ticket. "First ferry ride is free for you; you'll want to buy a punch card when it's time to make a trip to the mainland. It'll save you some money, especially if you plan to make frequent crossings. Now hang on, I'll call one of my boys over here to get those suitcases."

Chapter Three

The air was fresher, that's the first thing she noticed once she disembarked from the ferry and got away from the docks. She inhaled deeply, trying to take it all in, and smelled nothing but pine. A shift in the breeze brought the delightful scent of fresh roasted coffee, perhaps wafting from the bakery on the corner. She would definitely investigate that place later.

The road into Whispering Pines Village was paved, which she hadn't expected. When she read that there were no cars on the island, she just assumed the streets would be dirt or gravel. It was busier than she expected too, with bicyclists and a solitary electric cart vying for the right of way amongst all the pedestrians.

"It's probably always like this when the ferry arrives," she said out loud to herself and then looked around to make sure nobody noticed. That was a habit she needed to break.

She had booked an apartment, sight unseen, but it should be easy to find. *Look for the drugstore, it's upstairs*, the email from the landlord said. *Stairs go up the side of the building.* Yes, there it was. *Laska's Drugs, Est. 1971.* All of the buildings on this stretch of road were two stories, with the second story set back creating a wide balcony. That's what sold her on the apartment, the idea of sitting on her balcony sipping her morning coffee and looking out over the small town. She took a step backward for a better view, but something yelped under her foot, and she almost lost her balance.

"Christ, lady, watch where you're going!"

"I'm so sorry!" She had nearly stepped on a small corgi. Its owner knelt down, to smooth its fur and glare at her. He looked out of place here, with his shaggy sun-kissed blond hair and his Hawaiian shirt and cargo shorts. Vacationer from California maybe?

"Be more careful," he snapped. "Lucky for you Tristan moved out of your way."

"It's okay, he's probably just having a bad day. It has nothing to do with you," she told herself, then realized she had spoken out loud.

"Excuse me?"

"Sorry, I'm not mentally ill. I promise. I've just driven two days to get here and had nobody to talk to so I guess I've developed the habit of talking to myself. Don't worry, I'm not some crazy person wandering the streets." She laughed to show that she was joking, and expected him to smile back. After all, small towns were friendly, and she hadn't actually hurt his dog. She reached out to pet the corgi, but the man scooped him up in his arms before she could.

"Well I'm glad to know you aren't mentally ill. Wouldn't want anyone like that walking around, would we?" He stormed off, and she watched him go, chagrined. She hoped her first encounter wasn't a portent of what was to come. At least he was a tourist and not a local, so she didn't embarrass herself in front of anyone she'd have to see again.

She sighed and rolled her suitcases toward the stairs. Home. This was her home now. She swallowed the sudden lump in her throat and began dragging her luggage up the wooden steps.

Whispering Pines Island #3
If This Were a Love Story

She's an alcoholic. He won't touch a drop. Will her struggle with sobriety uncork more trouble, or be the road to true love?

Amanda O'Connell tries to drown her problems with vodka. So when an attempt to lie her way out of a DWI goes wrong, her family intervenes and sets her up with a summer job on remote Whispering Pines Island. Painting the town red on her first night there, she meets a hunky, tattooed drummer... who promptly rejects her drunken advances.

Everett Ryan wishes he could trade his late father's ferryboat for a Coast Guard cutter. And while Amanda brings a breath of fresh air to his boring island life, he's not interested in anyone with the same addiction that killed his dad. But when she's sober, he can't resist their red-hot chemistry.

Determined to win over the man of her dreams, Amanda vows to break up with the bottle. But Everett fears even if she manages to stay on the wagon, their love won't survive the end of the tourist season.

Can Amanda and Everett conquer their demons and chart a course for a beautiful new relationship?

Made in United States
North Haven, CT
23 June 2023

38101250R00225